AGAINST HER WISHES

Grace stood quietly in the earl's embrace, her surging heartbeat slowly returning to normal. She felt drained of all sense. As sanity began to return, she realized with humiliated chagrin that she had acted like a common strumpet, pressing herself against him and returning his ardor with virtually no resistance. She closed her eyes and laid her flushed cheek against his soft linen shirt, the sound of his heart racing as wildly as hers comforting her for a moment, then, with a sudden rush of clarity, making her face a horrifying truth.

God help her, she wanted more!

Deneane Clark

Grace

LEISURE BOOKS   NEW YORK CITY

A LEISURE BOOK®

November 2007

Published by

Dorchester Publishing Co., Inc.
200 Madison Avenue
New York, NY 10016

ISBN 10: 0-8439-5997-5
ISBN 13: 978-0-8439-5997-0

Printed in the United States of America.

10 9 8 7 6 5 4 3 2 1

Visit us on the web at www.dorchesterpub.com.

For my 10th grade English teacher, who made me keep a journal,
And who taught me much more than correct grammar.

Mrs. Manetta, have I told you lately...?

Grace

Prologue

Late August 1800

*I*n the neglected, long-forgotten hunting lodge, an important event was about to take place. Most residents of the dwelling in the woods, creatures of the creepy six-legged variety well used to the layers of dirt and the musty smell of rotting wood, kept a silent, respectful distance from the ceremonial proceedings. The reason for their discretion likely lay in their fear of ending up popped into an empty preserves jar for use in some brilliantly obscure scientific experiment—a justifiable fear.

Unfortunately for the hidden insects, one of the ceremony participants was having a great deal of difficulty achieving proper appreciation for the solemn nature of the situation. Her bubbly, infectious laugh rang merrily through the trees that surrounded and shaded the little weathered cottage as she tried, with little success, to capture a frightened cricket that kept hopping just out of reach of her chubby little hands. The creature managed to gain the open door and quickly jumped outside, scrambling under a large, conveniently fallen maple leaf just as Grace emerged from the cottage on her grubby hands and knees.

Inside the dilapidated building, an increasingly annoyed-looking blond boy of about ten glowered sternly at the little girl with the unruly cap of disheveled red curls. Cheerfully she gave up looking for the cricket and returned to sit facing him. Her short crossed legs were clad in a faded pair of his cast-off breeches, topped with a once-white shirt smudged and torn from a glorious summer morning spent climbing trees and chasing butterflies.

Catching Henry Belden's baleful look, Grace did her dutiful best to look appropriately grave. Despite her valiant attempt, she failed in her efforts to repress the uncontrollable urge to giggle. She clapped both hands over her mouth to contain her mirth, but still her bright blue eyes sparkled at him with engaging glee.

Henry shook his head and sighed in exasperation. "Grace," he admonished in his severest tone, "you simply mustn't laugh. This is really quite important." He reached across the small space that separated them and roughly grasped both of her hands, pulling them firmly away from her face. With gallant effort, Grace finally schooled her features into some semblance of solemnity, though an irrepressible dimple still managed to peep through.

"Now," Henry instructed in his most serious voice, "you must say precisely what I say."

She nodded, eager as always to impress the boy she considered her own private hero, for he did the most impressive things. She remembered the time he had spent an entire morning showing her how he could mount his horse at a full canter, a trick she was certain she could master if she could only get her pony to do so much as *trot* when she was not already mounted. "I swear," he began, tugging her back from her momentary daydream.

"I swear," Grace echoed in her high, childish voice.

"That I will marry only you."

"That I will marry only you," she repeated obediently, then spoiled the effect by dissolving into giggles again.

Henry looked down in lofty disdain at the seven-year-old girl who now rolled on the dusty floor in unrestrained hilarity before he, too, succumbed to the inevitable and began to laugh. Gales of high-pitched children's laughter echoed through the empty room and drifted out into the bright sunshine. Birds chattered in alarmed reaction. An owl perched in a maple tree lazily opened one round eye, then closed it again when the silly birds abruptly noted his regard, stopped chirping, and wisely took cover.

"What do you find so funny about this?" Henry asked, when he finally managed to stop laughing and catch his breath.

Grace sat up and wiped the tears from her eyes, leaving wide streaks of dirt on her cheeks. "You," she said, in a voice breathless from the exertion of laughter, pointing a small, pudgy finger in his direction. "You looked *exactly* like Reverend Teesbury just then. You know, the way he looks when he stops bellowing in the middle of a sermon and looks one directly in the eye, simply to make one squirm?" She made a face in a quite good, if irreverent, imitation of the tall, dour clergyman, then erupted into yet another round of giggles. She was so carried away with her own wit, she failed to notice that Henry had stopped smiling.

He put his hands on her shoulders and stepped closer, giving Grace an odd squirmy feeling in her tummy. "W-what are you doing, Henry?" she stammered.

"Now you have to kiss me," he said. His voice sounded thick and strange, and his eyes on hers were hard.

Grace wrenched her shoulders free and took a step back. "Yuck, Henry Belden. I'm not kissing you or any other boy!" She backed another couple steps away toward the

Chapter One

March 1813

*I*n the boisterous atmosphere and oppressive heat of the village inn's crowded dining room, two gentlemen enjoyed a leisurely after-dinner brandy. Dressed in immaculate, well-tailored clothes, they appeared out of place, though not ill at ease. The men exuded a sense of self-confidence and smooth urbanity that came only with either impeccable breeding or great wealth, giving them the ability to fit in no matter their locale. They had strikingly similar appearances, from their well-above-average heights, taut, athletic builds, and dark coloring, to their auras of deliberately leashed power and authority, attributes that marked them both as noblemen. When one considered their eyes, however, the comparison abruptly ground to a halt.

Sebastian Tremaine, the new and very reluctant Duke of Blackthorne, possessed a pair of startling golden-amber eyes that should have struck one as warmly compelling. Instead, they were cool, aloof, and forbidding, somehow reminding one of a large, predatory cat. Rumors whispered among the young daughters of the ton held that his eyes hid a dark past, a past never discussed but often wondered about. Most young ladies shivered deliciously when they encountered him at social functions or while out driving in the park, their young hearts beating with both hope and dread that the duke would single them out for conversation. Only the previous week, someone reported that one extremely timid young miss had taken to her bed in stark fear. She had seen her father conversing at a ball with the mysterious new duke, and had become certain they discussed a possible betrothal contract between herself and the frightening, powerful man with the golden gaze.

By contrast, one would never describe the Earl of Huntwick's eyes as cool. Trevor Christian Caldwell had a flashing dark green gaze that held a subtle hint of seductive promise, a great deal of smoldering warmth, and more than a trace of rich humor. When the earl looked upon a young lady, she always had the flattering impression that the entire world had fallen away, and that, for a moment, nobody else mattered to him. Few women could resist the potent combination, especially when added to the legendary charm that had reportedly brought the ladies to his side—and his bed—in record numbers. The lure of unimaginable wealth and the promise of the title "Countess of Huntwick" that came with the earl's hand served only to make him more irresistible. The fact that he did not profess an inclination toward settling down and getting about the business of siring an heir inspired great disappointment each year. Yet, as another Season inevitably came to a close with the earl still unattached, mamas with marriageable daughters breathed a collective sigh of relief, certain that, next Season, the earl would finally notice her child.

Finishing his brandy, the duke glanced across the smoke-filled room toward the door. He gave an almost imperceptible nod to the footman, who stood waiting for just such a signal. The man disappeared, slipping outside to alert the coachman of Sebastian and Trevor's impending departure so that he could have the ducal coach readied and brought around.

Tipping his head back, Trevor emptied his glass, then pushed his chair away from the table to stretch his long legs before him. He lit a slim cheroot with a practiced hand and inhaled deeply, regarding his friend through the thin haze of fragrant, gray-blue smoke that curled up and over his head. "Are you certain you wish to continue traveling this evening? The roads will be dark and hazardous soon."

Sebastian nodded without hesitation. "I'd like to finish my business at Blackthorne tomorrow and be on my way back to London the following day, if possible."

Trevor shook his head at his friend's bland tone. "Most men would be overjoyed to have inherited a dukedom, especially one for which they had no idea they were in line. Yet you refer to settling your new estate as mere 'business.'"

Sebastian looked with disinterest at the glowing end of his cheroot. "A dukedom," he said dryly, "marred by a series of lecherous, degenerate dukes who have bled the estate dry and left the new duke with staggering debts."

Trevor raised his eyebrows in silent amusement as Sebastian stamped out his cheroot and stood. He himself followed suit, and both men walked toward the door, the openly curious eyes of the entire tavern upon them. The duke paused momentarily to pay the innkeeper and thank him for his hospitality, then followed Trevor, who had preceded him into the yard.

Pulling on his gloves, Sebastian strode toward his waiting chaise. Named heir to the late Duke of Blackthorne only the previous month, he had not yet had the shining burgundy-lacquered door emblazoned with his new seal. He would see to that as soon as he returned to London, he mused, as a footman put down the steps and opened the door for him. Placing one booted foot on the step, he stopped and impatiently scanned the inn yard to see what kept Trevor.

He located the earl standing near the door to the inn with his hands clasped behind his back, his dark head bent as he listened intently to a lad who looked to be about ten years old. The boy spoke rapidly, gestured in the direction of Sebastian's coach, and then, strangely, held out his hand, his curly head tipped back to look earnestly up into Hunt's face. Sebastian watched with bemused interest as Trevor reached, not into his pocket for a handout, as Sebastian had supposed, but for the child's outstretched hand. He shook it gravely, as though closing a deal with a respected business acquaintance. Quickly the lad disappeared in the direction of the stables, his red hair gleaming in the fading light of the setting sun. Trevor sauntered over to the coach, an amused grin tugging at the corners of his mouth.

"Making friends with a local boy, Hunt?" Sebastian asked, settling back into the luxurious smoke-gray velvet squabs of his chaise.

Trevor sat down across from him, stretched out his legs as far as possible in the close confines of the coach, and quirked an eyebrow at the duke, his grin widening into a genuine smile. "Yes," he confirmed with an odd look. "Showed quite an interest in your cattle." He paused, then added, "Your Grace," in a low, teasing voice.

Sebastian let the irksome reminder of his new rank pass without comment. "He's a stable boy, then?"

"I don't think so. The child's speech is as cultured as yours or mine."

"The son of a landholder, no doubt," Sebastian said dismissively, gazing through the window as the darkening landscape began to roll by. The glow of the small village quickly fell behind them. The coachman slowed the horses imperceptibly in an effort to better see the road in the deepening dusk.

Unnoticed by the duke, Trevor's smile widened still further. "No doubt," he agreed, then also looked out the window, falling into a companionable silence with one of the few men he considered a trusted friend. As always when he was left with time to think, his thoughts turned to the latest of his varied business affairs. He recalled a mining investment in the American colonies he had taken under consideration. Despite some inherent risks, it looked like quite a promising venture, and he remembered he had intended to invite Sebastian to join him, certain the duke would find it as interesting as he had. Just as he opened his mouth to speak, however, a sudden shout came from outside the vehicle. A sickening lurch knocked him from his seat, slamming his shoulder heavily into the side of the coach. He scrambled to brace himself as it tilted precariously on two wheels for what felt like an eternity, then suddenly righted itself, skidding to a halt amid shouting footmen and terrified horses.

From his uncomfortable position on the floor, Trevor looked to see if Sebastian was unharmed. The duke had already recovered his footing and bounded out the door. Trevor followed a bit more slowly, rubbing his shoulder. He blinked in the sudden light of the burning carriage lamps, then looked toward the horses. They also appeared unhurt, so he glanced over his shoulder and noticed a knot of footmen and outriders gathered about forty paces behind the coach, talking excitedly and pointing at something that lay on the ground in their midst. Curious, Trevor watched as Sebastian strode up to the group, which immediately opened to let him through. The duke knelt for a moment, then gathered the object up into his arms. He returned to the coach carrying what looked like a small bundle of rags. As Sebastian drew near, the earl realized the bundle was actually a small figure that looked strangely familiar. With a start, he realized why.

"It's the lad from the inn," Sebastian said grimly.

Chapter Two

Trevor and Sebastian sat in tense silence as the swaying carriage sped back toward the inn, somberly watching the unconscious child, who lay motionless on the seat across from them. Clad in faded, almost threadbare breeches and a rather coarse gray shirt that was yards too large, the child looked all of nine or ten years old, and small for his age at that. Ridiculously long, sooty eyelashes lay in curly fans upon pale skin marred only by the ugly, already purpling lump just above his right eyebrow. He lay so still that Sebastian feared he had died until, with more relief than he cared to admit, he saw the subtle rise and fall of the boy's thin chest.

In no time at all the coach pulled back into the yard of the small inn, where the innkeeper waited for them in the dancing shadows of the torchlit yard with the outrider the duke had sent ahead. Before they had come to a complete stop, Sebastian impatiently flung open the door and motioned for the man to come near. "Do you recognize this child?" His tone was demanding, harsher than he intended. He indicated the small, prone figure on the seat opposite.

William Jones nervously leaned in the door as a footman held up a lantern behind him to illuminate the interior of the coach. The light fell across the boy's face as a sudden breeze lifted the auburn curls from his forehead, highlighting the ugly, swollen knot above his eye. Jones peered closely at the child, then sucked in his breath with a sudden hiss, his wide eyes riveted on the unconscious figure. "Mercy!" He exhaled forcefully and looked up at the tense, set face of the duke. "It's the youngest child of the Ackerly brood, Your Grace."

Sebastian nodded, dismissing the man. "Give my coachman directions to the Ackerly place, and send for a doctor to meet us there immediately," he instructed in a clipped, authoritative voice. "We'll take the urchin home, then expect rooms for the balance of the night. I'll want to be quite certain the child recovers before I'm on my way." He leaned back in his seat, his face set in determined lines.

"Aye, Your Grace," said Jones, bowing and hastily backing away as the footman closed the door. After a brief pause while the innkeeper spoke with the driver, the coach began moving again, eliciting a small, low moan from the prone figure opposite.

Sebastian moved across the interior in an instant, gently lifting the child's legs, then sitting and settling them gingerly across his lap. Although he had not driven the coach himself, he employed the man who had. Additionally, at Sebastian's instruction, the coach had been traveling much more quickly than prudence dictated on a rapidly darkening road. Because of this, he felt a keen sense of responsibility for the child's condition. Softly, Sebastian smoothed back the mop of unruly red curls, his brows drawn together with concern. As he watched, a sudden spasm of pain crossed the ashen face. With another moan, the boy began to flutter his eyelids. Sebastian glanced uncertainly at Trevor, whose face reflected as much worry as his own, then looked back down at the child.

What he saw made him stiffen in sudden shock. The

child's eyes had opened and locked on Sebastian, eyes the deep, dark blue of the sky at twilight, eyes enormous and frightened in the small, pale face. Eyes that definitely belonged to a girl.

A sudden snort of laughter came from the other side of the coach. Sebastian tore his gaze from those huge blue eyes and looked in Trevor's direction, one eyebrow quirked in accusation. "I take it you knew?"

His smile fading, Trevor nodded. "Yes, I did. Before the accident I thought it a great joke that you had no idea. In all the excitement, however, I had completely forgotten until now." Sebastian glared at him, quite taking Trevor by surprise. His taciturn friend rarely gave away his thoughts with so much as a flickering change of facial expression. A bit put out by the accusatory look thrown his way, Trevor glared back at him.

At a weak, rasping whisper from the young girl on the seat, both men quelled their annoyance and focused on her. "Wh-where am I?" she asked, trying to lever herself up on her elbows. She settled back, groaning deeply when her throbbing headache abruptly made itself known.

"You are in my coach," said the man she had first seen when she opened her eyes. His voice was deep and resonant. He was almost unbearably handsome, with thick, dark hair and sharply perfect features. His cool amber eyes held no expression. They appeared sad to her, though she couldn't imagine what about this powerful man would make her think he would ever allow such a weak emotion.

"How did I get here?" she asked in a low, halting voice.

"You had an accident on the road beyond the inn," the second man said gently from the opposite side of the coach.

She looked at him in momentary confusion, then closed her eyes. He was quite nearly as handsome as the first man. "Yes, I remember," she said weakly. "The duke with the team of magnificent bays." She tried sitting up again, succeeding this time with a slight, taut grimace. Leaning back against the soft velvet seat, she opened her eyes once more and regarded the man seated across from her, recognizing him for the first time as the man with whom she had spoken outside the stables.

Trevor's eyes twinkled as he encouragingly smiled back at her. "I knew you liked Blackthorne's horses," he teased, "but I didn't think you would make an attempt at highway robbery to obtain them."

She managed a small smile, then winced as yet another wave of pain shot through her forehead. Sebastian drew her up against his side without thought, cradling her head gingerly on his shoulder. "That's about enough activity, urchin. We're taking you home, and the innkeeper has promised to send the doctor to meet us there." A bit surprised at his own actions, the duke regarded the curly top of her head in silence, trying to assess the strange, protective feelings she elicited, feelings almost foreign to him. She smelled elusively of youth, a nearly forgotten combination of sunshine-kissed hair tousled by fresh breezes, and the clean-earth scent that followed a summer shower. "How old are you?" he asked, suddenly curious about this intriguing girl who roamed the English countryside dressed as a lad.

"I'll be thirteen in two months," she answered faintly, her strength obviously diminishing as she became tired. "My name is Mercy. I'm happy to make your acquaintance, Your Grace." She lifted a small hand briefly, then let it fall against his chest. Sleep claimed her.

Mercy.

Sebastian quirked a humorless smile. He had thought the innkeeper uttered the word in shocked prayer when he had seen the injured child, but it was really the urchin's name. He shook his head wryly and covered the small hand that rested on his chest with his own large, warm one, still unable to believe the oddly paternal feelings this strange girl evoked. Perhaps, he thought, he should take it as a sign that the time had come for him to begin thinking of getting married and starting a family. After all, he now had the damned title and all its accompanying responsibilities to consider.

"Here's a picture I won't soon forget," his friend drawled, jarring him from his unusually domestic and wholly unwelcome thoughts.

"Let's just get her home," Sebastian replied, with a careful shrug so he would not disturb the sleeping girl nestled against him. "I find myself most anxious to conclude this unpleasant business and get on with our journey."

Trevor grinned broadly, but for once held his tongue.

The coach turned into a short cobbled drive leading to a large, picturesque country home. As they pulled to a stop, Sebastian carefully gathered Mercy's small, limp form into his arms so he could carry her into the house.

Trevor gained the entranceway, taking the flagstone steps two at a time, and rapped sharply on the large oak door. After a short pause it jerked open, revealing a slightly older and very annoyed-looking replica of Mercy. The girl gaped in surprise when the tall intimidating stranger on her doorstep smiled disarmingly and abruptly thrust the door open wider. A moment later she emitted an alarmed gasp as she saw her little sister carried in by an equally tall, imposing, and darkly handsome man.

Her momentary alarm gave way to a fierce, protective anger, which she directed at the man holding Mercy, automatically assigning the blame for her sister's unknown condition to him. "What have you done to her?" she demanded, glaring up at him, her hands firmly planted on her hips, gloriously unaware that she had just snapped at a man feared or respected by nearly everyone he knew.

Sebastian looked coldly down at the small girl whose bright blue eyes spit angry sparks at him, and wondered if any of the members of this odd family had an ounce of common sense. He drew his brows together and gave her a quelling look. "Do you have somewhere I can *put* her?"

In no way chastened, the girl dropped her gaze to Mercy's face. Her eyes widened when they settled on the large purple bruise above her sister's right eyebrow. She spun on her heel and said, "Follow me," in a considerably softer voice.

As Sebastian followed Mercy's unnamed sister up the curving staircase, the Earl of Huntwick glanced around the high-ceilinged entranceway for any sign of a butler, maid, or other servant. Seeing no one, he walked slowly to the end of the room, where double doors opened to a large, bright chamber that looked comfortable in a rumpled, large-family sort of way. A shining grand piano occupied the corner to his left, a Bach piece left open on the music stand as though the pianist had only just stopped playing. Two large chairs in a buttery soft maroon leather faced each other at right angles to the fireplace, where a cheery fire crackled away, inviting one to have a seat and read a book in cozy comfort. A couch upholstered in a beautiful rose-and-gold stripe graced the wall to his right, small pillows perfect for tossing at a sibling scattered haphazardly across its cushions. Next to a wooden rocking chair sat a small basket crammed with balls of yarn. Two wooden knitting needles stuck out at dangerous angles, presenting a distinct hazard to someone's unsuspecting ankles.

Directly above the couch hung a portrait of a child he assumed was Mercy. As he looked at the picture, Trevor found himself chuckling. From what little he knew of her, he imagined she must have hated the frilly confines of the ridiculously ruffled white organdy dress. A blue satin sash wrapped around the high waistline and tied in an enor-

mous bow that peeked jauntily out from behind her back
and exactly matched the wide ribbon running through her
short auburn curls. The perky ribbon looked entirely out of
place tied in a fat bow above the gamine face dominated
by those huge pansy-blue eyes.

A smile of pure enjoyment lurking around his mouth,
Trevor continued his leisurely perusal of the rest of the portraits that lined the cozy room. He glanced over a startlingly beautiful blond girl, a rather impatient-looking and
obviously scholarly older man who held the place of honor
over the fireplace, and next to it, a handsome though
somber-looking young woman. Then Trevor stopped. He
took a fascinated step closer to the next likeness, inexplicably drawn to the smiling young woman in the painting.

Without question this portrait depicted Mercy's older sister, for she possessed the same elfin face, the same large,
heavily lashed dark blue eyes, and the same curly red hair,
although this sister's hair was longer, shot through with
amazing highlights of shimmering gold, where Mercy's un-
tamed mop was nearly auburn. She had the glorious mass
of shining curls pulled back from her forehead, held in
place with a delicate sapphire clip at the top of her head,
then left to tumble in luxurious, flaming waves across her
shoulders and down her back. It was hair that begged to be
released so that he could bury his face and his hands in the
fiery tresses.

Her eyes, when he finally managed to wrench his gaze
from her lovely hair, enthralled him. Warm and compelling, they reached out to him from the canvas, catching
and holding his own with an irresistible lure. They were the
deep blue of the sea on a clear and cloudless day, and contained a great deal of passionate emotion in their shining
depths, passion that tempted one with far more warmth
and glowing promise than the cold, deep ocean. They
pledged light and love, laughter and sharing, and, as he

lost himself in that promise, Trevor decided that, from the way she looked out at him, whoever had painted this portrait had obviously meant a great deal to the girl depicted on the canvas.

Just as he reached up, unable to resist the urge to touch the girl's painted face, he heard the sound of soft footsteps approaching from behind. Feeling suddenly foolish at being carried away by a mere portrait, Trevor quickly dropped his hand and turned to face the newcomer.

The same girl who had greeted them at the door entered the room. Something had changed about her, an intangible something he could not quite identify. It was not her demeanor, he thought, as she walked toward him with a gracious smile, though that had certainly improved since she had first opened the door. She held out a delicate hand in polite greeting. "I'm Amity, my lord, Mercy's older sister." She curtsied as he took her hand. Trevor started to reply, but Amity continued in her soft voice, "And you are the Earl of Huntwick, as His Grace has just told me."

"Please call me Trevor," he said smoothly, bringing her hand to his lips as he bowed over it in his most charming manner. She blushed prettily, and he again noted the incredible family resemblance between Amity, Mercy, and the fascinating but still unnamed girl in the portrait.

Amity nodded in agreement to his invitation for her to use his given name, then gently pulled her hand away. Moving with a natural, fluid grace, she walked across the room to a sideboard of polished mahogany laden with beautifully cut crystal decanters and glasses. "May I offer you a drink, my lord?" She glanced over her shoulder at him as she turned over a glass from those upended on the tray.

He nodded. "Brandy, please. How is your sister?"

Amity poured the drink, replaced the stopper in the decanter, and walked over to hand him the glass. "Mercy is resting comfortably. I wanted to thank you for bringing her home, my lord. The doctor is with her now, and she appears to be doing quite well." Amity's clear blue eyes gently shone with deep gratitude.

Trevor smiled warmly, but waved off her thanks with a dismissive gesture. "It was really Sebastian who cared for her. I was hoping to speak with your parents." He fell silent when he noted her expression change, her face clouding slightly for a brief moment. Her polite smile reappeared so quickly that Trevor thought he must have imagined the fleeting look of sorrow momentarily darkening her bright blue eyes.

"My father escorted my older sisters to a dance in the village tonight. My mother died almost thirteen years ago," she said quietly.

Mercy's weak voice came back to him. *I'll be thirteen in two months.* His eyes softened to warm jade with sudden understanding, and his voice deepened gently. "How many sisters and brothers do you have, Miss Amity?" he asked. It was difficult to believe the girls he had seen in the portraits that lined the room had no mother.

Amity's voice immediately brightened. "There are six of us, all girls," she began, gesturing toward the portraits. Beginning with the only male picture and moving on to the sober-looking woman on its right, Amity began to tell him of her family, the obvious love in her voice making Trevor feel he had somehow missed out on something precious. He had no brothers or sisters, none of the sense of family that this room, this very house was steeped in. "That's Papa there over the fireplace, trying to look as stern as he possibly can, though he doesn't manage nearly so well for real. Next to him there's Patience, my eldest sister, and Grace on the next wall," she continued, pointing toward the picture of the girl that had captivated him. Amity's voice faded to the back of his mind as Trevor looked again at her likeness, mentally assigning her name to her face. *Grace,* he repeated to himself as his eyes lingered on the soft, inviting lips curved in a winsome smile. Although they had never met, the girl's name settled comfortably in his mind along with her face, somehow feeling just right.

Amity's voice abruptly brought him out of his reverie. "And, of course, you've met Mercy, the baby of the family, perpetually petted and spoiled by all." She smiled up at him, pointing at the picture above the couch. "She hated posing in that frock. We teased her the entire time she sat for the portrait, and it took weeks to finish because she fidgeted so much." Amity fell silent for a moment, then laughed out loud at a sudden memory. At Trevor's questioning look, she explained: "Once, Grace actually rode her horse right up to the window of the room Mercy posed in and made faces at her behind the artist's back. Mercy laughed so hard that the painter threatened to quit before he'd half finished the painting."

"She'd much rather have been painted in breeches and shirtsleeves, I gather," Trevor put in with a smile.

"Oh, yes, but you see, Patience knew that Mercy had spoiled Papa's dissertation on the possible medicinal uses of fungi native to this area by spilling an entire bottle of ink while she was playing at his desk. Patience threw it away, and Papa thought he'd simply misplaced the dissertation, but Patience confronted Mercy with the truth, so she had to agree to wear that horrid dress."

"Mercy seems the sort who would rather come clean than be subjected to that sort of blackmail," put in Trevor. His curiosity was piqued by the quaint stories that surrounded the members of this family.

"Oh, no!" exclaimed Amity. "It's not that Mercy doesn't prefer honesty. It's just that Papa sort of lives in a world of his own sometimes, and none of us cares to spoil it for him—especially Grace. She seems to think that if we intrude on Papa's world with too much of this reality of ours, we'll lose him as we did Mama. It isn't true, of course, but then, nobody's ever been able to change any notion of Grace's."

The mention of Grace's name a second time in conjunction with that of Mr. Ackerly brought Trevor's mind back to the problem at hand. "Where might I find your father?" he asked, his expression turning serious once more.

"He took Patience, Grace, and Faith to a dance at the Assembly Rooms in the village. I don't expect them to return until late."

"I really feel as though I should let him know what has happened to Mercy," Trevor mused, not adding that he also wanted very much to meet Grace. "Will you give me directions so that I can go find him?"

"Of course." Amity smiled. "You just go back the way you came, toward the inn. When you reach the fork in the road, take the right fork rather than the left, which would lead you back to the inn. That will take you into the village, about a half mile beyond."

Trevor took Amity's hand in both of his and smiled down at her, his green eyes warm. "Thank you, Miss Amity," he said. "I've enjoyed meeting you."

She blushed again and shyly pulled her hand away, then walked with him to the front door. As he opened it, she bade him good night with a graceful curtsy, then turned and went back up the stairs.

Again struck by the acute differences in this Amity from the one who had opened the door, Trevor stood for a few moments, watching her sedate progress up the staircase. In that moment, Trevor finally figured out what had changed about her; she wore a different dress. He frowned, for it struck him as rather a strange thing for her to do, given the circumstances. When, he wondered, had she found the time to do it? Shrugging it off as just another oddity in this strange evening, he pulled the door closed behind him and went down the wide steps to Blackthorne's coach, which, Sebastian having failed to issue his coachman any new instructions in his haste to get Mercy inside, still stood in the drive where they had left it. Pausing to give directions to the driver, Trevor climbed in and sat down. As the coach pulled out and turned down the driveway, the portrait of Grace again appeared in his mind, and he leaned back with his eyes closed, his arms stretched out along the back of the seat, a smile of anticipation slowly sweeping across his face. He looked forward with pleasure to meeting this Ackerly sister in particular.

Chapter Three

*T*aking great pains to avoid detection, Grace peeked through the decorative gold fringe that adorned the tied-back red velvet curtains separating the small alcove in which she hid from the glittering assembly room beyond. Six such alcoves marched along two sides of the large room, but this was the first she had found unoccupied of the five she had already checked. Her eyes quickly skipped over the familiar faces of her friends and neighbors until she spotted the person from whom she was attempting to hide.

Sir Harry Thomas stood on the other side of the room, his narrowed eyes impatiently scanning the crowd of couples that moved gaily around the dance floor. He looked for Grace, an irritated scowl marring his usually handsome face. As his eyes swept toward her hiding place, she quickly pressed herself farther back into the alcove. She breathed a momentary sigh of relief, then looked around and frowned. Observing the small space in which she stood, she realized that when Sir Harry got around to checking the alcoves— and he *would* check the alcoves, she knew—she would be immediately discovered. Worse, she would have no avenue of escape.

She leaned back against the wall, chewing on her lower

lip in consternation. It would not take Harry long to begin looking in the alcoves, so she knew she would have to think quickly. Sure enough, when she chanced another look into the crowded assembly room, she saw Harry's unmistakable blond head, easily three inches taller than those of the room's other occupants, as he moved decisively along the opposite wall, pulling back curtains and checking the alcoves there. He had obviously realized she was not out on the floor dancing, or off to the side talking in one of the small, gossipy groups clustered around the room.

Ducking back in and flattening herself against the wall, Grace released a sigh and reflected again on how her life had come to this.

At the age of seven, she had lost her mother to complications incurred during the difficult birth of her youngest sister, Mercy. With Bingham Ackerly spending a great deal of his time working to keep his large family out of debt while also trying to deal with the sorrow of losing to an early grave the gentle woman he adored, the daunting task of raising the five younger sisters had fallen squarely on the shoulders of twelve-year-old Patience. Occupied with a new baby, irrepressible three-year-old twins, and a shy, frightened five-year-old still very attached to her late mother, Patience had had little time to tend to Grace.

So, with daily instructions from her harassed older sister to stay out of trouble, Grace had found herself free to wander about the village and the surrounding countryside as she wished. She had taken to visiting the neighbors and inhabitants of Pelthamshire, most of whom readily took her in with their own children, for everyone had loved her mother and wanted to help the now motherless Ackerly girls as much as possible.

Her favorite playmates quickly became the Belden boys, their nearest neighbors' four rambunctious sons. The youngest, Henry, was four years her elder. At first it had annoyed the brothers to find themselves followed about by the "carrot-haired pest," as they had taken to calling Grace, and they had done all they could to avoid her. Always, though, the harder they tried to get away from her, the more determination she poured into seeking them out. If they decided to go fishing, Grace showed up on the banks of the pond with her own pole, stoutly declaring that she would catch a bigger fish than any of them. Once, when the boys had hidden in the hayloft to try to discover what the upstairs maid did in the stables with the head groom every Tuesday afternoon, Grace had come looking for them, loudly calling out to them just as the *most* interesting things had begun to happen.

Gradually they'd grown accustomed to having Grace around, and even to look forward to the time she spent with them, for she was an engaging little thing for all her odd ways. Soon it became a common sight around Pelthamshire to see them all together. Grace so adored the boys she considered her own personal big brothers that she began having lessons with them, and often took meals with their family. For the whole summer following the death of her mother, one seldom saw the boys without her.

Oh, how she now longed for those free, easy days. Grace leaned her head back against the wall in her alcove and sighed again. When the boys, one by one, had left for school, their parents closed up the house and moved to London, no longer wishing to remain so far outside society now that they no longer had children to raise. With the boys had gone the tutor, and Grace missed her lessons so much that she spent hours each day closeted with her father in his study, learning subjects much better suited to a son than a young girl who would someday marry and start a family. The time she did not spend studying, she spent out-of-doors becoming an accomplished horsewoman. Although Patience despaired of Grace ever learning to comport herself in a ladylike manner, she'd had her hands full with little Mercy—a child unusually prone to sickness—and with Faith, who had convinced herself that if she lost sight of her eldest sister, Patience would disappear just as her beloved mama had. Patience had been relieved and grateful to know that Grace was safely looked after in their father's study.

Life had continued thus for years in the quiet village. Then, last summer, one Sir Harry Thomas had appeared in Pelthamshire and taken up residence in the old Belden home. Although the newcomer kept the details decidedly vague, he had somehow distinguished himself in the war, earning a knighthood before selling out his commission and moving to the small community. The village made quite a fuss over him, for everyone considered him a hero. Doing nothing to dissuade them, Harry enjoyed himself, basking in the glow of his neighbors' fawning admiration. The demands on his social time were great, and it was several months before a chance remark alerted him to the fact that his nearest neighbors were a widower with a house full of girls. He decided to ride over and introduce himself, happy for the opportunity to add to his bevy of admirers.

The breathtaking vision of budding womanhood who opened the door that afternoon bore absolutely no resemblance to the scruffy little waif who had run wild with the local boys years before. No longer did the hated freckles mar her countenance. They were replaced by a tawny complexion glowing with health from time spent outdoors. The mop of hair that had always needed a good combing had lengthened into piles of thick, shining curls the incredible, if unlikely, color of dancing firelight. Her eyes, which had always seemed too large for her small face, still dominated. Now, however, they were fringed with long, sooty lashes, and had become a startling color that shifted from a cold slate when she was angered to a deep sapphire when something amused her.

Harry was smitten. He had immediately begun his pursuit, his inflated ego making him certain Grace would simply fall into his arms, as had most of the other girls in the village. Grace, though initially friendly, quickly came to distrust and dislike the rather foppish knight and had, whenever possible, avoided him.

Now, again, she peeked out into the ballroom. Glancing furtively about while keeping one eye on Harry's progress, she looked for any possible means of eluding his notice. Her gaze settled on a pair of open French doors that led to the gardens, about a twenty-yard walk across the open floor from her alcove.

Feeling rather like a hunted rabbit, Grace emerged from her hole and began to walk, as sedately as possible, while keeping an eye on Sir Harry. He had turned to look into the last alcove on the far side of the room. If she hurried, she would make it outside and beyond sight before he started across the room to look in the alcoves on this side.

She could almost taste freedom when her progress was suddenly halted. She crashed headlong into a hard, unmoving male chest. Thrown off balance, Grace grabbed wildly at the man's burgundy coat, missed, and began to fall. She gave a small, quickly stifled cry as his hands closed like manacles around her upper arms. With a low chuckle, he lifted her as though she were a puppet and settled her securely upon her feet again.

Thoroughly embarrassed by her clumsiness, Grace raised apologetic eyes to the stranger's deep green ones and found herself arrested by their warmth. A face of raw male perfection met her gaze. He had slashing black brows over those incredible eyes, a decidedly firm chin, and a straight, aristocratic nose, all framed by well-groomed dark brown hair that looked as though it might have a tendency to curl if allowed to grow. As she continued to stare, his well-formed lips swept into a lazy smile, deepening the long dimples on either side of his mouth, transforming his face from chill perfection to warm male beauty. Grace felt her heart clench as he opened his mouth to speak.

"I've been looking for you," he said, in a deep, resonant voice that brought to mind the times she had curled up in her father's lap as a child, her ear pressed to his chest, listening to his rumble as he read her a story from her favorite book. She did not respond, just continued to watch his lips form meaningless words.

"Miss Ackerly?" He spoke a bit louder this time, his brows raised in silent question at her continued lack of response. Shaken from her reverie, Grace suddenly remembered her predicament. She glanced back in Sir Harry's direction just as he spotted her and began to head determinedly toward them.

"I beg your pardon, sir," she said to the man she had run into, belatedly letting go of his coat and pulling away toward the French doors, only to find herself stopped as his grip tightened imperceptibly on her arms.

"Please," she said a little desperately, looking back toward the approaching knight. She could still make it outside and have time to hide, if only this infernal man would cooperate. "Let go of me, sir." Another couple of seconds and Harry would be upon them. Her need to escape escalated to something near panic as she tried to pull away once more, then abruptly changed to annoyed displeasure when his hold on her tightened. She stopped struggling and looked up at the unknown man in irritated confusion.

"Why should I let go of you when I've only just caught you?" The man chuckled. When she saw her nemesis appear behind him, Grace gave the stranger a look of scathing contempt, then reluctantly composed her features to face Sir Harry.

"Is there anything amiss?" Harry asked evenly. He raked his eyes over the scene, taking in Grace's slightly flushed face and the hands of an unknown man closed with unsettling familiarity around her upper arms.

At the sound of Harry's clipped voice, the hands imprisoning her fell away and Grace took a quick step away from both men. "No, sir, everything's fine," she assured him hastily, then rolled her eyes skyward in exasperation as the stranger turned. The two men began to assess each other in the nauseating manner of all males who sensed competition.

"I'm afraid I haven't met your companion," Harry said to Grace, looking the stranger up and down rudely.

"Sir Harry Thomas," Grace began, before she remembered she had no idea of the identity of the newcomer; nor did she know from where he had come. At her questioning look, he smoothly stepped forward and extended a hand to Harry. "Trevor Caldwell," he said, then smiled at Grace with an air of friendly camaraderie as the two men shook. "There's no need to put my title in the way of your friends, is there, my dear?"

Feeling a bit dazed by the rapidly changing events of the last few moments, as well as by the lingering effect of the stranger's incredible smile, Grace automatically shook her head, then realized he had inadvertently given her the perfect opportunity to make her escape. "Why, of course not, Trevor," she agreed with a charming smile. She took a small sidling step away from the two men. "Now I'll just leave you two to become better acquainted." She dropped a haphazard curtsy in the general direction of both men, whirled quickly on one foot, and almost managed to step away. This time Harry's hand stopped her from leaving.

"I've come to claim my dance, Miss Ackerly," he said irritably, annoyed by both Trevor's familiar handling of Grace, whom he considered his exclusive property, and the intimate-sounding *my dear* the unknown nobleman had used when he addressed her.

At his statement, a look of revulsion crossed Grace's face, unnoticed by Harry, who watched Trevor, but noted with great interest by Trevor, who watched her. She kept silent for a moment, her nimble mind spinning frantically as she tried to think of a polite way out of dancing with Harry. When nothing came to mind, she looked at him with thinly disguised resignation and prepared herself to accept his request. Trevor once again stepped in to rescue her.

"I'm quite sorry, Harry, old chap, but Grace has just promised me her next dance," he lied smoothly, extending an aristocratic hand in her direction. "You understand, of course. Shall we, my dear?"

Glancing into Harry's scowling face, Grace placed her gloved hand on Trevor's arm and glided blithely away to the dance floor.

As they began moving together to the lilting strains of a waltz, Grace looked up into Trevor's eyes, which twinkled with amusement, and was surprised to find herself smiling back at him. "Whatever made you do that?" she asked.

Dazzled by the unexpected glamour of her unrestrained smile, Trevor was nearly unable to answer. Only seconds before he had thought Grace merely beautiful. With nothing more than a simple smile of unaffected warmth, she'd become utterly breathtaking. "Do what?" he managed, feeling like a boy with his first crush. "Ask a beautiful woman to dance?"

"No," she said, tilting her head to the side and giving him an arch look. "What made you decide to rescue a damsel in distress?"

He looked down at her, captivated. "Are you?" he asked.

She raised delicately winged russet brows. "A damsel?" she quipped.

"I meant," he asked, "are you in distress?" He grinned

wolfishly at her quick wit, and his green eyes deepened to jade as he realized that, within moments of meeting this girl, he desired her.

"Well, not exactly." She sighed and looked down. "I'm afraid Harry has rather fancied himself my beau since he arrived in Pelthamshire."

Trevor lifted his eyes from her entrancing profile and looked across the room at the stony-faced knight who still watched them. "And you're not."

"No," she said shortly, then fell silent.

They danced without speaking for several moments, gliding along smoothly to the music as if they often danced together. Trevor took the quiet moment to glance around the ballroom, noting with interest the openly curious stares of most of the room's other occupants. "Do your neighbors always take such an interest in your dancing partners?"

Grace shrugged and looked around, wrinkling her nose with the air of someone who really had no interest in what others thought of her. "You're a stranger to Pelthamshire. We don't get many of those here." She raised suddenly curious eyes to Trevor's. "You mentioned a title?"

"It's not important," he said dismissively, wanting to preserve the pleasant sense of companionship that had sprung up between them for as long as possible. He sensed that, once she knew of his nobility, she would be far less open and unassuming.

"But it is," she insisted, her brow furrowed in thought. "Why would a handsome, titled stranger suddenly appear in Pelthamshire, claim he was looking for me"—she paused, trying to think back to what he had already said, then narrowed her eyes, adding slowly—"and already know my name?"

"Do you really?"

"Do I really what?" she asked, distracted, as he intended, by the question that deliberately did not relate to the conversation.

"Do you really think I'm handsome?" He raised both eyebrows and cocked his head in an exaggerated, preening gesture.

Despite herself, Grace burst into sudden, musical laughter, causing the guests, who had begun to lose interest, to start watching their byplay with renewed attention. "All right, *my lord,*" she said with intentional emphasis. "Enough distractions. Now, really, how did you know my name?" Her eyes glowed with pure enjoyment as she tilted her head back to look up at him, her wide smile causing a distracting dimple to appear on each side of her mouth. "Did Faith put you up to posing as a nobleman? Or was it Patience? I know they both think that I'm at my last prayers, but really, I'm not, sir. If I marry, I'll marry when I'm ready and not a moment before." She looked through the crowd for one of her sisters, but did not see them anywhere.

Trevor stopped dancing and drew her hand through his arm, resolutely ignoring the fetching dents in her cheeks. He led her toward the French doors she had so desperately wanted to reach earlier, the curious eyes of the entire village following. Whispering began as soon as they stepped outside, most guests wondering about the mysterious man who seemed so familiar with Grace Ackerly. Those who had spent time in London and already knew his identity hastened to spread their knowledge. Before the doors had completely closed behind Grace and Trevor, nearly everyone in the room knew the noble identity of the handsome stranger who had just disappeared out onto the darkened terrace with Grace.

A few steps from the door, Grace stopped and pulled on his arm to halt Trevor, an inexplicable sense of alarm threading through her. He turned to face her, his eyes a deep, rich jade, gentle in the flickering torchlight from the gardens that bathed them both in a warm orange glow. He did not make her wait. "My friend and I are traveling to his new home, which lies about two hours west of here. We stopped to dine at the inn on the edge of the village and encountered your younger sister Mercy."

At this alarmingly ambivalent statement, Grace's eyes grew round, and Trevor took her hands in his, speaking hastily to reassure her. "She's just fine, Grace, really. She admired Sebastian's team, and when we left, unbeknownst to us, she followed us alongside the road on horseback for a short way. While she was trying to get ahead of us for whatever reason, she jumped a hedge onto the road in front of our vehicle and simply miscalculated just how close she would be to the coach when she landed. Her horse spooked and threw her, and she got a rather nasty bump on the head, but we got her home all right, and . . ." He trailed off at the sudden look of blazing anger on Grace's face.

She pointed a shaking finger at him, then actually poked him in the shoulder with it to punctuate each word. "What took you so long to tell me?" She whirled away from him, storming back inside in a flurry of green silk skirts to search for her father and sisters.

"The opportunity hadn't exactly presented itself," he muttered dryly. He strode after her, now oblivious to the renewed stares of the villagers, his long legs easily eating up the distance her furious pace had put between them. "Miss Ackerly, if you'll just slow down, I'll be happy to explain."

"Explain what? That you nearly killed my sister, and thought you'd slip that information to me between partners on the dance floor?" She tossed the words over her shoulder at him.

"You're hardly being fair, Grace," he pointed out reasonably.

"Fair!" she hissed. She rolled her eyes skyward and took a deep breath. "Well, at least make yourself useful and have our carriage brought around." She stopped walking and peered at the crowd in search of her father or one of her sisters, giving Trevor a second to stop and gather his thoughts, but before he could say anything, she rounded on him again. "I don't suppose you had sense enough to summon a physician?" Without waiting for an answer, she threw up her hands in disgust and hurried away.

Struck speechless by Grace's rapid veer from scathing contempt to unaffected friendliness, then to a demonstration of one of the quickest tempers he had ever witnessed, Trevor stared after her, then looked around the room at the now blatantly distrustful faces of the villagers. He shook his head and shrugged at them in rueful apology, then turned to do as Grace had told him and have the Ackerly carriage brought around. He smiled inwardly. He wondered what the ton would make of the powerful Earl of Huntwick meekly following the orders of a small, angry girl from the country.

Chapter Four

The Ackerly carriage careened into the drive and pulled up in front of the house, spewing gravel in its wake. It halted with an abrupt jerk just as Trevor stepped out of Sebastian's coach and started up the steps to the door. Trevor stopped, watching with interest as Grace hurtled out of the vehicle and ran past him up the stone steps without sparing so much as a glance in his direction. She burst through the front door and slammed it closed behind her with a loud bang, showing little concern for the fragile panes of expensive glass in the windows to either side. Trevor shrugged, shook his head with an inward smile, and looked back at the carriage. He watched as an older gentleman, whose face he remembered from the portrait room, stepped down from the carriage and extended a hand to assist the two ladies inside. Fully expecting to see two more Mercy look-alikes emerge from the dim confines of the small carriage, Trevor noted with surprise the tall, willowy blondes who stepped, one at a time, out onto the cobbled drive. Their faces set in grim worry, the trio hurried inside, followed at a more leisurely pace by Trevor, who already knew that they would most likely find Mercy sitting up in bed, cheerfully recounting the accident that had brought the two strangers into their home.

When he stepped inside, Trevor noticed Bingham Ackerly standing at the foot of the stairs, deep in conversation with Sebastian. Not wanting to interrupt, Trevor politely gave the two men a wide berth and instead went back into the portrait room in search of some refreshment. Finding the room empty, he helped himself to a glass of brandy. He smiled with wicked intent at the portrait of Grace on the wall above the piano as he poured. The young lady had proven far more interesting than he had even begun to imagine when he had first seen her portrait. He recalled her spirited fury at the Assembly Rooms when he had told her what had happened to Mercy. Giving her likeness a last, lingering look, he sauntered back to the open doorway and leaned a shoulder against the frame to wait for Sebastian to conclude his conversation.

Grace appeared at the top of the curving staircase. She still wore the dress she had worn to the dance, a simply cut high-necked gown of shimmering emerald silk. A wide ribbon collar of forest green velvet encircled her slender throat, then ran vertically down the front of the gown to border the hem in broad, sweeping scallops. Cut to loosely skim the contours of her body, the dress really had no waistline at all, only small darts to lightly cinch it in, giving one a subtle impression of the slender curves that lay hidden beneath. She wore no jewelry at all, and styled her bright hair in a simple loose knot at the crown. Several wayward strands had escaped to curl around her face and shoulders, dramatically softening what would have been a rather severe hairstyle on such a small girl into one that both flattered and allured. The tips of dark green velvet slippers peeped from beneath the hem as she gracefully held up her skirts to keep from tripping as she made her poised descent. Recalling the unladylike way she had rushed from the carriage into the house, Trevor grinned at the complete transformation she had undergone in the past fifteen minutes.

She stopped at the foot of the stairs for a moment, curtsied to Sebastian, then spoke quietly with her father, informing him of Mercy's condition and prognosis. She felt Trevor watching her as he lounged in the doorway across the room, and glanced toward him. She fought the sudden inexplicable urge to lift her skirts, turn her back on the smirking earl, and sprint back up the stairs to the safety of her bedchamber. But remembering the way she had shrewishly raged at him at the Assembly Rooms, Grace felt, at the very least, she owed him an apology. After all, the accident truly had not been his fault, and he *had* merely tried to help.

One brow raised in amusement, Trevor watched her surreptitiously glance in his direction and hesitate, biting her lower lip as if in indecision. He could easily read the direction of her thoughts, for the changing expressions on her candid face revealed nearly everything. She knew she owed him an apology for the way she had spoken to him, yet she remained angry with him for not letting her know right away the reason he had come to the dance, so she therefore felt that *he* also owed *her* an apology. Apparently she managed to sort it all out in her mind. She excused herself to her father and Sebastian, squared her shoulders as if to bolster herself for an unpleasant encounter, and began to walk toward Trevor, the former cloudy look on her face replaced with a gracious, apologetic smile.

When she reached Trevor, she curtsied prettily, then extended him her hand, her face tilted up to his, her blue eyes sincere. "Please, my lord, can you forgive my earlier behavior? Mercy and I are very close, you see . . ." She left the sentence incomplete, her eyes turning grave at the thought of what might have happened to her young sister.

He watched her swallow hard. "I just wanted to thank you for getting her home so quickly," she finished with a small catch in her voice.

The unshed tears that brimmed without shame in Grace Ackerly's enormous eyes turned them from glittering sapphire to a startling, luminous turquoise. Usually a woman's tears made Trevor feel one of two ways: annoyed when they were used as a manipulative tool by one of his mistresses, or very uncomfortable. Oddly, Grace's tears inspired a far different reaction. He had the urge to gather her into his arms to try to soothe them away for her.

"It was really Sebastian's doing," he said, checking the impulse. Instead, he smiled down at her tenderly. In his mind he bent his head over hers and took her troubled, upturned face between his hands, gently kissing her slightly parted lips until she trembled in his arms and forgot her worries. Grace looked suddenly uncomfortable, and the vision vanished. Trevor ruefully realized that, while he had fantasized about kissing her, he had kept her small hand warmly imprisoned within both of his. Reluctantly he released it, watching her reaction closely, as though observing some sort of wild, exotic bird he had just released, one that might flit fearfully away at any moment. Without removing his eyes from hers, he gestured toward the two large chairs near the fireplace in the room behind him. "Would you care to sit and talk with me for a moment?"

Grace hesitated. She looked down at his burgundy-clad arm, then nodded slowly and placed her hand gingerly in the crook of his elbow.

Such a distrustful little creature, Trevor thought as he escorted her to one of the comfortable chairs. He made certain she was properly settled before seating himself in the chair opposite. As he sat, he noticed, for the first time, the portrait that hung on the wall directly opposite the picture of Grace. He had not seen this one before because he had been so engrossed in Grace's picture while Amity had described the rest to him. What he saw in that portrait made him grin widely, a sudden lazy smile that swept across his lips, making the rugged planes of his face almost boyishly charming.

Grace saw him smile. Puzzled, she looked over her shoulder in the direction of his gaze, then back at Trevor quizzically. He gestured at the portrait of two identical girls with the now familiar curly red hair and laughing blue eyes. "That portrait answers quite a few questions," he said, shaking his head with a low chuckle.

"The portrait of Amity and Charity?" She raised a dubious eyebrow. "Whatever have they done now?" Amused tolerance softened her guarded features.

He gave a short, sharp bark of laughter when she said their names. "I've been introduced to Amity, and found her quite delightful, but I find it rather hard to believe that somebody actually named that little spitfire Charity." He shook his head, still laughing softly. "I gather she's a bit more excitable than her twin?"

Grace nodded, smiling warmly at him, always happy to talk about the members of her family. "They're nearly inseparable. Amity, who has a tendency to be quiet and withdrawn, seems to temper Charity's impulsive streak, though she has been known to instigate a prank or two herself. Charity, as I believe you've discovered, is anything but withdrawn, though she does manage to keep Amity from constantly burying her nose in a book and isolating herself from the outside world." She looked up fondly at the lone male portrait. "Amity is somewhat like Papa in that respect."

Trevor looked at her with gentle understanding. "Well," he said, "I've had the pleasure of meeting them both, though separately, and at the time I had no idea that there were two of them. It does explain how Amity was able to change her dress and her attitude so quickly from when Sebastian and I first arrived." Briefly, he described the reception they had received from Charity, and his subsequent conversation with Amity in this very room.

Grace laughed. "I can see why you were confused! They've always enjoyed pulling the usual twin tricks on our friends and neighbors." She looked into Trevor's warm jade gaze and marveled at how comfortable she felt with him, curled up here in one of her father's favorite chairs, cozily chatting with a perfect stranger just as though they had been friends for years. Deep inside, somewhere near the pit of her stomach, she felt the faint beginnings of a strange tingle as he returned her look. When his smiling eyes finally left hers and began skipping over the portraits once again, she felt free enough to allow her gaze to slowly wander over the amazing perfection of his features.

His face in profile was ruggedly beautiful, a face that might have inspired Michelangelo himself. She felt odd tingles build within her until something in her chest suddenly lurched. She hastily dropped her gaze to the floor. He lounged in the chair, his Hessian-clad feet stretched before him, legs crossed negligently at the ankles, one foot leisurely flexing back and forth. Her eyes slowly traveled up long, muscular legs encased in chocolate breeches that needed no false padding to improve their shape. A long-fingered, aristocratic hand lay across his lap, the nails neatly trimmed and buffed. His hands and face, more deeply tanned than those of the few other men in his class she had seen, indicated he likely spent a great deal of his time outdoors, either hunting or riding. The notion pleased her. She generally thought of society gentlemen as lazy and wasteful, almost prissy in both their attire and methods of entertainment. Certainly Harry Thomas was so. Trevor Caldwell appeared to be an exception.

Her gaze next wandered with admiration to his broad shoulders, his superbly tailored jacket of burgundy superfine fitting smoothly and perfectly over his crisp white linen shirt. Her composure now restored, she lifted her eyes once again to study his face. Her perusal skidded to an abrupt and immediate halt, her horrified gaze locked on his mouth.

Trevor was smiling rakishly at her, his wide grin revealing even white teeth, startling in contrast to his tanned skin. With dread she forced herself to look into his eyes, a rosy blush spreading hotly across her cheeks despite her frantic attempts to appear cool and unruffled. As she feared, his mocking eyes locked on hers with a look she had never seen, a look that told her he liked the way she inspected him, and that he was now thoroughly enjoying her embarrassment. Stubbornly refusing to allow him to intimidate her, Grace raised her small chin a notch and stared back at him, her embarrassment melting away into defensive antagonism.

Regretfully, knowing the few friendly moments of shared warmth between them were now gone, Trevor wisely decided to retreat to the relative safety of polite conversation. "You found Mercy quite recovered, I hope?" he asked in a deliberately neutral tone intended to defuse Grace's ire.

Greatly relieved that he appeared content to let her brazen inspection of him pass without comment, Grace managed to quell her anger. She nodded hesitantly. "She certainly seemed quite happy with all the fawning attention she's receiving." She lapsed into an awkward silence, then cleared her throat delicately, rather uncomfortable with what she wished to say next. "I wanted to thank you, my lord, not only for your help with Mercy, but also for what you did for me at the dance this evening." She paused awkwardly, chewing on her lower lip, as she often did when she felt ill at ease about something. "You know . . . with Harry."

Trevor lifted a shoulder in a small shrug eloquent in its negligence. "Please," he said. "Think nothing of it."

Sebastian appeared in the doorway. Grace rose quickly to her feet, her relief at being rescued from the awkward situation glaringly evident on her expressive face. Trevor also stood, taking the hand she offered and pressing it briefly to his lips. Unnerved by the sudden rush of sensation she felt when his lips softly brushed the back of her hand, Grace hastily pulled it away, then blurted out the first inane thought that entered her mind. "Did I also apologize to you for my earlier rudeness?" Instantly she felt like kicking herself. Her voice sounded breathless, awed and quite completely foreign, she thought in disgust.

Trevor reached out, lifted her chin with one long, aristocratic finger, and looked deeply into her eyes. "Again," he said, his low tone reminding her of sun-warmed honey, "think nothing of it." Her heart began to beat wildly as he slowly leaned in closer, his cheek next to hers. He lowered his voice still more to a whisper. "In fact, my dear, I rather enjoyed your close examination of my person," he said. His warm breath against her ear sent sudden chills skittering down her spine.

When the full import of his words finally hit her, her mouth dropped open. Trevor grinned, then straightened and strolled across the room toward Sebastian without a backward glance.

"My lord!" Her voice rang out much more loudly than she had intended.

Trevor turned, his dark brows raised expectantly.

"That wasn't what I meant," she said, her small chin jutting out defensively.

Trevor smiled. "I know," he said softly, then turned and walked from the room with Sebastian, leaving Grace standing stiffly beside her chair. She fumed at first, and then, after a moment, reluctantly smiled to herself. After all, she *had* been staring.

* * *

At Bingham Ackerly's insistence, they enjoyed a late supper. He invited the duke and the earl to stay at the Ackerly home rather than returning, at such a late hour, to the village inn, where neither the accommodations nor the repast would have been nearly as agreeable. They spent a pleasant hour at the table, especially enjoyed by Trevor, who had never had the experience of dining on good, simple fare with a large, loving family. He sat quietly, content to watch the sisters and their father pass plates of food to one another, laughing now and then at something somebody said, enjoying the good-natured banter that came easily to a family well used to communicating with one another. He found himself comparing this rather simple existence to the opulent manner in which he had grown up, and wondered which family he would describe as the richer.

Now, as he lay in his borrowed bed, staring through the inky darkness in the general direction of the ceiling, his thoughts once again centered on the amazing and self-possessed young lady whose fiery personality, although at such complete odds with her demure name, quite matched her glorious hair. "Grace," he whispered to himself, and decided he liked the way her name sounded as it rolled off his tongue. His lips curved in a fond smile as his mind's eye passed again over her vibrant features.

Her portrait did her no justice, he thought, sniffing disdainfully at the artist's obvious lack of talent. Although the rendering accurately depicted her features, it did not in any way capture her essence. In the space of a single evening, he had seen her large, expressive blue eyes reflect her changing emotions like very windows into her soul. One moment they darkened furiously in speechless anger; the next they sparkled with easy laughter. One moment they were shining brightly with gratitude; the next they clouded to a stormy blue-gray in frustration.

Tonight she had worn her hair pulled back in a sedate

chignon, a style a bit out of character and somewhat confining for someone of Grace's spirited temperament. It
would look much better unbound, he thought sleepily, exactly the way she had worn it in her portrait. Just as it
would look spread in a blazing fan across his pillows, he
added to himself as sleep finally claimed him. He dreamed
pleasantly of burying his face in those flaming tresses.

A few doors down the hall, Grace lay sleepless in her bed.
She pondered, with rapidly growing dismay, the various un-
welcome reactions she'd had to nearly everything Lord
Caldwell had said or done over the course of the evening.

For much of the past nine months, she had eluded the
unwanted bonds of marriage to Sir Harry Thomas by the
simple measure of avoiding the self-important knight as
much as possible. When she could not manage to evade
his notice, she kept him, both mentally and physically, at
arm's length. She had no intention of marrying anybody,
most especially not Harry Thomas. Having already reached
her twentieth birthday, she knew society considered her
well past the age at which most girls of her class should
have settled down.

From what Grace had seen of marriage within the limited circle of her small world, the institution held no attraction for her. The world, she had noticed, expected nothing
more from women than that they be submissive, demure
brood mares, allowed absolutely no rights or even opin-
ions of their own. Grace knew she would almost certainly
stagnate under such wretched restrictions. She thought of
the long, heart-pounding, full-out galloping rides she regularly took on her favorite mare, and of the pleasant philo-
sophical conversations she often held with her father over
a rousing game of chess, chats that lasted until late in the
evening, long after everyone else had retired. She could
not imagine any of the gentlemen of her acquaintance

actually deigning to spend time engaged in good-natured banter with her over the latest Parliament decisions reported in the slightly outdated London papers they regularly received in Pelthamshire.

Grace clenched her teeth in the darkness. That would *not* happen to her, she vowed. She would, at all costs, avoid marriage to anyone until society considered her safely on the shelf, quite beyond hope, and, most important of all, quite beyond interest. Once she reached official spinster status, she would travel, she decided with a deep yawn, finally ready to succumb to slumber. She rolled over, pulled the covers up over her head, and fell into a troubled sleep haunted by dreams of laughing eyes the many shifting colors of the forest.

Chapter Five

$\mathcal{B}$y force of habit Grace awakened early, opening her eyes when the first golden sunbeams moved lazily across the polished hardwood floor of her bedchamber. Feeling somewhat groggier than usual, she stretched her arms above her head, flexed her leg muscles, and sat up, inexplicably bothered by a sense of foreboding. She kicked off the covers, stood, and stretched again, then padded softly over to the window. She opened it and looked out pensively at what promised to blossom into a beautiful spring day.

Unable to shake the troubling feelings with which she had awakened, Grace turned away from the window and furrowed her brow in thought. She began to dress for the morning ride she and Mercy had lately made a ritual. As she stepped into the breeches she normally wore instead of a cumbersome habit, the events of the previous evening came flooding back, explaining the niggling warning at the back of her mind. She sat down heavily on the end of her bed and slipped an arm into her shirt.

Mercy would not join her today, she remembered, buttoning up the oversize cast-off garment of her father's. Worse, if she did not manage to get an early start, she ran the distinct risk of running into Lord Caldwell at breakfast. He, she absolutely knew, would undoubtedly decide to accompany her. Just the thought of the chaotic effect that particular man had on her senses made her hurriedly pull on her old scuffed boots and tie back her burnished hair with a length of wide ivory ribbon snatched from the top of her dressing table.

She left her room and peeked in on Mercy, who slept peacefully, then tiptoed down the dark back stairs to the homey warmth of the kitchen. "Good morning, Mary, dear," she said cheerfully, giving the plump older lady an affectionate squeeze.

Mary had come to cook for the Ackerly family shortly after the birth of Patience. A crotchety, sour-faced old darling, she constantly scolded, pecked at, and unashamedly ordered about the girls, who all good-naturedly ignored her, quite secure in the knowledge that Mary loved them all with as fierce a devotion as she would have her own children, had she borne any. Straight to the kitchen they had always gone in times of need, happily enduring her muttered admonitions as she taped up skinned knees, dried tears from grubby cheeks, or soothed someone's wounded pride with hot milk and pudding.

Mary looked sternly at Grace's attire. She shook her head and clicked her tongue disapprovingly, as she did every morning when Grace and Mercy appeared clad in their tattered but beloved male garments. "Lookin' a perfect disgrace, you are again, Miss Grace—an' with quality in the house, sleepin' above stairs just like we was someone." She gestured at the ceiling with the wooden spoon that never left her hand. "I been sayin' for years that nothin' good would come of you girls runnin' around in boys' clothes, and now look at Miss Mercy, all tucked up in her bed with a lump the size of a goose egg over her wee eye. Will she be joinin' you this mornin', or is her little head painin' her too much?"

Grace shook her head. "She was still sleeping when I

checked in on her, the poor darling. She'll likely sleep for hours yet."

Mary gave Grace a doubtful look. "Yer sisters will be hard put to keep her in the house and off the back of a horse, especially when she finds you've gone on without her." She turned back to the simmering pot of soup on the stove, dipping the wide spoon into the steaming liquid and stirring vigorously in unspoken dismissal. She looked over her shoulder and scowled when Grace did not move. "There's yer meat pie, missy, right there on the counter for you to take for yer breakfast. Now get on out of here and let me do my work." She frowned into the large black kettle, darkly muttering something about little girls running wild in boys' breeches.

Grace grinned good-naturedly at the woman's back, grabbed her wrapped meat pie, and left. She would take a long, leisurely ride through the countryside. With any luck, their noble visitors would have long since departed by the time she returned.

Two hours later Grace lazed on her back in the dappled shade of a leafy pin oak, trying to think of another original excuse to use for avoiding Sir Harry the next time she was unfortunate enough to come into contact with him. Her horse, Firefly, a beautiful and spirited chestnut mare, stood securely tethered across the glade near an old tree stump Grace would find convenient to use when remounting. She chewed on a long stem of grass with her eyes half-closed, one foot encased in its scuffed boot and crossed over her threadbare knee. An unexpected shadow fell across her face.

Certain the newcomer was Mercy directly disobeying the orders of both the physician and her sisters, Grace sat up and turned around, ready to scold the irrepressible young girl for getting out of bed. With a start of surprise, she saw one of the very people she least wanted to see, calmly settling down and leaning back against *her* oak tree. Without bothering to hide her annoyance, Grace plopped back down, refusing to acknowledge his presence.

"Good morning, Grace," he said in a pleasant tone.

Grace said nothing.

"You're out and about early," he commented.

Still no response.

Amused by her stubborn silence, Trevor tried one more time. "Have I done something to offend you?"

"No," came her terse reply.

Trevor fell silent for a moment. He regarded the top of her curly head with a thoughtful look while contemplating his next move. He cleared his throat in the stillness, then frowned when he saw Grace start in surprise at the noise. She was tense, strung as tightly as a bowstring, he thought, and wondered why. "Would you care to know why I've come to find you?" he asked. He stretched out on his side behind her, his dark head propped on one hand.

"To say good-bye?" Grace asked hopefully, without looking around.

Trevor chuckled. "No," he said, close to her ear, his warm breath tickling the fine hairs at the nape of her neck. Abruptly she scrambled up and stood over him, her hands firmly planted on her hips, her eyes spitting defiant blue sparks at him.

Trevor remained prone, lying on his side beneath her. He was able, from this angle, to properly appreciate every luscious curve revealed by the breeches that clung provocatively to her hips, thighs, and trim backside. He looked up farther, past the oversize shirt that hid any other attributes she might possess, to her small, set face.

"Perhaps we began badly, Miss Ackerly—"

"All the more reason to end well, my lord," she interrupted ruthlessly.

"Ah, Grace, but if we end our acquaintance prematurely, there will always be unanswered questions between us." He looked down and picked up the long blade of grass she had chewed upon, then deliberately caressed the toe of her boot with it.

She snatched her foot away. "I've no questions for you, Lord Caldwell. Ask yours so you may leave Pelthamshire with a free mind."

His eyes traveled back up her body to lock suggestively with hers. With satisfaction, he watched her expression go from defiance to wariness, then to sudden alarm.

Afraid she would take flight, he got to his feet in one fluid motion. He found her enormous blue eyes looking directly into his, silently beseeching, almost begging: *'Please don't ask me that!'*

I will, his eyes promised in return as he took a step closer, his intentions clearly written on his face.

Instinctively Grace began to retreat, more consciously aware of his nearness than she had ever been with any other person; then she bravely decided to stand her ground. She glared at him, her head held high in proud rebellion. A second later she knew she had made a tactical error.

Trevor reached out and grasped her upper arms, hauled her suddenly against the rock-hard length of his body, and brought his mouth down on hers. Despite the abrupt embrace, the lips that found hers were soft, cajoling. The more Grace struggled, the more closely Trevor held her, not wanting to hurt her, only seeking to calm her with his hands and his mouth as she fought more and more feebly to get away. Tenderly he coaxed her tightly compressed lips to part with his tongue, only to encounter the stubborn barrier of her clenched teeth. "Please kiss me, Grace," he said in a husky voice, willing her to stop resisting him, to give back with equal ardor the passion he so wanted to make her feel. "I've been dreaming all night long of kissing you."

Grace's head spun. Her senses were engulfed; his hands, his plundering tongue, his incredible, intoxicating scent, a beguiling combination of soap and leather and something indefinable. Everything about him made her want to ignore all her warning instincts, simply to let go and give herself up to the incredible sensations sweeping through her. She stood rigidly resistant in his arms, desperately fighting the overwhelming urge to give in to him. In helpless alarm she felt his hand move inexorably up her rib cage and stop when it came to the swell of her small breast. His thumb lazily caressed the sensitive underside, testing her reaction. Slowly he moved his hand to let her breast fill his cupped palm. Grace held her breath, unable to believe she was not pulling away from him. She gasped in shocked surprise when he slid his other hand deep into the thick curls at the back of her head and deliberately grazed his thumb across her already hardening nipple. The moment she opened her mouth Trevor deepened the kiss, tilting her head back and pushing his tongue past her teeth to the warm, moist softness within.

Liquid heat unfurled in Grace's stomach and spread, unrestrained, throughout her body, making her head spin and her knees weak. Slowly the rigid tension left her. She willingly opened her mouth to his, pressing herself with an urgency beyond her own understanding against his hard length. Her breast tingled where his thumb had grazed her nipple, and she felt a growing sense of need for something more, something she could not describe. Without realizing she did so, she reached around his neck and put both hands on the back of his head, instinctively pulling his mouth closer to hers, and then tentatively touching the tip of her tongue to his.

Trevor stiffened and groaned deeply at the light caress of her tongue. He felt the iron control over his rampaging desire suddenly break. He *had* to feel her against him. Expertly he unfastened the top buttons of her shirt with one hand and deftly slid it inside. The slightly rough skin of his fingers encountered the velvet softness of her breast. Trevor caught his breath, then centered her hardening nipple in the palm of his hand, lifting and kneading her tender flesh with ever-growing need. He slid his other hand from the back of her neck down her spine to cup her shapely buttocks and pull her fully against the rigid evidence of his arousal, his tongue plunging in and out of her mouth in ageless, primitive suggestion. He had never tasted anything so sweet, and knew that if they did not stop soon he would take her, here and now, out in the open beneath this shady oak tree. With a strength he did not know he possessed, he dragged his mouth from hers, flinching at her unintentional soft whimper of denial, and stared, sightless, over the top of her head, his mind fighting to command his thundering need.

Grace stood quietly in his embrace, her surging heartbeat slowly returning to normal. She felt drained of all sense. As sanity began to return, she realized with humiliated chagrin that she had acted like a common strumpet, pressing herself against him and returning his ardor with virtually no resistance. She closed her eyes and laid her flushed cheek against his soft linen shirt, the sound of his heart racing as wildly as hers comforting her for a moment, then, with a sudden rush of clarity, making her face a horrifying truth.

God help her, she wanted more!

Trevor gently closed his arms around her trembling body, sensing her frightened reaction to the incredible passion they had just shared in one simple kiss. He smoothed her tumbled hair, untangled the ivory ribbon that had somehow come undone, and pressed a kiss to the top of her head, humbled by the amazing tenderness she had awakened in him. He tightened his fist around the small scrap of linen he had removed from her hair. In that moment he made a decision he had never before even considered with any other woman.

He would marry Grace Ackerly.

Already a thread of possessive pride coursed through him. He held her imperceptibly closer, a smile of profound wonder stealing across his face at the passionate way she had responded to him. She was a natural temptress, unconsciously seductive and incredibly alluring. He could only hope she would never discover the power she held over him. Almost as soon as the thought occurred to him, he corrected himself. She *should* know, he thought, so that she could take pride in the way she made him feel, for he knew in his heart that if she ever loved him, she would never use that power against him.

While Trevor pleasantly contemplated their future, Grace grew more and more uncomfortable in his embrace, deeply unsettled by the way he had made her feel. Somehow this handsome stranger had entered her life and upset the carefully balanced existence that had defined her world, and she found that she did not like it—at all. Every instinct she possessed warned her that this man threatened her precious freedom, that she had to get away from him before she no longer could.

Her ear still pressed against his chest, Grace heard his preparatory intake of breath, and realized with horror that he intended to speak. Suddenly afraid of what he might say, she pushed with all her strength against his torso and stumbled back away from him, tripping on an exposed tree root and landing sprawled on her backside in the grass.

Pushing her hair out of her eyes, she looked up at him and saw that he was preparing to speak. Quickly, she blurted, "I won't marry *you*, either!"

Trevor closed his mouth in surprise, looking at the defiant beauty below him, her chest heaving with turbulent emotion, causing her mostly exposed breasts to quiver enticingly. With an effort, he looked away from the fetching sight to find her eyes shooting blue sparks at him. He raised an amused eyebrow as she fumbled with her buttons and extended a hand to help her up. "I don't remember asking you," he said calmly. He tilted his head and gave her a thoughtful, assessing look. "Have you had a great many requests?"

Sublime humiliation washed acidly through her, causing her ill humor to once again intensify. "No!" she snapped irritably, then closed her treacherous mouth before it could utter any more embarrassing statements.

"Perhaps, then, it's the customary thing to do around here after sharing a kiss," he mused, tapping an index finger on his upper lip. He gave her a reproving look. "If that's the case, my dear, you really should have informed me of the danger I faced before you returned my kiss."

"Returned your . . . I did no such thing," she said indignantly, knowing she lied even as the words left her mouth.

Trevor smirked.

Grace's hands clenched convulsively into tight little fists as she stared, speechless, at the infuriating man in front of her. Finally finding her voice, she took a calming breath and attempted to explain. "I don't intend ever to marry, you see, and I just wanted to disabuse you of the notion that our . . . our . . ." She gestured impatiently, searching for the proper word as she scrambled to her feet, pointedly ignoring his proffered hand.

"Our kiss?" Trevor supplied helpfully.

"Our *mistake*," she amended with emphasis, "that our mistake did not in any way indicate that I welcomed future . . . ah . . ."

"Mistakes," he reminded her.

"Future *incidents* from you," she finished severely, with an impressive glower. She tossed her head and marched resolutely across the wildflower-strewn glade to Firefly. She gathered the reins, stepped purposefully on the stump to mount, landed in the saddle, and spun away.

Trevor stared thoughtfully after her as she rode off. He recalled her almost desperate need to get away the evening before when Harry had approached. *I don't intend ever to marry,* she had said today. Pondering her strange behavior, he swung onto his own borrowed horse and galloped after her. Already he anticipated with pleasure his next mistake with Miss Ackerly.

Chapter Six

$\mathcal{W}$indblown and breathless, quaking inside from the turbulent feelings Trevor had awakened in her, Grace arrived back at the Ackerly stables still trying to bring her raging emotions under control. She skillfully eased Firefly into a canter, then further slowed her to a walk, transferred the reins to one hand and tentatively touching a trembling fingertip to her still-swollen lips. She felt an odd tension begin to build deep in her stomach as she recalled the way Trevor's lips had moved insistently over hers. Remembering the wanton way she had responded, how she had practically wrapped herself around him and brazenly returned his kiss, Grace groaned and felt her cheeks grow hot with shame. Hastily, she pulled the mare to a stop in front of the paddock and slid down, closing her eyes against the mortifying realization that she had thoroughly enjoyed what they had done.

She leaned forward and rested her forehead for a moment against the warm, comforting chestnut hide of her mount. No question remained in her mind: she simply could not allow such a thing to happen again. The sooner the Earl of Huntwick left Pelthamshire, the better. In the meantime, she thought grimly, she would have to do her level best to remain well away from him.

Hearing a shuffling footstep on the ground behind her, Grace abruptly straightened and shook her wind-tossed hair over her hot face. "I'll see to Firefly myself, Willie," she said without looking back at the young groom who had, she knew, automatically reached for the bridle. She wanted to remain alone for as long as possible, shamefully certain that anybody who looked at her would somehow know precisely where she had been—and worse, exactly what she had done. When the young man did not reply, she clicked her tongue and led the mare into the clean, roomy stall, gave her some water, and began rubbing her down with strong, sure motions, deliberately letting the rhythm of her movements push the disturbing encounter with the Earl of Huntwick to the back of her mind.

She became so absorbed in her task, she did not notice the visitor who entered the stables and leaned against the door to Firefly's stall, watching in silence as she continued to work on stabling her horse. Only when she had finished with the brush and turned to fetch a bucket of oats with which to fill the feed bin did she see Sir Harry leaning there, his blond hair gilded by a shaft of sunlight slant-ing through the hayloft, a determined smile fixed on his too-handsome face. Provoked by the events of the morn-ing, Grace stopped in her tracks and scowled at him for a second, then pushed open the heavy wooden door so it banged against the wall with a thud. She stalked over to the feed barrel in the corner without a word of greeting to the colorfully garbed, self-important knight.

Harry watched her deft movements as she filled the cedar bucket with the enormous scoop, then turned back to the stall. "Is the gossip I hear true?" He moved back a couple steps to protect his new bottle-green satin jacket when she pushed past him again with the rough bucket over her arm.

"What gossip?" Grace asked irritably, banging the bucket

against the feed bin in her haste to finish and get out of the stable, away from the unwanted proximity to Harry. Firefly, already nervous as she sensed the rapidly shifting moods of her mistress, shied in agitation and tossed her head in eloquent equine protest of the sharp sounds and raised voices.

"The gossip about you and the Earl of Huntwick, of course," he replied, watching her closely to gauge her reaction. He was not disappointed.

Grace stiffened and set her bucket down with another loud thud, finally giving him her full attention. "And just what is it they are saying?" she demanded, walking over to stand next to him, separated only by the wooden door of Firefly's stall.

Unable to retain his composure at the thought of Grace preferring anybody to him, Harry felt his perfect features twist a bit, betraying his carefully concealed ire. "What they're saying," he said, a bitter edge creeping into his voice, "is that his unexpected appearance at the Assembly Rooms last night was no coincidence."

"Well, that's certainly true," Grace supplied uninformatively. She turned back to her task, hoping he would pick up on the fact that she did not wish to have a conversation with him. She did not turn quickly enough. His hand shot out, and she gave an involuntary yelp as it closed painfully around her wrist. He spun her back around and pushed her up hard against the stall door.

"You're hurting me!" Grace cried out, struggling to free her arm from his iron grip. Firefly nickered nervously behind her. Grace tried unsuccessfully to stifle the small whimper that escaped her as pain shot up her arm from her wrist.

"They're saying," Harry said menacingly, his angry face, only inches from hers, turning a mottled shade of purple, "that you've known each other for years, that you're possi-

bly betrothed and probably lovers. Is that true?" he bit out
between clenched teeth.

In a flash, blind anger overrode Grace's momentary fear.
She tossed her head defiantly and glared straight into his
furious hazel eyes, ignoring the increasing ache in her
wrist. She opened her mouth to tell him that she belonged
to no man, that she never intended to marry, and most especially not him. Before she had a chance to utter a word,
Trevor stepped from the shadowy doorway near the tack
room and spoke.

"Now, if that *were* true," he warned in a calm, silky voice,
"how do you suppose I might react to somebody handling
my fiancée thus, and speaking to her in such an insulting
and abusive manner?" He took a threatening step closer to
Harry and looked pointedly at the hand still locked around
Grace's wrist.

Recognizing the steely glint in Trevor's eyes as possessive
fury, Harry let go and turned defensively toward the earl,
anger bristling in his narrowed eyes. Grace backed quickly
toward Firefly, safely out of reach of either man. She stood,
silently rubbing her wrist, as she watched the unbelievable
tableau playing out before her.

The two men stood facing each other warily, a study in
opposites, although quite similar in height and build. The
dark earl, attired in a subdued black coat and trousers over
a spotless white linen shirt, exuded an air of leashed
power and cool control. The blond knight, dressed in the
colorful, foppish finery of a town dandy, appeared weak
and somehow silly, despite his alleged exploits in the war.
Grace felt a shadow of alarm thread through her. A strange
sense of unreality descended upon the entire scene while
she stood holding Firefly's bridle. She stroked the nervous
horse's neck reassuringly and murmured soothing words
in a twitching ear, as much to calm herself as to settle the
animal.

As his anger began to dissolve into justifiable fear, Harry assessed the threat to his physical well-being, as well as to the new clothing he proudly sported. Wisely, he held up a placating hand. "Please understand that I'm merely concerned for Grace's reputation, my lord, as is the entire village," he said in an almost pleasant tone. "As she has no brother to keep her safe and defend her honor, naturally I feel as though I should assume the responsibilities of one."

Grace gave an unladylike snort of disbelief.

Trevor glanced at her briefly, then looked back at the now serenely smiling face of the knight. His hackles rose at the sight of the tasteless man's self-satisfied smirk. "Your brotherly services will no longer be required," he said shortly. He stepped aside so he did not block the door, making it blatantly obvious that he expected Harry to leave.

Anger once again flared in Harry's eyes. He gave Grace a long look of derision. She returned the look with belligerent scorn, lifting her chin and glaring down her nose in an obstinate gesture already becoming familiar to Trevor.

"So it's true, then," Harry drawled recklessly, looking her insolently up and down, his eyes purposely lingering on her long, shapely, breeches-clad legs. "I guess the only question that remains unanswered is whether his lordship is your fiancé . . . or your lover."

Firefly flinched at the sudden sharp crack that rang through the stable as Trevor's fist connected with Sir Harry's jaw. The knight grunted in pain as he careened heavily into the far wall and then slid slowly down to the straw-covered floor of the stable. With a small cry of shock, Grace released Firefly's bridle and ran to the door of the stall, looking over it to see Harry slowly raising himself up on an elbow, one hand ruefully rubbing his chin. She looked up at Trevor and physically recoiled from the blazing anger in his eyes. He crossed the floor in two long strides to stand over Harry.

"I should call you out for that, you bastard!" he said to the man on the floor in a lethal tone.

Harry shook his head with a wince of pain. "The slur to my parentage aside, I suppose that answered my question," he said, getting awkwardly to his feet and straightening his now hopelessly smudged and wrinkled jacket. "My apologies, Miss Grace, for my poor manners." He bowed stiffly in her direction, nodded shortly to Trevor, and strode from the stables.

Trevor watched him go, his lip curled in disgust at the man's distasteful attire. He turned back to Grace, who stood silent just inside the stall. She glared at him in anger, her hands balled into two small fists planted firmly on her hips. Trevor looked at those trim hips and immediately remembered the feel of their firm curves beneath his hands. His body tightened in instinctive response. A slow smile worked its way across his face.

That smile pushed Grace over the edge. "How dare you!" she flung at him, stamping her foot. "Do you have any idea what you've done?" She shook her head and stomped her foot again when she saw that he did not even comprehend the extent of the damage. When Harry returned to the village, he would tell everyone his version of what had transpired in the Ackerly stable. Soon the entire village would hear the tale, and would suppose that Grace actually *did* intend to marry the Earl of Huntwick. When the marriage did not come to pass, everyone would automatically assume the worst: that she had really been his lover all along.

Trevor thought she had lost her mind. "What would you have had me do?" he asked in disbelief. "Should I have allowed him to maul you in this stable, right before my eyes?" His growing frustration with her was evident on his face.

"You could have allowed me to take care of myself," she said hotly. "I've handled Harry before," she added, stepping out of the stall and latching the door firmly behind her. She started to walk past him, fully intending to escape into her room and not emerge until the earl and his friend finally left, but Trevor smoothly stepped in front of her, effectively blocking her exit. He looked down at her with a tender smile.

"You don't have to take care of yourself, Grace," he said, his voice turning deep and husky.

"I would rather do so, if you please, my lord," she returned in a tone drained of all emotion, unwilling to admit, even to herself, the almost magnetic effect his voice had on her. Tired from the battle of wills she had fought with this man almost from the moment they had met, she now wanted nothing more than to get away from him and from the way he muddled her senses. "Would you kindly move out of my way?" She looked up at him with weary patience.

Trevor gave her a long, assessing look, then stepped aside without a word. She pushed past him and walked out of the stables, her long hair swaying with each fluid step, her pert nose perched firmly in the air. He watched her go, gazing with admiration at the graceful movement of her hips. Grace did not look back as she crossed the yard and disappeared into the house.

Bingham Ackerly stood on the front steps, one arm curved protectively around his youngest daughter, bidding their noble guests a smiling good-bye. "I can't thank you enough for what you've done, Your Grace," he said with deep gratitude as he shook Sebastian's hand. Mercy stared unabashedly up at the handsome duke, her huge blue eyes shining at him with obvious adoration under the wide white bandage that encircled her small head.

With a rarely bestowed smile, Sebastian reached out to rumple her silky auburn curls, then chucked her affectionately under the chin, admonishing, "You stay out of trouble, urchin." Although he voiced it as an instruction, not a request, his tawny eyes held a rare gentle glint. This odd young girl had touched something in him he had previously not known existed. He bent and kissed her small hand with an air of gallantry, then went down the shallow steps to climb aboard the waiting coach.

Inside the house, clad in a pretty jonquil yellow morning gown, Grace stood at the front drawing room window, peering through a small break in the curtains. She watched as Trevor spoke with her father for a moment, then solemnly shook Mercy's hand and joined the duke in the shining burgundy vehicle. Through the coach's open doorway she watched Trevor settle into his seat, say something to the duke, then look directly at her window.

Instinctively, she shrank back. Although certain he could not possibly see her, she was unwilling to let him know she was watching him leave, and even more unwilling to admit that she felt an odd sense of loss at seeing him go. When she thought it safe to look again, the footman had already closed and latched the door. She watched in silence until the coach had pulled off and made its way down the short drive to the road. She turned away from the window, letting the heavy curtain fall back into place with a soft rustle.

"Miss Grace?"

Happy for any distraction from her unwelcome thoughts, Grace smiled at the young girl from the village who had just begun working in the household as a parlor maid. "What is it, Millie?" she asked in a pleasant tone.

"His lordship asked me to give you this after he left, miss." She handed Grace a folded piece of paper, then curtsied awkwardly and scurried from the room. She was so frightened that Grace did not have the heart to call her back and tell her that the members of this household did not require her to curtsy.

She also did not bother to ask which nobleman had written the note. A bit cautiously she opened it and scanned the brief contents. What she read made her clench her teeth in sudden, renewed annoyance. The earl had effectively gotten the last word. He'd written in a bold, sweeping hand:

> *You look beautiful in yellow, my dear Grace, although I think I prefer you in your breeches. I will be taking up residence in a week at my country estate. I will call upon you soon after.*
> *Yours, Trevor*

Furious, Grace crumpled the note and tossed it into the drawing room fireplace. The last thing she wanted or needed was for the Earl of Huntwick to live nearer Pelthamshire. She watched the edges of the note catch fire and curl into ash. When the last bit of paper disappeared in the flames, she nodded with grim satisfaction and stalked out of the drawing room in search of Patience. Her older sister had begun pressing her again this year to go to London for the Season. She and Faith had an open invitation from their mother's eldest sister. Until now, Grace had considered the idea of spending the entire spring in the city both distasteful and useless. But suddenly, she found the prospect of leaving the village very attractive. If Trevor insisted upon moving into her territory, she would strategically retreat to his. With luck, she would be far away from Pelthamshire long before the Earl of Huntwick returned.

As the stately coach again passed the little inn on the outskirts of the village, Trevor looked out the window, a thoughtful smile hovering around his mouth.

"I would not have imagined deflowering young virgins your style, Hunt." Sebastian spoke the words lightly, but his brows drew together in a disapproving frown.

"It's not," Trevor replied uninformatively, somewhat annoyed by his friend's erroneous assumption that his motives for seeking out Grace were purely sexual.

The duke remained undaunted. "Virgins," he stated flatly, "are nothing but trouble."

The earl raised his eyebrows at Sebastian. "Are you lecturing me, Your Grace? Speaking, perhaps, from the vast experience your age and travels have afforded you, my young, fledgling duke?" He turned back to the window. "Please. Spare me the sermon, Sebastian. You should be concentrating on perfecting your ducal glare of glacial contempt."

Sebastian ignored the jibe. "Making Grace Ackerly your lover would be a great deal more of an inconvenience than a pleasure, I can assure you," he warned emphatically.

An inappropriate parade of visions chose that unlikely moment to dance through Trevor's mind: Grace in her indecently distracting breeches, her hair unbound, a long blade of grass between her even white teeth, completely unaware of how alluring she looked; Grace tossing her head and defiantly declaring that she would not marry him, although he had not yet asked her; Grace as she would look in his bed, her glorious hair spilling across his pillows, her velvety blue eyes filled with passion, beckoning him near. . . .

Resolutely, he pushed *that* particular vision to the back of his mind and looked across the coach at his friend. "Making her my wife may well prove to be a great deal worse," he said softly. He looked back out the window at the passing scenery, therefore missing his normally unflappable friend's expression of shock.

Chapter Seven

The unmistakable clatter of carriage wheels in the drive took Wilson by surprise. The normally haughty Caldwell butler hastened to the front door in what could only be described as an undignified run. Even so, he managed only to arrive out of breath, too late to open it; the Earl of Huntwick already stood on the threshold of his spectacular estate, the Willows, grinning broadly at his slightly disheveled and quite embarrassed butler.

The small man drew himself up sharply and regained his usual ultradignified and lofty manner in a matter of seconds. "My lord," he intoned nasally, bowing ever so slightly. "Although we weren't expecting you for two more days, may I say how very good it is to have you home again?"

"I couldn't agree more, Wilson," said Trevor, clapping the older man solidly on the back. He walked in and looked around with satisfaction at the magnificent entranceway. The immaculate marble floor gleamed, and the walls paneled in satiny rosewood glowed with newly applied wax. The glittering crystal chandelier suspended three stories above his head threw a myriad of tiny rainbows around the room from the sunlight that streamed in the soaring arched windows, panes of glass that rose all the way from ground level to nearly the roof of the thirty-room estate.

Although Trevor employed a full complement of servants year-round in each of his estates, he also retained a small contingent of his most trusted staff, consisting of his secretary, cook, housekeeper, butler, valet, and coachman. This small, efficient group of people traveled with him, taking up residence in whichever home he happened to occupy. Since he followed a rather rigid daily schedule to which he strictly conformed, no matter his location, they had become very adept at anticipating all of Trevor's needs almost before he himself knew of them. As a result, their summons to relocate from London just as the Season began hardly surprised them. They managed, with their usual aplomb, to smoothly step in and take over the running of the household. Already their presence had made a vast difference in the condition of the long-unlived-in estate. This, the home of his childhood, was also the residence in which Trevor spent the least amount of time, so most of the rooms had been closed off for years. Although competently maintained by the steward, the household had acquired a rather deserted air. Now, however, everywhere he looked, Trevor saw servants busily working; shining silver and polishing brass fixtures, dusting furniture and cleaning the vast windows that covered a great deal of the front of the mansion.

In this home Trevor had grown up, a small boy lost in an immense, intimidating, coldly beautiful mansion. With no brothers or sisters, Trevor had only the servants for friends. As it was a rather remote residence, the Willows ran with complete self-sufficiency, requiring no local village to house its servants or provide its support. His parents, though loving, had spent much of his early childhood away from home, flitting glamorously in and out of his life on their never-ending cycle of travels and parties in the glittering capitals of Europe. Without the gentle guidance of the butler, Wilson, and the unobtrusive advice of Avery, a former footman who had eventually become Trevor's valet, the lonely young boy would never have gotten along as well as he had. It was no wonder he treated most of his personal servants as members of his family, rather than mere employees.

Despite the fact that he had led such a solitary existence, Trevor considered his boyhood happy and content. He spent his mornings in the schoolroom with his tutor, and his afternoons riding or fishing with footmen. He often followed one or two of his favorite servants about their duties, asking pointed questions that, from a very early age, betrayed an astounding intellect. All in all, he led a rather wonderful existence.

On Trevor's sixteenth birthday, word had come that the ship on which the Earl and Countess of Huntwick had most recently sailed had gone down in a storm, and all of the passengers, including Trevor's parents, were lost. When the London solicitors who handled his father's business affairs relayed the news to him, Trevor did not quite know how he should react. Since he had never really known his parents, he had, of course, felt sadness, though not grief, at their loss. He soon discovered, however, that he would now have to shoulder the burden and responsibility of vast business interests, as well as the day-to-day running of several estates and the livelihoods of a multitude of servants. To the inexperienced young man's credit, he quickly threw himself into the daunting task.

He'd traveled to each of the three estates he had inherited, spending most of the next two years becoming familiar with the various tasks involved in running them, and acquainting himself with the stewards and other household staff members in each residence. Possessed of a keen mind, he quickly learned the idiosyncrasies of each location and weeded out anything he judged inefficient or unnecessary. In short order, he improved the general productivity of all the estates and, in doing so, increased the already daunting wealth that had come with his title.

It was not until he finally traveled to London, though, that Trevor really *became* the Earl of Huntwick. With his ready wit and natural charm, he'd quickly become a favorite in the drawing rooms and at the dinner tables of London's elite. Already handsome at the age of eighteen, he had the bearing and presence of a much older man, thanks to a childhood spent almost exclusively with adults. At the many soirees, balls, and routs he attended, he came into contact with other men who shared an interest in many of the business ventures in which Trevor's father had involved himself. It did not take long for him to decide he would much rather handle his own affairs than have the London firm the former earl had hired continue to do so. Although they had done a competent job, he felt certain he could do better.

He'd done just that. His fertile mind, quick to pick up on the nuances of things said and left unsaid, cataloged and stored information about new investments, social trends, and shipping propositions. He possessed an uncanny sense of timing about which investments would pay off, and which would lose money. Time and again, the risks he took returned at a greater profit until, five years after the death of his parents, Trevor had become one of the richest and most sought-after young men in Europe. Possessing both lineage and good looks automatically brought him to the attention of all society mamas with daughters of marriageable age, but as the years passed and his wealth increased, his interest in marriage appeared to decrease.

His charm, however, remained legendary.

Among the young debutantes who emerged each Season, one heard whispered rumors that this girl or that woman or Lady Such-and-such had fallen into the Earl of

Huntwick's bed at a mere quirk of his aristocratic eyebrow. Every mama's heart raced with both hope and dread when a butler announced his presence at a ball, or when he made an appearance at the opera or the theater, especially when he attended unaccompanied. Never had he shown a partiality for any one particular lady, although everyone generally agreed that Trevor would have to marry soon, even if he did so only to beget an heir and continue his line.

Now, twelve years after he had first set foot in London, he was back at the Willows, pleasurably contemplating marriage to an unknown girl who hadn't the slightest interest in all he could offer her along with his name. He shook his head with an inward smile as he climbed the sweeping marble staircase and walked down the wide corridor to the master bedchamber, his feet sinking soundlessly into the thick blue Aubusson carpet that stretched down the endless halls.

"Good afternoon, Avery," Trevor said to the valet, who stood at the armoire unpacking several bags of the earl's belongings from London. Avery murmured a greeting and continued with his task, not really paying much attention to Trevor, who still stood at the threshold. The earl looked around in poignant wonder at rooms he had not seen in many years, thinking of the many things that had changed since then. The three estates, entailed and passed on to him, had all been greatly improved, and he had acquired three more: one in England and two in France. His wealth had increased more than four times in the period since he had become the Earl of Huntwick. He owned several shipping companies, and had business interests throughout the Continent, as well as in America. Until now he had not found anyone with whom he wanted to share it.

Abruptly shaking himself from his reverie, he looked across the room to a set of closed and firmly locked double doors. Although he knew exactly what lay behind those doors, he found himself irresistibly drawn to them. He walked slowly across the room, turned the key in the well-oiled lock, and pulled them open.

At the unexpected sound of the locked doors unlatching, Avery finally looked up from the drawers of the immense wardrobe, where he meticulously placed carefully folded cravats in precise rows. "My lord," he began to say, then stopped in surprised curiosity when he saw Trevor standing just inside the threshold of the open doors that led to the adjoining chamber. The earl slowly walked through the connecting bathing room to the suite reserved for his countess. Avery drew his brows together, then shrugged and returned to his task.

Trevor looked around the large chamber curiously, realizing with vague surprise that he had never actually entered this room before, not even as a child. Although it was a spacious, pretty room, he found he could not quite picture Grace in these delicate, fragile surroundings. He walked to the white-lacquered dressing table and ran a fingertip lightly across the polished surface, the movement reflected in the beveled mirrors that stood atop it. Behind him, framed in the center mirror, stood the canopied bed in which his mother had once slept.

He turned and slowly crossed the room, staring at the smooth blue silk coverlet and plump, untouched pillows. He fingered a gold tassel that held open the tied-back curtains hanging from each corner of the canopy. He closed his eyes and tried again to picture Grace curled up there, her hair a bright, curly flag on the light blue linen as she slept, but found he still could not.

A sudden realization struck him.

The fact that the frilly surroundings did not suit Grace's fiery personality had little to do with the reason he felt she did not belong there. It had everything to do with his expectations. From the first moment he had envisioned a future with Grace, he had imagined her only in his rooms, sleeping in his bed, wrapped in his arms.

She would never sleep in that bed, he vowed as he turned and strode briskly from the room to his own suite. She could use the chamber as a dressing room if she wished, but she would spend her nights in his bed, with him, where she belonged.

He walked back into the master chamber to find that Avery had finished unpacking and now stood looking at him in baffled wonder. Trevor grinned at the mystified valet and glanced back at the connecting doors. "Let's keep these open from now on, shall we?"

"As you wish, of course," Avery agreed, instantly recovering his usual aplomb. "Will there be anything else, my lord?"

"No, thank you, Avery," Trevor replied cheerfully, tugging at his crisp cravat to loosen it. Avery winced as he watched the earl pull on it. He held his breath until he saw the oblong scrap of snowy white linen flutter safely to the floor in one piece. He bowed and turned to leave, then looked back for a moment.

"Yes, Avery?" Trevor inquired before the butler could speak.

"It's good to be home, my lord."

"Yes, Avery," Trevor replied absently, lost in thought as he pictured confronting Grace in the morning. "It is good to be here."

Chapter Eight

When Trevor's coach pulled up in front of the Ackerly home the following morning, he prepared himself to have the door slammed in his face. He fully expected Grace to make things difficult, and even thought she might go so far as to refuse to see him. He did not expect to find her gone.

"She and Faith went to London for the Season," Mercy told him after she had invited him inside, the large bruise over her eye beginning to look yellowish around the edges as it healed. She gave him a puzzled look. "She didn't mention your return to me. I don't think she expected you, my lord."

Trevor grimaced with rueful irony. "I think she did," he muttered under his breath. Torn between amusement and annoyance at Grace's continued efforts to avoid him, he admitted to himself that he should have known she would try to do just that.

"I beg your pardon, my lord?"

Trevor glanced at the young girl and smiled tightly. He stood and began pacing around the salon, his hands clasped behind his back, his face a study of bemused reflection. "Nothing," he replied absently. He stopped before the window to stare at the rustic view of the stables. He raised a hand to his face, tapped his index finger thoughtfully against his lips, and stood in silence for another moment, his brow furrowed as he contemplated his options. Finally he made up his mind.

"Mercy," he said, turning. He almost collided with her, surprised to see her standing almost directly behind him. She looked up at him expectantly. He grinned, suddenly delighted. "I am going to marry your sister," he announced.

"Which one?" Mercy asked with a laugh. She arched a delicate brow, then winced as the movement irritated her bruise.

Trevor gave her a quelling look, but secretly praised the quick-witted answer that reminded him of Grace. "You know perfectly well which sister I mean."

Mercy's eyes began to dance. "Does *she* know?"

Trevor shook his head. His smile widened at the look of mischievous glee on Mercy's face.

"I think you should know that Grace doesn't take very well to being told to do something she doesn't wish to do," Mercy warned in a tone of sham gravity.

Trevor laughed and rumpled her curly auburn hair. "I can't imagine she does," he agreed.

Mercy ducked from under his hand with an irritated little scowl, then recovered her good humor and perched on the arm of an overstuffed sofa. "How will you manage it, my lord, considering Grace probably left specifically to get away from you?"

"Is that why you think she left?"

Mercy nodded. "I'm almost certain of it. Until a week ago she was adamantly opposed to the idea of going to London for an entire Season. She has always said she would rather spend three miserable months baking gooseberry tarts in hell than stifle in London for one single Season."

Trevor gave a sharp bark of laughter. That certainly sounded like something Grace would say. "She must have changed her mind about London when she received my note. Warning her of my intention to call appears to have been a bit of a strategic error," he said. He looked at Mercy and sobered. "I may need your help."

Mercy looked surprised. "What could I possibly do? I don't think Patience will let me go to London." She rolled her eyes and glanced down at her usual garb of breeches and boots. "Besides, I haven't a *thing* to wear."

Trevor smiled, and hesitated a moment. "I may need you to help me convince your father to sign a betrothal contract," he finally said.

At that, Mercy balked. "I don't know, my lord. I don't think I feel right about this. I mean, what if Grace really doesn't want to marry you, and you aren't able to convince her to do so?"

His eyes glowed at her with gentle humor. "I'm fairly certain that Grace really *doesn't* wish to marry me, but I'm completely certain that I can convince her to do so." Trevor's expression changed, sobering to add weight to his words. "I only wish to make her happy," he said, giving Mercy a steady look. "If I can't convince her to willingly marry me, I promise I'll leave her alone."

Mercy looked at Trevor for a long moment, trying to decide whether he really cared for her sister that much, if he truly wanted to make her happy. Trevor returned her stare, his look of sincere determination changing to one of concern at her continued silence. That fleeting expression of worry convinced her of what her sister meant to him. It was a young girl's first glimpse of tender emotion between a man and a woman, and her eyes unconsciously softened as she placed a small hand on the arm of the man who hoped one day to become her brother. "I'll do it," she said softly.

Trevor stretched his long legs across the coach and leaned his head against the back of the plush, dark green velvet seat, watching as the English countryside, decked in all the glorious colors of spring, rolled by. Every now and then he reached up and ran his fingers across the pocket of his dove-gray traveling jacket, the pocket in which the betrothal contract with Grace's father lay safely ensconced.

He had not found it an easy task to convince Bingham Ackerly to sign the papers he had asked his solicitors to draw up, even with Mercy's help. It had taken her a full twenty minutes of persuasive argument to get her father to even allow Trevor to discuss the possibility with him. On the night of Mercy's accident, Bingham had impressed Trevor as a man who had very little to do with the raising of his daughters. He could not have been more wrong, a misjudgment that surprised him.

Trevor usually had infallible instincts about those he met. Unfortunately, his preoccupation with winning Grace had caused his perception of those around her to cloud. Because of that, he went into the conversation with her father ill prepared and at a distinct disadvantage. Worse, Bingham had known immediately why he was there, putting Trevor in the uncomfortable position of having to explain himself without first preparing his opponent, as he usually did, for inevitable capitulation.

He found himself telling the quiet, scholarly man that he had become enamored of Grace on sight, and that he had felt more attracted to her with each subsequent conversation they had shared, and he therefore believed that they would get on well together as man and wife. In retrospect it sounded trite and rehearsed and perfectly nauseating. He knew he would forever remember the conversation that had followed, for he would always look back on it as one of the few times in his life he had been completely outmaneuvered.

Mr. Ackerly looked thoughtful for a few moments, then

floored Trevor by saying, "I believe my daughter has a very low opinion of you, Lord Caldwell."

Trevor was speechless, unable to find an adequate response to such a bald statement. He felt himself growing annoyed at being put on the defensive, a position in which he seldom found himself, although he knew he was entirely to blame for the situation. "I certainly wasn't given such an impression, Mr. Ackerly," he finally said in a neutral tone.

Bingham gave him a direct look. "My lord," he began in the superior manner of a schoolroom tutor speaking to a disruptive young student, "I distinctly recall riding home in our carriage after your first meeting with my daughter at the Assembly Rooms. She had quite a lot to say about her impression of you. I believe the most repeatable descriptor she used was 'deceptive cad,' although I can assure you she said a great deal more. She also looked most uncomfortable at the table with you that evening, and I couldn't help but notice her conspicuous absence when you and His Grace took your leave the following day. In addition to all of that," he continued, "Grace, who has been *most* outspoken about her deep aversion to going to London during the Season, suddenly developed a rather burning desire to go to that very place almost immediately after you and His Grace departed." Bingham shook his head in mock confusion, though his eyes had begun to gleam. "I'm curious, I must admit, as to what my daughter did to inspire this unexpected proposal from you, my lord."

Trevor stood quietly in front of the desk, listening to the man he hoped would become his father-in-law calmly spell out the very same reasons Trevor had already thought might keep Grace from agreeing to become his wife. His esteem for the older man rose with each passing second, and by the time Bingham Ackerly finished, Trevor wondered if he would have to convince Grace to oppose her father as well as try to make her fall in love with him. He hoped that it would not come to that. He remembered her glowing face as she spoke with obvious affection of the various members of her family, but knew that, regardless of the obstacles he would have to face, he fully intended to have Grace for his wife. She had not spoken of her father that evening, but Trevor knew instinctively that the respect he already felt for Bingham Ackerly likely ran strongly through the veins of his daughters.

Mr. Ackerly watched Trevor from behind his desk, patiently waiting for the earl to say something that would convince him the younger man had only honorable intentions toward Grace. Trevor finished gathering his thoughts, then spoke. "I understand, sir, that what you've seen would make you think that your daughter may neither welcome nor enjoy the prospect of a life with me." He paused and smiled, recalling the way he'd caught her slowly inspecting him in the portrait room the night they'd met, then continued. "But what you haven't seen, sir, is the way Grace looks at me when she thinks that I don't see her. What you haven't heard is how easily we converse when she doesn't put herself on the defensive. I can see how deeply she loves her family, and I know how much she would enjoy having a family of her own, children of her own, if God should choose to so bless us. When I look at Grace, I see a strong young lady who would be a wonderful partner in life, as well as a beautiful and gracious countess. All of these qualities make Grace the person she is. All I would like to have is the chance to learn more."

Bingham looked skeptical. "You gleaned all that in less than twenty-four hours and a few moments of conversation?"

Trevor searched vainly for a way to better describe the way he felt, his frustration mounting as he realized he could not possibly put what blossomed inside him into mere words.

Then, suddenly, he knew.

He was in love with Grace Ackerly. As the realization dawned his face changed, and his expression of awed disbelief caused Bingham Ackerly to look with new interest at the man who stood, tall and silent, on the other side of his desk. Ackerly knew, in that moment, that no matter what the Earl of Huntwick was about to say, he would allow Grace to become the man's countess if she so wished.

Trevor looked back at Mr. Ackerly, his green eyes suddenly grave and his face solemn with the incredible wonder of his newfound knowledge. "You already know I have a great deal to offer your daughter, sir, but I'm not going to stand here and tell you that Grace will be rich beyond her wildest dreams, or that she'll always live in the most luxurious homes I can possibly provide for her—although that may have been my intention when I first walked into your study. What I *will* tell you is that Grace will be rich in other, more important ways. I'll give her children, if she wants them, as many as she wishes, and she'll be able to live each day of her life knowing they're loved and will always be cared for." He paused and looked at Mercy, who had thus far remained silent, but now sat with a hand pressed to her chest, her eyes shining. He looked back at her father. "She will always know she is loved, sir," he finished, his unashamed, steady gaze locked with Bingham's.

Mr. Ackerly sat in silence for a moment, then looked down and cleared his throat gruffly. "All I've ever wanted for my girls is for them each to be happy in her own way," he said. "What I have always *hoped* for is for them to have the chance to experience a love like the one I shared with their mother." He stood and walked around the desk, reaching out and clasping Trevor's hand in a firm handshake. "You have my blessing, son, but I'm afraid that's only half the battle. I won't force my Grace to marry against her wishes. Convincing her to accept you is your job. Don't expect it to be easy," he warned. He shook his head at the thought of his headstrong daughter being told she had to do anything to which she was opposed.

Trevor smiled, relief evident on his face. "I doubt I'd enjoy it half so much if it were," he said, shaking the older man's hand. He looked down at Bingham's copy of the legal document on the desk, now signed, and sobered. "I did not know Grace wouldn't be here when I arrived. I intended to obtain your permission, sir, then take my time convincing her. Chasing her to London . . ." Trevor stopped and shook his head wryly, then continued. "Thank you for signing the papers."

"You might want to hold off on telling Grace of the transaction until she's made her own decision," Bingham advised. "I have a feeling she'll be of the view that she's been purchased."

Trevor chuckled. "Very good advice, sir."

He turned and saw Mercy beaming at him from the large overstuffed chair in the corner where she had curled up and watched the whole exchange. "I've always wanted a brother," she said happily. A sudden thought occurred to her. "When you marry my sister, you will invite the Duke of Blackthorne to the wedding, won't you?"

Bingham shook a finger at his youngest daughter while Trevor laughed at her audacity. Mercy looked undaunted. "Well, it doesn't hurt to ask," she muttered to nobody in particular.

Trevor felt the texture of the road change, smoothing out as they neared the more frequently traveled and well-maintained streets of London. He sat up straighter, smiling to himself at Mercy's marital plans for Sebastian. He would have to warn his friend to watch out, for he had a feeling young Mercy usually managed to get what she wanted, one way or another. A quality that appeared, he thought with an inner smile, to run in the family.

The carriage began to slow with the increased traffic on the cobbled streets. Courting Grace would definitely prove a tricky business. He fully intended to win her over first, to let her think she had fallen in love with him of her own accord. He would take things slowly and patiently. Somehow he had to make her fall for him, while still managing to keep the upper hand. It would never do for Grace to think she had command of the situation, because he knew that if she did, she would take the bit in her teeth and run like an untried colt.

Once he had won her over, they would hold the ceremony in church, with all the beauty, pomp, and celebration she deserved, for he knew she would be the most breathtaking bride London had ever seen. Trevor imagined her walking down the aisle, smiling radiantly at him, her face aglow with love, and his hands itched to hold her again as he had held her beneath the oak tree in the glade. After the wedding they would hold a lavish reception at the Willows. The Ackerly home was much too small to host such a grand event. Besides, when they retired for the night, he wanted it to be in his bed and in his home that Grace finally became his.

The coach pulled up and stopped before No. 7, Upper Brook Street. Trevor leaped out of the carriage and vaulted up the steps of the immense town house before a footman had even attempted to reach the coach door to open it for him. Wilson managed to get the front door open, but only because he had just arrived himself and stood near the door.

Trevor swept inside, his cape swirling around him. He issued instructions as he went, the beleaguered servants rushing to do his bidding before they had even had a chance to unpack. "Wilson, have my town carriage ready in fifteen minutes. I'll be going out for the evening. Has Avery arrived? I'll need him to lay out evening wear." Trevor stopped, thought for a moment, then continued. "Never mind, I'll tell him myself. Also, have the cook send up a tray of whatever he can find. I'm famished." He put one Hessian-clad foot on the oak stairs, then turned and added, "I'll also need flowers. Roses, I think, and . . . umm . . . daisies." He turned and took the steps two at a time, already bellowing his valet's name as he ascended.

Wilson watched Trevor disappear into the upper reaches of the house before he turned and directed a waiting footman to have the carriage readied. If the butler felt any trace of annoyance at the instruction to uproot his staff and head back to London after a stay in the country of only two days, he hid it well. Certainly, though, he must have wondered at the unusual actions of the normally predictable earl. Privately, when he received the summons to go to the Willows, he had felt a woman must lie at the bottom of it. Now, with Trevor's last instruction, he was convinced. High time, too. In his opinion, the earl had been alone for far too long. He stopped a maid and sent her to find one of the footmen who had traveled with the earl on this last trip. He would get to the root of all this, he thought staring up the stairs in the direction his employer had vanished.

"Avery!" Trevor called again before he reached his chamber. The surprised valet came running out just as Trevor strode in, very nearly colliding with him on the threshold. "Evening clothes, please, and quickly." He spotted a footman walking by the room. "Smythe!" The liveried man immediately reappeared in the doorway. "Have my secretary send up all the invitations we've received for events held this evening." Smythe nodded and bowed backward out of the room, then turned and ran down the hall in his haste to do his master's bidding.

Trevor turned back to Avery, who had a black coat and breeches already laid out and stood stooped over the bed, brushing nonexistent specks of dust from an impeccably pressed sleeve. "I'll need a shave, too," Trevor added, rubbing his chin.

Although he had yet to locate the bag that contained Trevor's shaving things, Avery managed to look as cool and unperturbed as ever.

Twenty minutes later, Trevor descended the steps in immaculate, superbly tailored evening clothes, his jaw smoothly shaved. He held in one hand a list of the evening's balls to peruse on his way to the address Grace's father had given him, and in the other hand a tasteful bouquet of pink tea roses and white daisies. Wilson swept open the front door and Trevor strode out. He gave his driver the address on Curzon Street, then settled into the coach with a smile, looking forward with pleasure to the company of his unknowing fiancée.

Chapter Nine

"Miss Grace is not in to callers."

"What do you mean?" Trevor snapped at the stooped, elderly butler who had answered the door at the home of Grace's aunt. After traveling across half of England, Trevor felt his lighthearted mood begin to deteriorate in the face of yet another setback.

Greaves drew himself up as much as his diminutive height would allow, deeply affronted at the earl's clipped, impatient tone. "I meant just what I said, my lord. Miss Grace is not in to callers."

Trevor took a deep breath and slowly counted to ten, reminding himself that this man did not purposely keep him from Grace. "And where might I find Miss Ackerly?" he asked in a more patient voice.

"Which, my lord?" the butler inquired with raised brows.

Trevor closed his eyes, again trying to quell his irritation. "Which what?" he asked.

"Which Miss Ackerly, of course," the old man said. He drew back into the house a bit and looked at Trevor as though he thought the young earl on the doorstep was bit batty.

Trevor's hands itched to close around the servant's neck, but he checked the impulse and forced himself to answer.

"Miss Grace," he bit out between clenched teeth, enunciating each word clearly in an effort to control his rapidly crumbling temper.

A look of baffled uncertainty crossed the butler's face. "I'm not quite certain I remember, my lord," Greaves said, scratching his bald head thoughtfully. "I know they went out, and I'm most certain Lady Egerton told me where they would go." He squinted up at Trevor for a moment, trying as hard as he could to remember, then visibly brightened, struck with a most brilliant thought. He looked at the earl eagerly. "Do *you* know, my lord?" he asked hopefully.

Trevor stared down at the smaller man in incredulity, unable to fathom why anybody with the slightest bit of common sense would employ this man, much less allow him to answer their door. "May I see Miss Ackerly's maid, then?" he finally managed.

Greaves immediately opened the door wider. "Of course, my lord. Which Miss—" he began.

"Miss Grace!" Trevor snapped. He stepped inside and removed his gloves as the elderly butler shuffled off. Trevor hoped the man would manage to remember what he had set out to accomplish. He walked across the entranceway and glanced into the first room he found, a frilly, feminine salon with intricately carved furniture and knickknack-covered tables, a fussy room of the sort Trevor hated. He noticed, however, a large sideboard of drinks near the fireplace. He walked inside, poured himself a generous brandy, then sat gingerly in one of the impossibly fragile chairs that littered the room, waiting for the maid to come from wherever Greaves had gone to fetch her. Fortunately he did not have long to wait. In a matter of moments a small, round, frightened-looking girl with her mobcap set crazily askew atop her head stepped into the room.

"My lord?" Becky curtsied, hiding her trembling hands in the folds of her black skirts. She was quite terrified at the thought of confronting the strange man Greaves had only just described to her as "rather unfortunately demented."

Annoyed, because whatever the butler had told Becky about him had obviously scared her to death, Trevor did not even look at the girl, merely held his glass up to the light and slowly moved his hand in a circle. "Who is your mistress?" he asked evenly, watching the amber liquid swirl in the flickering light from the candles.

"Miss Ackerly, your lordship," the maid immediately answered.

Trevor shook his head, smiling grimly. "Would that be Miss Grace or Miss Faith Ackerly?" he asked with a resigned sigh.

Becky blinked. "Both, my lord," she replied in confusion.

Suppressing a new urge to throttle the now conspicuously absent butler, Trevor moved on patiently. "Of course. Very good. Perhaps, then, you can be of some assistance to me. Do you happen to know where Miss Grace has gone this evening?"

"Almack's, my lord," the girl immediately replied, visibly relieved that she could answer his question. "And afterward they were to go to a ball at the home of Lord and Lady Seth."

Trevor nodded briskly. "Thank you," he said in a short, dismissive tone.

Becky stood waiting for a moment, then realized he no longer required her presence. She curtsied quickly and vanished, more than happy to take her leave of the strange nobleman.

Trevor watched her go and shook his head. Wednesday night. Almack's.

He took a final swallow of his brandy and gritted his teeth. The evening looked more and more grim. Of all the places he had hoped to find Grace this evening, he would have placed Almack's at the bottom of the list. The moment he set foot in those exalted rooms, he would find himself set upon by a multitude of matchmaking mamas and their sometimes less-than-demure daughters, all of whom hoped the same impossible hope: to snare the elusive Earl of Huntwick, considered the best matrimonial catch in England for several Seasons. Actually, he amended to himself without rancor, with Sebastian's newly acquired ducal title, Trevor would now be considered the second-best catch. He grinned for the first time since entering the Egerton house, happy to relinquish the label.

He set his glass on a table and walked slowly from the salon, toying with the idea of going to White's and playing a few hands, then catching up with Grace at Lord Seth's. After a moment's further thought, he decided against it. White's would likely be short of good company tonight. Lord Jonathon Lloyd, the Earl of Seth, and his younger brother, Gareth, two of Trevor's closest friends, would certainly not put in an appearance. If Amanda Lloyd planned to give a ball tonight, her husband would be at her side. She had probably roped in her young brother-in-law to help, as well. Trevor smiled affectionately at the thought of the staid Earl of Seth's beautiful, effervescent young wife. He would enjoy seeing them again tonight.

His mind made up, Trevor walked back to the front door. The elderly butler who had so annoyed him a few moments ago now sat in a chair near the entrance, snoring peacefully, his chin resting against his chest. Giving the sleeping man a scathing look, Trevor quietly opened the front door himself and stepped outside. With a great deal of satisfaction, he slammed the heavy door as loudly as he could. The resulting startled yelp from just inside the door was like music to his ears. Feeling vindicated, he walked down the steep steps to his waiting carriage, grinning widely.

"Almack's," he said to the footman who held open his door, "and quickly." He pulled his watch from his pocket and looked at the time. Nearly eleven o'clock. If he did not arrive before then, the patronesses would close and lock the door. Nobody, not even the influential Earl of Huntwick, could make it past Mr. Willis after that hour.

Grace looked around the crowded room with a gay smile, surprised at how glad she was she had come to London, regardless of her reasons for doing so. Thus far the balls and parties she had attended had been very grand, and the people she had met, with only a few exceptions, friendly and accepting. She was blissfully unaware of the fact that their unquestioned acceptance of her had been gained only by virtue of the position her aunt held in society. It would have surprised her to know that she and Faith would not have received a single invitation had Lady Egerton not sponsored them into the ranks of the ton. But sponsored they had been, and, with the dowager countess accompanying them, Grace had made a lasting and favorable impression on at least the younger set of polite society at the first ball they attended.

They had arrived at the festive affair, highly impressed and slightly awed by the decadent grandeur of the house and by the crowd of beautifully dressed people flitting around them. Faith had immediately received an invitation to dance; her quiet blond beauty was a magnet for many young men who implored their hostess to ask Aunt Cleo for an introduction.

While Grace enjoyed the sight of her sister gliding around the room on the arm of a handsome young dandy, one of the many men who had begged an introduction to Faith but not managed to secure a space on her dance card was struck with a brilliant notion: if he became friendly with Grace, it stood to reason that he would have a far greater chance of Faith looking upon him with favor. Immediately the young strategist turned to Grace. Although

Lady Egerton had presented him to both Grace and Faith at the same time, he had barely given Grace a second look, his admiration of Faith glaringly evident.

"Have you been enjoying yourself, Miss Ackerly?" he asked politely, still trying to keep track of Faith's movement around the room.

Grace turned and nodded, her face aglow with wonder. "This is my first London ball, you know," she admitted, smiling up at him when he flicked a distracted glance in her direction. She paused for a moment, then spoke again when he did not respond. "My sister and I have come for the Season," she confided unnecessarily, thinking that he, too, was likely new to town.

Lord Newcombe immediately seized upon the topic she offered, giving her his full attention for the first time. "Miss Faith, you mean?" When she nodded, he continued: "She is your younger sister, is she not?" His eyes followed Faith around the room with an admiring, hungry gaze.

"Yes, she is," Grace replied to the back of his head. Her eyes narrowed as she assessed the covetous look on the young man's face. She did not mind his interest in her sister, for she was very happy about Faith's instant popularity, but she most certainly *did* mind if he intended to use her as a stepping-stone to get to Faith. "She has a spotted, fur-covered tongue, you know," she added in an offhand tone, just to see what he would say.

"She's very beautiful," Lord Newcombe said in a reverent voice.

Grace raised her brows.

Suddenly he appeared to remember himself. "Such a trait seems to run in your family," he added hastily, in a belated effort at gallantry.

"Spotted, fur-covered tongues?" Grace's expression remained bland.

Newcombe looked confused. "No, I meant her beauty," he said.

Grace did not respond. A wicked thought struck her. She smiled up at him in a way that told him she expected to hear more.

Lord Newcombe looked down at her uncertainly. Used to the silly, flirtatious repartee with which most of the London debutantes of his acquaintance would have reciprocated, he had no idea of the depths into which he had just inadvertently waded. This young woman with the odd orange hair did not appear to know the unwritten rules of polite conversation. After a moment her direct stare as well as the continued lack of conversation began to unnerve him. "Is your mother as lovely as . . . er . . . you and your sister?"

Grace stifled a laugh. "Oh, no, my lord, I can't say that she is."

Newcombe was taken aback. *What a strange answer,* he thought. Faith danced by at that moment, momentarily distracting him. "Your sister must resemble your father," he said, then realized in horror that he had just implied that Grace herself must take after her mother, whom she had only just described as not attractive. He looked down to see if she had noticed his gaffe.

Grace inclined her head and raised an eyebrow, staring steadily back up at the fidgeting young man.

"Er . . . would you care to dance, Miss Ackerly?" he asked, feeling a sudden pressing need to make amends for his clumsy conversation. He would certainly never find favor with Faith if he angered her sister.

Dance? Did he think her daft? Grace glanced at Aunt Cleo, who nodded at her in a strange way, almost as if trying to convey some sort of message. Grace furrowed her brow until a brilliant notion came to mind. This self-important young pup needed a lesson in manners. She smiled conspiratorially at her aunt, then turned her most beaming expression on the young nobleman.

"Why, *thank* you, Lord Newcombe," she said, batting her eyes in an exaggerated imitation of some of the simpering debutantes she had seen in action this evening. The oblivious man looked dazed by her sudden eagerness. She gave him an even more dazzling smile and placed her hand on his arm. "I thought you'd *never* ask." She bobbed a quick curtsy and giggled behind her glove for good measure.

He reluctantly led her out onto the dance floor. The ever-curious eyes of the ton followed along, noting with interest how the newly arrived Ackerly sisters both danced with extremely eligible bachelors not long after their arrival.

Once they were on the dance floor, however, it became immediately apparent to Grace that, while Lord Newcombe danced with *her*, he still had his full attention on Faith, so much so that he stepped on Grace's toes twice, and once almost tripped her. When that happened, she heard a titter of laughter ripple through the crowd. Grace, who did *not* like laughter at her expense, realized her partner's absurd obsession with Faith had become embarrassingly transparent.

What she decided to do next was both shocking and unprecedented, and became *the* topic of conversation for an entire week. Seeing her chance when Faith and her partner danced close by, Grace abruptly stopped dancing in the middle of the floor, forcing Lord Newcombe to stop along with her. Thinking that she wished to leave the dance floor, Newcombe gratefully turned to escort her back to her aunt, but instead, Grace did the most extraordinary thing. She stepped out of Lord Newcombe's arms and put a restraining hand on her surprised sister's shoulder. Faith, afraid that something terrible had occurred, immediately stopped dancing and looked at her sister in alarm. Grace looked back at her with a determined, militant look in her eyes. "Oh, no," Faith moaned under her breath, even as Grace mouthed the words, *I'm sorry,* at her.

The music continued unabated, but those couples dancing nearest the little group that had inexplicably stopped in the center of the room sensed that something interesting was about to occur. They began to leave the floor in an obvious effort to better see and hear the action taking place. What they observed left them openmouthed with shocked amazement.

Grace reached back and drew the rigid and angry-looking Lord Newcombe up beside her. "My lord, please, once again meet my sister, Miss Faith Ackerly," she said with an overly sweet smile. "Faith, may I present Lord Newcombe? He appears quite anxious to make your acquaintance." With that, Grace proudly raised her chin and walked serenely away, leaving her sister smiling politely, if a bit uncertainly, at both men.

A frosty smile pinned to her face to cover her searing anger, Grace joined Aunt Cleo, who smiled widely, highly entertained by the entire debacle. "Good for you, Grace! I don't think I've enjoyed myself so much at one of these crushes in years." She nodded approvingly as she watched Faith very deliberately turn her back on Newcombe and ask her partner to escort her to the punch bowl for some refreshment. "Newcombe had it coming, too. He's become rather full of himself since his father fell ill. I think he'll come down a notch or two when the old geezer finally gives it up and Newcombe and the rest of the ton find out how much he *didn't* inherit." She thumped her cane and let out a bark of laughter. Grace clamped her mouth shut and lifted her chin, staring down some of the bolder spectators around the room with a glacial glare.

As the whispers began to die and the ball resumed, Faith immediately received another invitation to dance, but Grace found herself scrupulously and conspicuously avoided.

After thirty miserable minutes, she decided that London had proven just as disappointing as she had expected. She turned to ask her aunt if she could leave when she noticed a beautiful brunette girl dressed in a sumptuous royal blue silk gown walking her way. An entourage of still more beautifully dressed young ladies followed in her wake. She introduced herself as Amanda Lloyd, the Countess of Seth, and drew the slightly distrustful Grace into her circle of friends.

"That was really most awful of you, Miss Ackerly," Amanda said after introducing all her companions. She laughed, a pretty little unaffected laugh that chimed like bells. "Although, I admit I was watching you both before and during your dance, and Newcombe certainly had it coming. I only wish I could have heard what you were saying. He turned quite the loveliest shade of purple I've ever seen!" She laughed again, and so did some of the rest of the group.

Grace looked at the friendly brunette with a curious smile, her head tipped inquisitively to the side. "How ever do you do that?" she asked in an admiring tone.

Amanda stopped laughing and looked confused. "Do what?" she asked.

"Laugh like that. It sounds so pretty and feminine. Why, when I laugh, streams of tears invariably come from my eyes, and I make such awful snorting noises people are apt to come running with a gun to put the poor sick horse out of its misery."

The entire group laughed this time, and Grace looked slowly about at the young people around her, beginning to realize they did not condemn her for her actions on the dance floor; rather, they applauded her.

"Wasn't your sister mortified?" one of girls asked, her fascination evident.

"No, of course not," Grace replied with an impish smile, already becoming more comfortable with her newfound friends. "She's become well used to the rather odd things I sometimes say and do."

"She gave Newcombe the cut direct after you left the floor," the blond continued in disbelief. "Why, I've heard that when his papa dies, he'll have more money—"

"And fewer brains than a gifted goose," the countess cut in with a quelling look. She need not have tried to champion her new friend, though, for Grace simply shrugged with unconcern. "Faith knew I disliked him, and that was enough for her to distrust him as well."

The ladies moved on to other topics, automatically including Grace in their conversation. She had no idea that Amanda and her friends all hailed from the finest aristocratic families and moved only in the highest, most influential circles of society, but once everyone else in the room noted that they treated Grace's encounter with humor, the rest of the ton followed their lead. When the morning newspapers reported on the events of the previous evening, instead of describing Grace as a dismal social failure, the gossip columns would proclaim her an Original, her place in society secure. She never knew just how close she had come to complete social death. Now, thanks to Amanda Seth, people would regard her outlandish remarks and actions as humorous, if unusual. Less popular girls, striving to stand out in the unending throng of young ladies making their debut each Season, might repeat her words with admiration, hoping to achieve a similar effect.

So it was with the comfortable feeling of acceptance and an ever-growing circle of male admirers that Grace again watched her sister dance, this time at Almack's. As she did not seek marriage, Grace found it easy to not be jealous of her beautiful sister's popularity with the gentlemen. She also managed to hide her complete boredom in the exalted halls of Almack's, rooms she immediately judged as no more than a closed market offering young girls in mar-

riage to the highest bidder. The very thought left a bitter
taste in her mouth.

Anxious to move to a more festive atmosphere, she
stopped watching Faith and turned to her aunt to suggest
that they thank the patronesses and leave for Lord and
Lady Seth's ball. Before she could speak, however, a
strange hush fell over the room, followed by a wave of frantic whispering. All heads began to swivel toward the entranceway. The whispering grew steadily louder as excited
mamas began to push their suddenly nervous daughters in
the direction of the doors.

Curious, Grace tried to look over the heads of those now
crowding the doorway. When she could not see anything,
she glanced over at her aunt. "What's all the fuss about?"

Aunt Cleo, a full six inches taller, obligingly raised her
mother-of-pearl lorgnette and trained it across the room to
determine what had caused the commotion. "By the looks
of all the flustered girls and the hopeful mamas, I'd say our
most eligible has probably made an entrance—although
why a confirmed bachelor like him would dare enter the
marriage mart is beyond . . ." She trailed off thoughtfully,
then continued: "Unless someone drew him here." With that
ambiguous statement, she began scanning the crowd, looking for someone, anyone, who would not ordinarily attend.

Grace watched her and shook her head. Aunt Cleo
spoke in riddles. "Who are you talking about, Aunt?" Grace
asked in exasperation, noting that, although the music still
played, even the dancers had stopped to see what caused
all the excitement.

"The Earl of Huntwick, of course," her aunt replied, then
turned in surprise when she heard her niece suddenly suck
in her breath.

Grace looked toward the entrance in obvious trepidation. Sure enough, almost as soon as her aunt spoke,
Trevor's dark head appeared above everyone else's, his

jade eyes already skipping over the crowd as though looking for someone in particular. She watched as his sweeping
gaze paused imperceptibly at every red-haired girl, then
dismissed each in turn, obviously not seeing the person for
whom he searched.

Grace felt cornered. Almost in a panic, she began looking
for a place to hide. For lack of any other option, in an effort
to evade his notice she started to sidle behind Faith, whose
partner had only just returned her from the floor. At just that
moment his gaze collided with hers and her heart skipped
a beat. Ironically, her small effort to avoid detection had
drawn his attention. Pinning her in place with his eyes, he
strode in her direction, the crowd parting with ease to let
him through, then quickly filling in behind him as everyone
jockeyed for position, trying to see who had caught his eye.

As she watched the man she had so much wanted to
avoid bear inexorably down on her, Grace realized that,
although she cared little for what the gathered crowd
thought of her, she did care a great deal what she thought
of herself. She checked the sudden impulse to turn tail and
run. Instead she stood her ground, her chin raised a notch
in that telltale position of defense, her blue eyes glaring
into Trevor's with ill-disguised hostility.

He drew near, taking his eyes off hers only long enough
to request a formal introduction from Lady Egerton, who
grinned with malicious glee. She could almost see and feel
the sparks of animosity flying between her niece and the
Earl of Huntwick. Wondering how they had met, as neither
Grace nor Faith had even mentioned an acquaintance with
the earl, Aunt Cleo immediately decided that putting these
two together as often as possible would transform what
had promised to be a predictably dull Season into a most
diverting one. She accepted Trevor's request, turning to her
niece in delight.

"Grace!" she practically bellowed, deliberately ignoring

the imploring look directed at her. "May I present Lord Trevor Caldwell, the Earl of Huntwick. My lord, my nieces, Miss Grace and Miss Faith Ackerly."

Grace remained obstinately silent as the earl greeted Faith, then pressed her lips together as he turned to smile down at her. Aunt Cleo sighed with exasperation. A little prodding would be necessary, she saw. Leaning toward Grace, she hissed, "Do *not* embarrass me, miss!"

With chagrined surprise, Grace looked at her aunt, feeling immediate shame for her selfish behavior. Accustomed to doing precisely as she wished in Pelthamshire, where nobody cared if she romped about in breeches or spoke out of turn at afternoon teas, she had not realized that the way she acted here in town might reflect negatively on anybody else.

Guilt-stricken at the thought that she might cause her aunt embarrassment with her actions, and left with no other option, she reluctantly put her hand into the one Trevor still held out toward her. He raised it to his lips. Grace snatched it back from him as soon as she could do so without causing any more of a scene than they already had. "A pleasure, my lord," she said with a quick, halfhearted curtsy. Her wrist tingled where his lips had brushed it.

"Would you do me the favor of joining me in this dance, Miss Ackerly?"

Her eyes flashed. "I wouldn't dance with . . ." she began angrily, before she caught her aunt's stern eye and closed her mouth with a snap. Her mind searched frantically for a way out, then seized upon an easy—and luckily legitimate—excuse. She choked back her original sharp retort, and instead smiled sweetly at Trevor. "That is to say, I would love to dance with you, my lord, but I believe this dance is a waltz, and the patronesses have not yet given me their approval to dance the waltz." She did her level best to look contrite. She succeeded quite admirably until she saw

Trevor look across the room at Lady Sally Jersey, raise his eyebrows, and incline his head toward Grace. With escalating dismay, she saw the revered patroness nod her haughty approval, neatly and unknowingly maneuvering Grace into Trevor's trap.

She would find no way out this time, she realized as Trevor again held out his arm to her. Reluctantly she placed her gloved hand upon it and woodenly walked along beside him to the dance floor, glancing back in dismay at Aunt Cleo, who grinned in complete enjoyment of her predicament. Trevor pulled her into his arms and they began to move in time to the music.

The Earl of Huntwick danced very well, she admitted to herself after a few moments. He moved with the same easy grace and confidence she had noticed when she had danced with him at the Assembly Rooms in Pelthamshire, giving her a feeling of comfort that lulled her and allowed her to relax somewhat in his arms. She became so soothed by the easy motion that his next remark caught her utterly off guard.

"You look beautiful in women's clothing, my dear."

She stiffened, then frowned at his use of such a personal endearment, her momentary peace dispelled by their customary bristling animosity. She looked quickly around to see if anyone else had heard, and noticed that the fascinated crowd had focused their complete attention on Trevor and herself.

A wonderful, vengeful idea took root. She glanced furtively up at her partner and found Trevor smiling tenderly down at her in a way she could describe only as affectionate. With a surge of triumph, she averted her eyes to the general vicinity of his shoulder, afraid he might see by her changing expression that she planned to exact revenge.

From her experiences thus far in society, she knew that everyone watched everything everyone else did, and that everyone gossiped about everyone else all the time. She also knew that if Trevor continued to look at her in such a tender manner, she would have the power to make him appear a thoroughly besotted fool by looking as bored and disinterested as she possibly could. Quite suddenly the idea of dancing with society's most eligible no longer angered her, for it would allow her, quite effectively, to put him in a place he richly deserved. It would not escape the notice of the ever-watchful ton that the Earl of Huntwick gazed in what looked very much like devoted adoration at his dancing partner; nor would they miss seeing how very bored that partner appeared. Quickly Grace schooled her features into a mask of exaggerated ennui.

Unbeknownst to Grace, Trevor had watched her expressions change with amusement. He knew that she planned to do something, although he wondered just what machinations paraded through her agile mind. Whatever she plotted, it totally occupied her thoughts, keeping her very quiet. He frowned. She also looked rather bored. Suddenly he knew precisely what she intended to do. She thought that if she bored him, he might leave her alone. He grinned, admiring her ingenuity. The little minx! He looked around at the assembled crowd, most of whom watched them dance, and suddenly comprehended that Grace did not intend to bore him, but to make it appear as though *he* bored *her*. By the expressions on the faces of those assembled, her scheme had begun to work. He watched an attractive young lady turn to her companion, say something behind her fan, and giggle, actually pointing in their direction. His amusement faded as he realized that Grace had already enjoyed a fair amount of success. He looked down at her again and saw her pretend to stifle a contrived yawn. His jaw tightened in annoyance, even as he realized that she hoped for just such a reaction from him. Reining in his anger, he decided to finish in his own way the game she had started.

He began rubbing his thumb in light, feathery circles on her back. He felt her skin jump in response through the thin silk of her mint-green gown. "Some say the waltz is a dangerous dance," he said, his low-timbred voice sending chills skittering down her spine.

Grace forced herself to sigh in weary disinterest; then she squinted at his shoulder as if in deep concentration. Very deliberately, she reached up and flicked an imaginary piece of lint from his immaculate black jacket.

Trevor pulled her ever so slightly closer, his warm hand firmly pressed to the center of her back. "Such an intimate partnering," he continued in the same deep, sensual tone. "Almost an embrace," he added meaningfully.

Her heart began to pound so loudly she feared he could hear it. Making an effort to continue the charade she had started, Grace forced herself to yawn delicately again, then closed her eyes, trying in vain to shut out the evocative effect of the heat emanating from his hard body.

"It feels good to hold you in my arms again," he whispered, bending his head so that his lips moved very close to her ear, his warm breath stirring the tendrils of her hair that curled there.

Her eyes flew open at the disturbing images *that* statement brought to mind, images of his strong hands gently caressing her body, his lips moving softly against hers. In spite of herself, two bright spots of embarrassed color suddenly flared on her cheeks.

Trevor gave a low chuckle of satisfaction. "I see you remember as well as I the pleasure we found beneath that tree."

Having lost her battle to gain the upper hand, Grace raised angry eyes to the earl's warm jade ones and became lost in their sensuous, unwavering depths. Helpless, she softened in his arms, gliding through the rest of the waltz with ease, her eyes locked with his, that now-familiar ache deep within her stomach beginning to unfurl and spread throughout her body. She searched for words to describe that intangible something that felt so innately right about dancing in the arms of this one man, this incredible, infuriating man who looked down at her with tender, aching promise as the lilting music drew to a close. Then reality came crashing down on the spell he had momentarily woven around them.

Trevor led Grace back to her aunt, her eyes downcast to hide the dismay that was quickly turning to anger as she realized, with self-loathing, that she, not the tall, smugly self-assured man at her side, had behaved like a besotted little fool. By the time they reached Aunt Cleo, who waited to present her next partner to her, Grace felt once again the blazing fury that only Trevor managed to ignite within her.

Deliberately ignoring the baleful stare she directed at him, Trevor kissed her hand. "Thank you for the waltz, my dear," he said in a warm, low tone. He spoke politely to Aunt Cleo for a moment, then strolled off as though completely unaffected by their exchange on the dance floor.

Grace followed him with infuriated eyes. How could he act so cool and unruffled when his very presence always left her feeling utterly unsettled? She tore her eyes from his retreating back to face her aunt. Stiffly, she greeted the young, eager-looking man who stood there, and she automatically accepted his nervous invitation to dance. As she moved toward the dance floor, she saw Trevor now leaning against the far wall, smiling at her with a decidedly wolfish leer.

She lifted her chin and glared down her nose at him, then turned a deliberate, dazzling smile on her escort, Lord

Pattingson, quite taking him aback, for he had noticed, along with everyone else, that she had not graced the Earl of Huntwick with even a small smile. So vivaciously did she smile and flirt and chat with him during their dance that afterward he was heard to remark that, although Faith Ackerly was undoubtedly the more beautiful of the Ackerly sisters, Grace possessed both beauty *and* charm. On top of that, he pointed out, she had shown a decided preference for him over Lord Caldwell.

From that point on, Grace gave the appearance of a young lady having the time of her life. She danced every dance, flirted outrageously with her partners, and was so buoyantly charming that gentlemen of all ages and peer groups began to seek her out. The older gentlemen found her intelligent discourse on almost any subject refreshing, while the greenest of young dandies found they need not fear a rebuff if they screwed up the courage to speak to her. Even those gentlemen deemed prime catches by society found welcome respite from the ever-threatening claws of wedlock in her presence, for it stood to reason that if she had repulsed the attentions of Huntwick, the most eligible of them all, they certainly risked no matrimonial danger from Grace Ackerly.

As the circle of admiring males grew ever larger around Grace and her aunt, Trevor leaned against the wall and watched her, a small, indulgent smile lingering about his lips. He spoke periodically with friends who strolled by, and occasionally dutifully kissed the hand of a nervous young miss prodded in his direction by her chaperone, but his possessive gaze did not leave Grace for long; nor did he dance again that night, effectively putting the stamp of ownership on her just as surely as if his ring already graced her finger.

Shortly after midnight, Lady Egerton, Grace, and Faith took their leave. Trevor, too, left Almack's amidst whispering and gossip that flew on winged feet throughout the ballrooms and bedrooms of London. The earl, thoroughly satisfied with all he had learned this evening, decided to forgo the ball at Jon and Amanda Lloyd's, and instead returned to his house on Upper Brook Street. He did not notice the tall, shadowy figure on the corner who watched both his carriage and the Egerton coach leave Almack's.

The Egerton coach made its way through the dark cobbled streets to the ball at the Earl and Countess of Seth's home, the moods of its occupants quite different from Trevor's. Grace sat in tense, brooding silence, her earlier acts of lighthearted frivolity entirely dispensed with, while Faith sat on the seat directly across from Grace and watched her sister thoughtfully. Aunt Cleo simply looked smugly well entertained. Yes, Lady Egerton thought to herself as the coach drew up at the Lloyds' town house, the Season would prove *most* engaging this year.

The newspapers the next morning told the story for those unfortunate Londoners who had not already heard the extraordinary news. The *Times* reported that Miss Grace Ackerly had debuted her first public waltz with none other than the Earl of Huntwick, after which she had enjoyed an unprecedented popularity, and appeared to have had a wonderful time (which she had not). The *Morning Post*'s article read that, after dancing with Miss Ackerly, the Earl of Huntwick seemed perfectly content to prop up a wall and watch her dance (which, indeed, he did). The *Gazette* went a step further, boldly promising to leave space in its society column should the Earl of Huntwick find need for a future wedding announcement.

Trevor laughed uproariously and clipped all three articles to save and enjoy.

Grace reacted much differently. She threw the papers into the drawing room fire.

*   *   *

The tall man who had stood on the corner the evening before sat quietly in his rented rooms. He read each story,
then viciously cut each offending newspaper into very
small, precisely shaped pieces. Carefully he packed the
pieces away in a box and slid it under the bed.

Chapter Ten

Grace awoke the next morning with a pounding headache and an unsettled stomach. She suffered through breakfast and decided she did not feel up to the usual morning ritual of paying calls and receiving visitors. Instead, she spent a quiet morning in the garden reading *Pride and Prejudice,* the new book considered all the rage in town. She had just begun feeling better as the noon hour approached, when O'Reilly, one of her aunt's footmen, silently appeared next to the marble bench upon which she sat.

"Pardon me, Miss Grace."

"Yes, O'Reilly?" She closed the book on one finger to keep her place and smiled pleasantly at the short footman.

Both Grace and Faith treated the servants in the Egerton household kindly, just as they did at home in Pelthamshire. In addition to having actually learned each of their names, and often asking after the members of their families, Grace frequently had a nice word to say when she encountered them as they went about their daily duties.

Regardless of his affection for his young mistress, O'Reilly managed to keep his face appropriately solemn as he spoke. "You have a visitor, Miss Grace. I believe Greaves has put him in the blue salon."

"Him?" Grace inquired curiously. A bit surprised, she stood and shook out the wrinkled skirts of her lilac morning gown, wondering if she would have time to change before receiving her visitor. Until the night before, Grace had done absolutely nothing to cultivate the hope in any young man that she might welcome him as a caller, so she could not fathom who would want to see her. By contrast, her cool, unflappable sister collected admirers the way some children collected stray puppies, resulting in a steady stream of callers nearly every morning. "Are you quite certain he isn't one of Faith's suitors?"

"No, Miss Grace," O'Reilly said as they started toward the house. "I'm quite sure I heard the earl specifically ask for you myself."

Grace abruptly stopped. She looked with wide, frantic eyes toward the set of long windows that marched across the back of the house. Did one of them open from the blue salon? She clutched at O'Reilly's sleeve and pulled him behind a tall, leafy hedge, safely, she hoped, out of sight of the house. "Are you talking about the Earl of Huntwick?" she hissed.

"Well, yes, Miss Grace," the footman stammered, completely confused by her unusual behavior.

An unwelcome feeling of panic beset her at the thought of seeing Trevor again. The odious man had a horribly tumultuous effect on her thoughts and feelings, and she could never tell how she might react to anything he said or did. She thought hard for a long moment and tried, biting her lower lip in dismay, to figure a way out of the situation.

Unconsciously she twisted O'Reilly's sleeve, attempting to force herself to stop panicking and start thinking. Obviously he had already received the information that she was at home. She would have to think of a good reason why she might be in but not taking callers. After a moment's reflection, she settled on the weak but nearly truthful excuse of her earlier discomfort. "You have to tell him I'm indisposed, that I have . . . I have . . ." Her mind groped for a suitable way to phrase the message so it would be both honest and discouraging. She snapped her fingers. "Tell him I have a stomach ailment," she finished triumphantly. That could keep her down for days, she thought with a decisive nod.

"But . . ." O'Reilly started to say, before he remembered his place and closed his mouth. He bowed deeply instead and started back toward the house. As a servant, he had neither right nor reason to question her actions.

"I'll wait right here, O'Reilly," Grace called anxiously. "Please come and tell me when his lordship leaves." A pang of guilt at involving him in her ruse struck her as she watched him walk away. She sank down on another of the marble benches scattered throughout the garden, this one conveniently placed behind the boxwood hedge, and tried to muster the discipline to keep herself from peeking at the windows that opened from the back of the house. She now felt certain that one side of the blue salon actually *did* look out on the gardens.

Ten long minutes passed while Grace tried, with little success, to occupy her mind by resuming the reading of her book. She started and stopped, then started and stopped again, then sighed when she realized she'd read the same sentence several times. With a sharp snap, she closed the book. She felt horrible about sending O'Reilly inside with a story that, while not technically a lie, skirted dangerously close to deception. She battled internally for a moment, torn between doing what she knew she should, and fear of her odd inability to remain reasonable and objective around Trevor Caldwell.

The battle was short. Disgusted with herself, Grace squared her shoulders and started to walk to the house, intending to tell Trevor herself, firmly and politely, that she would rather not see him. She drew up short when she saw

O'Reilly emerge from the house and walk across the lawn, heading straight for her hedge. She sat back down on the bench, her face tight with self-directed anger. Contrite, she looked up as the footman approached.

"I'm so very sorry I put you in such an awkward position, O'Reilly," she said.

The small man looked surprised at the remorse in her tone. He shuffled from one foot to the other, unsure of what to say. His ears began to turn red.

Grace realized he felt a bit off balance and took pity. She wrapped her arms around her drawn-up knees, her lilac skirts spread about her in a brightly colored pool of silk. "Has he gone?" she asked hopefully.

O'Reilly nodded, grateful for the subject change. "Yes, Miss Grace, I watched him leave, myself."

Grace breathed a sigh of relief. "What did he say? Did he see me from the window?" Her voice was rushed and breathless. When O'Reilly looked a bit taken aback, she softened her voice. "Please, you have to tell me his exact words."

"Well," the little footman began, scrunching up his rather bulbous nose in an effort to recall the conversation. "When I went back into the salon, he was looking out the windows with his back toward me, so I couldn't see his face."

"You mean the windows that open to the garden?" Grace asked, holding her breath.

"Yes, miss, but his lordship didn't seem to have seen you, or at least, he didn't mention it."

Grace let out her breath slowly. That did not mean that he had not seen her, she knew. "Go on," she prompted.

"He was quiet for a few moments, and just stood looking out that window while I told him what you asked me to say to him." Grace silently congratulated herself for not succumbing to the urge to peek around the hedge. "Then he turned, smiled rather oddly at me, and bade me give you his best wishes for a quick recovery."

Grace drew her brows dubiously. "How 'oddly' did he smile, O'Reilly?"

The footman thought a moment, his mind stirred by long-forgotten memories. "It was rather like the way my father used to smile at me when he knew I wasn't being truthful," he said slowly. "He never actually accused me of lying, and yet I knew he thought I was."

Grace propped her chin on her knees, guilt assaulting her again. "And that was all?" she asked quietly, her mind searching for unexpected traps in Trevor's few words.

"Yes, miss."

Well, she thought, it really made no difference whether or not he believed her. It was not likely he would take it upon himself to come up to her chambers and see for himself if she was ill.

"Thank you, O'Reilly." She smiled at the waiting footman, then watched as he bowed and turned to walk back toward the house. She sat in pensive silence, her smile slowly fading. Her almost-lie had not come without consequence. It would obligate her to spend her evenings at home for a few days, for fear of encountering Trevor at some ball or at the theater. Grace grimly accepted her fate, then peevishly sought to lay the blame at his feet. Why, she wondered, did this man take such perverse pleasure in tormenting her? She thought back over the few times she had seen and spoken with the earl and could not remember anything she had either said or done to encourage him. She shook her head. If anything, he should have developed a decided dislike for her by this time. With the exception of a few brief moments in the portrait room at home, she had really behaved in a rather sulky and, on occasion, downright rude manner to him. That realization made her frown. Why *did* she comport herself in such a way toward him?

Her mind inadvertently returned to the heated moments they had spent together beneath the tree in the wildflower glade. She felt a hot blush slowly spread across her face. Her hands flew to cover her warm cheeks, as if she could control the direction of her thoughts by hiding the evidence of her embarrassed chagrin. Perhaps Trevor felt she would welcome more advances of that nature. Deeper mortification flooded through her as she recalled the lascivious way she had pressed herself against him that day, and the way she had melted in his arms only the previous evening at Almack's.

She dropped her forehead to her upraised knees, trying to block the thoughts of Trevor from her mind, but images of his hands kept coming into her head, his strong, long-fingered, comforting hands. She remembered how secure she'd felt when they had kept her from falling at the Assembly Rooms in Pelthamshire, and how gently they had touched her when he'd caressed . . . Hurriedly, her mind skittered away from *that* thought.

"O'Reilly told me I'd find you out here."

She jumped in surprise. Her younger sister smiled down at her, as usual the perfect picture of smooth serenity. Grace looked down at her own wrinkled gown and the comfortable, if unladylike way she sat. Spotting a new grass stain on the toe of her lavender slipper, she hastily drew the offending foot beneath her skirts. "Does nothing ever fluster you?" she asked.

Faith sank gracefully onto the bench next to her sister, her own pale pink skirts settling around her in precise arrangement, like a well-disciplined extension of herself. Grace noticed her sister did not have a single hair out of place, and unconsciously reached up to smooth a bright, wayward curl (that never *would* stay where it belonged) from her own forehead.

Faith ignored her sister's question and asked one of her own, giving Grace a direct, no-nonsense look. "Did I hear correctly that the Earl of Huntwick was here to pay a call on you?"

Grace raised her chin. "He was. And you may as well know," she said defensively, "that I had O'Reilly tell him I was ill and couldn't see him." She looked like a child caught with her hand in the candy jar.

"I know," said Faith softly, her gray eyes gentle. She paused, then added, "He has sent you flowers."

Grace rolled her eyes heavenward in disbelief. "Already? He only just left. When did he have time?"

"Would you like to see the note? I brought it out for you." Faith held the envelope toward Grace, who took it and glanced at her name written in the familiar bold, flowing hand. She tossed her head and gave it back to her sister, unopened and unread.

"You read it," she said in a deliberately offhand voice. "I don't know why he even bothered. He must know I will not appreciate them."

Faith gave Grace an amused look. She pulled the card out of the small blue envelope and smiled at her sister's unconvincingly blasé attitude. She began reading aloud: " 'I'm sorry to hear you're ill. I shall miss seeing you this evening. Please allow me to call upon you tomorrow morning in the hope that I might find you feeling better. With deepest regard, Huntwick.' "

Grace shot up from the bench with a muffled curse. "That insufferable man! 'With deepest regard'!" She snorted with derision, her momentary guilt forgotten. "Why can he not just leave me alone?"

"Have you asked him to?" Faith inquired.

Grace stopped blustering for a moment and looked blank.

"Have you asked him to leave you alone?" Faith repeated.

"I shouldn't have to," Grace muttered obstinately. Faith said nothing, just looked steadily at her sister. Grace stared back for a moment, then gave up because she knew Faith had a perfectly good point. She threw up her hands and stalked back to the house, muttering angrily to herself all the way, looking like a thundercloud as she swept through the hall on her way upstairs.

When she reached her chamber, the first thing she noticed was the tasteful bouquet of pink tea roses and white daisies arranged in a beautiful porcelain vase on her dressing table. Although they were pretty, the sight of them only reminded her that she allowed him to make her feel unsettled enough to behave in ways she normally would not. Her original determination to get rid of the Earl of Huntwick hardened to a steely resolve.

The shadowy figure lounging in the darkened doorway across the street from the Egerton town house surreptitiously tugged the brim of his hat lower to hide his face as the Earl of Huntwick's coach rolled past. He looked up at the small round window on the second floor. *She* had appeared there the day before, sticking her head out and calling a happy farewell to her sister, who had set off on an outing with one of her many callers. He had spent hours in this deserted doorway since, hoping for yet another glimpse. He settled back down against the steps to continue his vigil. He would wait as long as necessary.

Chapter Eleven

*T*revor scowled as the door to the Egerton town house thudded to a purposeful close behind him again. For three consecutive days now, he had come to pay a morning call on Grace. Each morning she had sent her maid with a prettily worded note thanking him for the flowers and concern, but begging him to excuse her for yet one more day of recovery. A note that Becky had, all three times, fearfully handed to him, while the increasingly impertinent Greaves stood by with an annoying smirk of satisfaction.

This time Trevor quickly recovered his good humor. He grinned at the door despite his third dismissal. Not for one moment did he believe Grace was really ill. Further, he questioned whether she had ever been sick to begin with. Doubtless she had begun to feel like a caged animal by now, he thought. Cheerfully he waved his carriage away and sauntered around the corner to the side of the house.

Upstairs, Grace held her breath as she lay in her bed, the beautifully embroidered satin bedclothes pulled all the way up to her chin. She listened for the heavy thud of male footsteps as she closely watched the door, perfectly certain the infuriating and persistent earl would eventually come upstairs to properly assess the situation for himself. She tensed as the door opened, then relaxed when the round, cheerful face of Becky appeared in the opening.

"He's gone again, miss," she said, bustling into the room with her plump arms full of Trevor's latest floral offering.

Grace wrinkled her nose in aggravation at the exquisite arrangement of roses and daisies, then briskly threw back the covers and hopped out of bed, landing lightly on the polished hardwood floor. She wore a lovely morning gown of peach linen trimmed with ivory lace that perfectly complimented her coloring, set off her burnished hair, and made her pure complexion appear impossibly creamy. She shook out her wrinkled skirts and went to the small, high window that opened out onto the street. She climbed up onto a smoothly polished oak chest and pushed the window open, looking out just in time to see Trevor's shining carriage pull away and disappear from view.

She turned with a smile and clapped her hands, hopping off the chest and glancing with naked longing toward the warm sunbeams streaming in the larger windows that opened out onto the side gardens. She snatched up her book and a length of ivory lace from the box on her dressing table. Handing the book to Becky, she haphazardly gathered her bright curls into the ribbon, tying it in a smart bow at the nape of her neck. "I am going to go out into the sunshine," she announced firmly. "I've been cooped up in here for three of the longest days of my life, and I'm positively dying for some fresh air." She dropped a kiss on the pink cheek of her plump abigail, retrieved her book, and swept through the door, her spirits high at the thought of having outwitted the earl once again.

Becky watched her go, then sighed and turned to make the bed for the second time that day.

Grace took a long, deep breath as soon as she stepped outside, tipped her face up to the sunlight, and held her arms wide, glad of the chance to enjoy the beauty of the day after confining herself for so long to her self-imposed prison. She found the utter lack of access to nature the most difficult thing about living in the city. She missed the opportunity to simply mount her horse and gallop for miles through the open countryside. Sitting in the garden during the quiet, cool hours of the morning came closest to satisfying her yearnings for her daily rides in Pelthamshire. Although they could not possibly compare for excitement and exercise, the peace and beauty she found here at least equaled that which she found at any of her favorite quiet spots in the country.

She walked across the garden with a jaunty step, stopping here and there to notice some of the flowers that had opened during the past few days, before finally rounding the hedge she had hidden behind when Trevor had first come to call three days ago. Cheerful at the recollection of how she had outsmarted him that day, she whistled the lighthearted opening bars of a colorful ditty she knew, then came to an abrupt halt. Her whistling trailed off and she narrowed her eyes.

Lounging on the marble bench—*her* marble bench!—and looking for all the world as though he belonged nowhere else, sat the maddening, smug Earl of Huntwick, his long legs stretched before him, his booted feet crossed at the ankles, a small bouquet of flowers on the seat beside him.

Picking up the bouquet, Trevor stood and walked toward her, his wide, satisfied smile betraying the pleasure he took in outmaneuvering her. Grace took an involuntary step backward as he drew near, then stopped, inwardly cursing herself for once again allowing him to see how he managed to affect her. She raised her chin, hoping he could not hear how loudly her heart was beating.

"I'm glad to see you're feeling better, my dear," Trevor drawled, one lofty brow arching in sardonic accusation. He sketched her a mocking bow, then held out the flowers. "These are for you," he said, looking down at her with a smile. "I hope you like daisies. The glade where we first began to know each other was strewn with them, you know." His voice deepened imperceptibly. "I think they'll always remind me of you."

Grace looked at the flowers with thinly veiled contempt, unable to believe he continued to allude to that particular incident. "Have I not made myself plain?" she asked, irritation evident in her scathing tone. "When have I ever encouraged you to continue this bizarre . . ." She fumbled for the right word, as flustered as always around him.

"Courtship?" he offered.

Her eyes widened as he uttered that word, and she shook her head in vigorous denial. "Is that what this farce has been to you? A courtship?" She scoffed at him, then added in a taunting voice, "Most suitors would have given up the first time their advances were rebuffed."

"Ah, but my dear, you haven't rebuffed my advances." Grace skeptically raised delicately winged russet brows as he continued in a silken voice, "You have responded to me in ways that vehemently deny your words."

Grace gasped in shocked surprise at the images conjured up by that statement. "You cannot mean the way you assaulted me that day in the glade?" she choked out.

He looked amused. "Do you really consider what we shared that day an assault?" His amused smirk softened to a fond, gentle smile.

Grace blushed as she recalled the way she'd reacted to him. She pushed past him, her chest heaving with emotions she did not care to identify—part arousal, part fear, intensified by the fact that she could never keep a thought straight in her head around Trevor. "I don't know what you're talking about," she said, standing stiffly, her back to him, her hands clenched into small, tense fists at her sides.

Trevor walked up behind her and placed gentle hands on her slender, trembling shoulders. When he spoke, his low, husky voice fell softly very near her ear. "I'm speaking of how well we fit together, Grace, from the very first time we danced, and of how aware we are of each other whenever we're together. I'm talking about the wonder I feel each time I touch you, and how the mere scent of your hair makes me insane with wanting you."

Her breath caught in her throat as he slowly turned her to face him. His eyes searched the luminous sapphire depths of hers to see if he had somehow gotten through to her, but her gaze reflected only taut wariness and frightened distrust. That glimmer of fright made him continue speaking, for he instinctively knew it was not a fear of him that put that emotion there, but a fear of herself, or perhaps of how he made her feel. "Don't you see, Grace?" he asked softly, his voice taking on an earnest huskiness that caught at her heart. "I'm talking about perfection. You and I, we're perfect for each other, my dear."

Grace turned her head away, pulling her eyes from his compelling green gaze with more effort than she cared to admit. "I have no wish to be perfect for anyone, least of all you." Her harsh words lacked conviction, though, for his words and his voice were full of promise, and she very nearly ached to believe him.

Trevor put two fingers under her chin and brought her mutinous blue eyes back to his. "Give me a chance to show you how wonderful perfect can be, won't you, Grace?" he asked gently, as cajoling as a little boy on Christmas Eve.

She closed her eyes.

"At least let me show you we belong together."

Grace opened her mouth to protest again, but this time

Trevor swiftly brought his lips to hers, effectively silencing whatever comment she might have made. Her own lips parted in a gasp of dismay, and Trevor took immediate advantage, parting his own and using them to mold and shape her mouth to his.

Grace thought her heart would explode as a lightning bolt of pure desire shot through her entire body. She felt her knees weaken and grasped Trevor's arms in a desperate attempt to keep her balance, even as his tongue began flicking gently at her lips, fanning the longing ache that had begun with his whispered talk of perfection. Heat blossomed low in her stomach. She slowly slid her hands upward to the nape of his neck, where her fingers entwined, despite herself, in the short, dark curls that lay there. Almost unconsciously, she touched her tongue to his. When she did, the kiss went wild.

Trevor felt unbridled lust ignite within his loins the moment she yielded her mouth to him. He tugged her closer, one arm encircling her waist while the other hand plunged deep into her fiery curls, tangling on the ribbon that held them captive. He pulled the ribbon out as he tilted her head back to deepen the kiss, his tongue plunging into her mouth; it was met by hers, shyly imitating his actions in a way that drove him out of his mind with need. The last threads of his self-control deserted him, but he did not care. All that mattered was this incredible woman trembling in his arms.

Unable to think, only to feel, Grace eagerly pressed herself closer to the hard length of Trevor's body, her hands moving restlessly up and down the tightly bunched muscles of his back. "Please," she whispered when his lips moved across her cheek to a sensitive spot just behind her ear. "Tell me what you want me to do," she murmured into his neck.

"Just touch me." He groaned and slid his hand down to cup her bottom as if to show her how.

Grace pushed his jacket open, slipping her arms inside and around his waist to copy his actions. "Like this?" she asked, not really needing an answer.

An unstoppable yearning to touch her more freely rocked through Trevor. Swiftly he bent and scooped her into his arms, then settled her gently on the soft grass beside the bench. He knelt next to her. She leaned up on an elbow to meet his descending lips, reached one hand around his neck, and pulled him down beside her. Quickly he loosened his cravat and undid the studs of his shirt, then came down atop her, sweetly crushing her with his body. Grace let him push her back down into the grass, the fingers of one hand reaching up and trailing across his cheek to where their lips met. He turned his head and caught her smallest finger lightly between his teeth, then deliberately sucked it further into the wet warmth of his mouth. Grace gasped and threw her head back as sensation shot up her arm from that finger, then traveled with lightning speed to that secret place at the juncture of her thighs. She shifted her legs fitfully and dug her fingernails into the tight sinews of his muscled chest, feeling his flesh convulse in response to her touch, secretly delighting in her ability to evoke such a reaction.

Unable to believe the innocent ardor Grace so unabashedly shared, Trevor ran his tongue down the vulnerable column of her throat to the tops of her breasts, where they strained against the scooped neckline of her dress. Impatiently, he tugged one side of her bodice down. The ripe, enticing mound was suddenly exposed to his hungry gaze, her small, rosy nipple jutting proudly up into the midmorning air. Reverently he cupped her soft fullness in his hand, and then bent his head to suckle the offered tidbit.

Grace gasped and clutched convulsively at his head, twining her fingers in his hair, not wanting him to ever stop. "Please," she moaned as she felt his teeth lightly nip at the sensitive morsel. "Please tell me there's more."

Trevor froze at the provocative innocence of her whispered words, suddenly remembering where they were. With heroic effort, he rolled onto his back and pushed her away from him. He heard her gasp in shocked surprise, and quickly pulled her protectively back into his arms. He held her tenderly cradled against his chest, one hand unconsciously smoothing her tumbled red-gold tresses as he felt his thundering heart beat with insistent need. With a level of control he did not know he possessed, he forced himself to lie still for a few moments, allowing his heartbeat and his breathing to return to normal.

When he finally spoke, his voice sounded deep and reassuring to Grace as she lay with one ear pressed to his chest. "If you'll just give me a month . . . ," he began, his voice still hoarse with passion.

"A week," she interrupted in a quavering voice.

Heady triumph soared through Trevor as he realized she would finally give in. "A month," he insisted, smiling up at the clouds scudding by in the clear sky.

Grace adjusted her bodice and pushed herself away from his chest, self-consciously sitting up and smoothing her hair. She raked her fingers through the tangled strands in a vain search for her ribbon. "Well, two weeks, then," she averred, then immediately felt peevish when he swiftly nodded, making her sure that he had hoped for a fortnight to begin with. "I have some conditions," she stated, holding up a warning hand before he could speak.

Trevor closed his mouth and looked at her in inquiry.

"First of all, there will be no more kisses," she emphatically declared. "I mean it," she added sternly when he looked as though he would protest. She blushed a bit. "I can't think when you kiss me."

Her inadvertent admission so pleased him that he agreeably nodded his assent to her first condition.

"Second, if you cannot prove to me that we belong together within the space of two weeks, you must promise to leave me alone."

"Completely?" he teased.

Grace refused to rise to the bait. "I want your promise," she said firmly, looking around on the ground for the scrap of fabric that had held back her curls.

Trevor thought guiltily of the betrothal contract in his desk at Upper Brook Street. He carefully worded his answer. "I promise you things will be just as they were the day I arrived in London."

Grace's eyes narrowed suspiciously. "Before you came to Almack's?"

Trevor laughed at her skepticism, then reached out and fondly ruffled her hair. "Before I came to Almack's," he agreed, then quirked an eyebrow and handed her the missing hair ribbon.

She blushed again.

"Shall we begin this evening, when I arrive to escort you to the Tildens' ball?" Without waiting for an answer, he stood, helped her up, then walked over to the garden wall. He easily scaled the structure, then dropped down and disappeared on the other side.

Grace took pity on her trembling legs and sank down on the bench, her book lying forgotten on the ground. She stared for a moment at the area of crushed grass where she had lain with Trevor, then dropped her hot face into her hands. What had she allowed him to do to her? Worse still, what had she agreed to? The thought of how she had again responded to his every caress horrified her nearly as much as the fact that she had not wanted him to stop.

Resolutely, she pushed the images that flooded her senses to the back of her mind. Every time she found herself alone with Trevor, she somehow ended up in his arms. Well, no more, she told herself firmly. She picked up the bouquet of slightly crushed flowers and smiled ruefully as she remembered what he had said about the daisies. Funny, but she had always adored daisies. She wondered if he had somehow guessed that. After a moment's reflection, she was sure he had. He instinctively seemed to know things about her that she usually would not admit even to herself, not the least of which was this: never, in her entire life, had she allowed herself to back down from a challenge.

Chapter Twelve

Grace's head was high, her mood light as she gracefully descended the staircase at Lord and Lady Tilden's ball a few steps behind her aunt and sister. Determined to forget that she entered on the arm of the Earl of Huntwick, she winced only slightly when the haughty butler stationed at the top of the steps bellowed out their names, and six hundred pairs of eyes swiveled with open curiosity toward them.

As they neared the foot of the stairs, Trevor covered her small hand with his own large, warm one, lightly rubbing his thumb along her wrist. Resolutely ignoring the caress, Grace looked out across the sea of upturned faces to see if Amanda had arrived. She picked out the people here and there whom she knew and smiled a greeting at them. She deliberately pretended she did not see the incredulous looks dawning on their faces as they recognized the man who escorted her.

She had no idea of the real reasons for their surprise: although Trevor had accompanied many beautiful women to ton functions, seldom had he appeared with someone so new to town, and never had he focused his attention on a debutante. Of all this Grace remained blissfully unaware, never knowing that nearly any woman in the room would have happily traded places with her, never knowing that attending any function with the Earl of Huntwick was an event considered a chore only by herself. She was simply abiding by her agreement with Trevor to allow him to escort her to functions, and she was determined to enjoy herself.

Glancing down at the beautiful girl on his arm who had thus far thwarted his every attempt to forge a relationship, Trevor easily picked up on Grace's good mood. His lips unconsciously curved into an appreciative smile at her appearance—a smile marked with glee by the other young eligibles present, and with increasing dismay by the many aspiring countesses in the room, for that smile held more than a hint of fond, possessive pride.

Grace was positively radiant. She wore a gown of deep sapphire silk that wrapped sumptuously around her upper body, the neckline square and low, the puffed sleeves practically nonexistent. The skirt fell in a straight line to the floor, elegantly simple, giving only a hint of the flawless figure hidden beneath the yards of rustling silk. Her burnished curls shone, piled in artful disarray at the top of her head, a strand of glittering sapphires the exact shade of her eyes woven through the gleaming mass. Her face was flushed with happiness and excitement as she turned and spoke with a young man her aunt had just introduced to her.

Trevor found it difficult to take his eyes off her. As he watched her friends, both male and female, come eagerly to greet her, he realized that, although he considered the endless round of parties and balls that typified the London Season simply a chance to conduct business, Grace embraced it with pure delight. She belonged here, he thought, among the most beautiful people in England, and knew, with great pride, that she would make a wonderful countess.

As though she could read Trevor's thoughts, Grace turned away from Lord Grenelle, the young man with whom she conversed, and briefly allowed her eyes to meet his. Something about the way that he gazed at her, a poignant look of aching tenderness that came from deep within his fathomless jade eyes, reached out to her heart. She softened toward him long enough to give him a winsome smile before she remembered the reason she stood here with him. Her smile faded, and she turned her attention back to the viscount.

With a slight shake of his head, Trevor gave the would-be suitor a speaking look over the top of Grace's head. He watched as Grenelle stammered an implausible excuse and abruptly took himself off, leaving Grace standing alone, perplexed. A scant second later she realized what Trevor had done. She gave him a scathing look and simply walked away, hoping he would not follow.

Trevor watched her leave, appreciating the natural, fluid way she moved, until the crowd of people around the dance floor swallowed her. He did not follow, for he wanted her to enjoy herself. Instead, knowing she would do her best to spar with him at every opportunity if he remained at her side, he had simply scrawled his name across one of the waltzes on her dance card, fully intending to leave her in the company of her aunt and sister while he played cards in one of the rooms Lord Tilden provided for his male guests, adjacent to the ballroom.

He had not realized just how difficult he would find it to leave the ballroom, however, as he caught sight of her again. He watched as the gentlemen began to flock around her like moths to a bright flame. He began to feel the first faint stirrings of jealousy, and was so caught up in watching her that he did not notice when an older, distinguished-looking gentleman approached him. Trevor almost flinched when the hearty gentleman began speaking in a booming baritone.

"It's good to see you back in London, Hunt. Hoping I

would find you here tonight. Didn't know you'd taken to escorting the young butterflies. In the market for a wife, I suppose?" Lord Anthony Galesworthy peered nearsightedly across the room in the direction Trevor stared, but could see only a blur of brilliant blue surrounded by the deeper hues of gray, navy, and burgundy.

Galesworthy was among the men Trevor had hoped to see tonight. The well-to-do baron participated as a partner in many of the ventures in which Trevor himself had an interest. Trevor had wanted to discuss with him the same mining investment upon which he had already secured Sebastian's agreement, but found himself completely unable to concentrate on the ensuing conversation. Twice he had to ask Galesworthy to repeat a question. Then, after giving him an answer that had nothing to do with mines, coal, or even investments, Trevor swore under his breath and rudely walked away. He swooped down on the unsuspecting group surrounding Grace and physically moved a young buck he thought stood a bit too close and stared a bit too eagerly at her low-cut neckline. His mission accomplished, he returned and calmly concluded his conversation with Galesworthy.

For the next few hours, the ton watched in fascinated amazement as he repeated the action several times. After each interruption, Trevor invariably returned to his colleagues, leaving an increasingly frustrated and angry-looking Grace behind. As a result of his intervention, fewer and fewer gentlemen sought Grace out, rightfully afraid of incurring the wrath of the powerful earl.

By the time Trevor appeared again to escort her home, Grace was fuming, prepared to give him a thorough tongue-lashing as soon as they got away from the prying eyes and ears of the ton. Once they were seated inside his coach, however, Aunt Cleo surprised her by entirely monopolizing Trevor's attention. She prattled on about everything she could think of, from the current style of men's coats to the deplorable lack of manners in the younger set. This last comment she directed at Grace, who at that moment was quite rudely glaring across the coach at Trevor.

It was the last straw for Grace. Her lips thinning into a furious line, she sat and stewed in silent anger while the conversation ebbed and flowed around her. As soon as the carriage pulled up in front of the house, she jumped out, ran up the front steps, and disappeared inside.

Trevor watched her go, smiling politely as he helped Aunt Cleo and Faith alight. He climbed back into the carriage, his fixed smile fading quickly. He had absolutely no reason to have behaved the way he had tonight. At the very least, he had managed to push Grace even farther away with his possessive actions, when he had intended only to charm and cajole her. When he had seen her laughing and enjoying the attention of the many gentlemen who admired her, however, something inside him had snapped. He found himself repressing the urge to drag her from their midst, to take her to his home and soundly kiss her until he was utterly certain she could not possibly think of any man except himself.

He slapped his gloves in a steady cadence against his thigh, his fury directed entirely at himself. He would have to regain control of the situation. He had no doubt that Grace would find some way to punish him for his behavior this evening. He would think about it tonight, before he showed up tomorrow to take her for the ride in Green Park he had planned. Surely he would find a way to rein in his jealousy before then.

"Just what did you think you were doing?" she asked, her even, modulated tone at complete odds with the angry glint in her sapphire eyes.

Trevor felt his blood warm as he looked at the tempestuous beauty who stood several steps above him, glaring down at him with militant ire. He smiled benignly. "Let me see," he mused, rubbing his chin thoughtfully. "I stopped for you at precisely ten o'clock yesterday evening and cooled my heels for approximately fifteen minutes in your aunt's uncomfortably small and overly warm blue salon before you decided to grace me with your presence. After that, I believe I escorted you to the Tildens' ball, at the conclusion of which I returned you home, quite safe and sound, at not quite two o'clock in the morning." Having blandly summed up the evening, he looked at her inquiringly. "At some point within that timetable, did I do something that caused offense, my lady? Perhaps you found fault with the comfort of my carriage? If you'll pardon me a moment, I'll have the springs on the phaeton checked at once. I would hate to think you might be subjected to a drive in the park in what could possibly be an inferior conveyance." He turned and headed purposefully for the door.

"My lord!" Grace's voice rang out, shrill in the high-ceilinged room. She took a deep breath and slowly let it out before speaking again in a more normal tone. "I found no fault with the transportation. It was your company I found lacking."

He walked back toward her as she descended the last three steps, and offered her his arm, which she took without comment. Neither of them spoke again until she settled comfortably into her seat and Trevor set the well-matched grays in motion. He spoke first. "You would, perhaps, have preferred the theater, Miss Ackerly?"

"I would have preferred a chance to enjoy myself last night," she snapped, unable to contain her resentment with even a facade of civility. "By deserting me as soon as we arrived, you made it appear as though escorting me were some sort of repugnant chore an older brother was required to perform. And, as if that weren't enough, you then made it your sworn duty to descend upon me like a hungry hawk and frighten off every man who so much as *looked* at me. In the meantime, *you* had Lady Maria Monfort hanging off your arm, her vulgarly displayed bosoms nearly falling out of her bodice as she flirted outrageously with you, just as if her seventy-year-old husband weren't propped up with his cane in some dim corner of that very room." She took a deep breath, prepared to continue her angry tirade, then realized she had nothing left to say. She closed her mouth with a snap, then sat staring resolutely forward as though fascinated by the ears of the horses, her hands folded properly in her lap.

"I did not desert you," Trevor pointed out in a reasonable voice. He glanced sideways at her flawless profile, and had to bite back a shout of laughter at her prim pose. "I had no idea that you were so jealous, my dear."

"Jealous!" she cut in indignantly. She felt her pulse begin to pound with a fresh surge of fury.

"Had I known you were jealous," he repeated, as though she had not spoken, "I suppose I would have paid you a bit more attention."

"I was *not* jealous," she protested hotly. "I simply don't like being made to look a fool." Belatedly, Grace remembered that she had attempted to do that very thing to him at Almack's. She lapsed into a guilty, uncomfortable silence. Self-consciously she looked away, nodding and smiling occasionally as they passed acquaintances and friends who also drove or walked in the park. As they plodded along, her ire began to slowly subside.

Several minutes passed before she spoke again. "You have a splendid team, my lord," she said quietly, nodding toward the grays. "And you handle them beautifully."

Trevor accepted the offered truce, noting the sincerity in her voice and the genuine admiration in her eyes. "My lady, would you care to try your hand at driving them?"

Grace looked at him in disbelief, eagerness evident in her shining eyes. She cheerfully disregarded his possessive address, her gloved hands already reaching for the proffered reins. "May I really?" she asked, looking for all the world like a child offered a brand-new toy.

Trevor smiled at her unabashed happiness and handed her the reins. He considered his carefully laid plans for her seduction and chuckled to himself at the simple pleasure she found in this small gesture. Had he but known . . .

She handled the horses expertly, he noticed with pride, guiding them with a firm, gentle touch. Trevor watched in amazement as the horses sensed the new hand on the leads, stretched their necks out, then began to almost prance down the cobbled street.

Grace's lips curved in a smile of unrestrained joy. "Animals know when you love them," she said in a confiding voice. She glanced sideways at the earl, who looked at her in the alert way that always made her spine tingle.

"Do they, now?" The husky note in his voice made Grace look away hastily.

Trevor smiled to himself and decided to change the subject. "You won't have to abide my presence for long tonight. I'll have to leave the entertainment a bit early for a prior engagement later in the evening. I hope I may prevail upon your aunt to escort you home."

Grace felt a sense of relief at the new topic of conversation, oddly accompanied by a small thread of wistfulness she could not quite explain. "You don't have to feel obligated to escort me somewhere every night, Lord Caldwell."

In truth, he hadn't intended upon an evening out at all, but he wasn't about to give Grace a night off from their arrangement. "It's not a difficulty for me to do both. I am simply having some friends in for cards."

"Cards," she said. An odd regret was washing through her.

"Yes," he said, then added politely, "Do you play?"

"My sisters and I have occasionally played for fun, but not for stakes," she answered.

Trevor smiled. "Are you a good player?"

"I think I play well enough. Mercy was the one we had to watch out for. She often cheated, you know." Grace laughed. And then she had a scandalous, wonderful idea. She turned impish eyes on him. "Perhaps I could join you?"

He shook his head, astonished that she would even propose such a thing. Her next words drew him up short.

"I could come in disguise."

He suddenly pictured her in a comically large mustache, her hair tucked up in a hat, half her face obscured behind the high starched points of a dandified collar. An unbidden smile came to his lips, a smile Grace noted immediately. Wisely she kept silent and allowed his thoughts to persuade him. It didn't take long.

"I suppose you could be my cousin visiting from Cornwall, come to London to acquire some town polish," he said. He still looked dubious.

She slowed the horses, then brought them to a smooth halt in front of her aunt's town house. "Who will be there?" she asked.

"Just two others. A possible third later on." He considered the damage such an adventure could do to her reputation. "I assure you each of these men can be trusted. Not that I have any doubt in your ability to pull it off." He shook his head and his tone turned wary. "Come now, Grace, you must admit this is a bad idea." He reached for the reins.

Grace sighed theatrically. "All right, my lord. I understand. You haven't the stomach for it."

The gently thrown challenge floated between them. Trevor hesitated only a second before grasping it with both hands. When he looked at her again, Grace knew that she had won. She smiled happily and asked, "How will we manage it?"

"Leave it to me. I'll make all the arrangements and tell you of my plan when I see you at the ball tonight." He touched his hat as a footman assisted her descent, then watched as she went slowly up the steps and into the house. He began whistling cheerfully as he flicked the reins and drove away down Curzon Street.

The hidden watcher cursed in frustrated fury. The usurper appeared every day now, and spent more and more time with his love. Eyes lifted again to her window, he decided it would have to be tonight. He was running out of time to rescue her. He would go in tonight, and he would take her home, to where she belonged.

With him.

Chapter Thirteen

Grace did her best to appear as though she were not looking for anybody in particular as she searched the milling crowd in the Havershims' ballroom. Clutching Faith's arm, she stood on tiptoe in a vain attempt to see over the heads of those surrounding her, then sighed in exasperation and turned to her sister. "Faith, you're taller than I am. Do you happen to see Huntwick anywhere?"

Faith looked down at her elder sister with cool appraisal. "Why? Are you still trying to avoid him?" she asked.

Grace averted her head from her sister's probing gaze, grimacing at Faith's usual excellent perception. "I suppose I can't hide anything from you, can I?" she said, hoping they could simply let the matter drop. A futile hope.

"Why do you wish to know where he is? He can't bother you here." Faith pinned her with a look. "Unless, that is, you allow him to bother you," she added reasonably.

Grace snorted inelegantly. "His mere *presence* bothers me," she retorted, but her eyes still searched the throng.

Faith raised dubious brows. "You know, it almost appears to me as though you are looking *for* him, not trying to *avoid* him."

Grace sighed and turned back to look at her sister. "What makes you say that?"

Faith shrugged gracefully. "Pure logic. In the past you've always tried to escape when we've encountered him. A mere three days ago, you went so far as to feign illness in order to keep him from calling on you. Yet tonight you're acting as though you're expecting to see him." She smiled, then bent down and whispered in Grace's ear, "And I think you're looking forward to it."

On impulse, Grace turned and looked for Aunt Cleo. She spotted her a few paces away, deeply engrossed in conversation with a small group of matronly ladies. Whirling back around, she grabbed Faith's hand and pulled her behind a nearby pillar. "Since it seems you're going to figure it all out anyway, I suppose I could use your help." Briefly, she explained the contest between herself and Trevor, glancing around to make certain nobody else could hear. As she talked, she began to realize how ridiculous the entire scheme sounded. She watched as Faith's expression changed from interest to dismay, and finally to shocked disbelief. She finished her explanation with a lame, "What do you think?"

"What do I *think?*" Faith hissed, her usual calm logic deserting her in the face of her headstrong sister's latest escapade. "Have you lost your minds? The only advice I could possibly offer is for you to act as if you have a brain in your head. Do you realize what people would *say*?" Grace began to look mutinous as Faith continued: "How in the world did you think I could possibly help you with this harebrained idea?"

An interruption saved her from having to come up with a plausible answer. "Good evening, ladies."

The honeyed, golden tones of Trevor's low-timbred voice deliciously touched, as always, a spot deep within Grace. Firmly she dismissed the warm feeling, saying irritably, "Must you always sneak up on people and pounce in that provoking fashion?"

Faith inclined her smoothly coifed head at him and smiled, but her alert gaze registered Grace's suddenly heightened color and bright eyes, as well as the way Trevor's eyes softened and the corners of his mouth quirked up. *Why, she is already half in love with him!* Faith thought to herself, her assessing eyes darting quickly back to Trevor's face. Did he know of her sister's budding feelings? she wondered, peering closely at the handsome earl. No, she decided, as she watched her sister continue to verbally spar with the man, but he certainly felt the same way. His affection showed in the way he looked at Grace, in the tone of his voice as he spoke with her, and in the tender way he treated her.

"Pounce?" Trevor quirked one of his eyebrows up in a way that never failed to infuriate Grace. Luckily, Aunt Cleo chose that moment to appear. Trevor wisely took full advantage of the distraction. "Ah, Lady Egerton, I'm so glad you've joined us. I was hoping to gain your permission to dance with Miss Grace." He sent his prey a rather triumphant look, bowing charmingly over Aunt Cleo's outstretched hand.

Aunt Cleo scowled in mock irritation and pulled her hand away. She thwacked him squarely on the shoulder with the silver top of her cane. "*Do* stop that infernal simpering at me, young man," she commanded.

Grace stifled a horrified giggle as Trevor winced in pain. She hastily composed herself as her outrageous aunt turned to look at her. "Grace!" she barked, in a voice that carried halfway across the ballroom despite the din of more than seven hundred guests.

"Yes, ma'am?" She gave Lady Egerton her best look of abject obedience.

"Will you kindly dance with this gentleman before he injures his back with all that wretched bowing and scraping?" And without waiting for a response, Aunt Cleo swept away, the large purple feather on her turban bobbing help-lessly along with her.

Grace gaped in astonishment after her aunt, then slowly looked sideways at Trevor. He, too, stared after Aunt Cleo, a broad grin wreathing his face. With a shake of his head, he turned and held out his arm to Grace, politely asking Faith if she would excuse them. Too perplexed to argue, Grace put her hand on his arm and allowed him to lead her away.

Once on the dance floor, they moved effortlessly into each other's arms. For a few moments they danced without speaking, in the fluid rhythm that came so naturally to them. Unwilling to bring up the subject that concerned her most, Grace chewed on her lower lip while Trevor watched with carefully concealed amusement. He could almost see the direction of her thoughts. She wanted to talk about the plan, but was unable to broach the subject without appear-ing too eager, so she hoped he would bring it up.

He did not miss his guess. Curiosity demanded that Grace ask him, but pride kept her silent. She jumped in sur-prise when he finally spoke. "Are you trying again to make me look dull, as you did last week at Almack's?"

She looked up at him with a swift, startled laugh, re-lieved to see by his expression that he was teasing her. "You're really horrid to bring that up again," she admon-ished. He looked solemnly back down at her, but a teasing grin played about his mouth, and his jade eyes held a de-cided glint. Grace realized he knew exactly what con-sumed her thoughts.

Trevor watched in amazement as a sudden impish grin lit her features. The moment she smiled, her already beau-tiful face transformed into something of flawless, breath-taking perfection. She opened her mouth slightly, offering Trevor a tantalizing glimpse of her even white teeth. He was just envisioning those teeth sinking gently into his lower lip, when she spoke, startling him from his momentary reverie. "All right, Huntwick," she said. "Let's hear this plan."

Wondering how she would react if she knew of the plan currently taking shape in his mind, Trevor pushed away his amorous thoughts. "First, is there no way I can talk you out of doing this?" He watched as she began to look stubborn, and sighed. "I thought not. Can you manage to leave here early?" Grace nodded slowly, her nimble mind already racing ahead to a possible excuse for going home.

Trevor watched her brows draw together. "I think 'twisted ankle' might suffice," he supplied helpfully, again correctly interpreting her thoughts. "That should get you home early, preclude a large amount of fussing, and you can miraculously heal overnight with a minimum of raised eyebrows."

Grace gasped in startled laughter, merriment shining in her eyes. "I'll wager you plagued your poor tutor half to death when you were still in the schoolroom, my lord," she accused good-naturedly.

"Several," Trevor returned, smiling pleasantly as he nodded at an acquaintance who danced nearby.

"Several times?" she asked when his attention returned to her.

"Several *tutors*, my lady," he corrected solemnly. Grace laughed, causing those dancing nearby to notice that, once again, the Earl of Huntwick appeared to enjoy himself immensely with the elder Miss Ackerly.

Aunt Cleo had also noticed that Grace and Trevor greatly enjoyed their dance. If she was suspicious when, moments later, Trevor led a limping Grace up to her, she did not bat an eye. If she wondered why, thirty minutes later, Grace gamely hobbled alone up to her chamber, firmly insisting that nobody fuss over her, she did not ask any questions. And if she heard, sometime during the night, some suspicious bumps and whispers coming from the room across the hall, she merely shrugged it off, rolled over, and went back to sleep.

"I can't believe you're actually going through with this insane idea," said Faith as she walked into Grace's room through the small dressing area that connected their bedchambers.

Grace looked up from where she sat on the floor, gave the tasseled Hessian a final tug, and experimentally wriggled her toes inside the shiny black boots. Rising gracefully, she struck a dandy's pose. "How do I look?"

Her sister slowly took in Grace's attire, from the tips of the boots gleaming in the moonlight that streamed in the open windows, to the dangerously high points of the heavily starched white linen collar. She shook her head, hiding a smile. "You look exactly like you did when you were a little girl playing dress-up with Papa's clothes," she said.

Undaunted, Grace grinned. "That's because you know what you're looking for." She added an unfashionably outdated light brown wig with a short clubbed ponytail to the ensemble, tucking in several wayward red-gold curls, then topped off the entire ensemble with a curly-brimmed hat. Her smile widened with each addition to her costume, until finally she laughed aloud at her finished reflection in the full-length, gilt-framed mirror.

"Do you mind telling me what this idiotic escapade is supposed to accomplish?" Faith asked mildly, seating herself primly on the edge of the bed.

Grace began walking back and forth in front of her sister. "This 'escapade,' as you term it, is going to accomplish absolutely nothing. I am simply going out for an evening of cards with some friends; that's all. Do you ever do anything simply for the pleasure of it?" She stole a quick look at her sister, noting with a touch of annoyance that Faith's composure remained intact. She altered her stride a bit in an effort to move in a more masculine manner, and walked a couple more times back and forth in front of Faith. She frowned. "Do you think I walk like a girl?" she demanded, looking over her shoulder into the mirror as she walked away from it.

"You *are* a girl, Grace," Faith pointed out reasonably. She tried another tack. "Do you really think it's wise for you, a girl, to go alone to the home of Lord Caldwell, a man, dressed like *that,* to play cards with a group of men you don't know?"

Grace experienced a sharp pang of guilt. The social repercussions, for herself and for her family, could be huge. "Trevor wouldn't let anything happen to me," she assured Faith.

Seeing that her attempts to appeal to Grace's sense of propriety would go completely unheeded, Faith gave up and changed the subject. "Where did you manage to get the clothing?"

"Trevor had a footman deliver it to O'Reilly—all wrapped up, of course. It was right here waiting for me when we came home, just as he told me it would be."

Faith gave her sister a level look, then rose and walked back toward her own chamber. At the door she paused a moment and turned back. "I do hope you enjoy yourself, Grace," she said. "You'll come tell me when you return home, won't you?"

Impulsively, Grace ran across the room and hugged her. "I'll be fine, Faith, really." She picked up a discarded cane she had found in a closet, making it her own addition to the costume. "Now, I'm off!" she said, dramatically flourishing the ebony stick with a jaunty air.

Faith rolled her eyes and closed the connecting door. Grace took a deep breath and eased the bedchamber door open just a crack to view the corridor. Carefully she peered out into the gloomy hallway. Seeing no one about, she stepped outside, closed the door behind her, then tiptoed through the darkened house to the moonlit garden.

The garden was bright in comparison to the gloomy interior of the house, the damp night air just slightly chilly, although Grace hardly noticed it as she walked through the shadowy maze of well-kept flower beds and neatly trimmed hedges. She found her way unerringly to the hedge that concealed the low marble bench from the house, half expecting to see Trevor already waiting for her on the other side. To her surprise, he had not yet arrived. She sat down and crossed her legs, thoroughly enjoying the freedom of movement that wearing men's clothing allowed her, a luxury she had not indulged in since coming to London.

As she waited, Grace allowed herself to think again about the enormity of what she planned to do. In Pelthamshire, where she did as she wished with no thought for the possible results, her neighbors would frown upon but ultimately forgive such a venture. The same did not hold true here in London, where the daunting consequences for breaking the rules kept most young women from daring to act with anything even resembling impropriety. Suddenly the whole adventure struck her as a very bad idea. What if someone recognized her? Grace's stomach clenched as she thought of how quickly such a delicious story would spread. It would upset and anger Aunt Cleo, Faith would not have a prayer of making a suitable match, and the ton would consider the entire Ackerly family a laughingstock.

"I see you're ready," came Trevor's low, mocking voice from out of the darkness.

Grace jumped quickly to her feet, her heart beating a quick staccato. "Damn you, Huntwick, you startled me!" She glared at the shadowy figure leaning lazily against the garden wall.

Trevor chuckled at her unladylike language, then patted the smooth wall behind him, easily ten inches higher than his own six feet, two inches. "Do you think you can make it over this?" he asked, knowing she would likely try to scale a building if he said he thought she could not.

Sure enough, Grace's head snapped up and her small chin jutted out in a way that became daily more endearing to Trevor. "Of course I can," she shot back immediately, completely forgetting that, only moments before, she had considered backing out of the entire scheme. With a confident toss of her head, she walked over to the wall, handed Trevor her cane, then gave the barrier an appraising look. It suddenly looked much higher than it had only a few moments before. Backing up a few feet, she took a couple of running steps and leaped at it. She managed to get her hands up and around two of the decorative iron spikes that marched along the top of the wall. She hung there in triumph for a moment.

Then she promptly ran out of ideas.

Trevor watched in mirthful enjoyment as Grace first tried bracing her feet against the wall, but found that the slick soles of her new boots could not get a purchase on the equally slick marble. He let her struggle for a few moments, admiring the unobstructed view of her trim derriere in breeches. Realizing she would continue to attempt, unsuccessfully, to climb the wall unless he intervened, Trevor finally took pity on her plight. He stepped up behind her and gave her pert backside a firm upward boost.

Surprised, Grace landed and perched catlike between the spikes atop the marble wall, glaring down at Trevor. "I would have made it myself," she hissed hotly.

"Of course you would have," he agreed, vaulting easily to the top of the wall beside her, then jumping down on the other side to the street below. "Now jump."

She hesitated.

"Don't worry. I'll catch you," he promised in his most reassuring voice, infuriating her further with his condescending attitude. He held out his arms encouragingly.

So Grace jumped—not lightly into his arms, as Trevor

had expected, but straight down at him, knocking him off balance so he ended up sprawled on the street with Grace sitting on his chest, glaring down at him in belligerent scorn. She tossed her head disdainfully. "I could have done it myself," she reiterated.

The watcher crept through the darkened house to the second floor. He listened intently at each door, but heard no movement within the rooms. He reached the end of the hall and eased open the door to the last room on his right. Slipping inside, he softly closed the door, then turned and headed purposefully toward the bed. He stopped short when he saw it was empty and unslept-in.

He looked around in confusion, certain he had seen her come home, limping slightly, with her sister and her aunt. He walked to the high round window that opened to the street, suddenly unsure whether he had entered the correct room. Stepping on the chest beneath the small aperture, he looked down, saw the street below, and knew he had gone to the room he had intended.

A movement caught his eye. Two men came around the corner and walked in front of the Egerton town house. The watcher immediately recognized Trevor Caldwell as one of the men. He narrowed his eyes. The other man had an unusually small stature, and walked with a decidedly feminine gait.

He sucked in his breath, cursing inwardly as the pair disappeared down the street. He knew he would never make it outside in time to follow them.

The smoke hung in a thick haze above the green baize–covered table. A tomblike silence enveloped the dark room, punctured by the quiet clink of chips, the shuffling of cards, and the occasional low murmur of men's voices placing bets. The only illumination came from a gas lamp suspended just above the playing surface around which the four figures sat.

After Grace had wormed her way into attending the card party, Trevor had carefully revised his guest list. The men who remained invited to this card party were chosen for their proven loyalty, unquestionable friendship, and, above all, their unerring discretion. He knew he could count upon both men to keep to themselves anything that might happen this evening. More important, he knew they would also protect Grace, should the need arise.

Grace had felt a momentary pang of dismay when the first guest arrived and she found herself looking into the eyes of Gareth Lloyd, the younger brother of the Earl of Seth. He was Amanda Lloyd's brother-in-law, a man to whom Grace had previously been introduced, well-known throughout the ton for his reckless—though rather successful—gambling habits. Amiable and charming, an unapologetic prankster, he could be counted upon to bring life to any gathering, and was thus quite a favorite addition to any guest list. Relief washed through her when his face registered no surprise at her introduction as Grant Radnor, Trevor's young cousin from Cornwall. But her alarm again escalated when she discovered the Duke of Blackthorne would join them as well. After the completion of the introductions, she turned angry eyes on Trevor, who met her glare with laughter lurking in his.

After a few moments of uneventful play, Grace began to relax. She felt more secure in the knowledge that her disguise was intact, blissfully unaware that Sebastian, at least, knew precisely who she was. She was comfortable, she played well, and she had thus far managed to thoroughly enjoy herself.

Trevor watched with a sense of pride as Grace played her role to perfection. She spoke little, but managed to create an air of quiet confidence rather than one of shyness. She appeared, in fact, just a shade too comfortable, Trevor thought, as he watched her rake a pile of chips from the center of the table and deftly begin sorting them into neat piles. He grinned to himself. Perhaps she could use a little shaking up. He glanced toward Wilson, who had stationed himself near the door, then nodded his head toward the decanter-laden sideboard at the far end of the room.

At his employer's unspoken command, Wilson walked across the room on silent feet and began pouring the drinks, already well accustomed to the preferences of the earl's close friends. He poured a glass of port for Gareth, then filled two glasses with brandy, one each for Trevor and Sebastian. He paused a moment with the brandy decanter poised over the fourth glass and looked at Trevor in inquiry. At the earl's almost imperceptible nod, Wilson filled the remaining glass and brought the drinks to the table, serving them and returning immediately to his post by the door.

Grace peered with suspiciously narrowed eyes at the amber-colored liquid in the glass at her elbow, then looked at Trevor. He had laid his cards facedown on the table and pushed his chair back, his long legs stretched before him.

"Something wrong, Radnor?" Gareth asked with a quirky grin. "Don't they allow you to drink brandy in the wilds of Cornwall?"

Grace glared at Gareth, biting back the sarcastic retort that rose unbidden to her lips. Again she looked toward Trevor and found him watching her with unconcealed challenge. Unable to back down from his unspoken taunt, she snatched the glass of brandy from the table and drank the whole thing down in three triumphant swallows.

Seconds later she gasped in pain as the fiery liquid burned a searing path straight to her stomach. Tears filled her eyes. She struggled in vain to control her violent reaction to the potent drink. Through the loud ringing in her ears, she heard shouts of male laughter. She tried to focus on Trevor's face. It took a while.

"Brandy is meant to be sipped slowly," he advised when her senses had finally cleared enough for her to understand him. Grace opened her mouth with the full intention of giving him a blistering setdown, but stopped when she felt a curious and wonderful warmth begin spreading out from her stomach all the way to the tips of her fingers and toes. She wiggled them experimentally, smiling at the strange tingle she felt as they moved. She looked up to find Gareth watching her steadily. She gave him a wobbly smile and leaned over to peer intently into his glass. "And what are you drinking, if I may ask?" she inquired, grimacing in distaste at the smell and wrinkling her nose in a very feminine way after a delicate sniff.

His mouth twitched. "Port," he replied blandly.

She leaned her head upon a hand and pointed one tingly finger at him. "Can't handle brandy, huh?" She gave him a sympathetic look.

His mouth twitched again as she picked up her empty glass and waved it in the air. "A man's drink," she informed him loftily, looking toward the other men for confirmation.

Sebastian's face remained, as usual, impassive, but Trevor wore the superior smirk she had always found so infuriating. Strange, but tonight it did not bother Grace in the slightest. She cocked her head to the side and smiled at him, completely unaware that, when she smiled, no costume in the world could dim the glamorous perfection of her features.

"Why do you do that?" Grace asked him.

"Do what, *cousin?*"

"Smirk at people," she replied, "as though you know something perfectly awful about them."

Trevor looked amused. "Why do you ask? Do you have some terrible secret you think I may know about you?"

Grace flushed and shifted uncomfortably in her chair. She looked at Gareth, who appeared deeply engrossed in the cards he held, then at Sebastian, who looked as bored as ever. Did they know her real identity? she wondered.

She picked up the cards that lay facedown on the table before her and pretended to have an absorbing interest in rearranging them. That done, she looked cautiously over the cards at Trevor. He looked back at her, still smirking. Then, of all things, he winked!

Suddenly she felt closer to him than to anyone else in the world. Because of this man she sat here in his study, playing cards, drinking brandy, and gambling the night away, something she would wager none of the other debutantes in London could ever say. Feeling a strange sense of kinship with the man she usually considered her foe, she winked back, then returned her wavering attention to her cards, gloriously unaware of the small victory Trevor had just won in his war to win her hand.

Grace hiccoughed.

She stood unsteadily in the street with Trevor, her head thrown back, looking in dismay at the impossibly high garden wall around Aunt Cleo's town house. "This is truly where I live?" she asked, her voice uncertain. "I'm quite positive our garden wall was much lower than this."

"No, my lady, this is it, I'm afraid."

Grace did not even have to look toward him to know what his expression held. "Stop smirking," she said, then hiccoughed again. "And I'm not a 'my lady,'" she muttered irritably.

Trevor's smirk widened into a grin. He had to stifle a laugh as Grace began running a numb hand over the wall as though trying to find nonexistent toeholds in the smooth marble surface. He stepped forward. "Please allow me." He bent and cupped his hands together as if offering her a leg up on her mount.

She placed one booted foot in his cupped palms, then tentatively touched his shoulder. "My lord," she said softly.

Trevor looked up at her, still bent at the waist with her small foot in his hand.

"I really enjoyed myself tonight. Thank you, Trevor." She hiccoughed again.

Pleasure washed through him at her use for the first time of his given name. He knew he could no longer trust himself not to reach for her and kiss her senseless. Without warning, he gave her a sudden boost, sending her not to the top of the wall, as he had hoped, but completely *over* it. A second later he heard a muffled thud as she landed on the other side. "Grace," he called anxiously, ready to climb the wall himself to see if he had hurt her. "Are you all right?"

"Mmm-hmm," came her muted response. He heard nothing further for a moment, and Trevor thought that she had gone into the house. Then she called softly, "Good night." He heard her running footsteps recede into the depths of the garden.

"Good night, my lady," he replied to the garden wall.

From across the street, the hidden figure watched the byplay between Grace and Trevor with clenched teeth and fisted hands. He did not enjoy entrée into the circles in which they moved, and had not yet found an opportunity to speak with Grace. He knew, however, that it was only a matter of time. When Grace saw his devotion, he knew she would never look at the damned earl again.

Chapter Fourteen

Grace." The voice came to her as though from very far away as she slowly swam up from the depths of unconsciousness. "Grace, wake up."

She frowned in her sleep. The voice prodded at her, annoyingly persistent. Worse, the person to whom it belonged had now begun to give her repeated jabs in the ribs with a very pointy and insistent finger. Reluctantly, she rolled onto her side and forced open one heavy eyelid.

Big mistake.

The instant before her eyelid slammed closed again, she caught a glimpse of a blurred but very grim-looking Faith standing over her, arms crossed on her chest in a way that could only mean trouble. Unfortunately, she did not have a chance to try to discover who had incurred her sister's wrath; the very next instant a horrid little man, who had somehow managed to climb into her head, began hammering away at her skull.

Grace groaned in pain and reached automatically for the satin coverlet, intending to pull it over her head to try to shut out both Faith and the little man. When her groping fingers encountered nothing, she settled for smothering herself with a pillow.

"You're lying *atop* the coverlet, Grace," came Faith's voice, now fortunately muffled. All voices should be muffled, she decided.

"Fully dressed."

Dressed? Grace wondered.

"With your boots on," her sister added in a dry tone.

"Go away, Faith," she said. She moaned when the effort to speak sent another wave of pain cresting through her head. She heard nothing else for a moment, then felt the bed dip as Faith sat down next to her. Her sister briskly plucked the pillow from Grace's face, letting in the agonizing brightness of the morning sun. "Sit up."

Reluctantly Grace obeyed the command, delivered in her sister's best no-nonsense tone. She gratefully accepted the glass of cool water thrust into her hand. Her mouth had never felt so parched; nor had it ever tasted so horrid. She managed to bring the glass to her lips and take a small sip without opening her eyes.

"You smell just like Papa after a night at the inn."

Grace finally opened her eyes a mere sliver and squinted at Faith. Her fastidious sister was staring at her with her usually perfectly straight nose wrinkled in sublime distaste. "I like the way Papa smells," Grace croaked. She had always loved the smell of tobacco and leather and fine brandy that clung to her father's clothing, had loved it ever since the not-so-long-ago days of her girlhood, when she had curled up in his lap for her nightly bedtime story. The scent comforted her, in much the same way Trevor's scent did. The realization surprised her. She winced as the little man gave her head an extra hard tap.

"Lord Caldwell came to call about an hour ago," Faith said, as though reading Grace's thoughts.

Trevor. She closed her eyes again and pinched the bridge of her nose in an unsuccessful effort to alleviate some of the pain. "What time is it?"

"Well past noon." Faith paused a moment. "I heard you come in last night."

"Sorry," Grace mumbled. "Did I wake you?"

"You were singing."

Two more sharp taps with the hammer. An unexpected wave of nausea washed over her, and she took a quick sip of the water. "Did I wake Aunt Cleo?"

"She didn't say," answered Faith, watching with concern as Grace began drinking the rest of the water in large gulps. "She did tell Becky not to bother you this morning."

Grace tipped the glass up and swallowed the last of the water.

"Perhaps you ought not drink that so quickly," she advised.

Grace's already peaked face paled further. She stood unsteadily, holding tightly to the bedpost as the room began to tilt alarmingly.

"It might make you sick," she finished lamely as Grace lunged suddenly for the chamber pot.

An hour and a half later, a more sedate though still wan Grace appeared in the dining room, garbed now in a very becoming peach gown. "Good afternoon, Aunt," she said in as cheerful a voice as she could manage, walking across the room to give her relation a quick peck on the cheek.

"I see your injury hasn't slowed you down, my dear."

Grace looked at her aunt blankly for a moment before she remembered her feigned ankle injury of the evening before. "Oh, yes, Aunt," she stammered. "I think an evening of rest was just what it required." She felt a telltale blush heat her cheeks. She moved quickly to the sideboard and began to fill a plate with food, in her flustered state hardly noticing what she selected.

When she felt a bit more composed, she returned to the table and seated herself across from her aunt. She stared down at the unappetizing food, perfectly certain her still-churning stomach would not accept a morsel. She gingerly tried a bite of ham, then cringed as her stomach lurched in protest.

Aunt Cleo watched in amused silence as Grace struggled valiantly to finish her unwanted luncheon. She readily recognized the telltale aftereffects of an evening's drinking, and wondered again what sort of scrape her niece had gotten herself into. That it had something to do with the Earl of Huntwick she had no doubt. He and Grace had conspired, thick as thieves, at the ball the previous evening, and he wore his feelings for her plainly enough for anyone to see. For some reason, though, Grace resisted him. Cleo could not fathom why. Huntwick would make the perfect husband for her, if she would but open her eyes.

Aunt Cleo cleared her throat, causing Grace to look up from the creamed potatoes with which she was toying. "Huntwick called upon you this morning."

"Yes, Aunt. Faith told me." Grace looked back down at her plate, certain her aunt's sharp eyes could see right through her.

"He seemed a bit concerned that you hadn't come down."

"That was kind of him," said Grace noncommittally.

Aunt Cleo slowly buttered a roll, watching Grace's reaction to her next words carefully. "He probably felt a bit responsible for your condition."

Grace dropped her spoon to the table with a loud clatter. She looked up at her aunt in alarm.

"After all, it was quite awkward of him to tread upon your foot like that," said Aunt Cleo with a sly look.

Grace slowly let out her breath. "Actually, it was I who quite clumsily tripped over *his* foot, Aunt," she corrected in relief.

Cleo shrugged her shoulders and waved a beringed hand

negligently in the air. " 'Always the man's fault' is my motto," she sang airily. She pointed her fork at both of her nieces. "Never accept responsibility for anything if you can blame it on a man."

Grace quite forgot her pounding head and laughed in startled surprise. "Why, Aunt Cleo! What do you have against men? You and Uncle always seemed especially to care about each other. He practically doted upon you, as I remember."

"Bah!" said the older lady with a shake of her head that set the feather on her turban bobbing. "I just had him well trained, you see. Your uncle Charles was a rake in his younger days. It took quite a while for me to bring him to heel." She looked sideways at Grace. "Huntwick rather puts me in mind of your uncle, when he was young." Her eyes turned at once tender and laughter-filled. "Properly trained, he'd make someone a good husband." She gave Grace a direct look.

Grace deliberately ignored her aunt's eyes as well as her words, though a blush stole across her face. "How did you do it, Aunt? Uncle Charles never acted as though he'd been 'brought to heel.' "

Cleo leaned across the table, her alert blue eyes twinkling. "I chased him until he caught me," she confided, "and then I allowed him to *think* he was in control." She stood up. "Men need that, you know," she advised. "Try it on your young man."

"Trevor's not my young man," Grace protested, quite unaware that she had inadvertently let her use of his given name slip.

Aunt Cleo looked over her shoulder on her way out of the room. "Were we still talking about Huntwick?" With that she swept out the door, leaving Grace to her headache, queasy stomach, and unsettled thoughts.

* * *

Ablaze with lights, the theater glittered, crowded with splen-
didly garbed men and beautifully gowned women, all of
whom had simply come to put themselves on display and
gossip about their neighbors. Most of them likely had no
idea what would appear on the stage for their entertainment; nor would they watch once it started. Instead, they
would watch the more enlightening tableaux presented in
the extravagant boxes held by the members of London's
elite.

Grace, Faith, and Aunt Cleo had already entered their
box and were busy greeting a steady stream of visitors,
Faith with her usual unruffled charm, and Grace with a
slightly strained smile. During the day her stomach had finally settled, but the throbbing in her head had only intensified. Using her nonexistent ankle injury as an excuse,
Grace had done her best to get out of their plans for the
evening. Aunt Cleo had smiled at her in a strange, knowing
way, and announced that they would all attend the theater
instead of a ball, so that Grace could sit and rest her ankle,
rather than have to miss an entire evening out.

So here she sat, smiling dutifully at each haughty dowager and wizened old gentleman to whom she received an
introduction. She prayed for the moment when everyone
would find their own boxes and the gaslights would dim,
thus allowing her a small amount of relief.

Just when she thought she could stand it no longer, the orchestra finally began tuning up. One by one people began
to take their seats, and the last visitor slowly left their box.
Gone until intermission, Grace thought wearily. She prepared to take a much-needed nap as the lights went down.
Just as she closed her eyes, Faith poked her in the ribs.

Grace looked at her sister in surprise. Faith was rarely so
indecorous as to actually poke someone. She saw Faith
staring in shock across the theater at a box above and to
the left of the one they occupied. Curious, she followed her

sister's gaze, then sucked in her breath. The Earl of Huntwick had just seated himself beside a beautiful lady Grace did not recognize.

The unknown woman was lovely in a calm, sedate manner—lovely, in fact, in every way that Grace was not. She had shining dark hair pulled back into a smooth bun at the nape of her neck, and she wore a pale pink gown of simple, elegant lines that bespoke sublime breeding and great wealth. As Grace watched, the lady leaned over and spoke to Trevor, resting a graceful hand familiarly on his arm. Trevor grinned in response to whatever she said, that quick, slashing smile that always made Grace weak in the center of her stomach.

Grace felt her heart begin to pound rapidly. She stood up without knowing she did so, her hands gripping the railing of the box so hard that her knuckles turned white. She stared across the theater at the evidence of Trevor's betrayal.

Vaguely, she heard Faith hiss at her from behind to sit down, but Grace stood stock-still, oblivious as she watched Trevor lean over and whisper something in the lady's ear that made her laugh aloud. His gaze skipped across the boxes without really registering their occupants. Until his green eyes collided with Grace's furious blue ones.

Even across the room, Trevor could feel her blazing anger reaching out to him like a coiled whip, tangible, real, and deadly. The sudden realization of what prompted her ire sent a soaring sense of triumph through him. He smiled across the space in satisfaction, well pleased with this evidence of the fact that Grace was jealous.

If Grace had been angry before, she became positively livid when she saw the smug, self-assured smile sweep across Trevor's handsome face. She knew, with vile self-loathing, exactly why he had smiled, and that she herself had provided him with the ammunition he wanted and needed to use against her. "Bloody hell," she muttered, and dropped back into her seat in an unladylike heap. She leaned back in her chair until Aunt Cleo's enormous turban obscured her from Trevor's line of vision.

"Who is she?" Faith asked without taking her eyes from the stage, her lips barely moving.

"Who cares?" said Grace, her voice petulant.

"You care, dear sister. What's more, the entire theater knows it." Faith nodded toward the rest of the boxes, where people whispered, some glancing and even pointing in their direction. "Sit up straight now, and swallow your pride, Grace. By midnight the rest of the ton will know, too."

She spoke the truth. Pride dictated that she compose herself and give the gossips no more fodder than she already had. She straightened her shoulders and turned her face toward the stage, which was nothing but a blur. Her mind raced feverishly. She considered and rejected several plans by which to extricate herself from the agreement with Trevor.

The thought of returning home to the peace and quiet of Pelthamshire was more than tempting, but the realization that Huntwick would certainly follow her marred that possibility. Refusing to see him had not worked in the past, and besides, she hardly relished the thought of barricading herself in her room for days on end. Ten days! Ten days still remained of the original fourteen she had promised Trevor. She could find no solution. She would just have to grit her teeth and stick it out.

Then a flash of inspiration struck and she sat up straighter in her seat. She would find spending time with Trevor much easier if she had a goal, a definitive reason for doing so. Grace smiled to herself. She could suffer now for the greater reward of beating him at the game. She would simply kill him with kindness. She would be so utterly agreeable, so nauseatingly adoring, that one of two things would happen: Trevor would either be smugly certain of his victory, which would make handing him his defeat all the sweeter, or he would realize he could not stomach her presence even if he *did* manage to win the wager.

Elation soared through her. She turned to look again in the direction of Trevor's box. Just as she had expected, he was still looking directly at her. She gave him a sweet smile and a little wave, which he acknowledged with a slightly surprised nod. Grace returned her attention to the stage and concentrated on enjoying the rest of the opera.

Chapter Fifteen

"What are you doing?" Faith asked.

Grace sat quietly upon the third step from the bottom, elbows on her knees, her small chin propped in her hands. Her eyes were fixed on the massive front door at the end of the long foyer. "I'm sitting," she replied.

"Why are you sitting?" Faith asked with a puzzled frown. She sat down on the step next to Grace, leaned forward, and peered at the front door in confusion for a moment. The door looked just as it always had to her.

"I'm waiting, of course."

"For what, please?"

"For whom," corrected Grace.

"All right, for whom?" Faith amended patiently.

Grace smiled pleasantly at the door. "A low, morally corrupt, conniving, degenerate scoundrel." Her voice was congenial. She might well have said she was waiting for the morning post.

"Lord Caldwell?"

"The same."

Faith searched her sister's composed face for any sign of the anger that should have accompanied Grace's colorful description, but could find nothing unpleasant in her calm, unruffled features. "How do you know he's coming?"

"He sent flowers with a note stating his intention to call at eleven to take me driving in the park." A sudden thought occurred to her, and she looked away from the door for a moment to address her sister. "Would you like to go with us?"

"That depends," said Faith with a direct look.

"On what?" Grace glanced again down the foyer. Her face brightened as she heard a conveyance pull up in front of the town house.

Faith shook her head. Whatever freakish plot her sister had contrived in order to punish Trevor, she knew from the way Grace was acting that she would certainly see it through. Nevertheless, she tried to divert her from what was surely a reckless path. "It depends upon what you intend to do about his lordship's choice of escort last night."

Grace grinned, her dimples flashing impishly. "Nothing," she replied. The sound of the knocker echoed through the foyer, and Greaves shuffled toward the door. "Nothing at all," she added under her breath. She stood and fixed her most dazzling smile on the tall man who stepped through the door.

"Good morning, Grace," Trevor said. He smiled with pleasure at the breathtaking vision moving toward him, her face radiant, both hands outstretched in welcome.

She wore a high-waisted cream silk walking dress accented with tiny cobalt ribbons tied in cunning little bows at intervals on the scooped neckline, around the cuff of her small puffed sleeves, and along the scalloped hemline. A wide sash in the same lively shade of blue ran beneath her breasts and tied in a flat bow in the back, the ends falling in long, trailing streamers that reached almost to the floor, fluttering gaily behind her as she walked. Perfectly matched slippers and gloves encased her dainty feet and hands, and she wore her flaming hair pulled back from her face, secured at the crown with a blue filigree clip, then left to fall in riotous abandon well past her shoulders. The effect was simple, fresh, and incredibly alluring.

Trevor caught her gloved hands in his, bringing them both to his mouth for a kiss, unable to take his eyes from her entrancing smile. Her skin tingled above the gloves where his lips brushed her wrists. Grace fought the overwhelming urge to snatch back her hands, to turn and run. Instead, she smiled up at him in what she hoped would pass for adoration. "Good morning to you, my lord," she said.

Although he had not set out the previous evening with the intention to do so, Trevor decided that making Grace jealous had been a good move. He had fully expected to find her coldly furious, spoiling for a fight. Instead, she stood before him this morning voluntarily holding his hands and practically simpering. He frowned, his pleasure turning to suspicion, suddenly unable to reconcile this previously unseen side of Grace. He narrowed his eyes. "What's wrong with you?"

Oops! thought Grace. She must have laid it on a bit thick. Deliberately, she made herself look puzzled. She reached up as though checking her hair, then looked down at her dress in distress. "This isn't all right for our drive?"

Faith shook her head and rolled her eyes, her sister's ploy suddenly plain. Yet Trevor fell neatly into the trap. He hastily assured Grace she looked as lovely as always, then asked solicitously if she would like to depart. Faith nearly snorted in disgust.

Grace brightened. "Oh, yes, my lord," she said with bubbling enthusiasm. "Would you mind terribly if Faith joined us? After I described your beautiful horses to her, she said she simply *had* to see them for herself. Isn't that right, Faith?" Grace asked, turning to her sister for confirmation.

With Trevor and Grace looking at her expectantly, Faith searched for an answer both truthful and in keeping with her sister's story. "I've heard they're quite something, my lord," she managed politely, mentally throttling Grace for involving her in this deception.

"Of course you must come with us, then," agreed Trevor. He gallantly held his free arm out to Faith. Grace quaintly wrinkled her little nose and batted her eyes up at Trevor, while clinging to him as though she never intended to let him go.

As he handed both girls up into his landau, Trevor mentally scrapped his tentative plan to get Grace off alone somewhere for a few moments of tender persuasion. He almost groaned in disappointment as he looked up at her, talking animatedly with her mostly silent sister. He longed to push his hands into her heavy hair and turn her face to his for a deep kiss. Resolutely, he swung up and seated himself across from the two girls, and the spirited team sprang into motion at the command of Trevor's coachman. The horses settled into a smart trot and headed toward the park; Grace was already controlling nearly all of the conversation.

How strange, Trevor thought, that he had never noticed Grace's talkative nature—the first characteristic of hers he found he disliked. She prattled on endlessly in a mindless monologue, leaping from topic to inane topic with astonishing speed. He felt himself growing annoyed. When she switched from discussing the latest gossip and began to describe and critique the clothing of the friends and acquaintances they passed along the way, he found he could no longer stand it. "Miss Ackerly!" he broke in.

"Yes, my lord?" both young women said in unison.

"I was speaking to Miss Faith, my dear," he said to Grace. She gazed at him. The rapt, adoring expression in her sapphire eyes reminded him of a cocker spaniel. She looked crestfallen, but obediently subsided with a pretty little pout.

"Yes, my lord?" Faith repeated in her quiet voice, her calm gray eyes leveled at him.

"Are you enjoying the Season?"

Faith opened her mouth to answer, but Grace immediately piped up. "Oh, yes, my lord, she's having the most *perfectly* wonderful time! Such scrumptiously lavish parties and balls, and so many invitations that one can hardly *begin* to decide which of them to attend, for, of course, one couldn't *possibly* have time enough to get to them all. And, of course, nothing was at *all* fun until you arrived in town, my lord. Oh, I know that I was rather difficult to deal with at first, but you quite surprised me with your sudden interest, especially when I am used to such a quiet country life, with such quiet country activities and such quiet country pastimes. And could *anybody* else have possibly been so utterly patient and kind to me as you have been, my lord, putting up as you have with all my petty little temper tantrums?" She stopped to take a breath, laid a hand on his knee for a moment, then launched right back into speech. "Why, I shouldn't be at all surprised if you simply couldn't *abide* spending another moment in my terrible, sullen company, and wouldn't I just deserve it? Oh, look!" she exclaimed suddenly. "There's Lady Burton in a brand-new white carriage! Oh, isn't it *shiny!*" She half stood in the swaying landau and waved enthusiastically, nearly toppling out of the vehicle. She recovered her balance and sat down once again, hardly missing a beat as she began going on about Lady Burton's various coats, hats, and jewels.

It was then, as he watched Grace gesture and babble on in a way completely foreign to her, that Trevor finally figured out her game. Grace intended to either bore him or disgust him into giving up on their little wager. He let her blather on until she finally had to stop to take another breath.

"It won't work, Grace." He addressed her gently, but firmly. Faith stirred and looked at him with interest.

Grace stopped speaking in midsentence. She nearly scowled, but recovered nicely. "Why, my lord, surely you didn't think that I was trying to hint that I'd like some sort of gift from you? Why, I would never be so—"

Trevor cut her off. "I meant that your poorly executed imitation of an empty-headed widgeon will not work," he said calmly.

"Imitation!" Grace looked gloriously indignant. "My lord, if you don't like me as I am, then just say so, but please don't hurl unkind accusations at me. I am as I am, and you can just take it or leave it!"

Trevor shrugged. "I suppose I'll just have to take it then." His eyes twinkled merrily at Faith as he leaned past Grace to say conspiratorially, "She can't keep this up, you know."

Faith smiled back, inclining her head in deference to his excellent logic, a trait she particularly admired.

Grace sat furiously and rigidly silent. Trevor had always had the power to anger her, but the fact that Faith, her own sister, had defected to his camp so easily . . . How *could* she? She stole a glance at her sister out of the corner of her eye. Faith silently and serenely admired the passing parklands. Grace glanced at Trevor and found him quietly watching her, his smile smug. She snapped her gaze back to the front, glad to see they were approaching Aunt Cleo's town house. She pressed her lips together and resolved to stop trying to best him with plots and plans. She would simply ignore him for the next nine days.

Before the horses had come to a complete stop, Grace stood up. She brushed past Trevor's knees in her haste to get out of the vehicle and away from his irksome presence. She gained the ground without injury, then stalked up the steps and swept into the house without a backward glance at her treacherous sister or the irksome earl.

Trevor watched her go, a wide grin sweeping his features. He climbed down and held out a hand to Faith. "It has been a real pleasure, Miss Ackerly. Would you please tell

your sister that I look forward to escorting her to the Corwins' ball tonight?"

Faith gave him a direct look as she stepped down from
the landau. "You know she would rather die than go with
you this evening, Lord Caldwell."

Trevor raised his eyebrows. "Ahh, but she hasn't such a
choice, has she? Will you be there also?"

Faith nodded. "I'll be there with Aunt Cleo."

"Well, good, then. I shall have a chance to give your aunt
my regards." He tipped his hat to her and climbed back
into the landau. The vehicle pulled away, leaving a bemused Faith standing silently at the curb. She watched him
go, turned to walk up the steps, then stopped for a moment, her attention caught by a subtle movement in a dark
doorway across the street. She peered at the shadowed alcove for a moment, then shrugged and decided her eyes
were playing tricks on her. Her thoughts quickly returned
to the problem of her sister and the earl as she walked up
the steps and slowly entered the house.

As soon as she came in, Grace pounced on her like an
angry cat. "How could you take his side?" she accused furiously. "Against your own sister!"

Faith looked at Grace calmly as she pulled off her gloves.
"Think about what you're saying, Grace. What is it, exactly,
that Lord Caldwell has done that is so very terrible?"

Grace stubbornly pressed her lips together and averted
her gaze.

"He's done nothing," Faith answered with cool logic, "except escort you to balls, tolerate your temper, and gift you
with his time and undivided attention. In return, you've re-
peatedly deceived him, tried to make him look foolish before the entire ton on more than one occasion, and flayed
him with your tongue at every possible opportunity.

"Despite this, he continues to try to please you in every

way he can, which only leads me to believe that the man must genuinely care for you. What more could I ask for my sister than that she be cared for?"

Grace shook her head. "You're wrong, Faith. It is merely his desire to win that makes him continue with this farce. I'm nothing but a prize to him."

"My point exactly. If he wins—and let me point out that he's working quite hard to do just that—he gets you, Grace. If the prize weren't worth getting, why would he work so hard to get it? Why hasn't he quit if it isn't worth it to him?"

Grace turned away and walked slowly into the yellow salon, her thoughts jumbled as she processed the information she had known all along but stubbornly denied.

Faith followed her persistently. "I'll tell you why, Grace. He wants the prize."

Grace did not respond.

"Try being nice to him," Faith urged.

"I have no wish to marry, Faith—not even Lord Caldwell," Grace protested weakly.

"Just please try to be kind to him for the next nine days. At the very least, you'll be able to look back and say that you kept your part of the agreement honorably."

Grace sank into a chair, lost in thought. "I'll try," she promised her sister quietly.

Chapter Sixteen

✥

*T*revor sat uncomfortably in a delicate gold brocade chair in the yellow salon, his long legs crossed carelessly, his impatience evidenced only by the tapping of his index finger upon the intricately carved arm of the chair. He sat because he knew that if he stood he would pace, and if Grace caught him pacing, he would be forced to concede yet another small victory to her.

He had already cooled his heels for more than fifteen minutes before he'd decided to take a seat, choosing the gold brocade armchair because it looked like the only piece of furniture in the dainty, feminine room substantial enough to bear his weight. Even so, he felt like a great, hulking beast caught in a doll's house. He grimaced. Trust Grace to try to throw him off balance in varied and subtle ways before she drove the final dagger home at the end of the allotted fortnight.

Upstairs, Grace was pacing. Troubled by a nagging headache and an odd sense of weariness, she briefly considered writing a note begging him for the evening off, but was loath to use the fact that she did not feel well as an excuse, ruefully reflecting that she had already dishonestly done so. After several starts and an equal number of stops, she gave up and decided she would have to brave the inconvenient pain for the evening. She reread the last draft of the note:

> *Dear Lord Caldwell, I know you will understand when I say things have transpired rather quickly between us. I hope that you will therefore allow me some time alone to reflect upon the enormity of the steps we are taking. This is not something I treat lightly. . . .*

Grace shook her head and prepared to go downstairs, leaving the unfinished letter on her dressing table. Trevor had no idea of her thoughts since she had angrily left his vehicle. He deserved more than a simple note.

After he had waited for twenty-five minutes, Trevor finally heard Grace's voice in the hall. He stood, automatically composing his features into those of a gentleman who had nothing better to do than to wait for a woman to honor him with her presence.

A moment later Grace entered the room. She walked directly to him. She stopped a mere foot away and searched his features for a clue to his mood. What she saw appeared to satisfy her, for she smiled and held out a hand. "Good evening, Lord Caldwell," she said softly. "You look very nice this evening."

Trevor stopped in the act of kissing her hand, her fingers still pressed to his lips. He quirked an eyebrow, then let go, trying to reconcile this very agreeable Grace with the girl who had stormed out of his carriage without a backward glance only hours earlier. He found he could not. "I look very nice?" he drawled in exaggerated shock. "Why, Miss Ackerly, that was a *very* nice compliment. You look *very* nice, yourself. I expect we shall have a *very* nice time tonight, don't you?"

Her eyes glowed with humor. "I suppose I deserve that,"

she admitted with a little laugh. "Can you possibly forgive my wretched behavior the past few days?"

Trevor raised his other eyebrow in disbelief, certain his ears deceived him.

Grace saw the look and hastened to explain. "It's rather unfortunate and a bit embarrassing, but I'm afraid I have a very bad habit."

More and more interesting. "Go on," he invited.

"You see, I very much hate to lose."

"Doesn't everybody?"

Grace blushed. "But most people don't try to cheat."

"You cheat?"

She nodded in sublime discomfort. "When I'm not certain of winning."

"And you don't feel certain of winning our wager?"

Her eyes flashed and her chin lifted proudly. "Of course I'm sure I'll win," she stated, then grinned a trifle sheepishly. "But it doesn't hurt to take steps to ensure I do."

Trevor looked down at Grace. He took in her jaunty smile, her gloriously flushed cheeks, and her dancing blue eyes. A wave of tender, possessive pride swept over him, startling him with its intensity. He returned her infectious smile with one of his own. "Shall we begin anew then, my dear?"

Relief visible on her face, Grace held out a compromising hand. "Shall we round off the days already used, my lord? We can say one week remains on the agreement, beginning today. Care to shake on it?"

Trevor's lips twitched as he looked at her proffered hand, then back at her face. He gave her a pointed look, then reached for her hand and pulled her against him. His arms closed around her as he bent his head and whispered in her ear, "No, my dear, the original deal stands. We have nine days left." He pushed a hand into her hair, tilting her face up to his as he had wanted to that afternoon. Her heart hammered wildly as he lowered his mouth to hers and murmured against her lips, "I think we'll seal this agreement with a kiss." His lips brushed hers as lightly as a butterfly lands on a flower.

Grace caught her breath, hoping he would not hear the wild thundering of her heart. "We originally agreed that there would be no more kisses," she protested weakly, angry with herself for standing quietly within the warm circle of his arms.

"I believe I'm entitled to bending the rules just this once. *You* did," he pointed out to silence her when she started to protest. "Besides," he continued, his eyes turning forest green with desire, "that wasn't a kiss. *This* is a kiss."

He claimed her mouth with insistent, searing tenderness, molding and shaping her lips to his. Grace held herself rigid in protest for just a moment, then gave in and melted against him with a small, surrendering whimper. He gathered her more closely. Helpless, she slid a hand up the broad expanse of his chest to clutch his shoulder for support, clinging desperately as the world spun away beneath her.

Her touch fanned his carefully banked passion into flames of wanting. He ran his tongue insistently between her lips, teasing them, coaxing them to part. When they did his tongue plunged into her mouth, and she met it with her own. The kiss exploded, each of them feeding an urgent need in the other, a need that defied explanation. As she pressed herself more tightly against him, Grace felt the rigid evidence of his arousal between them, and gasped in involuntary shock.

Afraid he had frightened her, Trevor tore himself away and walked across the room, looking out a window with his back toward Grace, his raging emotions betrayed only by an occasional twitch of his clenched jaw.

Grace stood in the center of the room where he had left her, her head down, fighting the overwhelming urge to go to him, to wrap herself around him and lay her cheek against his back. Her arms felt strangely empty as they hung at her sides. Not knowing the real reason he had pulled away so suddenly, she said in a small voice, "I know that I deserved that."

Trevor released a breath he did not know he held. "But who is punishing whom?" he muttered. Turning, he faced Grace. "Perhaps we should both play by the rules from now on," he suggested. "Shall I escort you to the Corwins' ball now, my dear?"

Not trusting herself to speak, Grace nodded. Trevor walked across the room and held out an arm. Although he noted that the hand she placed on it shook just a little, he somehow managed to keep from pointing that out.

Grace winced. Everything was glaring and blazing. The tiniest sounds seemed amplified. The smell of the wax from the chandeliers accosted her senses, and the voices of too many people crushed into a hot room that was much too small pounded upon her ears. Even the music blared, too loud for her to handle tonight.

When they arrived at the ball, Grace and Trevor had almost immediately separated, she to go stand with her aunt and sister, he to join some friends in the adjacent room for cards. Grace had watched him go, his dark head and broad shoulders easy to follow because of his height. As soon as he disappeared into the other room, she found, to her surprise, that she felt somewhat bereft.

She accepted a dance from a stammering young man, and managed to work her way through it without either of them incurring an injury, hoping she had uttered the appropriate responses to his clumsy attempts at light conversation. Next she danced with an older gentleman her aunt had waited to introduce to her. Midway through that dance, her small headache suddenly intensified. Blaming the heat and the noise, she mumbled an excuse to her partner, then made a hasty exit onto the terrace through the doors that opened from the ballroom, hoping the relatively cool night air would do her some good. She sat down upon one of the stone benches placed at intervals near the balustrade and closed her eyes with a sigh, grateful for the slight breeze that gently lifted the tendrils of hair that framed her face.

Her thoughts returned to the kiss she had shared with Trevor just before the ball. For the first time she found she could not deny her feelings for him, even to herself. Did she look the same after he kissed her? she wondered. Her lips tingled in remembered sensation and she reached up to run a trembling fingertip across them, then jumped in surprise as she heard booted footsteps ring on the marble terrace. They stopped for a moment, then began walking slowly in her direction.

Knowing she had no hope of remaining unseen, Grace reluctantly opened her eyes and looked in the direction of the approaching footsteps. She found herself caught in the strange golden gaze of the Duke of Blackthorne. For a moment he said nothing, just looked at her in disquieting silence, giving Grace the alarming feeling that he might pounce and devour her like a large, predatory cat. He finally spoke. "Good evening, Miss Ackerly." His voice was deep and resonant with an underlying note of command— a combination not unlike Trevor's. For some reason, though, Sebastian Tremaine's words left her feeling chilled, while the mere sound of Trevor's voice sent shivers of delight coursing through her body.

In deference to his rank, Grace stood and curtsied. Her nagging headache erupted at once into a fearsome pounding. A wave of sudden nausea swept her, but she managed to utter, "Good evening, Your Grace," before sitting back down heavily on the bench. A thin sheen of perspiration broke out on her upper lip and forehead.

Sebastian's hooded look turned speculative. "Have you been drinking, Miss Ackerly?" he asked. A look of disapproving accusation crossed his normally impassive face.

Had she felt better, Grace would have taken immediate offense to his high-handed attitude, but right now she did not have the energy. She simply shook her head. "I'm fine," she lied, giving him a wobbly smile as if to prove it. When she saw his eyes narrow on her pale complexion, she hastened to change the subject. "You know, Mercy plans on becoming your wife, Your Grace," she told him.

Sebastian looked puzzled for a moment before he remembered Mercy's identity. A look of fleeting distaste crossed his face before the expressionless mask returned. "A bit young, isn't she, to already have aspirations of becoming a duchess?"

Grace smiled fondly, despite her increasing discomfort. "Mercy has no such aspirations, Your Grace," she assured him. "I think she'd want to become your wife even if you swept chimneys." A sudden wayward image of the staid Duke of Blackthorne covered from head to toe in soot entered her mind. Grace found herself repressing a smile as she continued: "I should warn you, my little sister is more than a trifle stubborn once she gets her mind set upon something."

A familiar voice came from the shadows. "A trait that apparently runs in the family."

A banner of warmth unfurled in Grace's stomach at the sound of Trevor's warm, rich voice. He stood just outside the doors that led from the ballroom, a shoulder propped negligently against the stone wall. As he straightened and walked toward them, Grace caught her breath in awe. Truly, a more handsome man she had never seen. His eyes glowed a deep emerald in the semidarkness, shining with a tender warmth that made her feel as though she and Trevor were the only two people in the world. As she watched him approach, Grace realized he could have nearly any woman in London at his beck and call, that almost any of them would trade places with her in a second. And yet, he wanted *her*. The wonderment of that reflection washed through her as she stood again, deliberately forgetting her earlier dizziness, resolutely ignoring the now steady throbbing of her head.

He clasped both of her hands and bowed to her, disregarding the presence of his friend the Duke of Blackthorne. "May I still have the waltz you assured me of earlier, Miss Ackerly?" he asked, his voice low and full of the same promise she could see in his eyes.

"Of course." Grace smiled up at him, although she knew that she had pledged him no such thing. "I was just waiting for you to ask, my lord," she said, her eyes glowing in the pale moonlight.

The Duke of Blackthorne lit a cheroot as he watched his best friend lead Grace back into the ballroom. *Poor sod,* he thought to himself. *Practically leg-shackled. Positively hurtling down the road to matrimony.* He exhaled slowly, allowing the slight breeze to carry the gray smoke out across the dark garden.

Quite a little schemer, he decided, the Ackerly chit. He remembered what she had said about her little sister, that simple, unaffected little urchin he had met only two weeks ago. Apparently, little Mercy had already received some coaching from her older sister on how to snare a noble title. He shook his head. A pity time would change that unspoiled, straightforward child into a woman. He had rather liked her, remembering fondly her outlandish breeches and wide-eyed innocence. His affectionate smile turned abruptly sardonic. How unfortunate, he thought, that little girls had to grow up.

Trevor stood next to his coach, watching as Grace walked up the steep front steps to the front door of her aunt's town house. She turned and gave him a last wave and a gay smile before letting herself into the darkened foyer. She closed the door, leaned heavily against the cool wood, and raised a shaking hand to her aching forehead.

The throbbing had now sharpened into a screaming pain. She had managed to hide the agony from Trevor, as she did not want anything to spoil this first night of understanding between them, certain he would not have believed her anyway. Not after all the excuses she had used since they had met in order to avoid spending time in his company.

Grace wearily pulled herself upright, sighed, and began the long trek upstairs. Her legs felt heavier with each step, and she grasped the banister so tightly her knuckles were white. Somehow she managed to make it to her chamber. She slipped inside gratefully, wanting nothing more than to climb between the cool sheets and lose herself in the comforting embrace of sleep. With the intention of having a quick drink of water, she crossed the room to the table that held the pitcher and a small glass, but her hand shook so badly she found she could not pour it. Before she could set the pitcher back down, the room began spinning. Her vision blurred and her ears filled with a strange ringing. She took one step toward the door before she lost consciousness and crumpled to the floor.

Chapter Seventeen

*T*he sun was high, shining with cheerful brightness in the midday sky when Trevor pulled up in front of the Egerton town house and jumped down from the seat of his phaeton. He was anxious to show Grace his recent acquisition, looking forward to watching her learn to drive from the seat perched precariously high above the cobbled street. He bounded up the steps of the town house, whistling with a lighthearted air, and knocked on the front door, well pleased with the progress he had made in his courtship. He remembered the charming and candid way in which she had confessed her wrongs to him the previous evening, and the sweetness with which she had melted into his arms just moments later. In only eight more days he would ask her to become his wife. He could just imagine her happy response.

The fond smile that played around his mouth faded slowly when he realized he had been waiting for some moments and had not received a response to his knock. Regarding the still-closed door with a trace of annoyance, he rapped on the knocker once again, certain Greaves stood just on the other side, ignoring the summons. He would have to do something about that man, Trevor thought, his animosity increasing when the door still did not open. He made a fist and brought it thundering down once on the oaken panel, only to have the door suddenly jerked open by an out-of-breath and very flustered-looking O'Reilly.

Happy that Greaves was not standing in the doorway scowling at him, and determined that the recalcitrant servant would not spoil the beginning of the day he had planned for Grace, Trevor swallowed his ire and smiled cheerfully at the short, round footman. "Good morning, O'Reilly," he said in a jovial tone. He stepped inside and plopped his hat at a rakish angle on the balding man's head, his former good humor magically restored. "Have you been made underbutler, or has Greaves finally been most deservedly relieved of his duties?" Without waiting for an answer, Trevor strolled away, saying over his shoulder, "Would you please inform Miss Grace that I've arrived? I'll wait for her in the yellow salon, as usual."

O'Reilly followed the earl into the salon, wringing his hands in an agitated fashion. "I'm afraid I cannot deliver your message, my lord."

Trevor's good mood evaporated. He turned and looked at the fidgeting footman in surprise. Certainly, he thought, after the unspoken truce of the previous night, Grace would not begin playing games with him again. "Why not?" he asked, his voice dangerously soft. His narrowed eyes glittered ominously at the nervous footman.

"Miss Grace won't be receiving any visitors today, my lord," O'Reilly stammered bravely, then recoiled in fear at the look of blazing anger he received.

Trevor's jaw clenched. *Quite the clever little actress,* he thought. He pictured Grace as he had seen her the night before, adoration dawning in her eyes, a winsome smile on her lips. She had firmly convinced him of her sincerity last night, when she had apparently been setting him up for yet another pointed rebuff. "Did Miss Grace manage to provide you with a reason?" he asked, his calm voice belied by the angry glint in his eyes.

"Miss Grace is, er . . ." O'Reilly paused, not quite certain of the story he had been told to give callers, or whether Lady Egerton had intended that they include the Earl of Huntwick in the short list of people who knew the gravity of the situation. A muscle worked in Trevor's jaw as he waited, with obvious impatience, for the footman to finish his explanation.

O'Reilly brightened as the proper term finally floated into his worried and befuddled brain. "Miss Grace is *indisposed*," he finished, with the loftiest air he could muster from his diminutive height.

That particular phrase sparked immediate and instant antagonism in Trevor. O'Reilly instinctively stepped back from the fierce anger that blazed in the earl's eyes. "Indisposed?" His tone remained even.

"Y-yes, my lord," O'Reilly stammered.

"As she was for three days last week when I called to see her?" Trevor continued in the same dangerous, silken voice.

O'Reilly blanched at the memory of Grace's little deception and the part he had played in it. "N-no, my lord," he stammered, then flinched when the earl reached out and snatched back his hat, still comically perched on the footman's bald head. Trevor left the room with long, ground-devouring strides.

"Tell Miss Ackerly . . ." bit out on his way to the front door, then stopped and thought better of it. "Never mind, O'Reilly. I'll tell her myself." He spun around and headed toward the curved marble staircase with purposeful intent, his boots ringing out in the high-ceilinged room with each step he took.

O'Reilly trotted after him. "My lord, please wait!" he called in vain.

Trevor ignored him, taking the steps three at a time. When he reached the second floor, he began jerking open doors, startling a young chambermaid who was busy dusting the second room into which he looked. "Where is Miss Ackerly's chamber?" he demanded, terrifying the poor girl into momentary silence.

"Which Miss Ackerly, my lord?" the frightened maid asked when she finally found her voice, trying to curtsy with a feather duster in one hand and a waxing cloth in the other. The door was rudely slammed closed again before she finished uttering the words.

O'Reilly caught up to Trevor, his face red from the exertion of running up the stairs and down the hall. "My lord," he panted, "if you would only wait . . ."

"Where is she? I'll not ask again." Trevor's voice was low and ominous.

A door opening near the end of the corridor spared O'Reilly the necessity of answering. Faith stepped into the hallway, her face haggard and pale with worry—a fact that escaped Trevor's notice as he strode wrathfully toward her. "Is this your sister's room?" he demanded, pointing at the door she had just closed behind her.

In her exhaustion, Faith did not wonder about his presence in this part of the house. She mistook his mood for one of troubled concern and nodded. Before she could explain about Grace's illness, Trevor burst through the door, sending it crashing back against the wall with a resounding boom. In three long strides he covered the distance from the door to the bed, where Grace lay perfectly still beneath the pale blue satin coverlet, her aunt and an unknown young gentleman rising in startled shock from their seats on the other side of the bed.

"Quite a fetching picture, my dear," drawled Trevor sarcastically at the motionless figure on the bed.

"My lord," Aunt Cleo began, then gasped in alarmed outrage as Trevor snatched back the coverlet and unceremoniously jerked Grace to a sitting position. The horrified look on his face when he felt the shocking heat emanating from the limp form he held did nothing to appease Cleo Egerton's righteous fury. She drew herself up indignantly and, without warning, smartly whacked him on the head with the shining silver knob at the end of her cane. She marched around the bed, brandishing the ebony stick like a weapon. "Who do you think you are, young man, to come bursting into this room abusing my niece, who has done nothing to deserve it, save for the fact that she may have somehow inconvenienced you with her illness? Just what gives you the right—"

"I have every right where Grace is concerned, my lady," Trevor cut in tautly, forgetting for the moment that none of the occupants of this room knew of the secret betrothal between Grace and himself.

"Pah!" Cleo thumped the floor with her cane for emphasis. "Because of some silly, ill-advised wager you made with her? I don't think so."

"No," said Trevor, his jaw clenched. "It is much more complicated than that." At a small rustling sound, his eyes snapped back to the bed where Grace was thrashing fitfully. He turned his back on Cleo and bent with growing concern and sudden fear over the bed. Grace looked so frighteningly pale. The unnamed gentleman had moved to her side and tried to coax her into drinking something from a spoon.

"Who are you?" Trevor asked in a tone bristling with animosity. An unwanted surge of jealousy coursed from nowhere through his veins.

The stranger looked up for a moment at the tall, ominous-looking earl. Unconcerned, he returned his attention to Grace. "I am Dr. Wyatt," he said. He added a belated, "my lord," after a sizable pause.

Trevor looked as though he intended to say something else, but Lady Egerton chose that moment to remind him of her presence by poking him sharply in the side with her cane. "Have you had an edifying look at my niece, young man?" Cleo barked at him. Trevor raised his eyebrows.

"Good," she continued, as if he had answered. She swept her cane toward the door in blatant command. "Now get out!" When Trevor did not move, she swung the cane at his shoulder, intending to batter him out the door if necessary. He caught the end firmly and held on, staring down its shining length at the furious older lady. When Cleo raised her chin and stared fiercely back in a way that poignantly reminded him of some of his more fiery encounters with Grace, the sheer absurdity of the situation struck him. Despite the dire circumstances, a rueful smile lit his features as he contemplated how ridiculous he must look, locked in battle with a woman twice his age and half his size. He released Cleo's cane and gave her a mocking bow of exaggerated gallantry.

"As you wish, my lady," he said, and bestowed upon her the lazy smile that never failed to charm women of all ages.

Cleo slowly lowered her cane. Against her will, she felt herself soften with the warmth of his gaze. She beckoned to Faith, who stood quietly near the door. "Take Lord Caldwell down to the yellow salon, dear. He can wait there for news of Grace's condition." With a nod of regal dismissal, she walked back around the bed to take up her former position, her remaining anger dissolving into renewed concern as she reached out and took Grace's small, hot hand between hers.

The earl gave the motionless figure on the bed a final, lingering look. "Will she be all right?" he asked Dr. Wyatt in a gruff voice, pinning the young physician with his eyes.

"We'll know more in a few hours, if her fever breaks." The worry he saw on Trevor's aristocratic face tugged at him, and he added gently, "There's nothing you can do here, my lord." Trevor slowly nodded and reluctantly left, followed immediately by Faith.

"What happened?" he asked quietly when they reached the hall, his face sober as he recalled the way Grace's hot, limp body had felt in his arms. A shudder went through him at the thought of the possible outcome of this sudden illness.

Faith stole a glance at him, noting the expressionless mask hiding his tortured thoughts. "We don't know," she said haltingly, her beautiful face haunted. "I heard a strange thud from Grace's room last night, only moments after we had returned home. Since I didn't think that you had brought her home yet, I went into her room to investigate and found her lying unconscious on the floor by the window. By the time Dr. Wyatt arrived, she was burning with fever and mumbling incoherently."

"Has she regained consciousness at all?" Trevor asked. His alarm escalated.

Faith wrung her hands in an uncharacteristic outward show of emotion, emphasizing to Trevor the seriousness of the illness. "For a while after Dr. Wyatt arrived, she was talking strangely, mostly about things she did when we were children. Dr. Wyatt said the fever was making her delirious."

They had descended the staircase and walked across the foyer while they talked. Trevor fell silent as they entered the salon. O'Reilly appeared. "Can I get you some refreshment, my lord?" The footman hovered nervously, hoping to undo whatever damage he had done earlier with his bungled answers to Trevor's questions.

Trevor started to shake his head in the negative, then abruptly changed his mind. Something to drink might help dull the deep dread that had begun to quake through him. "Brandy, please," he told the footman. He crossed the room and stood gazing out the window to the busy street below, his thoughts returning to the previous evening. Grace had seemed fine, as cheerful as ever, almost shy in the glow of her new feelings for him. He saw her standing on the Corwins' terrace, her beautiful face aglow when she realized he had come looking for her. In retrospect, he thought that her eyes might have looked a little overbright, her smile a bit forced, facts he had noticed and attributed to an awakening awareness of what they had begun to mean to each other.

Faith stood silently aside, watching the emotions play across his handsome face. He cleared his throat in the stillness. "Did she ask for me?" he asked without turning, his profile impassive.

Although he asked the question quietly and without emotion, Faith sensed how very much her answer meant to Trevor. She looked at his ramrod-straight back, then at the muscle working in his jaw, betraying the growing fear he tried so valiantly to hide. Her tender young heart went out to him as she realized that he cared about the answer a great deal more than he wanted to admit. Knowing the proud man standing with his back to her would prefer simple truth over conjecture as to why Grace had not asked for him, Faith said, "No, my lord. She didn't ask for anybody."

"Thank you," he replied quietly after a moment's pause; then he resolutely turned and faced her. "You'll send immediate word if there's any change." It was a command, not a question. Faith nodded, then silently disappeared, leaving Trevor to wait alone in tense resignation.

He sat, at first, with apparent patience and outward composure, as the endless minutes dragged by. Before long he was drumming his fingers on the marble-topped table beside the gold damask-covered chair upon which he sat. When he caught himself doing so, he forced his hand to still, then sat quietly for a few minutes more. Inevitably, though, his mind returned to Grace, his heart lurching again in remembered shock at the way her limp, hot body had felt.

With a muffled curse at his once-again-drumming fingers, Trevor stood and began pacing the room, no longer caring if someone walked in and witnessed his growing agitation. He jumped at each noise he heard in the hall, turning to receive news, good or bad, with an underlying sense of dread. Each time, the noise he heard had a perfectly plausible explanation: a servant in the hall, going about his daily duties, or the rattle of a conveyance going by on the street.

After waiting for nearly two hours without word, Trevor finally lost patience. He strode to the closed doors of the salon and jerked them open, sending them crashing back against the fabric-covered walls. Servants materialized from everywhere as the resounding noise echoed in the tomblike silence of the worried household. "O'Reilly!" he bellowed at the top of his lungs.

The stout little footman magically appeared, running down the hall as quickly as his short, bowed legs would carry him. He skidded to a halt in front of the earl, trying to bow and keep his balance at the same time. "Yes, my lord?" he inquired breathlessly.

Trevor glared down at the small man. "I've heard nothing of Miss Grace's condition."

"I'm sorry, my lord. Word has not yet been sent."

Trevor clenched his teeth in an effort to control his angry frustration. "I want someone sent up immediately to inquire as to how she is doing." O'Reilly nodded, turning at once to go up himself.

"O'Reilly!" The servant halted at the sharply barked command, obediently turning to face the glowering earl once more. Trevor strode across the floor to tower over the quaking footman. "I also want a report on her condition, changed or unchanged, every fifteen minutes," he added. "I want to know if she improves or if she does not. If she so much as coughs, I want to know about it. Furthermore—"

"Furthermore, young man, if you feel you simply *must* exert your authority, I'll thank you to do it elsewhere. There is no need to bully *my* servants when you have perfectly good ones of your own."

Trevor spun at the sound of the outrageous harridan's voice. Cleo stood regally on the landing with Faith, one hand resting on her niece's arm, the other clutching the silver-topped walking stick she had used so effectively on Trevor's head two hours earlier. He looked up at her, his eyes anxious.

Faith looked at Trevor's grim, set face and took pity on him. "The fever has broken, my lord," she said in her calm, low-pitched voice. "Grace is resting quietly now, and Dr. Wyatt hopes she will improve from here."

Trevor hesitated for a split second, staring up at the ladies in momentary disbelief, then vaulted up the stairs. He pushed past Aunt Cleo and Faith and ran up the second flight of stairs, disappearing down the hall in the direction of Grace's bedchamber. Faith turned, moving immediately to follow him, but her aunt's firm pressure on her arm forestalled her. "Let him go," Cleo said quietly.

"But it's hardly proper for him to be alone with her in her chamber," protested the ever-correct Faith, already envisioning the sort of gossip that could arise from this situation.

"Dr. Wyatt is with her. Besides, he'll do nothing to harm Grace or to hurt her reputation," Cleo pointed out with a satisfied smile. "He's in love with her, you know."

Faith smiled too. "Well that's just as well," she remarked, helping her exhausted aunt down the last few steps to the foyer, "for she loves him, too, although I doubt you'll ever get either of them to be the first to admit it to the other."

Cleo patted Faith's smooth white hand with assurance. "But when they do . . ." She smiled with remembered joy at the deep love she had felt for her husband for the many years they had shared before he died. She knew she would look forward to watching such a love unfold once more in Trevor and Grace.

Chapter Eighteen

Grace blinked rapidly. The bright afternoon sunlight slanting in the west window bathed the room in a golden glow that hurt her eyes and set a dull ache throbbing in her head. A tall, dark figure stood quietly beside her bed, frustratingly blurred beyond recognition. Her efforts to try to focus upon his face created a sharp, agonizing pain that felt as though it would split her forehead in two. She closed her eyes for a moment of blessed darkness, waiting for the horrible pain to subside. When it finally did, she slowly and timorously reopened her eyes, cautiously allowing them to adjust to the daylight before trying to use them again.

Slowly the room swam into focus. Gingerly she turned her head on the pillow toward the person she had seen moments before. Although she could now see him clearly, she still did not recognize him. He smiled down at her, and she automatically began to smile back before she realized, with horror, that she was in her bed, clad only in her night-clothes, and that a perfect stranger—an unknown *man*, for that matter—was the only other occupant of the room.

Uncharacteristic terror filled her enormous blue eyes as she tried to push herself into a sitting position. She found, to her dismay, that she was weak as a kitten, unable to do more than raise her throbbing head a fraction of an inch from the pillow. She looked a little frantically toward the bellpull that seemed miles away across the room, wishing she could somehow reach it to summon someone to come help her.

The strange man followed her frightened gaze, realized the reason for her trepidation, and hastened over to pull the golden rope himself. "Please don't be frightened, Miss Ackerly. I'm your physician, Dr. Wyatt. You've been quite a sick young lady, I'm afraid."

His quiet voice was kind and reassuring, but still Grace kept a wary eye on him until Faith came hurtling into the room a moment later. At the sight, Grace's eyes widened yet again. In all her life she could never remember Faith hurtling anywhere. When she saw Grace watching her alertly, her sister calmed down and approached a bit more sedately. She perched gingerly on the edge of the bed and took Grace's hand in hers with a gentle smile.

Grace tried to speak, but found she could not force a sound beyond the unbearable dryness of her mouth. Her hand fluttered to her throat in a mute gesture of need, and she pointed weakly to the pitcher and glass that stood on the bedside table. Faith quickly poured her some water, then helped her to sit up, propping several pillows behind her head and back so that Grace could nestle comfortably into their welcoming softness. Grace gratefully accepted the glass of water as the physician hovering anxiously behind Faith admonished with a warning frown, "Small sips at first, Miss Ackerly." His kind eyes smiled with encouragement, though, and Grace found it difficult to stop drinking once she started. When she had finished, Faith took the glass from her, setting it on the bedside table. She took both of her sister's hands again.

"How do you feel, dear?" she asked, peering closely at Grace's wan face.

Grace closed her eyes and sank thankfully back against

the pillows. "Tired," she said with a sigh. "How long have I been ill?"

Faith and the doctor exchanged a glance. "Four days," replied Dr. Wyatt in a gentle voice. Grace's eyes flew open in stunned disbelief, and the doctor hastily assured her, "You're quite on the mend now, Miss Ackerly, and I see no reason why you shouldn't be up and about within the next couple of days."

Grace suddenly felt exhausted again, and knew sleep would soon overtake her. A ghost of a smile touched her lips as she struggled to keep her eyes open for just a few more minutes. "Huntwick?" she asked Faith in a near whisper, squeezing, with frail urgency, the hand that still held hers.

"He was here every day," Faith assured her, thinking Grace wished to see the earl. "I've already sent word to let him know you've awakened."

Grace weakly shook her head. "Tell him," she whispered, then stopped for a moment to catch her breath before continuing: "tell him that I said he has only a few days left." With that, her eyes closed and her breathing became long and regular as sleep claimed her in its welcome, healing embrace.

A scant fifteen minutes after receiving Faith's note telling him Grace had awakened, Trevor knocked urgently on the door of the house on Curzon Street. "Good evening, Greaves." He greeted his nemesis with a good-natured grin, so happy with the news that Grace would recover that he felt moved to treat even the infuriating Egerton butler with kindness. As he handed over his hat and coat, he noticed the old man's rheumy eyes also had a happier glow, and that the oppressive, tense air that had permeated the house during the past few days had disappeared. He marveled at the loyalty and love Grace inspired in those who knew her. Even in himself, he thought. He shook his head as he recalled the way she had fought him tooth and nail before he could claim even a small victory in his battle to win her hand. Yet each conquest felt the sweeter for the battle, and he savored each heady triumph as a small step toward his goal of her inevitable surrender.

Courtesy dictated he call upon her aunt first, although Trevor would have liked nothing better than to go straight up to her room and gently kiss her awake. Quelling his impatience, he turned to Greaves and politely asked after Lady Egerton, then followed the shuffling elderly butler to the sunny parlor that overlooked Grace's favorite haunt, the garden to the west of the house.

"The Earl of Huntwick, my lady."

At the sound of Greaves's gravelly voice, Cleo and Faith looked toward the open doors. Faith came to her feet with a welcoming smile, while Cleo remained seated at the small desk where she sat writing a letter, although she, too, smiled with pleasure at the sight of the earl.

Faith came quickly forward to greet Trevor, giving him a proper and very pretty curtsy, as befitted his rank. How did it happen, Trevor wondered wryly as he looked down at Faith, that two sisters raised together could grow up to have such very different temperaments and personalities? He mentally shook his head, chuckling to himself as he tried to imagine a circumstance in which Grace would curtsy to him willingly and sincerely. Not surprisingly, such an occasion did not come to mind. As Faith straightened and smiled, Trevor reflected momentarily that she would likely have proven much easier for him to woo. He quickly dismissed the thought. He would not have found the effort nearly so enjoyable.

"My lord?"

With a start, Trevor realized that Faith had spoken to him while he had gotten lost in his thoughts. "I'm sorry, Miss Faith. You were saying?"

She smiled, a knowing little smile. "Would you care for a drink, my lord?" Although he wanted no such thing, wanted only to go upstairs and see Grace, he nevertheless nodded, accepting Faith's offer of a cup of tea. She poured it for him, and he sat sipping the tea and exchanging polite pleasantries with the two women.

At long last he cleared his throat and put his teacup down with a little clink that rang out startlingly loudly in the quiet room. "I understand Miss Grace is somewhat recovered, ma'am." His jade eyes went to Faith's gray ones, silently thanking her for notifying him so quickly of her sister's recovery. She inclined her head slightly and gave him a small smile.

Lady Egerton nodded happily. "She was awake for nearly an hour this afternoon, although she is still weak, of course, and unable to get out of bed."

"That's wonderful news!" Trevor stood and smiled charmingly at both ladies. "I'll just stick my head in and, if she's awake, say hello before I take my leave." He gave them a gallant little bow. "Thank you for the tea and the pleasure of your company, ladies." Just as he turned to leave the room, Lady Egerton's voice snapped out at him like an uncoiling whip.

"Oh, no, you don't, young man!"

Trevor stopped in the doorway. He composed his features to conceal his impatience, his eyebrows raised in mute inquiry.

"It was quite one thing to allow you to go up to Grace's bedchamber when we weren't . . ." Cleo paused momentarily, and when she continued her voice trembled slightly. "When we were unsure she would recover. Since she has begun to do so, however, I'm afraid that it would be nothing short of the height of impropriety for you to visit there now, my lord."

Trevor's jaw tightened as his impatience swelled into annoyance. He sent a quick glance toward Faith, but she demurely kept her eyes on her embroidery. "I see," he said shortly, bringing dangerously sparking eyes back to Lady Egerton, who bravely stared back, certain she was helping Grace further her suit with the earl by giving him a bit of a challenge. "When might be a better time for me to visit Miss Grace?" Faith looked up in alarm at the earl's voice, which was, to her ears, ominous.

Cleo's quavering voice became firm again. "The doctor has told us that Grace could be up and about in a couple of weeks, perhaps as soon as one week, if we are careful." Trevor watched as Faith leveled a direct look on her aunt, who raised her chin a defiant notch in a way that distinctly reminded Trevor of Grace. He narrowed his eyes at the older lady, but said only, in an even voice, "Please give her my best wishes for a speedy recovery, ma'am," and bowed stiffly once more.

"I'll see you out, my lord." Putting aside her embroidery, Faith gave her aunt a reproachful look and hastily stood to walk Trevor to the front door. She tried, in vain, to keep up with his long, ground-devouring strides as they went down the corridor to the foyer where Greaves stood. He smugly held out the earl's hat and coat in a way that left no doubt he had listened to and enjoyed the conversation in the parlor.

Trevor ignored Greaves completely. "Does Grace know I've been here to visit her during her illness?" he asked in a clipped voice. His stared at Faith.

She hesitated only a second. "Yes, she does, my lord," she answered softly.

"And what was her reaction when she was told?"

In a rare show of discomfort, Faith flushed and looked away, knowing how Grace's words would sound to the angry man at her side. "She said . . ." Faith paused, trying to think of a way to make her sister's thoughtless words sound kinder.

"Yes?" Trevor prompted impatiently. Greaves shuffled closer and held out the coat and hat more insistently.

Faith sighed in resignation. "She said to tell you that you have only a few days left, my lord." She winced as Trevor's jaw clenched and his eyes filled with cold rage, and she added hastily, "I'll send word to you as soon as she can receive visitors."

He gave her a look of scathing disbelief. Without answering, he turned his back on her and walked out the front door, leaving the smirking Greaves still holding his garments. Faith looked after him sadly, wishing she could take back the words Grace had said so lightly.

Trevor stood for a moment on the steps after the door had closed behind him. That Grace had come up with the idea to put him off for another week he had no doubt. Though he knew she had not planned on her illness, he also knew she would have no qualms about using it as leverage in order to win their wager. She would not balk, either, at enlisting her aunt and sister into helping her to pull off the ploy in the process. She had admitted to him herself that she would cheat if she felt she had to do so in order to win, but after the conversation they had shared in the salon the night of the Corwins' ball, he found her methods unpalatable. Poor Faith could barely bring herself to speak, the farce in which Grace had compelled her to participate troubled her so.

"Home!" He flung the command at his startled coachman as he boarded the shining carriage and slammed the door almost before the footman had a chance to put up the steps. He stretched his long legs across the limited space between the velvet seats and scowled out the window at the beautiful mansions of the social elite.

He was tired of playing Grace's games. He had demonstrated endless patience, nauseating charm, and deep accommodation for much too long, he decided. For his troubles, he had received only blatant disrespect and thankless deception. On top of that, all of London knew he had finally set his cap for someone, and would now also know that she had turned him down flat, although that, admittedly, he could blame only upon himself.

Well, he decided grimly, it would not happen again. There would be no more game playing.

The watcher stared as Trevor stormed out of the house. Something did not feel right. Grace had not left the house in days, and the Earl of Huntwick came and went, looking like a thundercloud. Paranoia flooded through him, settling a knot of fear in the pit of his stomach. Faith Ackerly must have seen him that day in the street, he thought. Suddenly alarmed, he waited for Trevor's carriage to roll out of sight, then slunk away to his shabby rented rooms. He would have to find another place from which to watch her after dark. This one no longer felt safe.

Chapter Nineteen

*T*revor walked on silent feet across the dim room from the window through which he had just climbed. He stopped quietly by the bed to look down at Grace where she lay in peaceful slumber. Her beautiful burnished hair glowed as though lit from within wherever the moonlight streaming through the window touched it, the tousled curls scattered across her pillow and about her face. She looked so fragile and angelic in sleep, so utterly without guile. Trevor almost managed to convince himself that she could not possibly be the treacherous liar he had come to know.

Almost.

Somewhere in the distance a dog barked. Trevor automatically tensed. He held his breath as she moved restlessly in her sleep, then let it out slowly when she settled once again on her side, her long legs drawn up to her chest, one hand curled beneath her cheek. Quietly Trevor moved to the window he had left open when he entered the room.

He had found it ridiculously easy to gain access to Grace's room. For the third time since he had known her, he had simply climbed the garden wall. From there all he had to do was walk up the shallow terrace steps, step on the stone railing, and climb into the lower branches of a conveniently placed elm. That gave him access to a narrow ledge that ran the length of the house beneath all of the second-floor windows. He found Grace's room behind the first window on his right and had, to his surprise, discovered it unlocked. The window pushed easily inward at only a light touch.

Now, as he closed that window with a gentle click, Trevor ruefully reflected that, between the garden wall and the tree he had just scaled, he had done more climbing since meeting Grace than he had done as a lad of ten. He turned away from the window and approached the bed again. She looked so beautiful as she slept, her curly lashes splayed in dark fans against her cheeks, her full lips parted slightly. A ghost of a smile played around their corners, indicating that her dreams were pleasant. He remembered the feel of those soft lips on his, and his jaw clenched. This time he directed his anger at himself. Although he now knew of her treacherous and false nature, the passion she had shown in their few stolen kisses had seemed achingly real.

He still wanted her.

Visions paraded through his mind, taunting him as he considered the enormity of what he would do tonight, sweet memories of Grace indelibly stamped in his head. He had thought himself intrigued by her when he had first seen her portrait, but she'd positively captivated him when they met, this blue-eyed spitfire with the face of an angel. What possessed him to want so very badly the one woman immune to his charm, who cared nothing for his money, and even scoffed at the title he could offer? She scorned with such passion the very things most women in England would have sold their souls to acquire. In the end, she had stooped to trickery and deceit simply because she could not abide him long enough to adhere to their bargain, and she was not honorable enough to tell him, face-to-face, that she wanted out.

So he had decided to give her what she wanted. He would release her from the wager.

As he felt his anger begin to mount again, he tore his gaze from the girl on the bed to look around the softly feminine room she occupied, not knowing exactly for what he searched. A clue, perhaps, to the woman he knew as Grace, something, anything, that might help him gain insight into the girl he had read so inaccurately. He had felt instinctively drawn to her from the start, sensing a strong streak of conviction in her, a streak he had mistaken for loyalty and honor, but which had instead proven to be callous selfishness, stubborn will, and cowardly artifice. Trevor despised one thing above all else: cowardice.

He found the fact that she hid in her room to avoid the conditions of their bargain an act of sublime cravenness, one of which he had not thought her capable. Worse, she had used her aunt and her sister as go-betweens, thus eliminating any chance for Trevor to discuss the situation with her, effectively removing any possibility for him to try to change her mind. That, he found, he could not tolerate. He expected loyalty, honesty, and integrity from his friends. He would require those same traits in his wife.

Seating himself next to the bed in an ecru velvet–upholstered chair, Trevor watched Grace sleep for nearly an hour. Somewhere within the house a clock struck the hour of four. The distant sound reminded him that, sometime soon, the servants would wake and begin moving around, going about the business of making the lives of their employers easier and more comfortable than their own. He sat up straighter and leaned over Grace, gently smoothing back a lock of hair that had fallen across her cheek. God, she was beautiful. He almost could not bear the knowledge that he would never again have a chance to watch her sleep like this, not in his bed or in any other. Abruptly, before he could change his mind, he pulled his hand away and sat back in the chair.

"Grace."

His ominous, quiet voice broke the stillness. He spoke her name only once, but somehow the sound pierced her consciousness. She dragged herself up from the depths of sleep, certain she had dreamed of hearing Trevor call to her. When her bleary eyes finally focused on the motionless figure sitting in the darkness next to her bed, she gave a start of surprise and sat bolt upright, protectively pulling the covers up to her chin.

Trevor smiled at her, a chilling, forbidding smile that did not quite reach his eyes, eyes that glittered a cold emerald in the subdued light. "You seem worried I might ravish you as you lie in your bed," he said. His voice dripped with disdain.

Grace looked a little frantically at the door that led to the hall and then to the one that led to the connecting dressing room between her bedchamber and Faith's, more worried that someone would discover Trevor in her chamber than for her safety. "What are you doing here?" she hissed at him.

"I came to see how you were feeling, my dear." His voice sounded strangely flat, lacking the customary warmth and resonance she loved.

"I-I'm feeling somewhat weak, my lord," she stammered in confusion. A look of cold revulsion crossed his face. "But the doctor says I *am* improving," she hastened to add, vaguely wondering how her illness could possibly anger him.

A muscle leaped in his jaw. "Yes, I can see that."

"Could you please tell me why you're here, my lord?" Her voice was small and bewildered. Again, Trevor marveled at her acting skills.

He stood. "I am now willing to release you from our bargain, Grace," he stated in the brisk tone of someone conducting a business transaction—as if he were not standing in her bedchamber in the middle of the night.

Already Grace's confusion had begun to diminish. She felt a growing sense of irritation at the way Trevor had rudely startled her from a comfortable sleep to subject her to this bizarre conversation in the small hours of the morning. Both the earl's tone and his brusque manner were uncalled-for. "Why?" she asked in a much stronger tone, her alert eyes narrowing on his shuttered face.

Trevor looked back at her with raised eyebrows. "Why, Grace, I can almost *see* your former good health returning, even as we speak," he said. His voice took on a taunting edge. The silence held for a long moment as she looked back at him steadily. "In answer to your question, as you will recall, you did not wish to be a part of our little experiment from the outset. I simply begin to think that you were right." He took a step closer to the bed and watched as Grace lifted her stubborn little chin, refusing to allow his towering presence to intimidate her. "There's only one thing about which I'm still uncertain."

Grace's eyes sparked at him out of the darkness. "And what, my lord, might that be?"

He leaned down to look her directly in the eye, placing a hand on each side of her hips, effectively pinning her beneath the covers. "This," he replied harshly. He took her lips in a crushing kiss that stole her breath and forced her back into the pillows. Her hands lifted to push weakly at his shoulders until he braced one knee on the bed for support and buried a hand in the tumbled mass of red-gold curls to cradle the back of her head. He raised his head a fraction of an inch to look deeply into her stormy blue eyes.

"I'll scream," she threatened against his lips, her chest heaving with the effort to drag air into her constricted lungs.

"Go ahead, my dear," he taunted. "Scream the house down. You'll get me out of here, if that's what you want. But you have to remember that the servants, as well as your aunt and your sister, will come running to see what could be wrong. Servants gossip. Your reputation will be in tatters."

"I could care less about my reputation," she flung at back at him. She managed, somehow, to square her slim shoulders in the meager space he had allotted her between the pillows and his body.

Trevor almost smiled at her bravado. "Ah, but you *do* care about the reputations of your precious sisters. A scandal of this magnitude would ruin their chances for making a good marriage, now, wouldn't it? Poor little Mercy would never get her duke. And only think of what this could do to your aunt. Why, she'd never be accepted in polite drawing rooms again."

"You're the vilest person alive," she hissed at him between her teeth.

"Well, then, I'm in good company," he countered.

Suddenly Grace could no longer fight him. Her hands fell to her sides in an uncharacteristic show of defeat. She wearily turned her head away from him, closing her eyes against the overwhelming weakness that threatened to overtake her. "Could you just go away now, please?" Her voice, small and hurt, barely reached his ears.

"No, my dear, I'm afraid I cannot. Not without saying good-bye." Trevor cupped her chin in his hand and brought her mouth to his again, gently this time, slowly stretching himself out full-length on the bed beside her. His lips moved insistently over hers, evoking, demanding her complete response. When she felt his tongue trace the full contours of her lower lip, she groaned in spite of herself, and gave in to the feelings already consuming her. She turned her body toward his in mindless surrender.

Automatically, Trevor deepened the kiss, filling her mouth with his tongue, pulling her more closely against him. His hand slipped down from her face to cover one small breast. Grace gasped as jolts of pure pleasure shot through her at his touch. Her nipple rose proudly against his palm as Trevor's lips moved along her jawbone to kiss the sensitive spot just behind her ear.

"Trevor," she moaned, a whispered plea.

He stopped long enough to whisper back, "If you want me to, I'll stay." When she did not reply, he began retracing the path his lips had taken before, his thumb gently teasing her nipple through the thin muslin of her nightdress.

Somewhere, far in the back of Grace's mind, warning bells had begun to ring, but they faded with each second she remained in his arms, with each melting kiss she returned with one of her own. He lifted his hand from her breast. Her eyes flew open at the sudden loss of warmth; then she gasped in shock as she felt him unbuttoning the front of her gown. At the small sound, Trevor stopped. He raised his eyes to hers, his voice unintentionally harsh. "Do you want me to stop?"

His hands had stilled in their action, but Grace could feel the trembling tension that coursed through them as they rested against the bodice of her nightdress. The knowledge that he was as affected as she by their nearness filled her with awe and a sweet sense of discovery at the great power all women shared. She closed her eyes. Even as her mind screamed at her to tell him to stop, that this was wrong, her body and her heart compelled her to allow him to continue what felt so right. In the end, her heart emerged the victor.

When she stirred beneath him, Trevor knew she would answer his question. Suddenly the answer meant so much to him that he found himself holding his breath. He watched as she slowly opened her eyes and looked into his. What he saw made his heart momentarily constrict, then begin wildly hammering.

Grace was looking up at him with such aching warmth, such tender, melting promise, that he felt rocked to the very core of his being. With a tortured groan he tore his eyes from her luminous blue ones, and quickly unbuttoned the rest of her gown. Impatiently he pushed it aside.

Her body was sheer perfection, glowing a dusky peach in the pale moonlight. Her nipples rose proudly, blushing pink on small breasts shaped to perfectly fit his cupped hand, begging without shame for his kiss. He bent to take one into his mouth. When he did, she arched against him with a gasp of pleasure.

He suckled at her breast with rough-tender strokes of his tongue, sinking his teeth gently into her soft flesh. She caught her breath as he lifted his mouth from one sensitive tip, then moved immediately to the other to give it equal attention.

Nearly insensible from the incredible feelings that rushed through her, Grace ran her hands fitfully up and down the corded muscles of Trevor's back, wanting to pull him as close to her as possible and just hold him there. He raised his head to look at her with passion-drugged eyes, and she felt a sudden, deep regret for the way she had initially treated him. She thought of all the wasted moments she could have had, simply spending time with this wonderful, incredible man. She laid a hand softly against his cheek and whispered with aching tenderness, "Trevor, I am *so* sorry."

Trevor jerked back as though slapped. He abruptly remembered why he had come, that the woman he held in his arms had proven herself nothing more than a conniving little liar. Deliberately he cupped a breast in each hand, rolling and teasing both nipples between his thumb and forefinger. He kissed the shadowed valley between. "Does that feel good, my lady?" he asked in a husky voice.

Urgently Grace nodded, reaching for him, needing to hold him close to her.

He eluded her touch. "There's more," he whispered. "Tell me you want it."

Grace opened her eyes to find his staring into hers, their centers dark and inscrutable. Her emotion-fogged mind spun in confusion. "I-I don't understand," she stammered, wondering why he would not let her touch him. She reached for him again.

He pinched a nipple in his fingers. She arched her back, dropped her hands, and groaned. "Oh, Trevor," she pleaded urgently.

"Tell me."

"Yes . . . yes, I do," she breathed, not knowing for what she asked. "I want it so very *much*."

Immediately Trevor lowered his head, his tongue flicking sensuously at the undersides of her breasts. He ran a hand down her silken stomach to the nest of soft curls that hid her secrets. At the convulsive tightening of her legs, Trevor raised his head and took her lips with a savage intensity. "Don't close me out, love," he murmured into her mouth, his fingers still splayed on her soft mound. "Open for me, darling."

Unable to resist him in her weakened and aroused state, Grace gave up and relaxed her legs. Trevor watched her face as he slid his hand between her thighs to cup her honeyed heat in the palm of his hand. His touch teased, light and aching, softly at first, his fingers gently seeking out her pleasure points. Grace reached for him again, but he caught both of her hands in one of his and held them above her head. His tongue thrust more insistently now, stroking and tasting hers as shock waves engulfed her body. She gasped against his mouth as he pressed the heel of his hand against the sensitive nubbin at the top of her slick folds and tenderly parted her with one probing finger.

"Trevor!" Grace gasped and arched against him, fearing

and reveling in the unbelievable sensations that had begun to thread through her. "More," she begged without shame. Quickly he complied, urgently stroking her most sensitive places until she writhed beneath him. She took a deep, shuddering breath that announced her coming fulfillment. Swiftly he covered her lips with his, taking her keening cry of pleasure into his mouth as she convulsed around him.

Then he waited.

Slowly her world stopped spinning. Her breathing began to return to normal. As sanity dawned, she realized that Trevor simply rested atop her, his face carefully blank as he registered her reactions. She smiled tenderly and reached for him, her face aglow with her newfound knowledge.

Trevor's handsome face hardened into a mask of cynical contempt. Abruptly he pushed himself off her and stood silently next to the bed, looking down at the girl whom, just the day before, he had feared he might lose forever. She lay on the bed without moving, openly vulnerable to his now cold gaze, momentarily stunned at his sudden change from a sweetly tender lover into this man she scarcely recognized.

"This," he said in a bitter, mocking voice, "is exactly how I'll remember you."

Plunged abruptly into horrified shock, Grace felt waves of humiliation wash over her. Suddenly ashamed of her nudity before the hard gaze of the man she had just allowed to remove her clothing, she quickly scrambled to cover herself. She knelt, trembling, in the center of the bed, holding the edges of her gown together with numb fingers, watching in dazed disbelief as Trevor turned coldly away and walked over to the window.

He glanced back at her once more, firmly pushing to the back of his mind the unwelcome thought that she looked like a heartbroken angel sitting there in defeated misery. "I release you from our bargain, Miss Ackerly." With cruel and deliberate harshness, he looked straight into her eyes and said, "I don't want you anymore." He opened the window, stepped out onto the ledge, and disappeared into the quiet of the predawn London mist.

For several long moments Grace sat motionless, her blind gaze rooted to the spot where she had last seen him. Slowly the numbness that had engulfed her began to recede, replaced with a screaming, paralyzing pain beyond anything she had ever known. With a deep, shuddering gasp, she wrapped both arms tightly around her stomach and began to rock back and forth in silence against the strange, horrible emptiness that slowly spread from within and surrounded her. Finally, unable to hold back any longer, she collapsed in a heap against her pillows and gave in to the flood of tears she had held back from the moment the man she loved had left her arms.

Chapter Twenty

*T*revor dropped lightly onto the terrace from the tree and moved grimly through the shadowy garden. The sky had just begun to lighten in the east. He found himself loathing the day to come. He already knew the cold light of day would bring nothing but torturous recrimination.

He headed purposefully toward the wall at the back of the garden, the same wall he had helped Grace scale the night of the card party. He stopped and placed a hand on the smooth surface. That night now felt like it had occurred an eternity ago, although it had, in reality, happened only a few days before. He took a step back, intending to jump to the top of the wall, but something held him in place. He cursed inwardly and clenched his hands into fists, angry with himself for his inability to leave, furious that he even cared. Unbidden images flashed through his mind: Grace laughing in his arms the first time they danced; Grace holding herself tauntingly aloof, then melting in his arms; Grace, her expressive face wreathed in wonder at the pleasure he made her feel; Grace, adoration shining in her eyes.

Grace, fragile and lost, clutching her gown to her naked body.

Trevor flattened both hands against the wall and closed his eyes, wishing he could stop the images, seeking to quell the tide of overwhelming regret washing through him. *My God,* he thought, *what have I done?* He lowered his head to the cold marble, waging an internal war with himself.

Logically, his mind told him he should let it go. He and Grace had found themselves at cross purposes from the moment they met, hurtling inexorably down the road toward this moment from the very beginning. His reactions to her had caught him up in their intensity, enthralled him, rendered him incapable of listening to his reasonable side.

He had listened to his heart.

Even now, after what had happened between them, his heart compelled him to go to her. His back stiffened with the effort it took to keep himself from turning and climbing back into her room. His arms ached to hold her, to comfort her, to beg her forgiveness.

Trevor's internal battle raged for some moments. When he finally opened his eyes, the sky had lightened considerably. He knew he could not leave things this way. He took a deep breath and turned resolutely back toward the house. Fixing his gaze on the second-story window through which he had just exited, he took a step toward the house, then stopped abruptly. A gas lamp had just flared to life in the room next to Grace's. He saw a shadowy figure moving around behind the gauzy curtains.

He stared at the dark window beside the lit one for a moment longer, then became aware that the morning birds were stirring. The pleasant sound of their song grated on his ears, and a shuttered expression came over his face. His chance had passed. Abruptly he turned and leaped to the top of the wall. He glanced back only once, then dropped down and disappeared on the other side.

His chance had passed.

The day dawned bright and cheerful, filling the spacious room with warm sunshine and vibrant color. The earliest birds had awakened and sang sweetly in the garden. Their happy sounds drifted into the house through the open window where Grace stood, already fully dressed in a simple, unadorned cream muslin gown.

She had not gone back to sleep after Trevor left, although she felt physically, mentally, and emotionally exhausted. She had cried for over an hour, the first time she could remember crying like that since her childhood, until finally she realized she had no tears left to shed. In the strange calm that often follows such an outpouring of emotion, Grace began to examine what had happened, began searching within herself for the reasons why.

The fact that Trevor had come to her room with the sole intention of hurting her went without question. The reasons he had done so puzzled her. The act defied logic, went against everything she had come to know about Trevor's nature. The more she thought about it, the less sense it made. Trying to reconcile his actions, however, forced Grace to face an unsettling truth: she had fallen in love with him.

Certainly nobody had ever made her feel the way he did. Every emotion she had experienced since she met him felt magnified, whether it was anger or sadness, happiness or longing. He had evoked extreme reactions in her from the outset, and she had fought each feeling fiercely, frightened of that which she could not control.

She sank down on the chintz-covered settee beneath the window, drew her knees up under her skirt, and rested her chin lightly upon them. She furrowed her brow, still thinking about the man she now realized she had somehow lost. He had cared about her, too. She knew that now.

Until last night.

Before last night he had reacted to each outburst of her temper, each ill-tempered verbal jab, each scathing rebuff with patience, gentleness, and humor. So why now, she wondered, when she had just begun to return his caring, did he do this terrible thing? She had asked herself that question at least a dozen times since he left, and still it made no sense to her. He had seemed so angry, so very bitter. Almost . . .

Hurt.

Grace heard the door to her room open softly. She fixed a bright smile on her face and turned away from the window to see Faith standing quietly by the door. "Good morning," she said as cheerfully as she could, beckoning her sister to come and sit beside her.

"You should be in bed," Faith admonished in a quiet voice as she crossed the room. Her troubled gray eyes searched her sister's placid face.

Grace let that remark go. She kept the frozen little smile fixed to her lips and turned back to the window, pretending a sudden consuming interest in watching a fat gray squirrel scamper across the terrace.

Faith looked at her sister's pale profile. She noted the bluish shadows under her luminous eyes, the cheekbones that had always been delicate made more prominent by her recent illness, the glow missing from her usually animated face. Grace turned suddenly from watching the squirrel, and Faith averted her eyes lest her sister catch her staring.

"What a pretty day it's going to be," Grace said with hollow enthusiasm. "I think I'd really like to spend some time outdoors. You can't imagine how terribly boring it is being cooped up in this room all day, waited upon hand and foot while the world goes on without me." She paused a moment to take a breath, her numb mind searching for topics to distract her sister from how miserable she felt.

"I know Lord Caldwell was here last night."

As though Faith had not spoken, Grace continued her haphazard, one-sided conversation. "I know that Dr. Wyatt said that I might go downstairs for a bit tomorrow, but I'm really feeling so much better today than I'm sure he thought I would be. . . ."

"Grace."

Faith spoke with quiet firmness. Grace subsided. She closed her mouth and looked at her sister with eyes so vulnerable it almost broke Faith's heart. She reached out and clasped both of Grace's hands in her own. "I don't know why his lordship was here, or what you said to each other, but I do know that I've never heard you cry like you did this morning after he left." Her eyes were filled with solemn sympathy, her voice full of gentle compassion.

Grace felt her resolve to remain strong crumble against the love and soft understanding on her sister's face. Slowly, in stops and starts, she told Faith what had happened, leaving nothing out, blushing only a bit as she described in a small, trembling voice the intimacies she had shared with Trevor. When she finished, she looked helplessly at her bemused younger sister.

Faith was silent for a long moment, staring out the window in deep thought before turning back to face Grace. "Why aren't you angry with him?" she asked.

Grace gave her a blank look.

"After all, he's treated you abominably, and with no apparent reason. It just isn't like you to simply accept—" She broke off. She looked into her sister's eyes in sudden comprehension, for the answer was there for all the world to see. Faith caught her breath. "Oh, Grace." She sighed. "You've only just realized you're in love with him."

Grace closed her eyes and nodded miserably.

Faith sat quietly for a moment, staring with heavy eyes at the rumpled bed in which her sister had cried out her heart only hours before. She glanced at Grace out of the corner of her eye, taking in the dejected air so foreign to her feisty older sister. She knew she had to do something.

Briskly she stood up. "All right, so you love Lord Caldwell. What do you plan to *do* about it?" She kept her voice deliberately offhand and light.

"Do?" Grace repeated numbly, her eyes widening.

Faith nodded decisively. "Of course. You want to get him back, don't you?"

That alarming statement brought Grace surging to her feet. "No!" Her voice rang out, shrill with alarm. "I don't ever want to see him again!"

"You're giving up?" Faith scoffed. "You'll simply allow him to waltz in here in the middle of the night, treat you that . . . that *way*, and then just let him walk off?" She peered intently into Grace's face with mock concern. "I guess that fever took more out of you than we thought," she said. "Why, the Grace Ackerly I thought I knew would never stand for that sort of treatment. At the very least, he owes you an explanation."

"But he doesn't want me," said Grace, exasperation and pain on her face.

Faith shrugged. "Suit yourself," she said. She walked over to the door, where she paused with her hand on the knob. "But if you ask me . . ."

"I didn't," said Grace crossly.

". . . I'd say that Trevor Caldwell probably loves you, too, and with an intensity that would astound you." She opened the door and started to leave, but turned back again at Grace's flat, misery-filled voice.

"You're wrong, Faith," she said. "It was all just a game to him. He doesn't care for me at all." She looked dully across the room at her sister.

Faith felt her heart break again, but her voice remained firm. "Of course he does, Grace. Only someone very much in love could hurt deeply enough to do what he did to you last night." With a final encouraging smile, Faith left the room, closing the door on her sister's stunned expression.

* * *

The object of their conversation was ensconced in his library at the house in Upper Brook Street, methodically imbibing fine French brandy from an ornate crystal decanter that had once belonged to a Russian prince. A matching bottle lay ignominiously on its side beneath his chair, already emptied of the whiskey it had contained. He sat precariously perched on the edge of the red leather armchair, his feet widely spaced, his elbows propped upon his knees, and his spinning head buried in his hands. He tried, unsuccessfully, to block the image of a shattered, red-haired angel, her sapphire eyes brimming with anguished tears, silently beseeching him not to leave her. He had begun to think that nothing short of death itself would ever wipe that image from his mind. As soon as that thought left his mind, he realized that even death might not bring respite, for he was perfectly certain he would spend eternity in his own personal hell, forced to relive, over and over, each moment he had ever spent with Grace. He groaned and slumped back in the chair with a muffled curse.

Gareth Lloyd, the Earl of Seth's brother, found him like that when Wilson showed him into the library at half past ten. All of the curtains were drawn, casting the room in a gloomy semidarkness. The only light emanated from a stubby candle that sputtered on the table beside Trevor's chair. Gareth looked at his friend in amazement, then walked to the nearest window and reached for the curtains, intending to open them and let in some light.

"Don't!" Trevor's voice rang out, harsh and unnaturally loud in the oppressive air of the still room. Gareth turned in surprise. Trevor straightened in his seat and reached for the decanter. He refilled his glass unsteadily, sloshing a bit of the amber liquid over the rim and onto the shining surface of the polished mahogany tabletop. "Care for a drink?" he slurred, holding the decanter toward Gareth, who shook his head. Trevor shrugged and put the bottle back on the table with a clumsy thud. "Fine," he said. "More for me."

Gareth calmly seated himself in the red leather chair opposite Trevor's. "May I ask why you seem bent on self-destruction at such an early hour, my lord?"

Trevor closed his eyes and leaned his head back, his face a mask of bitter remorse. "My God, I hurt her!" His voice was harsh with self-recrimination.

Gareth looked curiously around the dim room, half expecting to see a sobbing, huddled female form in some shadowy corner. He had never seen his friend so distraught, especially over a woman. "Who did you hurt, Hunt?" he finally asked.

Trevor leaned over and waved a hand underneath Gareth's nose. "I thought I could make her care, but all I did was drive her into lies." He looked at Gareth with sudden intensity. "Never lose your heart and your head at the same time, my friend," he warned in a thick voice. He blinked rapidly in an effort to clear his alcohol-fogged brain.

Gareth had a sudden recollection of Trevor, in this very room, winking at a disguised Grace Ackerly over a hand of cards. At the time he had thought that Trevor and Miss Ackerly, who had a reputation for her odd sense of humor, had merely decided to share a lark, harmlessly breaking the rules of society together. Now, however, as he watched his friend down another full glass of brandy without flinching, he read an entirely different meaning into that affectionate wink, as well as into her very presence at the table that night. It appeared that, after years of ambitious mamas with lovelorn daughters, and worldly, sophisticated matrons chasing him across half of England, Trevor Christian Caldwell, fifth Earl of Huntwick, Viscount Cavendale, second Baron Huntley, and Lord Allyn of Graveson, had fallen hard for a virtual nobody. A girl who, apparently, did not want him. Gareth chuckled to himself, not because he found his friend's predicament funny, but because of the amusing irony of the entire situation.

Trevor had slumped back in his chair again, his chin lolling against his chest. He lifted it at the sound of his friend's low laugh. He did his best to focus his bleary eyes on Gareth, but found he could not. He gave up and let his head fall back, murmuring, "I pushed her too hard." His eyes closed again.

Only through a lot of patient coaxing did Gareth finally manage to extract the whole story from the inebriated earl. When he eventually lost Trevor to a deep, alcohol-induced sleep, Gareth left. He instructed Wilson to tell the earl that he would meet with him later to discuss the business decisions he had originally come that morning to talk over.

As he stood on the front steps of the Upper Brook Street mansion, he thought about all he had learned in Trevor's library that morning. Gareth had met Grace only briefly before he had again made her acquaintance in the Grant Radnor disguise. In that one short meeting she had impressed him with her unaffected candor, and by how genuine she appeared in comparison with the usual crop of vain, vapid daughters the aristocracy trotted out for the Season. He could easily have included himself in the circle of Grace's admirers if he had any interest at all in the debutante set. Certainly, though, she had not seemed capable of the level of malicious deceit Hunt thought she had engineered.

Pulling on his gloves, Gareth walked down the steps to his phaeton, shaking his head again at the irony. Although Hunt had set out to punish Grace, he had so upset himself about hurting her that he had nearly drowned himself in alcohol trying to forget about it. Gareth vaulted lightly up onto the high seat of the vehicle, took the reins, and set the team in motion. Perhaps, he thought, something interesting would happen this Season after all. Unless he missed his guess, things had hardly ended between Miss Grace Ackerly and the Earl of Huntwick.

Chapter Twenty-one

With a breezy smile, Grace slid quietly into a chair across the luncheon table from her sister. She had spent most of the previous day in her room, grappling with her newly realized feelings for Trevor, then had fallen into an exhausted sleep. When she awoke she felt slightly stronger, physically. She also knew that she could not just let Trevor walk away.

Faith looked across the table and smiled back at Grace in satisfaction. Aunt Cleo, seated between them at the head of the table, also looked up and nearly dropped the knife with which she was buttering a roll. She recovered quickly and gave Grace a severe look. "Dr. Wyatt advised at least two more days of undisturbed bed rest for you, young lady," she said in her firmest tone, but her eyes glowed with happiness at her niece's greatly improved condition.

Grace waved an unconcerned hand. "Dr. Wyatt," she said lightly, "is quite overly cautious." Her eyes twinkled merrily in a face still too thin and pale from the ravages of the fever.

"You may be quite overly optimistic, Grace Olivia Ackerly." Aunt Cleo turned to Faith, counting on her younger niece's unfailing logic for support. "Talk some sense into your sister, miss," she commanded.

Calmly, Faith eyed Grace. "Well, she certainly *looks* healthier," she commented. She took a delicate bite of her superbly seasoned roast duck and turned innocent gray eyes on her aunt.

Cleo looked sharply at Faith, who looked back, as cool and composed as ever. When the older lady transferred her assessing gaze to Grace, however, she found her niece squirming awkwardly in her chair. She wondered at the girl's guilty air. Turning her attention back to the table, she feigned deep interest in selecting a muffin, glancing covertly at both young women while she did. Out of the corner of her eye she saw Grace sigh in relief, then dart a questioning look at Faith. Certain she would learn nothing from the girls if she tried to press the issue, Cleo reluctantly changed the subject, drawing both girls into a gossipy conversation about the latest *on-dits* among the members of the ton.

Grace smiled her thanks at the footman who set a filled plate before her. She sat quietly, listening to the fast-paced dialogue between her aunt and her sister. She did not feel the least bit hungry, ate only, in fact, to further convince her aunt of her recovered health. As she pushed the food about on her plate, she realized just how much gossip she had missed during her short confinement. Things happened quickly during the Season. Reputations were built and torn asunder with lightning speed.

She managed to choke down most of her food, ever mindful of the watchful eyes of her aunt, although she could not remember the last time she had felt so full. She bided her time carefully. As soon as she heard an appropriate lull in the conversation, she interrupted with a delicate cough. "It's a pretty and unseasonably warm day, I believe, Aunt. It feels as though I've not been outside in ages. I think I'd like to take a short turn about the garden, if someone wouldn't mind going along with me?"

Although the question was phrased to include both herself and Faith, Cleo could tell by the charged atmosphere that the girls really hoped for some time alone. "Not me," she declared cheerfully, then almost laughed aloud when she saw Grace relax in relief. Feeling wicked, Cleo widened her eyes in mock concern and reached over to clasp one of Grace's hands in her own. "Although I really think, Grace, that you ought not spend too much time outside just yet. You still look a bit peaked to me, dear."

Grace lightly chewed on her lower lip. She cast wildly about in her mind for an excuse, *any* excuse, to give her aunt, but before she could come up with anything, Faith resolved the problem with her usual aplomb. "Nonsense, Aunt Cleo, she'll be with me. We won't stay out long. If she begins to look tired, we'll come right back inside."

Taking pity on Grace, who was making a huge effort to keep from wriggling in her chair and further revealing her agitation, Cleo finally nodded her acquiescence. The girls quickly excused themselves and left the room before she could change her mind, Grace looking as though she might burst, Faith as serene as ever. Cleo watched them go with an indulgent smile, then sighed in disappointment. She could have eavesdropped much more easily if the girls had stayed inside. Standing, she crossed the room and leaned on her cane by the window, watching fondly as her nieces slowly strolled, arms linked, toward the hedge maze at the back of the garden.

Grace stood looking at the entrance to the well-manicured maze in pensive silence, wishing she found her own maze of emotions as easy to navigate. After a moment she sat down upon one of the stone benches flanking the maze entrance and drew her knees up under her skirt in her usual casual fashion, wrapping her arms about them.

Faith smiled and settled primly on the bench next to her.

"You shouldn't sit that way, you know," she advised gravely, looking down her nose with regal hauteur. "It isn't a bit la-dylike."

"Trevor liked me just as I was," replied Grace softly, but with a trace of her usual spunk.

Faith's look changed to one of smug satisfaction. "You've decided to win him back, haven't you?" she asked, certain she already knew the answer. The determined look on her sister's face gave it away.

"If I can," Grace affirmed with a nod.

Faith paused. "Have you given any thought to how you're going to do it?" she asked.

"Send him a note?" Grace queried.

Faith lifted delicate brows in disdain. "Saying what, pre-cisely?"

Grace shrugged. "Asking him to meet me here to discuss a matter of great importance," she offered.

"He'll ignore it," said Faith.

Grace's face fell, then quickly brightened. "Perhaps not. It may pique his curiosity. Besides, I could hardly go to him myself," she pointed out.

Faith gave her a direct look. "I think that's exactly what you'll have to do." Grace sucked in a breath and looked so alarmed at the possibility that Faith laughed and took pity on her older sister. "All right, Grace, assuming that Huntwick decides to obey your summons—" She broke off again when she saw Grace frown. "Well, that's precisely how he'll perceive it—as a summons."

Grace clenched her teeth in exasperation. "Go on," she said, her voice level.

"So, assuming that he actually responds, what do you plan to say to him once he arrives?"

"I'll simply tell him that I'm sorry, that I was wrong, and that I love him," replied Grace promptly.

"And then you'll stand there with your mouth hanging

open like a complete dolt when he either laughs in your face or walks out on you altogether."

Tired of Faith contradicting her at every turn, Grace set her small chin. "I'm sure he'll be resistant at first—," she began.

Faith cut her off, pointedly ignoring the venomous look Grace sent her. "Before you begin to plan this, try putting yourself in his lordship's place." When Grace clenched her teeth but did not respond, she continued: "Remember, he's been nothing but kind to you, from the first moment you met him up until the other night. *You*, on the other hand, have done your level best to thwart each attempted kindness in any possible way. Despite your lack of willing cooperation— or perhaps because of it—he persisted in trying to win you, and, in the process, managed to fall like a rock for a woman who didn't seem to notice or care for him."

"I did care," Grace mumbled, so low that Faith nearly had to lean over to catch it.

"Perhaps you did, Grace, but you didn't make it apparent to him. When you finally *did* begin to show some affection, he discovered you apparently didn't mean it at all, that it was still only a game to you, and that you had every intention of avoiding him when the allotted two weeks ended."

"He knew when he made the wager that there was a possibility he would lose," Grace protested weakly.

"But in his eyes, you did not play fair. You admitted as much to him yourself the night before you became ill."

Grace knew that her sister spoke the truth. Her shoulders slumped in defeat, but for only a moment. She did not consider losing an option, had never allowed defeat in anything she had ever set out to accomplish. Now, when the stakes were higher than ever, she was stubbornly determined not to falter.

Faith sat quietly, watching the expressions change on her

sister's face as she reasoned her way through the problem. When Grace looked at her again, it was with squared shoulders and a lifted chin. The decisive look in her eyes reminded Faith of stories she had read about knights of yore, bravely charging into battle when they obviously did not have a prayer of defeating their enemy.

"So," Grace said brightly, "you think sending him a note is a bad idea?"

"No, actually, I don't." Faith smiled. "I think sending him a note is a *good* idea. I just wanted you to be able to understand what may motivate his actions when he receives the note."

Grace looked at her younger sister with new respect. "How did you become so wise?" she asked softly.

Faith looked away and shrugged, betraying her discomfort. "I like to watch people," she said simply.

Knowing that Faith disliked compliments, Grace gave her sister a quick, impulsive hug; then they got to work, plotting their campaign to recaptivate the Earl of Huntwick. They planned the effort with a tactical brilliance Napoleon himself would have appreciated.

"All right," said Grace. "I'll send him a note. How shall I word it?"

Faith thought for a moment. "Simple and very straightforward. No sense wasting time on something that will merely be tossed away and ignored."

Grace glared at her sister in renewed exasperation. "If you're so certain he'll ignore it, why should I bother at all? Why don't we simply proceed to something he can't ignore?"

Faith shook her head. "No," she mused. "We have to make sure that he can't put you out of his mind. Small reminders are important while we plan something more elaborate."

Grace smiled suddenly, a widening grin of delighted hope. "He can't win, you know," she stated with a confident toss of her shining, red-gold head. "Nobody is as persistent as an Ackerly."

Faith looked grave. "You're absolutely right, Grace; he can't win. If Huntwick allows himself lose you, he's lost more than he'll ever know, so he couldn't really count that a victory. But *you* can lose, big sister." They looked at each other soberly for a long moment.

Grace stood and shook out her skirts with a determined air. "Well," she said brightly, "shall we go write that note? We'll send it, and if I don't receive a reply in two hours, we'll move on to step two." She paused. "What *is* step two?" she asked.

Faith had already begun walking back to the house, having no need to straighten her own unrumpled skirts. "That," she said calmly over her shoulder, "depends entirely upon his reaction to step one."

Trevor took the envelope from the silver tray his footman held out to him. He opened it in distraction as he mulled over a legal document that required his signature. When he reached a stopping point, he paused a moment in his work and glanced at the two lines the note contained.

> *Trevor,*
> *I have a matter of great importance to discuss with*
> *you. Please call upon me this afternoon.*
> *Grace*

His expression utterly blank, Trevor handed the note back to the waiting footman and returned to his work. "No reply is necessary," he said. The footman bowed and left the room, closing the study door silently. Lately, his lordship preferred everyone around him to be quiet.

Chapter Twenty-two

While waiting for Trevor's reply, Grace retired to her chamber and took a much-needed rest. When she awoke, she found that several hours had passed, for the sun had angled much lower in the sky. She stared out the window in sleepy confusion, trying to fathom the strange sense of anticipation that tugged at the edges of her consciousness. A wayward image of Trevor as she had last seen him, silhouetted against the moonlight from that very window, flitted through her mind. With a sudden rush of clarity she remembered the note and the plan, and realized the answer she awaited from the earl was causing her nervous expectation. Quickly she leaped out of bed and ran across the room, yanking so hard on the bellpull that Becky and two footmen appeared at a run, certain that something grave had once more befallen their mistress.

After convincing the footmen she had suffered no untoward incident, she impatiently shooed them out of the room and turned to her glowering maid. "Have I received any messages?" she asked breathlessly, ignoring the censorious look in Becky's narrowed eyes.

"Lord above, Miss Grace, I don't know! What's gotten into you, to go about scaring us all half to death like that? I was sure I'd find you in a heap on the floor again."

Grace managed to look contrite. "Nobody has called either, I suppose?" she persisted in a hopeful tone, although she knew that if Trevor had called, Faith would have made certain someone awakened her.

"I don't know that, either. I've been above stairs the whole time you were sleeping, miss."

"Well, then, I'll just have to go and see for myself." Grace hurried to the door, then stopped at the sound of Becky's hesitant voice.

"If you don't mind my saying so, Miss Grace, your dress is looking like it was slept in. And your hair could use some attention too."

Grace opened her mouth to tell Becky that she could care less about her appearance, when a sudden thought struck her. She stopped in her tracks, one hand on the doorknob. If, by some miracle, Trevor decided to answer the missive in person, looking her very best was probably a good idea. Reluctantly she turned back. "All right," she agreed. "But please hurry." She slid into the chair before the vanity mirror and allowed Becky to brush the riotous tumble of burnished curls into some semblance of order.

Fifteen minutes later Grace walked into the blue salon her aunt favored because she could watch the setting sun through the windows overlooking the garden. Grace appeared calm, freshly dressed in a becoming russet day dress, her hair smoothed into shining waves held off her forehead with an amber clip. Inside, her stomach was doing flips. She looked at Faith in inquiry, who shook her head, indicating that she had heard nothing. Although Grace had hoped for better news, she had not really expected it. She shrugged cheerfully and crossed the room to the chair near the windows in which her aunt sat.

"You certainly look refreshed after your nap, dear," said Cleo.

Grace perched on the arm of the chair and leaned down to give the older lady an affectionate kiss on the cheek. "I feel better with each passing moment," she assured Cleo. "Have you any plans for the evening, Aunt?"

"I thought perhaps the opera," Cleo mused. She leaned forward so she could see past Grace to the settee where Faith sat with her needlework. "What do you think, Faith? Shall it be the opera?"

Faith lowered the embroidery hoop and looked up. "You go with some friends, Aunt. I think I'll stay and keep Grace company."

Cleo looked distressed. "Perhaps we should both stay in tonight, dear. Some quiet entertainment at home will be just the thing."

"No!" Grace blurted, then hastily tried to cover her outburst. "I mean, I won't be the least bit bored with Faith for company, and besides, it will be a nice night for you to do something you would like." She looked to Faith for support, but her sister was busy counting stitches and was not paying attention to the course of the conversation. Grace reached down and covered Aunt Cleo's hand with her own. "You've spent all of your time chaperoning us, and we *do* appreciate it, but you must want some time to yourself, perhaps to spend with some friends?"

Aunt Cleo looked shrewdly from one sister to the other, then patted Grace's hand, saying, "You were always such a sweet child." She got up with the help of her cane and started toward the door. "Perhaps I'll ask Edna Fariday to join me at the theater. I've scarcely seen her all Season." Her voice trailed off as she left the room and made her way toward the stairs.

Filled with a strange exhilaration, Grace began pacing back and forth in an effort to decide what step they should take next. When she began mumbling to herself, Faith finally put aside her embroidery and regarded her sister. "I'm not sure what you expect to accomplish with all that pacing, Grace. You'll tire yourself."

Grace stopped in midpace and plunked down in a chair across from the settee. "I'm going to go see him," she announced.

Faith raised her brows. "Alone?"

"No. With you."

Faith shook her head. "I think you should let him know you intend to pay him a call."

"So he can simply refuse to see me?" Grace sighed in exasperation. "No, thank you."

"He may still refuse when you appear uninvited on his doorstep."

Inspiration struck, and Grace sat up straight. "I could always dress up again and go as Grant Radnor. He may see me then, if only because I've shocked him into it."

"Yes, you could do that—and you could also hope that nobody else sees you and recognizes you on the way to his town house in broad daylight," pointed out Faith. "Besides, he already knows you rather well. I don't think anything you do will shock him at this point."

Grace gave Faith a barbed look. "If you're only going to contradict every suggestion I make, the least you could do is to come up with ideas of your own." She fumed, her growing frustration evident on her face and in her tone.

"I did."

Grace snorted. "Another message? I told you before we sent the first one that it wouldn't work."

Faith leaned forward. "It's perfect; don't you see? If you tell him you'll come to him if you don't get a response by a certain time, you're forcing him to at least acknowledge you. And that means he *has* to think about you."

"But it's only making him angrier."

"Precisely."

Grace looked at Faith in complete bewilderment for a moment before comprehension dawned. A slow smile spread across her face. "I have to make him feel something for me, right? And anger is *much* better than indifference." She looked at Faith, her excitement mounting. "I can do this."

"Of course you can," said Faith. She picked up her needlework and sighed as she began counting stitches again from the beginning.

Grace sat down at the desk, twirling a strand of red-gold hair around her index finger as she contemplated what to write. She considered and discarded several ideas before she came up with a message that suited her. She frowned, unsure of what she should use as a salutation. She had simply written his name at the top of the first note, but now thought it had sounded a bit too personal, especially as she rarely called him by his name, even when he had still liked her. *My lord* sounded as if she pandered to him, and she thought *Huntwick* sounded too masculine. She briefly toyed with the idea of writing *Hunt* at the top of the note, as she had heard Gareth Lloyd and Sebastian Tremaine address him, then realized he did not consider her a trusted friend, as he did both of those men.

Finally, she turned to Faith for an opinion. "Tell me how this sounds: 'There are things we must discuss. I will call upon you this evening at seven o'clock unless I hear otherwise from you before that.'" She looked at Faith. "I'm undecided on how to address him or how to sign it."

Faith kept working. "Be yourself," she advised without looking up.

Grace thought for a moment, then resolutely turned back to the desk, wrote *Trevor* at the top and signed it simply, *Grace*, as she had done before. That finished, she sprinkled the note with sand, folded it, and slipped it inside an envelope. She sealed it with a bit of wax, then hurried off in search of O'Reilly. She wanted someone she trusted.

She found him stocking the liquor cabinet in the library, and said, "O'Reilly, could you please take this note to the Earl of Huntwick for me? It's quite important that he receive it today, so please track him down if you must."

"Yes, Miss Grace," said O'Reilly, feeling unaccountably pleased that she had specifically chosen him to carry out this task.

Grace smiled in thanks. "Please tell whomever you speak with that you've been instructed to deliver the note personally. I need you to watch his lordship closely and tell me how he reacts."

If her request sounded strange, the servant hid it well, nodding as Grace continued with her instructions. "From the moment he sees you until the moment you leave, watch him and try to remember the expressions on his face, as well as his words. Can you do that for me, O'Reilly?"

"Yes, of course, Miss Grace."

"Thank you." And with another sweet smile, she walked away.

Chapter Twenty-three

When O'Reilly knocked on the Earl of Huntwick's door in Upper Brook Street, Trevor was at his favorite table in White's playing cards with his friends Gareth and Jonathon Lloyd. It took an inordinate amount of persuasion before the footman finally convinced Wilson to part with that information. It would take far less time for Wilson to regret doing so.

After Trevor had drunk himself into oblivion the previous morning, he'd slept the afternoon away, awakening with a pounding headache and the grim determination to forget that he had ever set eyes on Grace Olivia Ackerly. As if to prove to himself how easily he could do just that, he dressed for the evening and went to the Dunworthys' ball. Once there, he set out to charm as many young ladies as possible, once again raising the hopes of every mama in London who had previously seen her aspirations dashed by the exclusive attention Trevor had paid to Grace.

An hour after he arrived he encountered Melissa Porter, a friend from childhood, attending the ball in the company of her mother. As he often did when he saw Melissa at a town function, he courteously asked her to dance. Her calm friendliness and cool beauty washed over him like a soothing balm after his short, tumultuous relationship with

Grace. He felt so at ease in her presence that, after their dance, he remained by her side. He spent the better part of the evening talking and laughing with Melissa's mother and their friends, to the great disappointment of all the matchmaking mamas whose hopes had momentarily risen.

The sight of Melissa's gloved hand on his arm, and the fond smile on Trevor's face as he looked down at her, definitely qualified as a titillating new topic for the gossipers. The whispers and suppositions began, further fueled by the rumor that had occasionally circulated over the years about a possible match between Trevor and Melissa, whose father owned property that marched along the boundaries of one of the estates owned by Trevor. Additionally, some of the assembled guests recalled that Trevor had, only a few days before, escorted Melissa to the theater. Still others remarked upon Grace's conspicuous recent absence from society. Few knew she had been ill, and those who did know wondered if she were simply home nursing a broken heart.

The morning following the ball, Trevor paid a short call on Melissa, and found himself further impressed with her pleasant demeanor. If he gave any thought to Grace at all, he firmly pushed it from his mind.

Just after one o'clock, he'd received the first message from Grace, which he pointedly ignored. As the afternoon wore on, however, he found it increasingly difficult to concentrate on his work. Wayward images and unbidden thoughts of Grace kept popping into his head. Finally, with a snort of disgust, he'd quit working and gone to White's for some cards and diverting conversation.

He had brooded, nearly silent, for the past hour, systematically divesting Gareth and Jonathon of their funds, remaining stoic despite repeated attempts to break him out of his mood. Trevor had just won yet another hand, causing

even the irrepressible Gareth to frown at a diminishing pile
of chips, when the Duke of Blackthorne pulled up a chair.

"Oh, perfect," Gareth muttered. Sebastian signaled for
one of the circulating footmen to bring him a drink. "Good
to see you, Thorne. You're just what we needed to liven up
this table." The staid duke ignored him. Trevor, who usually evened out the mood of the group, remained quiet,
gloomier than Gareth had ever seen him.

A footman arrived with Sebastian's drink and set it on
the table in front of him. He quietly made sure the other occupants of the table did not need anything before he vanished. Sebastian caught Gareth's eye, nodded toward Trevor,
and raised an inquiring eyebrow, prompting him for an explanation.

Gareth shrugged good-naturedly. "I can always count on
big brother here to dampen my spirits—and upon you,
Tremaine, to wet-blanket any entertaining notion I can
come up with. Usually Hunt will oblige me by not being
quite so morose, but I've yet to hear him utter more than
the words 'cut,' 'deal,' 'pass,' or 'fold' in the last hour." They
all looked at Trevor.

The earl picked up the cards Jonathon had just dealt
him. He steadfastly ignored Gareth's jibe, an action that
caused Sebastian to go so far as to raise *both* his eyebrows
before turning his attention to his own cards. At a questioning look from Jonathon, Sebastian laid two cards facedown on the table, indicating he would like two more.
Trevor shook his head, and Gareth took three cards. Sebastian waited a moment for everyone to reassemble their
hands, then spoke. "I trust the Ackerly chit is recovering
from her recent illness?"

Gareth looked at Trevor, who did not react, although a
muscle tightened in his jaw momentarily. "I'm sure she's doing fine," he said with an indifferent shrug, then smoothly

raised the opening bet of seventy-five pounds by two hundred more. Jonathon and Sebastian immediately folded and sat back in their chairs to watch Gareth and Trevor play out the rest of the hand.

Gareth met Trevor's upped bet with one of his own. "Two hundred seventy-five? Shall we make it an even three hundred?" He added his chips to the steadily increasing pile in the center of the table. "So, Miss Ackerly was fine when you saw her last?" He asked the question casually. He had no idea whether Trevor even remembered their conversation of the previous morning. He got his answer seconds later when Hunt's eyes registered nothing more than cold anger, and he answered with a curt nod.

Gareth grinned as Trevor called the bet and laid down four kings. "Take your winnings, Hunt," he said cheerfully, pushing back his chair and stretching his legs. "And I'm afraid I'll have to call it a night after that disastrous hand," he added. Frowning at the empty space on the table where his chips had been stacked, he lit a cheroot and inhaled deeply.

Laying down his cards and leaving the pile of chips he had won in the center of the table, Trevor did likewise. He turned to signal a footman for a drink, then suddenly stiffened. A short, bowlegged footman in Egerton livery was approaching, accompanied by the proprietor of White's. Trevor immediately recognized O'Reilly. The pair stopped in front of Trevor. The little footman bowed nervously, visibly trembling at the look of eloquent displeasure on the earl's face.

"I was instructed, my lord, to deliver this to you directly." O'Reilly bowed again and handed an envelope to the earl, who looked at it with blazing contempt. Short of making a scene that would set the tongues of the ton wagging for weeks, Trevor knew he had no alternative but to take the envelope and open it. He pulled the single sheet of paper out of the envelope, scanned it, then pinned the proprietor with a scathing look. "Get me something to write with," he snapped. "And a bottle of brandy," he added to the man's hastily retreating back.

O'Reilly stood quietly, watching Trevor closely as Grace had asked, but also trying to take in as much of the famous club as he could. As far as he knew, nobody of his station had ever stepped foot inside the place.

Within moments a footman came running back with the requested items. He placed the writing utensils on the table in front of Trevor, opened the brandy, and poured it into the earl's glass. He glanced surreptitiously around the table, wondering if his lordship wished to share the bottle with his companions.

Without noticing or caring about the servant's consternation, Trevor hastily scrawled a reply on the back of the note Grace had sent, shoved it back into its envelope, and thrust it at O'Reilly. The proprietor escorted the small man from the building with all due haste.

As soon as the door closed behind him, buzzing whispers began filling the room, each man present vying to beat one another in the race to report the extraordinary news that the impulsive Miss Ackerly had chased the Earl of Huntwick into the exclusively male domain of White's. When the shameless gossiping reached an unprecedented level, Trevor finally lost his patience. He tossed down the remainder of the brandy in his glass and stood abruptly. He gave the entire room a sweeping glare of blazing fury, effectively silencing everyone. As soon as the whispers ceased, he turned and stalked out of the club, his winnings left in a pile in the center of the table.

The stillness held for a moment after his footsteps receded. Everyone stared in amazement after the usually imperturbable earl. Then, as if by collective agreement, they all made a leap for the famed betting book, leaving Gareth, Jonathon, and Sebastian almost alone in the room.

"I'm surprised you didn't go with them, Gareth," the Earl of Seth said with a reproving look at his grinning brother. "I'd have thought you'd be the first in line at the book."

Gareth stood. An alert footman rushed over with his coat and hat. "I was," he informed Jonathon loftily. "I placed my bet yesterday." And with that quelling statement Gareth strolled smugly off, leaving his brother scowling. Blackthorne, looking bemused, quietly watched him go.

Chapter Twenty-four

Grace, Faith, and Amanda, the Countess of Seth, were in the sitting room enjoying a relaxing cup of tea when O'Reilly finally returned. He handed the envelope, now torn and slightly crumpled, to Grace. She ripped the note from inside and read the two small words aloud. " 'Don't bother.' " She turned the piece of paper over to make certain she had not missed anything, then looked at O'Reilly. "What did he say? How did he look? Was he angry?" The questions tumbled from her lips in rapid succession.

"Well, Miss Grace, he never really said anything at all, and I think his immediate reaction when he saw me was shock, not anger."

"Shock?" Faith asked, perplexed. That particular reaction had not occurred to her.

O'Reilly reflected a moment, then nodded. "Yes, it was shock, although now that I think about it, it could have been because I'm probably one of the last people he expected to see in White's."

"White's!" the girls cried. Now all the ton might know of Grace's pursuit.

"Yes, and he looked just as you do now, Miss Grace!" O'Reilly pointed at Grace, happy to have an example in order to save himself the description.

"Oh, my God," said Faith, with more feeling than she'd intended. She bit her lip and wished she had not said it as she watched the color drain from her sister's stricken face.

Grace sank down limply on the settee, too stunned even to think. Amanda sat next to her and put an arm about her friend's shoulders. "What did he *do?*" Amanda asked O'Reilly, patting Grace's hand soothingly. Faith handed a cup of tea to her sister, which she automatically drank, though she hardly tasted the warm brew.

"Well," said O'Reilly slowly, looking in confusion from one girl to another. They were not reacting at all as he had expected.

"Go on, O'Reilly," Grace prompted. She gave a weak but encouraging smile.

"He looked quite angry when I handed him the note, although it seemed to be the note itself he was angry with, not me."

That made perfect sense to Grace, even if it did not to O'Reilly, so she nodded for him to continue.

"Then he asked one of those hoity-toity servants for a bottle of brandy and something to write with. When those came, he wrote the answer, handed me the note, and I left."

Grace turned stricken eyes on Faith and Amanda. "It's early yet," Amanda soothed, giving Grace's slim shoulders an encouraging squeeze. She gave Faith an anxious look over her friend's head. "Perhaps the club wasn't very crowded," she added, with more conviction than she really felt.

"Oh, yes, it was, my lady," supplied O'Reilly, eager to give as much information as possible. "We had to work our way through many filled tables in order to reach Lord Caldwell's. They were sitting quite in the center of the room, you see, so it was most difficult to reach them from any direction."

"They?" Faith asked. She closed her eyes, certain she really did not want to hear with whom Trevor had shared his table.

"Lord Caldwell, the Duke of Blackthorne, your husband, and his brother, my lady," he said, turning toward Amanda.

Grace and Faith immediately turned imploring looks in Amanda's direction. She stood in a flurry of pink silk. "I'm going," she said grimly. With a reassuring look, she left to summon home Jonathon and Gareth for some damage control.

O'Reilly returned from seeing Amanda to the door and stopped hesitantly near the two quiet figures seated in the parlor. "Miss Grace, did I not do precisely as you requested?" His voice shook with concern.

Grace's heart went out to him. He had only tried to do what he thought she wanted. With a valiant effort, she smiled up at him sweetly and replied, "You did exactly as I asked, O'Reilly, and I thank you."

Much relieved, the footman bowed and left the room, his step light as he returned to his duties.

Grace watched him go, then turned to Faith. "Trevor will never forgive me for this. It'll be the topic of gossip for weeks." Her voice was glum, as she'd lost the hope that had sustained her for the past two days.

Faith looked equally grim. "That's the least of your worries," she stated flatly. "Your own reputation will suffer when it becomes known that you sent O'Reilly into White's to appeal to Huntwick. Society is well used to women chasing after Trevor, but there are rules, and I'm certain no one else has been as brazen as that. We'll have to hope that since he was in Egerton livery, it will be supposed that O'Reilly was there on business for Aunt Cleo."

Grace looked skeptical. "And what do you think the chances of that would be?"

Faith shook her head. "His lordship has made no secret of his attraction to you. That information, combined with the way he publicly reacted to your message, leaves me very discouraged, indeed."

As it turned out, Amanda did not have to track down her brother-in-law. As soon as she entered the house Desmond, the Seth butler, informed her that Lord Gareth was waiting in the library and that he had asked for her. Amanda thanked him and handed him her cloak before hurrying through the foyer to the library.

Gareth had just poured himself a drink when she threw open the doors. He took one look at her face and reached for another glass. "Shall I pour you one also, my lady?"

"Sherry." She nodded. "Tell me it isn't as bad as I think it is."

He handed her the glass. "It's worse. How is it that you already know?"

"I was with Grace when that misguided footman of hers returned," she said. "Is there any chance nobody knew who employs O'Reilly?"

Gareth shook his head. "I'm afraid not."

Amanda sat down in a winged leather chair, one foot tapping furiously as she tried to think. "The message didn't necessarily have to have come from Grace. For all anybody knew, it could have been from Lady Egerton regarding some business venture for which she needed advice, or an investment she had immediate questions about."

Again Gareth shook his head. "There are two reasons nobody would ever believe that. The first is that Hunt was quite obviously furious about the message. Since there are only ladies living in the Egerton town house, it will be assumed that the message came from one of them."

Amanda's face fell, and Gareth continued.

"Lady Cleo would hardly have sent a message that would have inspired such a reaction in Hunt, so obviously the message had to have come from one of the younger ladies." He paused and smirked a moment. "Can you imagine our incomparable and ever-so-correct Miss *Faith* Ackerly pulling a stunt like that?"

Miserably, Amanda shook her head.

"Neither will anyone else," Gareth finished. He swallowed the last of his port and poured another.

Amanda took a restorative sip of her sherry, then remembered what Gareth had said. "You said there were two reasons that everyone would think it was Grace who sent the note. What is the second?"

Gareth closed his eyes, his cocksure, arrogant attitude gone for the first time since Amanda had known him.

"What is it?" she asked in alarm.

"The second reason is entirely my fault," he began, his voice heavy.

"Yes, it is," came a voice from the doorway. The Earl of Seth stood there, glaring at his younger brother with cold displeasure. "Please," he invited scathingly, "tell my wife what you've done to her friend."

Gareth's chin rose. His eyebrows snapped together as he glared back at the earl in a clash of wills that had begun years earlier. "You tell her," he said coldly, then strode from the room. He slammed the door behind him. A moment later they heard the front door slam, too.

"Really, Jonathon," Amanda chided, "You leave him no choice. It can't be all that terrible."

"Perhaps you should reserve judgment on that score, my dear, until you've heard what he's done this time." He helped himself to a glass of brandy before seating himself in the chair opposite his wife. "Yesterday my reckless little brother placed a public bet in the sum of one thousand pounds." He paused. "The entry reads, 'Miss Grace Ackerly will bring the Earl of Huntwick to heel within one week.'"

Amanda gave a gasp of horrified laughter. She quickly stifled it at the quelling look from her somber husband. "Oh, my," she said, unable to manage any other response.

"Quite," said Jon. "By this evening your friend will be known as an extremely fast and bold young lady. On top of that, because Hunt left White's almost immediately after receiving the message, everyone will assume he left to obey her summons, making him look like a fool in leading strings."

That statement deeply alarmed Amanda. She caught her breath. Trevor would hate Grace for making him look so foolish, leaving her little if any chance of ever winning him back. She knew her friend could care less about her own reputation, but she also knew Grace cared a great deal about the reputation of her family, and even more about what Trevor thought of her. Considering the situation a moment, she could come up with no new ideas. In frustration, she gave up and changed topics. "Must you ride Gareth so hard?"

Jon's scowl deepened. "He must learn some responsibility, Amanda. Had he thought this through before placing the bet, he would have seen the most likely possible consequence and not done it."

"But, Jon, he feels terrible already. You couldn't possibly make him feel worse, and I'm afraid you'll drive him away from us again."

The earl fell silent a moment. That possibility had occurred to him as well. He well remembered the year immediately following their father's death, when Gareth had fought the control Jon had tried to exert over him. That year had ended with Gareth running away to join the army, only to come home nearly dead after taking a bullet fighting Napoleon.

Her husband remained silent, so Amanda pressed her momentary advantage. "He's a grown man, Jon, needing to make his own choices and mistakes. Stop trying to control him or he'll do something drastic. I heard him discussing a possible move to the American Colonies only the other day."

Jonathon looked at the earnest face of his beautiful wife.

His eyes turned tender. "Marriage would settle him down, you know."

Amanda stood and walked to her husband's chair. She settled herself comfortably on his lap. "I couldn't agree more, darling." She wrapped her arms around his neck and rested her head against his chest, then tipped it back to look up at him. "I'll have to give it some thought," she murmured, then promptly forgot Gareth, Grace, and Trevor as Jonathon's lips claimed hers.

Chapter Twenty-five

Grace stood before the full-length mirror in her bed-chamber, tugging on her clothes and finding critical flaws in her appearance where none really existed. She wore a shimmering gown of turquoise satin, a shade that exactly matched the bright blue of her eyes and set off to perfection her creamy complexion. Becky had fussed with her hair awhile, but in the end Grace decided to wear it down, held back from the sides of her face with mother-of-pearl combs. Long satin gloves in the same shade of blue as her dress encased her arms, ending just above her elbows. The gown itself had no adornment, elegant in the simple style Grace liked best, cut straight across her chest with short, square sleeves, a row of darts beneath her breasts and across her back. From the insert of each dart, a panel of teal chiffon fell in gossamer folds, forming the effect of an underskirt that just brushed the tops of her soft turquoise satin slippers.

Amanda gave Grace a final appraising look. She took in the girl's delicate cheekbones, made more prominent by the weight lost during her illness. Her slightly tilted eyes appeared larger, and her face was still a bit paler than normal, but the combination gave Grace an exotic and vulnerable look. Amanda was counting on that vulnerability to help pull off the scheme she had concocted with Gareth.

Grace gave her bodice another tug, uncomfortable with the low, square neckline, above which her rather smallish breasts swelled enticingly. "I can't do this," she said. She took a deep breath in an attempt to calm the nerves that were making her stomach do flip-flops.

"Nonsense," soothed Amanda, "you look beautiful. You have nothing to fear. They're just people."

"It's not the people who worry me," muttered Grace.

"Trevor's just a person, too," said Faith, as pragmatic as ever.

Grace glared at her sister in the mirror. "You're wrong," she said flatly. "He's two people, and right now I'd much prefer if he were the Trevor who chased me, rather than the one I'm chasing."

"You could have had him then, girlie," said Aunt Cleo from the doorway. She moved into the room, inspecting her niece's appearance through a lorgnette. "Although I think you'll appreciate him more now when you get him." She stopped before Grace and nodded. "I suppose you'll do. You all will. Let's go." She rapped her cane on the floor in impatience.

They rode to the ball in Aunt Cleo's well-sprung carriage, Amanda rattling off last-minute instructions. "Gareth, Trevor, and Sebastian should have been there for at least an hour by now. Gareth and Jonathon have been putting about the word that the whole incident was a simple prank of Gareth's, which should be believed, since he is always pulling stunts like this. Gareth has also promised to convince Trevor to go along with the plan and to behave toward you, Grace, as he always has."

"He won't do it," said Grace, a note of despair beginning to thread itself into her voice as the carriage neared their destination. "Trevor won't give a hang about what people think of him, and he'll be more than happy to see my reputation suffer."

"Stuff and nonsense," barked Cleo from the corner of the carriage, her voice loud in the closed space. "Huntwick won't tolerate people thinking he's a fool. Men don't, you know. Can't abide it." She nodded wisely.

Faith, who had remained quiet until this point, finally spoke. "Lord Caldwell will go along with the plan," she said quietly. Three pairs of eyes swiveled in her direction. Faith sat primly erect in her corner, her hands folded in her lap, a small smile on her composed face.

"How can you be so sure?" Amanda asked.

"Because I took the liberty of sending your brother-in-law Gareth a message as soon as you told us what you had planned."

When her niece did not elaborate, Cleo lost patience and thumped her cane on the floor. "Spit it out, girlie! What did you tell him?"

Faith smiled tolerantly. "Well, it's perfectly obvious that if his lordship's ability to handle a mere female is questioned, his business partners may also question his ability to select sound investments."

Cleo, Grace, and Amanda stared in openmouthed amazement.

"It's true," Faith insisted. "Lord Caldwell's business reputation is entirely based upon his uncanny ability to judge whether or not an investment will reap good returns. Among the wealthier members of the ton, he is viewed as having rather a golden touch, because he seldom makes a poor business decision."

Amanda shook her head in admiration. "How do you know all this?"

Faith raised disdainful brows. "Because," she said loftily,

"there is a great deal *more* to a newspaper than the society section." She turned her head to look out the window as the carriage came to a stop.

Making a mental note to ask her husband more about Lord Trevor Caldwell, Amanda quickly got back to the subject at hand. "Does anyone have anything to add?"

Faith remained silent. Grace shook her head, her face a taut mask of misery. The footman opened the door. She took a deep breath and prepared to step out of the carriage into a crowd of people who would immediately begin whispering about her.

Aunt Cleo suddenly checked Grace's exit with her cane. "It won't work!"

Amanda and Faith turned their heads sharply in her direction. "Why not?" Amanda asked.

Aunt Cleo gestured at Grace, who remained grimly by the door, steeling herself to face the crowd. "Huntwick can agree to be his most charming, and young Gareth can spread all the rumors in the world," she declared, "but it will all be for nothing if Grace walks in there looking like a sacrificial lamb." She leaned toward Grace for emphasis. "I don't care how you manage it, but you go in there with your head high, your spine straight, and you smile, missy. If you don't, they'll slaughter you within moments—" She broke off as the footman lowered the steps and held out a hand to help them alight.

With a last, long look at her aunt, Grace raised her chin, squared her shoulders, and stepped down, followed immediately by Aunt Cleo, Faith, and Amanda. They had not walked ten feet before heads swiveled toward them and whispers began. With a fixed smile, Grace offered her arm to Aunt Cleo, who took it and leaned in with a last bit of advice before they entered the lion's den. "Just remember this, my dear: if tonight goes badly for you, Huntwick will still have his title, his money, and entrée into the highest circles of society. You, however, will be dropped so fast your pretty little head will spin." Cleo felt Grace's spine stiffen beside her, and watched as the intimidated look in her eyes changed to one of angry resolve. *Much better,* Cleo thought with satisfaction as they entered the beautiful Upper Brook Street mansion. Huntwick would not know what hit him.

They gave their wraps to one of the footmen stationed just inside the door, then ascended to the third-floor ballroom. Grace felt her stomach tighten again as they neared the top. The music spilling from the entranceway grew louder, along with the din of the more than six hundred invited guests. Just outside the entrance she took a deep breath in an effort to calm her rampaging nerves.

Grace felt an encouraging squeeze on her hand. "Are you all right?" Amanda asked in a low voice, as Faith and Aunt Cleo entered the ballroom ahead of them.

Grace nodded, determined to ignore the butterflies in her stomach. She pasted a serene smile on her face, then stepped up to the entranceway with Amanda. The butler bellowed out their names, and they began their slow descent.

Those nearest the entrance responded with blatant immediacy. Heads turned sharply toward the top of the staircase, then back toward their neighbors. The news that Grace Ackerly had arrived spread in an ever-widening arc of whispers. Grace fixed her eyes on a point just above the blurred sea of faces and continued her poised entrance into the room.

Across the ballroom Jonathon Lloyd watched them enter. He nodded above the crowd at Gareth and Trevor. All three men headed through the throng toward the small group of women now gathered at the bottom of the stairs.

Amanda greeted her husband with a kiss on the cheek and then turned to her friends. "You remember Miss Grace and Miss Faith Ackerly, my lord?" The girls curtsied to the earl, and again Grace wondered what had attracted Amanda to such a stern, serious-looking man. She always had a hard time envisioning Jonathon Lloyd as anything but staid and boring, yet Amanda's adoration was obvious.

Gareth and Trevor chose that moment to join the group upon which so much public attention had focused. Lord Lloyd performed all the necessary introductions. Grace executed a perfectly correct curtsy, as befitted Trevor's rank, although her knees trembled and her mouth felt as dry as cotton. She almost collapsed in relief when she saw Trevor smile down at her in that lazy way of his. Then she looked into his eyes and her heart plummeted: they looked right through her, as cold and expressionless as shards of green glass.

Trevor went through with the farcical reintroduction to Grace. He had thought himself immune enough to her to manage to get through this evening without feeling overly affected. His heart had clenched, however, when he saw her, a breathtaking vision in blue gracefully descending the wide staircase. When Seth presented her to him, he even found himself smiling warmly down at her. Then, just when he had almost forgotten his animosity, Grace dropped into a perfect curtsy. The simple act reminded Trevor of the day he stood in Cleo Egerton's parlor, trying to think of a circumstance in which Grace would willingly curtsy to him. He managed to keep the smile pinned to his face as she rose, although he knew the revulsion he felt at having to play this role was reflected in his eyes.

Shaken by the undiluted disgust in Trevor's gaze, Grace watched as he secured her aunt's permission to dance with Faith, as had been prearranged by Gareth and Amanda. Cleo gave him a nod, and the couple glided off to the dance floor.

The whispering immediately increased. Gareth, who had remained with the small group of people that included

Grace, had a hard time keeping a straight face. "Right now," he said to her, "six hundred people are busy declaring to anyone who can hear that you certainly never sent Hunt a message at White's."

Grace looked dubious.

"They now know," he continued, "because I told them, that Faith is also a possible candidate, and that your aunt Cleo is most fond of tracking Hunt down and summoning him to advise her on financial matters at the drop of a hat. Since everyone knows how very abrupt your aunt is, and how very correct your sister is, I'd say that most of these people are about to come to the conclusion that they were quite wrong about you."

Just then two matrons standing across the room caught Grace's eye, staring at her in blatant disapproval. When they realized she had noticed them, they coldly and pointedly turned their backs. Grace looked up at Gareth and inclined her head in their direction. She gave him a sad smile. "There are those, however, who will choose to believe the worst. Some people will always remain convinced of my guilt."

Gareth looked momentarily sober. "I'm afraid I did you a grave disservice, Miss Ackerly, by placing that bet at White's."

Grace noticed for the first time how much he resembled his older brother. He looked so terribly contrite that her heart went out to him. She smiled warmly. "Please, my lord, don't vex yourself on my behalf. I really don't care what these people think of me. I never did." She swept an arm in a wide arc that encompassed the entire room, then turned troubled eyes on the handsome man dancing with her sister. "But I do care very much what they think of Lord Caldwell," she added quietly.

Startled by the depth of feeling in her voice, Gareth followed her gaze. He saw Trevor leading Faith off the dance floor, courteously directing her back toward her aunt. In that instant he knew what he had to do. Considering the damage he had done to them both, he thought it only right. He excused himself and walked away in search of Amanda.

Trevor dutifully returned Faith to Aunt Cleo, then stood for a moment, talking and laughing quietly with them. Finally he turned to Grace. She stood to the side, a gracious smile pinned to her face, feeling rather like an awkward interloper. Courteously he held out an arm and gave her a smile. "Would you honor me with a dance, Miss Ackerly?"

Grace held her breath for a moment, then remembered her audience and let it out slowly. Returning his smile with a dazzling one of her own, she executed another graceful curtsy, then nodded and rested her gloved fingertips lightly on his arm.

The orchestra had just begun a waltz as they stepped out on the floor. Trevor immediately swept her into the crowd of couples dipping and swaying in the lovely dance. She danced with him in silence, staring at his burgundy superfine-clad shoulder, not quite trusting herself to begin the conversation.

After they had glided around the room in silence for a second time, Trevor finally spoke, his low, angry words at complete odds with the pleasant, almost relaxed look on his handsome face. "If you don't wipe that damned look of bored disdain off your treacherous face, I'll resort to one of your infamous tricks and leave you standing in the middle of the dance floor."

Seconds of shocked silence passed before Grace found her voice. She forced herself to smile up at him in a very plausible imitation of a simpering debutante. "And destroy all the work Gareth and Amanda have done to restore our respective reputations? Really, Lord Caldwell, that would be most ungrateful," she admonished.

Trevor ignored the impulse to smile, once again genuinely impressed by her control. He whirled her around the room again, angry with himself for the weakness he felt each time she entered his sphere. "You and I are going to finish this dance," he bit out between clenched, bared teeth, "and then I'm going to ask your aunt to dance. And after that, Miss Ackerly, if you ever speak to me or approach me again, I will take great pleasure in publicly humiliating you. To hell with anyone's bloody reputation!"

Numb, Grace made herself smile as though he had just given her a flowery compliment. Only she and Trevor would ever know that her eyes were bright with unshed tears.

True to his word, Trevor next took Aunt Cleo for a romp around the dance floor. Grace watched for a moment from the sidelines, then left the ballroom, searching for a quiet corner in which to compose herself and try to stop the suddenly uncontrollable quaking of her limbs. She found the darkened library and slipped inside. She sank down on a low, cushioned stool near one of the soaring windows that lined one side of the room. There she finally succumbed to the tears that raged within her.

Unobserved by Grace, Amanda had followed. She watched as Grace entered the library, observing from a quiet post by the door as her friend sat down and seconds later buried her face in her hands, sobbing in anguish. Amanda withdrew, hurrying back to the ballroom to find Gareth and her husband.

Her tears finally spent, Grace sat looking out the window at the strolling couples in the gardens below, wondering how she and Trevor had come to this point. They had found themselves at cross purposes from the moment they met, each wanting the same thing. They had simply wanted it at different times.

Until now.

Now they wanted precisely the same thing: for this to be

over. Trevor had already put Grace from his mind. As the tears slipped slowly down her cheeks again, Grace decided that she would do the same. No more schemes or plans for winning him back. No more games. She would put the Earl of Huntwick out of her mind, and she would start by going back to Pelthamshire. Tomorrow.

The door crashed open. The man she had resolved to forget only seconds before stormed into the darkened room. He stalked past the window where Grace sat, straight to the sidebar laden with decanters and glasses. There, Trevor poured himself a glass of brandy, drained it, then quickly poured another. He walked across the room to the fireplace and set the drink on the mantel. He braced one hand against the wall for support and ran the other through his thick, dark hair.

Grace had come quickly to her feet as he strode past, her heart thumping wildly in her chest. As he stood by the fireplace, his aristocratic profile outlined in stark relief against the white marble, Grace realized that he did not know she was there.

Moonlight mingled with the illumination from the gas lanterns in the garden below to spill through the row of tall windows that lined an entire wall in the room. Grace stood in the shadows to the right of the window farthest from Trevor, but he stood bathed in that light. The look on his face and the vulnerability of his stance made Grace catch her breath.

His head was tipped forward in profound anguish, the lines of his handsome face harsh and angular, his eyes closed against the emotion that quaked through him. He had loosened his cravat at some point since she had last seen him, and the snowy white ends dangled in stark contrast to the deep burgundy of his jacket.

He did not move for several moments. Grace's tender heart constricted painfully as she felt a nearly uncontrollable impulse to go to him, to put her arms around him and to comfort him. She had actually taken a step forward before she thought better of it, then turned to leave quietly before he noticed. But her one step forward had brought her into the moonlight that streamed through the windows, and the subtle rustle of her gown caught Trevor's attention; out of the corner of his eye he saw her turn to leave. He stiffened and whirled to face her.

"I thought I'd warned you to stay away from me!" he ground out.

Grace stopped and turned toward him, suddenly angry at the entire situation. "I was here first!"

She looked like a defiant angel as she stood across the room, her chin outthrust and her hands curled into tight little fists at her sides. Her blue eyes flashed, her hair a fiery red halo created by the moonlight. A reluctant grin of admiration tugged at the corners of Trevor's mouth as he looked at her. It widened when she stamped a dainty satin-shod foot.

"Will you kindly cease laughing at me, Trevor Caldwell!"

The grin slowly left his face. He belatedly took in the two bright spots of color flagging her cheeks and realized that her fury had escalated beyond reason.

She proved it a second later when she advanced on him like an angry young tigress. "I have had it with you, my lord. You swoop into my life after nearly killing my sister and magnanimously declare that you are going to marry me, which forces me to run to London like a hunted rabbit in an effort to avoid you. I couldn't even lose you in a city this size, though, because there you were, popping in for uninvited visits, following me to functions, making a complete nuisance of yourself!" She stood nearly toe-to-toe with him now, jabbing him in the chest with a long, tapered finger to add emphasis to her words. "And *then*," she continued, spreading her arms wide in an exaggerated shrug of mystification, "when I finally admit to myself that I've fallen in love with you, I get sick, which *you*"—another jab—"found so inconvenient that you couldn't even wait for me to recover before expressing your tender feelings to me so very eloquently in my bedchamber in the middle of the night!"

She turned away, feeling suddenly deflated, and failed to notice the expression of dawning amazement in Trevor's eyes. Her voice trembled, small and weak, when she spoke again. "I thought you were just angry with me for the way I'd treated you, that you still cared for me, that perhaps I'd deserved it. But I hoped that if you loved me just a little before, then perhaps you could love me again." She looked down and scuffed the floor with the toe of her slipper, desperate to keep him from seeing the tears that had welled to overflowing and now slipped silently down her cheeks.

"I do."

He uttered the two small words softly but firmly. Grace refused to turn and look at him, certain her ears had deceived her. A second later she felt his hands on her upper arms. He turned her around, then crushed her against his chest. She almost sobbed in relief as he pressed a kiss to the top of her head. They stood quietly like that for long moments, neither able to speak through the tide of emotions that swept through them.

Finally Trevor pulled out of the embrace and took a small step back. "May I speak?" He grinned wryly. Grace nodded, then held out both of her hands to him. He took them in his.

"First," he began, "I did not declare that I was going to marry you that day, though I'll admit the possibility was foremost in my mind. *You* informed *me* that you wouldn't marry me before I even had a chance to do the asking." He smiled tenderly down at her as a faint blush stole over her face; then he sobered and tilted her face up to his. "I'm so sorry I hurt you." His voice caught, and he cupped her face in his hands and looked deeply into her eyes. "The night you fell ill, you seemed to have given in to me. For the first time it all felt right. I was terribly worried that they wouldn't let me stay with you for very long when you were so sick. I visited every day. Then, when the fever had passed and you were recovering, your aunt suddenly denied me visits. But even all of that wouldn't have made me do what I did."

"What did?" asked Grace.

"As I was leaving, Faith gave me your message."

Grace looked confused.

"You told Faith to tell me that I had only a few days left our agreement," he reminded her.

Grace's face cleared as she remembered when she had spoken those words. "But . . . I said that in jest!"

He gently placed an index finger on her lips. "I believe that now," he said, "but only moments before, your aunt had informed me that you would not see visitors for at least a week."

"So you sought to punish me by doing that terrible thing," she said, hurt. Immediately she wished she had not spoken. Trevor looked so anguished by his actions that she tried to smooth things over. "It's all right," she began, laying her hand on his cheek.

He caught her hand in his. "No," he said quietly, "it's not all right. We've hurt each other. The only way to go on from here is to face it and put it behind us."

Grace looked up at Trevor, and he caught his breath. The love she felt for him glowed in her eyes, shining brightly, deeply, and without shame.

"I already have," she whispered, just before his lips claimed hers.

Chapter Twenty-six

The next three weeks flew by in a whirlwind of activity for Grace, although they dragged endlessly for Trevor. He had at first insisted upon getting married immediately, before, as he put it, anything else could possibly happen to keep them apart. However, Grace, who was rather inclined to agree, had had second thoughts when Faith, as logical and prudent as ever, pointed out that it would hardly be fair of them to get married without the rest of the family present.

Trevor, who had no immediate family, had scowled. He'd opened his mouth to protest, then saw Grace's guilt-stricken face and remembered how much the six mother-less girls meant to one another. His face softening, he'd asked, "Would you like for your family to be here, darling?" He'd looked at Grace tenderly, willing to bear anything, even postponing their wedding night, in order to make her happy. She'd nodded gratefully and given his hand a little squeeze. Quite pleased with himself, Trevor had promptly decided the happy look was ample reward for waiting. He'd magnanimously announced that since they had to wait anyway, they might as well do the thing right with a formal church wedding.

Now, weeks later, Trevor felt a bit less generous. The plans for the impulsively offered church wedding, which

Trevor now privately considered a circus, had all but taken Grace away from him. During the few secluded moments Trevor managed to steal with her, Grace was distracted, crossly complaining about lists.

"What lists?" Trevor asked, laughing when Grace muttered darkly about making somebody eat the bloody things.

"Faith!" Grace threw her hands up in exasperation as she walked beside him through the garden. "She has made me a list for everything! So far she has given me a guest list, a list of thank-you notes that I must write, a list of menu items for the wedding breakfast, and a list of errands that must be run. *That* list has a sublist specifying the order in which I must run the errands."

The corners of Trevor's mouth began to twitch. Grace glared at him. "Don't you *dare* laugh, my lord." With visible effort, Trevor composed his face, and Grace continued: "This morning, though, was the last straw. Would you believe Faith actually gave me a list that detailed which list I must attend to first?"

Trevor turned, but his shoulders began to shake suspiciously. Grace stopped, planted her hands on her hips, and gave him a severe look. "I think you should know, my lord, that on none of my lists will you find an entry that reads, 'Waste time strolling in the garden with Lord Caldwell.'" She elevated her nose and turned to go back into the house.

Finally unable to contain his mirth, Trevor gave a shout of laughter. In two long strides he reached Grace, snatched her up in his arms, and whirled her about until she laughed, too. When he set her down, her eyes were glowing with love and the pure pleasure she felt from simply spending time in his company. Instantly Trevor's mood shifted from gaiety to desire.

Sensing the change, Grace put her hands up as he stepped forward to close the small distance that separated them. "Trevor," she said, her voice turning breathless. "What are you doing?" He bent his head to hers, his lips lightly brushing her cheek en route to the sensitive skin behind her ear.

"I'm making a list," he murmured.

"What kind of list?" Grace whispered back shakily as he lightly nipped her earlobe, sending a surge of desire through her. She felt her knees weaken.

His lips moved down along her jawbone. "A list," he said in a melting voice, "of all the places I am going to kiss you." He took her lips in a sweet exchange that made Grace forget everything: the lists, the plans, even the wedding. She lifted her arms to pull him closer, opening her mouth at the insistent caress of his tongue, returning his kiss with equal ardor. She groaned as his lips left hers, then arched her neck and tilted her head back as she felt his moist mouth move down the column of her throat to the shadowy hollow between her breasts. She gasped and pushed her fingers into his dark hair as she felt his tongue lightly probe there.

"Good heavens!"

Grace and Trevor jumped apart and looked down the path toward the last turn they had taken. There stood Mercy, grinning impudently at them, garbed in, of all things, a dress. "It's a good thing, I think, that the two of you are already planning on getting married. If Papa saw you kissing like that, he'd have had you in front of Reverend Teesbury faster than you could blink."

Her face bright red, Grace glanced at Trevor. He was openly glaring at her little sister. Hastily she smoothed her hair and dress, laid a restraining hand on Trevor's arm, and went to give Mercy a hug. "My goodness, look at you," she exclaimed, taking Mercy's hands and spreading her arms wide to get a good look at the dress. She laughed and fingered a puffy silk sleeve. "It's pink!"

Mercy scowled. "Patience promised I could come visit you and Lord Caldwell in London after the wedding, so long as I behave like a young lady." She wrinkled her little nose in distaste.

"You're off to a bit of a rocky start, aren't you?" Trevor walked up behind Grace and placed his hands on her shoulders. He glowered at Mercy dampeningly.

She shrugged with an impudent grin. "What Patience doesn't know won't hurt her." She turned to walk out of the maze, then looked back as a sudden thought struck her. "You won't tell her, will you, my lord?"

Trevor simply raised his eyebrows and shrugged. "Well, since it would be *my* house you invade on your intended visit, I suppose I would have to weigh the relative value of my silence, wouldn't I?"

Mercy gave him an assessing look for a moment, then, amazingly, stuck her tongue out and flounced away. Grace watched her leave, then looked back at her glowering fiancé. "You wouldn't tell on her, would you?"

"No."

"Then why do you still look so put out?"

"Because," he predicted grimly, "with a house full of Ackerlys, and only a week until the ceremony, I seriously doubt I'll have another chance to be alone with you until our wedding night."

As it turned out, Trevor was right. He seldom, if ever, saw Grace alone. When he called at the Egerton town house, he invariably had to wait long moments, or had to swallow his ire as Greaves reported, with obvious satisfaction, that Grace was "otherwise occupied." If Trevor did manage to see her, he often received only a hurried kiss before one of the many female Ackerlys whisked her away.

More often than not, Mercy appeared in the parlor when she knew Trevor was waiting. She said it was so she could keep him company, although she admittedly had another, more selfish purpose: she shamelessly pumped him for details about her hero, the Duke of Blackthorne, whom she still insisted she would someday marry. Trevor, who could already glimpse a great deal of Grace's stubborn spirit in her younger sister, simply shook his head with amusement. He hardly knew what he looked forward to more: watching his enigmatic friend deal with the adoration of this elfin girl with hair too short and eyes too large, or the prospect of leading his young sister-to-be a merry chase in her quest for Sebastian's hand. Either way, the entire situation promised to be entertaining, for he did not see Mercy giving up her crush any more than he saw Blackthorne falling prey to it. So he usually patted her atop her curly head, asked her to take Grace a message from him, and left, finally giving up waiting for his fiancée to appear.

A few days before the wedding, after spending the afternoon in the gardens with Mercy, Trevor went to White's for a drink and a hand of cards. He had not been back since the incident with the betting book, so he steeled himself for the inevitable jokes and snide remarks he knew he would receive about being apparently "brought to heel," as Gareth had predicted. Strangely, though, nobody even mentioned the notorious entry as he made his way to the table customarily occupied by himself and his friends. Sebastian had already arrived and sat enjoying a cheroot and a glass of brandy.

Trevor nodded a greeting to him and pulled up a chair. "Don't tell me everyone has forgotten about that infamous bet," he said, indicating the room's other occupants with a tilt of his head. "When the wedding announcement hit the papers, I assumed tongues would be wagging for weeks about how Grace really *had* brought me to heel."

Sebastian shrugged. "Gareth neatly took care of that situation."

Trevor accepted with a nod of thanks the glass of brandy a footman brought to the table. "How do you mean?"

"He publicly declared he'd lost the bet."

The thought of his devil-may-care friend announcing to all of London that he had made a mistake momentarily stunned Trevor. "He did what?"

"He simply said that the two of you seemed to have brought *each other* to heel, then paid his note and left the building."

Trevor rubbed his chin. He looked at Sebastian with raised brows. "That," he said, "was well-done of young Lloyd."

Sebastian nodded. "I rather thought so, myself." He motioned for a footman to bring them a deck of cards. "So, do you still intend to go through with this wedding?"

Trevor grinned. "You look positively grim when you say the word. Don't be surprised if you find the bonds of matrimony written in *your* future. Grace's little sister is of the idea that she will marry you someday."

"So I've heard. Quite young, don't you think, to be already so active in the title hunt?" Sebastian's lip curled in sublime displeasure.

"I think the child means what she says. Perhaps you should take this a bit more seriously," Trevor advised.

"I'm hardly in danger of being forced to marry a thirteen-year-old child."

"Ah," said Trevor, "but there is one very good reason I think you should heed my warning."

Sebastian merely looked bored. "And what might that be?"

"Mercy," said Trevor, "reminds me a great deal of Grace."

Sebastian did not answer, but Trevor noticed that his face grew just a touch grimmer as he shuffled the cards.

Trevor smiled.

Chapter Twenty-seven

May 15, 1813

Trevor shrugged into the black velvet jacket his valet held up for him, then stood patiently while the man brushed nonexistent specks of dust from his shoulders and back. After pulling and tweaking at his master a bit more, Avery stood back in satisfaction, then handed Trevor a pair of immaculate white gloves. "There you are, my lord." He bowed stiffly. "May I take this moment to offer my sincerest congratulations?"

Trevor looked at the man who had dressed him from babyhood, then grinned and hugged him, clapping him soundly on the back. Avery stiffened further. "My lord!" He extricated himself from the uncharacteristic show of affection and busied himself again with Trevor's attire. "You'll wrinkle your jacket."

"Never mind the jacket, Avery," he said, stepping away from the red-faced valet. "I intend to get a good many of that sort of wrinkles in this jacket today." He turned back to the mirror one last time to inspect the closeness of his shave and the intricate folds of his cravat. Finding no imperfections, he dismissed Avery with a nod, then smoothed on the gloves, flicking a glance at the chair where the Duke of Blackthorne lounged patiently.

Sebastian spoke. "You're nervous." He did not state it as a question, merely as an observation to which Trevor chose not to reply. The duke raised sardonic brows. "Well, I certainly hope you don't intend to hug *me* today."

"My lord, the Earl of Seth and Lord Lloyd have arrived." Wilson stood stiffly in the doorway, but his lined face glowed, wreathed in a smile that stretched from ear to ear.

Shaking his head at the informal way Hunt allowed his servants to behave, the Duke of Blackthorne stood; then the two men went downstairs to leave for the church.

Trevor spoke little on the way. He had not slept all night, tormented by visions of Grace changing her mind and not showing up. His most horrible imagining consisted of her making an appearance, only to run from the church—and from him—in the middle of the ceremony.

Gareth somehow managed to sense Trevor's fears. He teased him the entire way, despite the censorious stare of Sebastian and the obvious annoyance of Jonathon. The jibes hardly mattered. Trevor, lost within his own thoughts, scarcely heard.

Several blocks before reaching the church, their conveyance slowed, then stopped altogether. After a moment the door opened, and one of the footmen stuck his head inside. "My lord, the road between here and the church is completely blocked."

"Has there been an accident?" Trevor asked. "Why don't we just go another way?"

"*All* the roads are blocked, my lord."

Trevor drew his brows together. "Well, then," he said. "We shall walk." He stepped out of the vehicle, followed by Sebastian, Gareth, and Jonathan. He looked up and down the street in disbelief. "Where in the world did these *people* come from?"

Jonathon spoke. "I imagine they are on their way to a wedding."

Trevor's jaw clenched. Despite the modest number of invited guests, the ton had apparently decided to turn out in force, drawn by the public and tumultuous courtship preceding the wedding. He turned back to the waiting footman. "Send a man to Lady Egerton's home to warn them of the traveling difficulties." The footman bowed and turned away. Trevor looked up at his driver. "When you manage to get to the church, see what you can do about getting the problem solved so we can get out after the ceremony." And without waiting for a reply, Trevor turned and began walking toward the church.

Gareth walked quickly and drew even with Trevor. Just as he opened his mouth to continue his teasing, Jonathon stuck his foot out and smoothly tripped him. Gareth stumbled, then managed to regain his balance before falling to the cobbled street. "Don't," said Jon in a pleasant voice as he walked past. Gareth scowled.

When they arrived at the church, they worked their way through the throng of people waiting to enter and walked around to a side entrance. The bishop waited for them just inside, wringing his hands in agitation. Jonathon and Gareth stopped and spoke quietly with him while Trevor walked across to the door that led out into the church proper. He opened it a crack.

The pews had already filled to capacity, and Trevor could see even more people waiting outside the massive front doors. He felt a movement at his side, and turned to find Sebastian looking out into the church beside him. "There must be six hundred people out there," said Trevor with more than a trace of irritation. "Who invited them?"

His friend shrugged with disinterest. "I can only imagine," he said, "that people flock to a wedding for the same horrible reason they flock to an execution."

Trevor openly glared at the duke while the organ began tuning up in the other room. Gareth, who had overheard Sebastian's cynical comment, gave a sharp bark of laughter. His brown eyes danced. "And what exact reason would that be?"

"A morbid curiosity for the irrevocable," replied Sebastian.

A slight breeze carried the songs of birds into the room where Grace dressed for the most important day of her young life, surrounded by the people who knew and loved her best. Patience, Faith, and Amanda attended her, beautifully gowned in simple silk dresses of the palest green. They would carry bouquets of pink roses and white daisies, flowers that some might consider unfashionable but that would always be the most beautiful flowers in the world to Grace.

She stood solemnly before a long mirror as Amanda attached the long, weblike veil of silver net to the delicate wreath of flowers that held her flaming hair away from her face. She draped the folds artistically around Grace's arms, then let the veil fall from her fingers to shimmer in waves to the floor. She stepped back to admire her friend. What she saw reflected in the mirror nearly made her gasp. Although Grace wasn't smiling, her peaceful face reflected the quiet inner joy she felt, and her blue eyes shone radiantly with the love she had for the man to whom she would pledge herself for eternity.

The gown she had intended to wear hung forgotten in the closet. Instead she donned the gown her mother had worn when she married Grace's father. Patience had first proposed the idea, and the whole family agreed that it felt right for Grace to wear it. Everyone had always said she looked exactly like her mother. Grace had found that hard to believe as a child, and even harder to fathom when she became an awkward adolescent. She remembered people telling her how beautiful her mother had been, how kind and gentle and wise, and Grace had always smiled politely and said thank-you. Then, when alone, she would creep away to her room to open the miniature portrait she secretly kept in her drawer. She would look in the mirror and try very hard to find a resemblance, but would give up when she saw the image that stared back at her: a skinny teenager with carrot-colored hair and the multitude of tiny brown freckles that came from spending all of her time out-of-doors.

She looked in the mirror now and caught her breath. Somehow, it appeared, all those people had not just said those things to be kind. She stood still as Patience bent down to straighten her hem, and caught Amanda's eye in the glass. Amanda smiled. Grace glowed today, and she felt that glow to her very soul. Her face reflected utter serenity, as though she knew that nothing and nobody could possibly spoil this day.

Although dreadfully out of fashion, Grace's pale gray gown looked just right. Long, sheer chiffon sleeves hugged her upper arms and gradually widened to bells at her wrists. A double row of glittering diamonds beautifully accented the square neckline, cut low in the front and the back. The bodice, tight to her waist, made Grace look even smaller than usual, and the skirt fell in frothy layers of dove-colored chiffon from her trim waistline, all the way down to brush the floor.

She had left her hair unbound, save for a diamond clip that held back the burnished curls from her face, because Trevor had once told her that he always imagined her with her hair down. She had added the clip only because she wanted Trevor to be able to see her face as she walked down the aisle, wanted him to understand that she came to him with pride, with joy, and without a trace of uncertainty.

They heard a hesitant knock on the door. Becky opened it and cautiously stuck her head inside. "Miss Grace?"

"What is it, Becky?" Grace turned and smiled at the little maid, beckoning for her to come into the room.

"Mr. Ackerly asked me to come up and tell you that it is time to leave. His lordship has already left, and sent word that the roads around the church are nearly impassable."

"Well," said Patience past the lump in her throat, "I suppose we're as ready as we can be." She crossed the room to where Grace stood, and laid her hand on her sister's cheek. "Shall we go?"

Grace shook her head. "Why don't you go on down? I think I'd like to be alone for a few moments." Patience smiled and bent to give her sister a quiet kiss; then all the girls filed out of the room.

Grace watched them go, then looked around the quiet chamber. Her eyes filled with nostalgic tears. Never again would she have a bedchamber exclusively hers, a room she could call her own. Always, from now on, she would share her space with her husband. She walked slowly around the pretty room, running her fingers across some of the furnishings, picturing in her mind the times she and Faith had curled up together on the bed after returning from an evening out to talk and laugh over the things that had happened.

Grace thought of her smaller room in Pelthamshire. She realized, with a funny little tingle in her stomach, that the next time she slept in that room, Trevor would sleep with her. She smiled to herself, looking forward to sharing the home of her childhood with the man she loved.

Another thought occurred to her. Leaving her chamber and walking down the corridor to the room occupied by her father, she knocked quietly. "Papa?" She listened for a moment, then pushed open the door when nobody responded. Grace stepped in and was immediately transported back in time by the smell she always associated with her father. She caught her breath. Papa would give her away today. Never again would they share the same type of relationship.

She crossed the room to the bureau and ran her fingers over the carved handle of the brush that lay atop a folded sheaf of papers, noting the glint of silver mingled with the strands of blond caught in the bristles. It was funny, but she had never thought of Papa as growing older. He never seemed to change as the years passed. She picked up the brush with a smile. The top fold of the papers that lay beneath it popped up. Grace caught sight of Trevor's signature, the bold, distinctive handwriting she had come to know so well leaping from the page. Curious, she picked up the papers, unfolded them, and began to read.

It was a document outlining her betrothal to the Earl of Huntwick, signed by her father and by Trevor. It was dated just two days after she'd left for London. One day before Trevor had followed her here.

Bemused, she walked out of her father's chamber and back into her own room. She sat back down at the dressing table and considered what the document meant. Then she smiled. Trevor could have compelled her to marry him from the outset. Instead, he had chosen to court her, had allowed her the opportunity to develop feelings for him. Still, she wondered why he had not told her of the betrothal after they had reached their understanding.

No matter. Grace stood again with the papers, intending to return them to the top of her father's bureau. As she turned to leave the room, she caught sight of the sudden movement of a figure behind her. Just as she opened her mouth to scream, a large hand clamped around her mouth. Before she could react she was struck sharply on the back of her head with a blunt object. In an instant her world exploded in shards of blinding pain. The betrothal contract fell from her limp fingers to the floor as she slowly slid into oblivion.

"She's late." Trevor's face reflected nothing.

"The roads," said Sebastian.

"I sent word."

"She'll be here."

Trevor looked out the window. The snarl of carriages and conveyances had finally untangled, and he could see no reason why Grace would not already have arrived at the church. He turned away, his jaw tight, intending to summon a footman to go look for her, when he heard an urgent knock upon the door.

Really, he knew right then that she wasn't coming. Before Jonathon had opened the door and spoken to the unseen man outside, before he had even turned to give Trevor the news that Grace was missing, he knew. Gareth stood by awkwardly. Sebastian looked, as always, impassive, and Jonathon looked sober. The bishop rustled in and tried to say a few words, but Trevor dismissed him immediately.

"Was there a note?"

Jonathon held up his hands in a gesture that indicated he didn't know, so Trevor looked around and said simply, "I suppose we should escape before someone informs that throng in the church that there will be no wedding." He nodded curtly to a footman, who scurried off to summon his carriage to the side door. "I'm going to the Egerton place."

Sebastian spoke up: "I'll stay and see to things here with Gareth." The younger Lloyd nodded in agreement.

"I'll come with you," said Jonathan. "My wife is there, in any case."

The two left and rode without speaking. When they arrived, Greaves opened the door before Trevor knocked. Trevor walked straight to the study, where he knew the family had likely gathered. As he entered, Mercy looked up with red-rimmed eyes. "This is all my fault," she said, then ran past him and up the stairs.

Trevor looked at Bingham Ackerly, who said, "Grace found the betrothal contract. We discovered it on the floor next to her dressing table."

"And Grace?" One might have thought Trevor was asking about the weather. Faith watched him closely, noting the carefully shuttered look in his eyes.

Patience stood and walked toward him. "This was on her dressing table." She handed him a single sheet of paper.

Dear Lord Caldwell, I know you will understand when I say things have transpired rather quickly between us. I hope that you will therefore allow me some time alone to reflect upon the enormity of the steps we are taking. This is not something I treat lightly . . .

He folded the note and placed it inside his jacket pocket. The words *some time alone* were, at least, encouraging. "All right," he said. "You're her family. You know her best. Where might she have gone?"

"Home," came a small voice from the doorway. Mercy had come back quietly. Trevor thought a moment, then said to Bingham, "Mercy is right. Grace is headstrong but not foolish. Take the family back to Pelthamshire. I'll come in a couple of days, unless you send word sooner." He stopped a moment, then continued, "She has asked me for some time alone. The least I can do is to give her that."

Chapter Twenty-eight

Grace awoke with a tortured groan when the rough jarring of the coach suddenly worsened, causing her injured head to bounce painfully against the side of the vehicle. Cautiously opening her eyes, she struggled to sit up, but found she could not. Nor could she move her hands or feet. With that realization, her memory came rushing back.

Hastily stifling a terrified whimper, Grace recalled the horrific feeling of a large male hand unexpectedly clamping across her mouth, and then nothing else from that fleeting moment in her chamber until now. As her throbbing head began to clear, she ascertained that she could not move her arms and legs because something bound them securely together. Worse, much worse, she had absolutely no idea of her whereabouts, nor of how long she had been unconscious. And she discovered, for the first time in her life, that deep fear also made her searingly angry. She clenched her teeth in outraged fury, resolutely ignored the throbbing pain in her head, and began kicking her bound feet with all the strength she could muster against the side of the carriage.

"Hey!" she yelled. "Whoever's out there, you'd better let me out!"

The rocking coach stopped immediately. She heard the

creaking sounds of someone climbing down from the driver's seat, then the shuffling of feet on the ground. A second later the door near her feet opened, and a familiar figure stepped into her line of vision.

"Harry!" Grace gasped as she recognized the man who stood, framed by the moonlight, smiling down at her. Sir Harry Thomas of Pelthamshire.

"Welcome home, Grace," he announced, just as if she stood proudly beside him instead of lying in an ignominious heap on the dusty floor of his coach. "Would you like for me to help you down?"

Incredulous, Grace stared at him, sudden alarm threading through her at the pleasantly vacant look on his face. She echoed, "Would I *like* for you to help me down?" Her voice rose. "You want to know if you can help me down? By all means, Harry, *please* help me down. And when you're finished helping me down, could you also help me to remove these ropes from my hands and feet? Then you could really help by *taking me back home!*" She was nearly shouting by the time she finished. The pounding ache in her head intensified.

Harry shook his head as though at a child throwing a temper tantrum, then bent down and effortlessly scooped her into his arms. "Shhh," he crooned. "You're home now, darling." He turned toward a building that looked vaguely familiar to Grace. She frowned as she tried to recall where she had seen the dwelling before. With a start she recognized the old, no longer used hunting lodge on the very edge of her father's property. She had often played there as a child.

Slightly relieved to know she would be in familiar territory when she managed to escape, Grace settled herself down with a deep, calming breath. "Put me down and untie me, Harry." She spoke softly but firmly, hoping to establish some sort of control over this bizarre situation.

Harry continued walking as though he did not hear her.

"If this is supposed to be some sort of prank, I don't like it at all, and I can promise you my fiancé will like it a good deal less than I."

Harry's vacant face suddenly hardened into a mask of cold displeasure. He glared at her. "You will have no husband other than me," he hissed through clenched teeth. He turned, kicked open the cottage door, and strode inside. He unceremoniously deposited Grace on the only piece of furniture in the room, a stiff-backed wooden chair that offered little more comfort than the floor of the coach.

As he helped her to sit upright in the chair, Grace held her breath, hoping he also planned to untie her wrists and ankles. When he straightened without touching her bonds, then walked over to the window and leaned his elbows on the sill to peer outside, she realized he had no intention of freeing her. A fresh surge of anger coursed through her, but she squelched it with concerted effort, and resolved to try a different tactic. "Harry," she said softly.

At her now meek tone, the man turned away from the window and stood in a shaft of moonlight that allowed her to see his face quite clearly. He regarded her somewhat warily.

Grace purposely allowed her shoulders to droop as if in surrender. She hoped shadow blanketed her face so that he could not tell how utterly disgusted this helpless act made her feel. "I'm really quite stiff and sore from being jostled on the drive over here. I certainly don't mean to complain, but I think that if I could just stretch my arms for a moment, it would really be an enormous relief." She gave him her best look of defenseless appeal, then hung her head and chewed on her lower lip.

Hesitantly he walked toward her, searching her carefully blank, downcast face for any sign of duplicity. Finally he nodded as if satisfied, and loosened the ropes around her arms and feet, unable to believe a mere female could out-smart him.

Rubbing her chafed wrists, Grace slowly stood on weak legs, careful not to let the triumph she felt show on her face at accomplishing her small goal. Harry kept a watchful eye on her as she walked around the large room. It was empty except for the lone wooden chair and a small box that lay on the floor beneath one of the windows.

"You know, Harry, I can remember when I used to play in here as a child," she commented, smiling a bit and keeping her tone deliberately light.

A strange glow crept into Harry's eyes. He smiled back at her, a frightening smile that chilled Grace. "I knew that you would remember our promise, darling, just as soon as I brought you here." His eyes grew more demented.

"Our promise?" she asked cautiously.

His smile began to fade. "It was here that we first prom-ised to marry each other. Of course you remember that." He looked suddenly annoyed.

And then Grace recognized him. His name was not Sir Harold Thomas, as the villagers had all been told. "Henry?" she said incredulously.

"See?" He smiled again. "You do remember."

Grace's stomach lurched. The head trauma combined with the events of the day finally took their toll. She cov-ered her mouth with a hand and made a mad dash for the closed door. "Hey!" Henry yelled, grabbing her arm as she tried to push past him. He threatened, "Do you want me to tie you up again?"

Grace struggled to free herself with growing desperation. "Please," she implored. "I'm going to be sick!"

For the first time Henry noted her pallor. He scowled and pushed her impatiently ahead of him across the room and out the door.

Grace fell at once to her knees in the tall grass beside the doorway, her slim shoulders heaving violently with her stomach's efforts to empty itself. After a moment she stood and walked unsteadily back into the building, a sheen of cold perspiration breaking out on her face. She sank back into the chair and dropped her head into her trembling hands.

"Do you always have such a weak stomach?" Henry asked crossly. "Have you been ill, Grace?"

She shook her head miserably. "No, of course not. I've not eaten in a while, and—" She broke off at the look of blazing fury dawning on his face. She cringed inwardly as he stalked across the room to where she sat.

He leaned down, menacing and threatening. "Are you with child, Grace?" he asked, his tone dangerous. "Don't tell me you've lain with him."

Grace lifted her chin a notch and refused to answer, two bright spots of angry color flashing on her cheeks. She stared back belligerently at him, no longer able to maintain the facade of friendship. Henry cursed under his breath, grabbed her arms, jerked them painfully back behind the chair, and began to tie them tightly together. Grace did her best to pull away, a futile effort in her weakened condition. Despite her struggles, he tied her arms firmly behind her back and secured her ankles to the legs of the chair.

Grace shifted uncomfortably, then looked up at Henry with renewed ire. "Why are you doing this to me?"

Harry smiled bitterly. "You were supposed to marry *me*, Grace, supposed to carry *my* son."

She pulled at her ropes again. "And this is supposed to convince me to marry you?"

His sardonic smile turned into a sneer. "No, Grace. Not anymore. You're ruined now that you carry another man's brat in your belly." He waved a hand in her direction. "This is just to keep you here until we can be together in the only way left to us."

She narrowed her eyes. "What do you mean?" she asked, not bothering to deny his accusations.

Henry walked back to the window and bent to pick up the polished wooden box. He rubbed his hands lovingly across the top as though it contained a great treasure. "Once I'd heard you'd agreed to marry that damned earl, I knew there was only one thing I could do." He slowly opened the box.

Grace sucked in her breath at the sight of the two gleaming dueling pistols that lay inside, snugly encased in soft black velvet. A knot of cold fear settled in her stomach.

"You see, darling? There's one for you, and one for me." He snapped the case shut. "But not quite yet." He tucked the wooden box under his arm, picked up the lone candle from the floor, and strode across the room toward the door.

"Where are you going?" Grace cried, hating herself for sounding so terrified.

Henry did not answer. He snatched her fallen veil from the floor and used it to gag her. After completing that odious task, he did not even look back; he simply stepped out the front door and closed it with a resounding thud, leaving Grace to the torture of her imagination in the dark silence. A moment later the sound of the shabby coach pulling away broke the stillness.

Resolutely Grace buried the panic that threatened to rise and take over. As the rumble of the carriage wheels faded, she began to work on the ropes that bound her wrists.

Chapter Twenty-nine

$\mathcal{T}$he late spring full moon was just rising in the inky night sky when Trevor's shiny black carriage pulled into the short circular drive in front of the Ackerly home. As his conveyance came to a rattling halt, Trevor slammed the door open and erupted from within, striding up the wide front steps and sweeping into the house. Ignoring the butler's greeting and brushing aside the hand outstretched to take his cape, Trevor stalked grimly across the hall to the drawing room, where he heard voices engaged in conversation. Sebastian followed more slowly.

The summons had come at midmorning. Bingham had wasted no time when it was determined that Grace had not come to the house in Pelthamshire. He'd hastily penned the necessary note and given it to the man Trevor sent along for that very purpose. Riding hard on dark, dangerous roads, he'd reached London in record time. Trevor sent for Sebastian, and the two had been on their way to the small village by early afternoon.

His gaze swept the room. He saw Patience reach blindly for one of the twins' hands. The other twin, he supposed Charity, glared angrily at him, as though she somehow held him responsible for her missing sister. Faith simply stood with a trembling hand pressed against her lips.

Mercy slipped in from the foyer. She took a step toward her father, then turned to Trevor. "Did you find Grace?" she asked.

A muscle worked in his jaw. He looked down at her but couldn't answer.

A little frantically, she looked at Sebastian. "Where is my sister?"

"We aren't sure, urchin," the duke answered.

She stood frozen for a moment, then abruptly rushed from the room. She pushed past both men, the beginning of a sob trailing in her wake. The sound of her running footsteps echoed loudly through the foyer, followed by the loud slam of the heavy oak door as she fled from the house.

Bingham started to follow, but Sebastian held up a restraining hand. "I'll go," he offered quietly. He exchanged a speaking look with Trevor, silently communicating that he wondered if Mercy knew more about Grace's disappearance than she had told the others. "Does she have a favorite place she often goes?" Sebastian asked.

Amity spoke up softly. "Sometimes Mercy takes the forest path from behind the stables to the wide part of the stream when she wants to be alone."

Sebastian gifted her with a grateful, encouraging smile, then took his leave. His long black cape billowed out behind him, his booted feet echoing a deep staccato as he crossed the hardwood foyer.

Patience stepped forward and looked at Trevor. "Please, my lord, tell us what you think happened to Grace." Her voice, thick with worry, sounded strangled.

Trevor shook his head in mystified frustration, unable to provide much more information. "Cleo has heard nothing from her. I made inquiries into possible means of transportation from the city, but nobody I spoke with remembers a lone woman of Grace's description on any hired conveyance." He looked at Bingham. "None of the Egerton horses are missing. I begin to wonder if she left of her own accord."

Faith spoke up then, her logical mind leaping nimbly to the glaring holes in his brief explanation. Her forehead furrowed in concentration as she asked, "Did anyone think to search the rest of Aunt Cleo's house?"

Trevor looked sheepish. "No, we didn't," he admitted.

Faith gave him a look of patient tolerance. "Grace has no enemies, my lord. Perhaps she never actually left London."

A sense of blessed relief began washing through him. Grace was likely still in the city this very moment. He shook his head and swore under his breath before he remembered the people around him. Christ, he had behaved like a lunatic. The time for speculation had passed. He had to get back to London right away, to find her as quickly as possible. To learn the truth.

Trevor turned on his heel and strode from the room. Unaware of his rudeness, or of the alarm his behavior was once more causing the assembled Ackerlys, he made his way from the house without another word.

The twins broke into excited chatter. Patience and her father exchanged worried, frightened looks. Only Faith remained unperturbed. "Grace is fine," she assured her family calmly. "Lord Caldwell is still unused to her unpredictable nature. That's all."

It was the first time in years the family could remember Faith's unquestionable logic failing her.

At first Sebastian did not see Mercy when he walked outside. He stood on the steps, patiently allowing his eyes to adjust to the darkness. Once he could discern details in the dim moonlight, he swept his glittering golden gaze across the woods bordering the property. After a moment he turned decisively and headed toward the stables. He was rewarded when he spied Mercy outside the far end of the low building. She was riding bareback, astride the same showy gelding she had ridden the dark night all those weeks ago when his coach had nearly killed her. Without a backward glance she urged her mount into a gallop, heading for a small bridle path that led through the woods.

Quickly Sebastian ran into the stable and began to prepare a mount for himself, knowing that only with the advantage of a saddle could he possibly outride the little hellion. She rode as if she were born to it, and he hoped he did not lose too much ground in the time it took to saddle the stallion. He had nearly finished when Trevor strode in.

"I'm taking a horse and going back to London, Thorne," he announced, a muscle working grimly in his jaw. "Will you bring back my coach and my fiancée on the off chance I'm wrong, and that she hasn't actually been in town the whole time?"

Sebastian nodded as he led his mount out into the corral and swung effortlessly up into the saddle. He gave Trevor a last hard look, then dug his heels sharply into the stallion's flanks. He galloped toward the bridle path down which Mercy had disappeared.

Trevor watched him go, then finished saddling his own horse and mounted. He directed the gelding down the drive to the London road, which ran along the Ackerlys' extensive property line for nearly a mile before forking at the inn. The left fork ran farther along the northern boundary of the Ackerly holdings, while the right fork headed east and then north, away from Pelthamshire and ultimately to London, where he hoped to find Grace.

Trevor reached the split in the road and pulled up. He looked toward the inn, trying to decide whether stopping and asking the locals within if they had seen Grace would have any value. After only a moment's thought, he rejected the idea. He turned his mount eastward, then pulled up in surprise. Behind him, from within the tall hedges that bordered the road and separated it from the Ackerly property, Trevor heard a distant, frightened scream. And then, ominously, the sound was cut off.

Sebastian galloped smoothly along the path. As the dark foliage whipped by him in the darkness, his eyes surveyed it for any sign of another path that branched away from the one he followed. He did not see one, however, before he reached the tall hedge that marked the boundary of the Ackerly property, where the path suddenly ended. A break in the hedge led him out onto a road. Looking to his right, Sebastian realized he had emerged on the left fork of the road that ran past the Ackerly drive. He could see the lights of the inn quite clearly in the distance, and he could also see the silhouette of Hunt mounted upon a black horse.

Sebastian realized Mercy could not have gone that way, for Trevor would undoubtedly have seen her and would have stopped her. That left only the road continuing west, which led eventually to Blackthorne Manor. He pulled gently on the left rein to turn his mount in that direction, preparing to urge the stallion into a gallop. The next instant, a terrified scream shattered the night.

Grace's head jerked upward when she heard the scream. It sounded so close.

Suddenly she heard scuffling noises outside the cottage. Henry thrust open the door and struggled into the room grasping Mercy. The child kicked and squirmed with all her strength, both hands furiously tugging and scratching at the hand he had clamped across her mouth to keep her from screaming again.

He managed to drag her inside and close the door, but not before one of Mercy's booted feet connected painfully with his shin. With a savage curse, Henry dumped her in a heap on the bare floor.

Mercy glared up at her captor, her small chin set at a mutinous angle, before she looked away and spotted her sister. She scrambled across the floor, closer. Her eyes widened in shock when she observed the thick knots that held Grace captive.

"My God, Grace, are you all right?" she asked breathlessly, scanning her sister's face with worried eyes. Grace nodded mutely from behind her gag. Her blue eyes stared at Mercy, hard and determined, glittering in the light of the single candle. Mercy reached up to pull the gag from her sister's mouth.

"Stop!" Henry commanded. His loud voice boomed in the stillness. Mercy flinched and snatched back her hands. He shook his head and sighed. "You're a rather unwelcome complication, brat."

"What are you doing here, Sir Harry?" Mercy asked, looking up at him in confusion. "Why did you tie Grace up?" Her hands hesitantly moved to the knots around her sister's ankles.

"Don't touch those!" Henry yelled, then visibly composed himself and raised his eyebrows. "Inquisitive little twit, aren't you?" He straightened from where he leaned against the wall and came toward them with slow, measured steps. Mercy began to shrink back, then bravely straightened her spine, mustering all the dignity she could while still seated on the filthy floor.

Henry chuckled. "You Ackerly sisters have so much spirit, don't you?" He stopped walking and stood before them, tapping a long finger thoughtfully on his chin. "The real question is what I should do with you now." He shook his head regretfully. "I'll have to give it some thought, as I have only two loaded pistols. I'd not planned on reloading. In the meantime, of course, I'm afraid I'll have to detain you.

I'm sure you understand." He picked up a spare length of rope and bent over.

Mercy's mind swung instantly from confusion to alarm when she heard him mention pistols. She scrambled frantically backward in an effort to get away, but he caught her easily. He grabbed her arm in a punishing grip and shoved her back down beside her sister's chair. "Don't try my patience, Mercy," he growled, his demented face inches from hers.

Mercy's fear and confusion abruptly vanished. She spit in his face.

Rage instantly mottled Henry's features; he turned a furious purplish hue in the semidarkness. Without another word he backhanded her with so much force her head snapped to the side. She cried out and tasted blood where her inner cheek split against her teeth. Never in her young life could Mercy remember anyone hitting her. With a pitiful little whimper, she subsided and allowed him to secure her to the legs of the chair with no further struggle.

Henry stood and wiped his face. "Somebody should have taken a strap to that brat long ago," he told Grace. He stopped suddenly and stood quite still, looking toward the window.

Grace heard it then, too: the staccato sound of hoofbeats approaching the cabin, more than one horse, moving fast. Instantly hope soared in her heart, and she looked swiftly down at Mercy. Her dazed sister still sat with eyes downcast. Grace watched Henry bend and quickly gag Mercy with his cravat. He blew out the candle and picked up the box holding the dueling pistols. He extracted one and stashed it inside his coat, then held the other loosely in one hand as he opened the door. He gave Grace a last warning glance, then went outside.

Henry's eyes focused intently on the path that led from the woods. He ran to Mercy's unsaddled horse and sent it trotting off into the trees with a sharp smack on the hindquarters. The dappled gray gelding had just disappeared from view when two riders appeared from around the bend. Hurriedly Henry hid behind his leg the hand that held the pistol. He immediately recognized Trevor Caldwell on one of the Ackerly mounts. The other man, though unfamiliar to Henry, also rode one of Bingham Ackerly's horses. Cursing inwardly, Henry gave the men a disarming smile as they pulled up before him.

Inside the darkened lodge, Grace pulled her hands free of the ropes she had managed to loosen when Henry left her alone earlier. She scraped the gag from her mouth, then bent down and went to work on the ropes at her ankles. She winced at the burning sensation from the chafed skin on her wrists, and vaguely wondered whether she would scar. "Mercy," she hissed urgently.

Her sister looked up, a purpling bruise already showing on her left cheek. Her eyes widened as she saw Grace kick away the ropes that had bound her ankles then kneel to remove the gag from Mercy's mouth.

"My knife," Mercy whispered as soon as she was able.

Quickly Grace pulled out the knife Mercy habitually carried in her boot. As she heard the hoofbeats outside draw closer and stop, Grace hastily sliced through the rest of Mercy's bonds. "Hurry," she urged, helping the child to her feet. "Before they leave." Together the sisters raced for the door, opened it, and stumbled outside.

"Good evening, gentlemen," Henry said with a wide smile. "Rather a dark night to be out for a ride. Is there anything I can do for you?"

Trevor studied the man. Something about his stance instinctively bothered Trevor. He looked somewhat familiar, and Trevor searched his memory, trying to place him. Finally he did. This was Sir Harry Thomas, he recalled, the soldier Grace had artfully avoided by colliding with him on the evening they met. The man he'd punched.

"Good evening, Thomas," he said, his eyes now scanning the surrounding tree line. "We're looking for Mercy Ackerly. We thought we heard a scream coming from this direction."

"I heard it, too." Henry nodded. "I was just coming out to investigate. I haven't seen little Mercy, though. I was under the impression that the entire Ackerly family was in London."

Sebastian looked around the clearing. "Isn't this Ackerly land?" His eyes narrowed on the unkempt lodge.

"Why, yes, it is," said Henry. "Bingham allows me to use this old lodge whenever I feel like hunting. Truth is, if I didn't use it, nobody would, what with Bingham having a whole passel of daughters. Wonderful neighbors, the Ackerlys."

The two men on horseback nodded, then exchanged a glance and prepared to leave. "If you would, Thomas, please keep an eye out for Mercy," said Trevor. Henry nodded again, still smiling, and stepped back toward the building.

At that moment, the door to the cabin crashed open.

Chapter Thirty

*T*revor's eyes widened in shock. Sebastian froze in stunned disbelief. Both men dismounted as Grace and Mercy stumbled out of the cottage and into the moonlight. "Trevor!" Grace choked, relief evident on her face.

Unfortunately, Henry stood between the girls and the men. At the sound of the cabin door crashing open, he spun around. In their flight from the cabin, neither Grace nor Mercy had taken notice of him standing just outside the door. They'd focused on reaching Trevor, Sebastian, and the promise of safety.

With an angry snarl, Henry lunged for the girls. He missed Grace entirely, but caught Mercy's wrist. Forcibly he pulled her from her sister's grasp. Mercy gave a small, involuntary yelp as she was hauled suddenly in front of him. She stiffened, and everyone went silent. The color drained from Mercy's face as she felt the cold, hard metal of Henry's pistol press against her forehead.

Grace fell, sobbing, into the refuge of Trevor's arms, then realized she no longer grasped Mercy's hand. She turned to look for the younger girl and gasped in horror. Henry held her little sister in front of his body like a shield. Mercy stared back at her with huge, frightened eyes.

Sebastian took a slow step toward Henry and Mercy.

Henry leveled his demented gaze upon the duke. "Don't even try it," he warned. He waved the pistol in Trevor and Grace's direction. "Move away from that horse."

Grace, frozen in fear for her sister, felt Trevor tug her away from his mount. Sebastian stood his ground. Henry quickly brought the muzzle back to Mercy's forehead. "Now!" he thundered.

With a deep scowl Sebastian moved aside, his hawklike, reassuring eyes never leaving the young girl's. Mercy swallowed hard and nodded imperceptibly at him. As though she had absorbed a measure of his strength, some of the fear faded from her eyes, replaced by a look of grim determination. As Grace saw her sister's expression change, she bit her lip and clutched at Trevor's arm.

Carefully keeping Mercy's body between himself and the others, Henry edged toward Sebastian's horse. With a mocking smile he removed the barrel from Mercy's forehead and jammed it into her ribs. She cried out in pain as he pushed her up onto the horse's back.

"You'll have to excuse us," he said in a pleasant, sugary tone. "I'm sure you understand. We really must be going." He moved as if to swing up onto the horse behind Mercy. For just a moment the pistol pointed at the ground. Mercy saw her chance and kicked out suddenly. Instant pandemonium erupted.

The contact of Mercy's foot with his wrist caused Henry's finger to tighten convulsively on the trigger. The gun discharged into the soil between the horse's legs with a sudden loud bang. The blast erupting beneath the already skittish stallion now spooked him completely. The animal reared up in sudden fear, dumping Henry heavily to the ground. Mercy frantically clutched handfuls of the horse's mane. Somehow she managed to hang on as the frightened horse bolted from the clearing. The loose reins flapped, useless and dangerous, around his running feet.

Mercy tried unsuccessfully to seize them with her right hand while desperately hanging on with her left.

Sebastian shot an anxious look at Trevor, who shouted, "Go!" with an outflung arm in the direction the horse had fled. Without a backward glance, Sebastian leaped on Trevor's mount to pursue the helpless girl. Grace watched Sebastian disappear from the clearing while Trevor purposefully strode toward Henry.

Just before Trevor reached him, Henry rolled over. He scrambled to his feet and reached inside his coat to retrieve his second pistol. Standing and drawing in one motion, he leveled the wide muzzle at Trevor's midsection. Trevor froze.

"Back off," Henry snarled. Bits of grass clung to his disheveled hair, and dirt smeared his face. "Don't make me shoot you!"

Trevor's eyes narrowed. His jaw clenched and his nostrils flared as he stared into Henry's eyes with a look of pure hatred. Henry's thumb calmly locked the hammer back, filling the taut silence with a threatening, metallic click.

Oddly, at the ominous sound Grace felt the fear drain from her mind, replaced with calm purpose. Set and determined, she began edging away from the men, sidestepping out of Henry's lines of fire and sight. Her eyes probed the clearing, questing, searching for something, anything she could use as a weapon. The moonlight illuminated a sharp-edged stone about the size of her fist a couple of feet away. Swiftly she bent and scooped it up. Then she spun and threw the rock in the madman's direction.

At Grace's sudden movement, Henry turned toward her. Her thrown rock sailed uselessly by, and he swung the barrel of his pistol around to bear upon her. There was a change in his expression. The madman closed one eye, as if taking aim, and minutely adjusted his pistol, leveling it at Grace's abdomen.

Trevor sprang. His fingers locked on Henry's arm in a steely grasp, and the momentum of his body weight and motion carried both men to the ground. The two hurled curses at each other and wrestled for control of the weapon.

Grace stood frozen, desperate to help, paralyzed by the realization that she could not. A strangled cry tore from her throat as she heard the men grunting and swearing. She wanted nothing more than to flee, but instead she moved closer, her eyes seeking out Trevor's face in the moonlight.

Henry grasped the pistol firmly with both hands. Trevor kept the fingers of his left hand locked around Henry's right wrist, pummeling his adversary's face with his right. Blood erupted from Henry's nose and mouth. Ignoring the blows, with a strength born of madness the man slowly brought his pistol to bear on Trevor's face. With a mighty heave, Trevor tugged down sharply on the barrel. The weapon vanished between them. Henry kicked out and rolled atop his opponent, spitting into Trevor's face, blinding his foe with blood and saliva.

The second she lost sight of the weapon, Grace's heart constricted with fear. An instant later the gun went off with a sudden, muffled bang. Her hand flew to her mouth in an impossible attempt to hold back a scream. For a long moment neither man moved. Then Trever gave a mighty push, kicking and shoving his motionless opponent from atop him. Blood covered the earl's face and chest.

At the sight of the stain spreading on her fiancé's white shirtfront, Grace gasped. She raced to Trevor's side. He tried to sit up, but she pushed him back down. Her hands tore at the fabric and clawed at the studs of his shirt in a terrified attempt to find the wound.

"Grace," he said.

"Shhh, darling, please. Just let me look at you." Her fumbling fingers finally managed to unfasten the uncooperative studs. With trembling hands she impatiently pushed his shirt open. Her fingers searched, roving over the bunched muscles and planes of his chest and stomach. She raised eyes filled with thankful tears to his grimly smiling ones. "It wasn't you," she choked out. Almost against her will, she turned toward Henry's still figure.

Trevor swiftly reached up and caught her face in his hands, forcing her once more to meet his eyes. "Don't look, darling. There's no need. You're fine, and I'm fine, and that's all that matters."

Grace began trembling all over. Trevor folded his arms tenderly about her as she buried her face in his neck. She began to feel safe once more. Against his collar she mumbled, "I never thought I'd see you again."

He sat up and pulled her onto his lap. "Don't be silly," he murmured in a soothing voice, stroking her tangled hair. "Although I do wish you'd stop going to such extreme lengths to avoid becoming my wife."

Grace pulled back indignantly, preparing to offer heated protest, when she spied Trevor's tender smile. "After all," he said with a victorious smirk, "I *did* win our wager."

Grace could not be angry with him for the gentle gibe, could not even find annoyance at the fact that blood had soaked her hands and dress. She simply took his face between her hands and kissed him softly. Relief flooded through her, expressing itself in happy tears that cut stark-white paths through the dust and grime covering her cheeks. "Trevor?"

"I know, darling." He smiled softly. "I know."

They turned in unison as slow hoofbeats approached the clearing. A familiar pair emerged from the trees, mounted together on the gelding, leading the lathered stallion behind them. Mercy was laid quite comfortably across a grim-faced Sebastian's lap, her arms wrapped happily about his neck. The duke stared fixedly ahead and looked slightly

Chapter Thirty-one

$\mathcal{A}$ hush fell over the enormous room. The crowd stared as four of the most powerful and influential men in England solemnly took their places at the front of the church, garbed in their finest clothing. The organ was silent for a long moment as the bridal procession assembled at the back of the church. An occasional sniffle punctured the silence, either from an emotional guest or a disappointed mama who had held out a final hope for her own daughter. Then the music began again, soaring through the church, filling the enormous room with sound. One by one Patience, Faith, and Amanda walked slowly down the aisle. When they had each taken their places opposite the men, Grace appeared at the end of the aisle on her father's arm. The pair started slowly on their journey to the front of the church. Little by little the dreadful knot that had formed in the pit of Trevor's stomach dissolved, replaced by a feeling of warm, possessive pride.

She was truly a vision to behold. Almost impossibly beautiful, she came toward him with regal grace, her head held high and her luminous blue eyes locked with his. *I did it,* he thought. *Somehow I made her love me.* His heart quickened at the thought, and his eyes softened with the wonder of it all. Before he knew it—though not soon enough—she stood beside him. Bingham Ackerly gently placed her small hand in his large one. Trevor smiled tenderly down at his bride, and they turned together to speak the vows that would make them man and wife.

Grace repeated her pledge in a strong, clear voice, her eyes never leaving his. Trevor felt something wrench inside him, and when it came time for him to say his own words, his voice caught on the word *love*. He paused a moment, swallowed hard past the lump of emotion in his throat, and continued. Grace squeezed his hand.

After the words were spoken, Trevor leaned over to softly kiss his wife and to whisper to her in a voice still choked with feeling, "You look absolutely ravishing, my lady."

Grace gave her husband an impish little smile, then stood on tiptoe to kiss him back. She replied in a low tone of mock solemnity, "I'm very glad you approve, my lord." She waited a heartbeat, then whispered, "I very nearly wore my Grant Radnor costume, you see."

The picture *that* statement brought to mind wrung a startled laugh from Trevor. Grace remained serenely composed. Still laughing, Trevor offered her his arm and they turned to walk together for the first time as husband and wife. And for weeks after the ceremony, those lucky enough to sit close to the aisle speculated as to why, when the Countess of Huntwick sailed blithely down the aisle, her face tranquil, her new husband walked beside her, his shoulders shaking with mirth.

They decided to hold the lavish reception at Trevor's town house for the sake of convenience. His ballroom, much larger than Cleo Egerton's, would more easily accommodate such a large guest list. The town house also contained more available chambers to house the many overnight guests who had come for the ceremony.

Grace and Trevor had stood in the receiving line for well

over an hour with their attendants, Aunt Cleo, and Bingham Ackerly, when the number of arriving guests finally began to dwindle. Gratefully, Grace accepted a glass of champagne and a gentle kiss from her husband, then rubbed her cheeks where the muscles ached from the effort of continuous smiling. She took a rejuvenating sip from the glass, leaned toward Trevor, and whispered, "Would it be all right for us to leave now?"

Trevor was pleasantly surprised. He had expected maidenly fears to have a prominent place in her mind this evening. "I think it is a bit early yet, darling. There would be talk, you know."

Grace sighed. "I suppose it *would* be rather rude," she said. She looked around the crowded room, but brightened as a thought occurred to her. "There are a lot of people here. Perhaps we wouldn't be missed?" She gave him a hopeful look.

Trevor couldn't believe she meant what he thought she did. Could she really be so eager to begin their wedding night? He searched her smiling face, but found nothing but love and trust in her shining blue eyes. She *had* grown up in the country, he rationalized to himself. She had likely watched her father breed horses all her life, and had, perhaps, even helped with the delivery of some. That would, of course, explain her frank attitude toward the consummation of their marriage. The knowledge rather relieved him. Although he looked forward to initiating his innocent young wife to the joys of the marriage bed, he did *not* enjoy the thought of frightening her. He smiled down at her, a wry grin on his face. "I'm quite certain our absence would be remarked upon."

"You're probably right," she said with a resigned little sigh. She looked up at her handsome husband and felt a sudden surge of complete, carefree joy. Playfully, she tapped him on the shoulder, then backed a couple small steps away from him. She clasped her hands innocently behind her back, an impish smile lighting her face. "Well, if we can't leave yet, I think we should make every effort to enjoy the time we must spend here, shouldn't we?"

Trevor looked into her dancing eyes dubiously. He took a step toward her as she continued to back away. Grace held up a warning hand. He stopped. "You're it," she gleefully informed him with a jaunty toss of her head.

A smile lit his face. He caught her joyous mood. "I'm what?"

"It," said Grace patiently. She backed two more steps away. A worried look crossed her face, and she took one step back toward him, suddenly remembering that he had never had brothers and sisters to play games with as a child. Staying just out of his reach, she explained: "You see, *I* just tagged *you*, and now *you* must tag *me*. Then I will be it. But you have to catch me first." With that, she spun away in a flurry of dove-colored silk skirts. She vanished with astonishing swiftness into the crowd.

Utterly enchanted, Trevor stared at the spot where he had last seen his bride of only a few hours, his face wreathed in a wide, silly grin. *I'm it,* he thought, and chuckled to himself.

Gareth materialized at his side. "Something amusing, Hunt?" He squinted and peered in the same direction as Trevor, but saw only a cross-looking old dowager in a shocking orange turban adorned with a large lime-green feather. He found the sight far more frightening than amusing. He looked back at his friend. "Care to let me in on the joke?"

Trevor's eyes scanned the room in clear delight. "I am it," he informed Gareth gleefully, then set off across the ballroom in search of his irrepressible countess.

Gareth watched him go and shook his head. Marriage, from what he had seen, had a very real tendency to make fools out of perfectly logical men. He caught sight of the Duke of Blackthorne engaged in reluctant conversation with a very nervous-looking young lady. Mercy Ackerly stood off to the side and watched, scowling. He decided to join them. Sebastian, he knew, wholeheartedly shared his opinion on the subject of marriage.

Three hours later, Trevor's amusement had nearly vanished. He'd had no idea—because he had never had cause to consider such a thought—how many places one could find to hide in a crowded ballroom. More than once, certain he had caught Grace, he'd found himself in possession of one of her laughing sisters, whose help in the game Grace had obviously enlisted.

For the first half hour she kept him busy by dispatching servants to his side, ostensibly to inquire about the various fictitious needs of some of the guests. He'd finally caught on when he glimpsed Grace speaking to a footman across the room, then pointing in his direction. Trevor caught his wife's eye and glowered good-naturedly at her, then dispatched the footman to have his problems solved by the capable Wilson. When he looked up again, Grace had vanished. Trevor found Wilson himself, and instructed him to order all the servants to ignore the countess's attempts at diversion. To Wilson's credit, the man's expression did not change at the odd command, though the corners of his mouth twitched once or twice. Trevor decided to pretend he hadn't seen.

Next, Grace resorted to using their friends and family to intercept and hold his attention, a new relation appearing each time he concluded a conversation and renewed his attempt to search for her. Trevor did not find much success in fending off these interlopers. Short of being rude, he simply could not walk away in the middle of someone else's speech. After yet another hour passed, he realized that most of the room's occupants now knew exactly what Grace was up to. Worse, they knew she was besting him.

Trevor changed his strategy. Each time one of Grace's saboteurs waylaid him, he launched into conversation on whatever boring subject occurred to him, making the intruder positively yearn to be away from him. This time *his* unsuspecting audience found themselves held captive. Whenever somebody tried to make an excuse to leave, Trevor would address that person directly, thus making it impossible for them to leave without appearing rude themselves. After another thirty minutes passed, word got around to avoid the groom at all costs. Trevor finally found himself blessedly free of their restrictive company.

However, the game was old. Taking his bride to bed now loomed foremost in his mind, but he had no idea where she had taken it into her pretty little head to hide. He knew she had not left the ballroom. Grace would never shirk the responsibility of attending to their guests, but exactly *where* she performed that duty was a mystery. So he decided not to look for her at all. He simply walked to the outer edge of the dance floor, glanced once around the room, then stepped around a column and disappeared.

Until that very moment, Grace's plan to evade Trevor had worked. She had kept him in sight, knowing his exact location at all times. But momentarily distracted by a distant cousin of Trevor's who commented on her gown, she looked away. When she looked back again, he had vanished. And for the first time all evening, Grace knew her husband had the upper hand. A delicious thrill coursed through her. With the knowledge that he likely now knew *her* precise location, she began looking for him, beginning with the place she had seen him last.

Trevor watched from his vantage point behind the pillar, waiting patiently as she approached. When she drew even with the column, he slipped quietly around it and came up behind her.

The hairs on the back of Grace's neck prickled. She whirled and found herself swept, helplessly laughing, into his arms. "Got you!" Trevor declared triumphantly. He turned and strode purposefully toward the ballroom steps, holding Grace firmly in his arms so that she would not escape again.

He nudged his way through the crowd, excusing himself as he went, to the great entertainment of everyone they passed. When he reached the wide, shallow steps, he took them two at time, then turned at the top to face the amused crowd. As the music came to a discordant halt and the whispering died down, he spoke.

"Grace and I would like to thank you for being our guests tonight. Please feel free to stay as long as you wish and enjoy yourselves." He smiled down at his wife, who beamed back at him happily, then looked again into the ballroom. "We do hope, however, that you will excuse us. Say, 'Good night, everybody,' " he told Grace.

"Good night, everybody!" She waved obediently; then Trevor turned and they left, amid laughter, applause, and shouts of encouragement.

Chapter Thirty-two

*M*y goodness," said Grace with a breathless laugh as her husband carried her effortlessly down the corridor to the suite that housed the connecting chambers of the Earl and Countess of Huntwick. "Our guests seemed almost happy to see us go."

Trevor raised sardonic brows. "I believe they may have expected us to go sooner."

"They did? But it's early yet." Grace wrinkled her brow in momentary confusion as she thought of the normally late hours the ton kept when in town, then shrugged happily. She nuzzled her face into Trevor's neck.

He considered the fact that she had been raised, motherless, by an elder sister who remained a spinster, and realized Grace might not have the best grasp on the concept of a wedding night and all it entailed. At the thought of her innocence, tenderness washed through him, and when they reached the door that opened into her chamber, Trevor easily hoisted her slight weight over to one arm and opened the double doors with a flourish. He carried her inside and gently set her down on her feet.

She looked around in wonder at the spacious, elegant room, unable to believe that it actually belonged to her simply because she had married this wonderful man. She turned shining eyes on her husband. "It's beautiful, my lord," she murmured.

Acres of pale green Aubusson carpeting covered the floor making Grace long to kick off her slippers and peel down her stockings, just so she could curl her toes deep into the velvety pile. She ran her fingers across the marble-topped vanity table to her right. Skirted in a sumptuous mint-and-pale-peach stripe, the fabric matched the draperies at the high windows and the coverlet on the large bed that stood in the center of the room. With a little laugh, she ran across the room and leaped onto the bed, rolling across linens fashioned of the softest silk, edged with scalloped cutwork lace.

Suddenly she remembered she was not alone in the lovely room. She flushed as she sat up and looked shyly at her widely grinning husband. Somewhat abashed at her childish behavior, she wriggled off the enormous bed, then turned to smooth the rumpled covers, allowing her cheeks a moment to cool in the process. She faced him when she felt his hands on her shoulders.

"I take it you like your chamber, my lady?"

Impulsively, Grace stood on tiptoe and threw her arms around his neck. "I shall never wish to leave this room," she declared with a laugh.

"Oh, but you must, my love," Trevor said gravely, inclining his head to the right. "That door over there connects this chamber with mine. I'm afraid I'd get rather lonely in there without you." He moved closer and lifted her chin with his finger, looking down at her in a way that made her heart race. She stood on tiptoe and pressed her lips against his.

"Can you keep a secret?" he asked. The words were a whisper against her lips, his tone confiding. Grace nodded gravely.

A light came into his eyes. "I'm rather frightened of the dark."

A sudden image of her large, powerful husband peeping from beneath his covers popped into Grace's head. Stifling a giggle, she looked up at him with mock sympathy, and laid a hand on his cheek. "What is it that scares you, my lord?" Her voice quavered with amusement.

He pulled her closer still, and slowly ran the tip of his tongue along the crease between her lips. As her knees turned to liquid, he murmured, "Monsters."

"My goodness," Grace said, pulling back. "Monsters!" She opened her eyes wide in feigned shock.

He nodded. "Great, big, furry ones. With claws."

Grace ran a finger down his jawline to softly tap his lower lip. "And where do these horrid monsters stay when it isn't dark?"

Trevor drew his head back and gave her a look that plainly said she had insulted his intelligence. "Why, under the bed, of course!"

She nodded sagely. "Of course," she returned, with such a grave look that Trevor gave in. With a shout of laughter, he scooped her up under her arms and lifted her over his head, spinning her around and around until she breathlessly begged him to put her down.

A small sound near the door made them both stop laughing and look around. Trevor set Grace lightly back on her feet. Becky had come quietly into the room to help prepare Grace for bed. The plump maid curtsied, still a bit self-conscious around the earl, not yet used to her new station.

Trevor took a reluctant step away from Grace, then turned and walked across the room to the connecting door. "After you've dressed for bed, my lady, would you care to join me for a drink in my chamber?" She nodded hesitantly; he opened the door and went into the room beyond.

Grace turned toward Becky with a helpless smile. "Well," she said, her stomach beginning to feel strangely jumpy. "I suppose those are for me." She indicated the frothy night-gown and dressing gown laid across a large, overstuffed chair in the near corner.

She had been looking forward to this night, but after she changed into the new clothing, Grace became certain that some sort of horrible mistake had occurred. The gown that Becky helped her into was positively transparent, and the matching robe didn't do much to help. She recalled the night he had come to her chamber after she was ill. With a sudden rush of clarity, she realized that the reason the gown was so filmy was that it was a nearly unnecessary garment. Suddenly nervous, she sat stiff and silent at the dressing table, unable even to gossip pleasantly as she usually did while Becky finished brushing her hair. She did not even notice at first when the maid set the brush down and left the room.

With clarity came logic. Trevor had undressed her that night. It stood to reason he intended to do so again tonight. This time, she was not yet passion-drugged and senseless. Tonight, she would participate willingly. The thought gave her a tiny thrill—until she allowed her thoughts to follow a natural progression. Her eyes widened in the mirror. If she were going to be undressed and in her husband's bed, wouldn't he also be unclothed? Her mind skittered away from *that* certainty.

After several moments passed, Grace stood. She wiped her damp palms on the sides of her gown and stared with growing trepidation at the door across the room, wishing fervently for her much more serviceable dressing gown, already packed for tomorrow's early morning trip to the Willows. But she took a deep breath, resolutely squared her shoulders, and marched across the room to knock firmly on the connecting door.

At her husband's pleasant, "Come in, my lady," she opened the door, slipped inside, and quickly closed it behind her, pressing her back against it and clutching the doorknob as though it were her lifeline to safety. She looked slowly around the room. Trevor stood near the fireplace on the other side, reaching up to replace a book he had obviously read to pass the time as he waited for her to appear. To her immediate right stood a table upon which a candle burned. Without thinking, Grace leaned over and blew the candle out. She glanced at Trevor to gauge his reaction and found him facing her. At his questioning look, she nervously stammered, "T-too much light sometimes hurts my eyes, my lord."

Trevor looked steadily at his wife, registering the expression on her face. He revised his earlier assessment of her frank attitude toward their wedding night. He began walking toward her, then stopped when he heard her gasp. He followed the direction of her stricken gaze and looked down at himself. He wore his favorite dark blue satin dressing gown trimmed in midnight velvet. Belted loosely at the waist, it showed a good amount of the crisp, curly black hair that covered his upper chest. He watched her flush a deep red and avert her eyes in embarrassment. He sighed with resignation. He would need to go slowly.

"Grace," he said softly.

She looked at him out of the corner of her eye, blushed deeper still, and looked away again.

"Look at my face, love, only my face, just as I am looking at yours."

Hesitantly Grace did as instructed. Trevor looked at her with gentle understanding in his dark green eyes, a look that reassured her nearly as much as his next words. "You are my wife. There is no need, now or ever, for us to have secrets from each other." He moved closer, took her hand and led her across the room, dousing candles as he went, until only the crackling fire and the two candles beside the bed illuminated the room.

Grace glanced covertly at those two candles. She wondered if Trevor intended to snuff them as well, then promptly forgot the candles as her gaze skidded to a halt on the enormous bed. It loomed before her like a monster on its raised dais. A long-forgotten memory of something someone had once wickedly told her about married couples and what they did in beds stirred faintly in her mind. She suddenly knew, without a doubt, that she absolutely did *not* want to get into that bed with her husband; she wasn't sure she was prepared.

When Trevor saw where her eyes had riveted, he smiled grimly to himself. He idly wondered if all females inherited an innate sense that told them to beware of finding themselves alone in a room with a man that also happened to contain a bed. "Remember, Grace, I asked you to look at me," he reminded her.

She turned obediently toward him. He could see the pulse beating rapidly in her throat. *Christ!* He had not even touched her yet. He decided to try another approach. "I've been thinking about how we got here, Grace." He kept his voice as deliberately pleasant and unthreatening as possible. "We've wanted each other at different times. First, I wanted you when you didn't want me, then you wanted me when I didn't want you. We've led each other quite the merry little chase, haven't we?"

Her face softened. She smiled and nodded.

"Now, here we are. You are my wife. I want you with me as much as possible. I want spend my days with you in laughter. And I want to fall asleep, every single night for the rest of my life, with you in my arms and in my bed." He cupped her cheek in his hand and kissed her forehead softly. "I think you want that too, Grace. Come to bed with me, darling."

Grace nodded. Before she could change her mind, he effortlessly scooped her into his arms and laid her gently against the soft pillows, then stretched out beside her. She lay stiffly silent, but looked at him trustingly. Trevor felt his heart wrench at the bravery displayed by the girl he had married in the face of something she did not understand. He gently smoothed a burnished curl from her cheek, then leaned down and brought his lips to hers.

She returned his kiss automatically. She felt her nervousness melt away, replaced with that odd sense of longing she always felt with this man, now her husband. Her stomach tightened into a knot of desire, although she had no idea what she wanted from him. With a small whimper, she closed her eyes and leaned into his body.

Trevor slowly untied the satin ribbons of her dressing gown, then pushed himself up on his elbows to look down into her face. Her eyes flew open as she realized what he planned. "Shhh," he crooned. "I'm going to take your clothes off now, Grace."

She thought fleetingly of the last time he had done that, and her eyes widened. Trevor ignored the look and continued speaking. "When you are undressed, you may get beneath the covers. I'll join you there after I take off my dressing gown."

Grace started to shake her head in denial, then remembered that he had said for her to trust him. Stoic, she lay bravely still as he pushed the gown from her shoulders, then gently lifted her arms from the sleeves. He pulled down the covers on her side of the bed, and she quickly scrambled beneath, moving all the way to the far side and pulling the sheets tightly up under her chin. She watched him warily. He stood and quickly removed his robe, then slipped into bed before he could startle her with the blatant evidence of his arousal.

With Grace lying silently beside him, Trevor turned on

his side and raised himself on one elbow, propping hi
head on his hand. He regarded Grace with a small smile
She now had the covers pulled all the way up under he
eyes. Those eyes no longer held any nervousness, and he
almost laughed at her mutinous expression, for if he had a
choice, he much preferred a Grace filled with passionate
anger to a timid and unsure one. At last she was reacting a
expected.

"Are you going to blow out those last two candles, m
lord?" She glared up at him hotly.

"No."

As she watched his lips form the denial, Grace's eye
brows snapped together. She narrowed her eyes at Trevor
then looked away. "I knew there was a reason I neve
wished to marry," she muttered under her breath.

"*You* may blow them out if you wish," he pointed out in a
reasonable tone.

Grace twisted her head around in an effort to see if she
could possibly snuff them without emerging from the safet
of the coverlet. She grimaced. Short of pulling the sheet from
its place tucked under the end of the bed, she did not see
how she could accomplish it. She gave the sheet an experi
mental tug, then glanced at Trevor triumphantly. She pulled
harder to gather it around her naked body.

With an amused chuckle, Trevor reached over and pinned
both of her hands together with one of his. She struggled
for a moment, then quieted and looked at him in exaspera
tion. "What is it you want from me?"

Trevor's grin slowly faded. The apprehension his wife
stubbornly tried to hide showed in her expressive eyes. He
felt a rush of admiration for her spirited show of bravado
and his eyes softened to a dark, velvety green. "All I want to
do is kiss you," he said.

She stuck her chin out and pressed her lips together in
mute rebellion.

"I *am* going to kiss you, Grace," he corrected firmly. While I'm kissing you, I am going to hold you as close to me as I possibly can, and I'm going to touch you. *This time*," he added, knowing that she still thought of that other night, "I'll show you how to touch me, too. And then, my lady, I am going to make love to you. It will hurt at first, but only for a moment, and after that I promise I'll never have to hurt you again."

Grace had quieted as he spoke, a long-forgotten memory stirring from her childhood. *Now you have to kiss me*, Henry had said, and she had giggled and run away. She had run from Trevor, too, at first. Something in his voice finally gave her the courage to trust him. He waited, staring back for a moment, and then released her hands. In that instant, she knew, to the depths of her soul, that she need never run from him again. She reached up with trembling fingers and gently touched his lips.

"I love you," she said.

She said it quietly and without emphasis. The impact of those three words nearly took Trevor's breath away, and left him, for a moment, speechless.

"I love you," she repeated in a melting voice, "and I would like for you to kiss me, and to hold me as closely as you possibly can, and to touch me and teach me how to touch you." Her fingers traced a slow pattern around his lips. "Please, Trevor, make love to me. I want you to show—"

The rest of what she said would never be known. Trevor's mouth came down on hers, silencing her. He kissed her deeply and completely, coaxing her lips to part with his tongue. When they did, he invaded her mouth with a primitive thrusting that awakened a need in Grace she did not know she had. She shyly returned his kiss as he had taught her. Each tentative touch of her tongue stoked the fire of Trevor's arousal.

Telling himself to slow down, he tore his mouth from hers and gently kissed her closed eyelids, the tip of her nose, and then, softly again, her lips. Her eyes fluttered open, and he caught his breath—they glowed with unabashed joy, all the love in the world reflected in their shimmering depths. He pushed the sheet slowly away from her body as she stared unflinchingly at him, offering herself with all the innocent ardor she knew. He raised himself on an elbow and looked down at her, at the soft, ripe mounds of her breasts, her nipples rising at the touch of his eyes, at the tiny waist and slim hips framing the flat planes of her stomach, and then down at the curling auburn triangle of hair still partially covered by the sheet. "My God, you're beautiful," he whispered hoarsely. He took her hand and pressed it to his chest.

She looked at him in wonder as she felt his heartbeat thundering against her palm, amazed that the sensation rushing through her body affected him as deeply. She reached down and grasped his hand, then brought it to her chest and covered it with both of her own. "Do you feel it too?" Grace whispered in an aching voice.

With a groan, Trevor nodded and slid his hand over to cup her breast, marveling at the way it just fit into his palm, almost as though made for that very purpose. Gently, he teased her nipple into a hard little knot of feeling. Darts of pleasure shot through Grace. She moaned as his hand lifted and his mouth took its place, alternately suckling on the erect nipple and laving it with long, slow strokes of his tongue. Gently he applied his teeth, making her gasp and arch her back as jolt after jolt of wild sensation rocked her. He turned his attention to the other breast, then let his fingers slip down the planes of her stomach to tangle in the curling hairs at the juncture of her thighs.

Grace jerked in shocked surprise. Instinctively she pressed her legs together, remembering the pleasure he had caused when he touched her there before. She shook her head wildly from side to side, fearing the same loss of control she had felt then. Trevor lifted his head and looked at her, his eyes dark with strained passion.

"Don't," he whispered hoarsely. "Please don't." His face was taut, his features harsh with the effort of keeping rigid control of his rampaging desire. He reached up and clasped the fingers of his other hand around hers. Grace stared back at her husband for a moment, and then bravely squeezed his hand and allowed her legs to relax.

His eyes still locked on hers, Trevor let his hand slide slowly lower, moving toward the slick folds that hid the entrance to her body. He stopped when he reached the little knot of flesh at the top of the aperture, then gently rubbed his index finger across it.

Grace caught her breath and bit her lip to keep from crying out. Intense, almost painful pleasure, nearly more than she could handle, enveloped her. A small whimper escaped when she felt his fingers move again, lower this time, to stroke between the crease that lay openly vulnerable to him. He watched her intently as he slowly slid a finger into her enshrouding softness, enjoying the changes on her expressive face. She closed her eyes in rapturous disbelief at the exquisite pleasure he evoked.

"Grace?"

Her eyes flew open again at the sound of his passion-thick voice.

"Do you think you could touch me, too?" His finger began moving deliciously within her. Grace nodded and closed her eyes with a rapturous moan, then opened them again to find his eyes still locked with hers. Tentatively she reached out to touch him. Her fingertips lightly brushed the crisp hairs that curled on his chest, then drew back as the muscles there jumped in reaction. Feeling braver, she touched him again, then flattened her palm on the taut muscles and began to caress him. With her index finger she curiously circled one of his flat male nipples. To her surprise, it hardened just as hers had. She looked at him again and realized that he had stopped stroking her, had almost stopped breathing.

Remembering what he had done to her, she shyly brought her lips to his chest and lightly licked the hard little nubbin of flesh. Trevor released his breath and began caressing her again, his fingers moving within her more urgently.

With a gasp Grace nuzzled closer still and began suckling harder on his nipple, her hands now more boldly exploring her husband's body. Her fingers slid through the dark hair on his chest, down across the smoother skin of his stomach. She moved with him now, finding a rhythm that matched his questing fingers. Her tongue laved his flesh, reveling in the taste of him, and her own fingers dipped into the hollow of his navel, stroking him there in time to the movement of his hands. Then her hand brushed against the rigid evidence of his arousal and she stopped. It felt like satin over steel. She lightly ran her fingers over him, then closed her hand around his maleness and looked up.

He did not move. His tightly closed eyes and clenched jaw worried her.

"Am I hurting you?" Grace whispered.

Unable to wait any longer to join himself with her, Trevor shook his head and moved over his wife, nudging her knees apart with his, his hardness poised at the entrance to her body. At the sudden change of position, Grace's eyes again grew apprehensive. She trembled despite herself and grasped his upper arms. As if trying to reassure him, she began speaking, smoothing her hands up and down his muscled forearms.

"This is the part where you said you would hurt me, isn't it?" At his regretful nod, she continued in the same self-convincing tone: "It will only last a moment?" She caught her breath as she felt him begin to ease into her tight, hot passage. "Well, I've sometimes thought," she continued bravely, "that the things that are the most important are often the most difficult."

Trevor reached the barrier that proclaimed her innocence. Any hope that this would happen easily for her died in his chest. Looking deeply into her eyes, he gave a slight push, then cringed as she gasped and squeezed her eyes closed.

"Grace, look at me," he said. She opened her eyes and smiled bravely at him. He lowered himself carefully to stretch out full-length upon her, so he could take her hands in his. He withdrew slightly, and whispered, "I love you." Then his lips descended on hers and he surged completely into her, breaking the barrier and muffling her small, involuntary cry of pain with his mouth.

After only a moment, the sudden sharp pain began to subside. Grace opened her eyes to see Trevor holding himself stiffly motionless, watching her face intently. She felt a surge of deep emotion and smiled tenderly up at her husband. "I think," she said in an aching voice as she tightened her fingers around his and he slowly began to move within her, "that I have never felt so completely whole in all my life."

His heart exploding with the sweetness of her words, Trevor began thrusting faster, urging her toward that peak she had scaled only once before, determined that they would attain it together this time. Instinctively she moved her hips with him, matching his thrusts, reaching with age-old knowledge for that pinnacle. Then, without warning, the world shattered into a million shards of crystal light, and she cried out in release just as he found his. He gathered her close as her body convulsed around him, making her his beginning and his end, melding with her, complete.

Some moments later he rolled onto his side, taking her with him, their bodies still linked in that most intimate of joinings. Breathing hard, he gazed at her passion-drunk face and was astonished to see her grinning at him. "What is it?" Trevor asked.

"Does it always feel like this?"

He smiled and nodded.

"And we get to feel this way each time we . . . do that?" She blushed and pulled lightly on the hairs of his chest.

"Each time we make love," he agreed, kissing the tip of her pert little nose.

"How," she said shyly, "How could I have ever run from this?"

With a low chuckle, Trevor rolled his wife onto her back and began moving within her again. "You ran," he returned, "so that I could catch you. Somebody had to, and it had to be me."

CONNIE MASON

The Black Widow

That was what the desperate prisoners incarcerated in Devil's Chateau called her. Whatever she did with them, one thing was certain: Her unfortunate victims were never seen again. But when she whisked Reed Harwood out of the cell where he'd been left to die for spying against the French, he discovered the lady was not all she seemed.

Fleur Fontaine was the most exquisitely sensual woman he'd ever met, yet there was an innocence about her that belied her sordid reputation. Only a dead man would fail to respond. Reed was not dead yet, but was he willing to pay…

The Price of Pleasure

ISBN 10: 0-8439-5745-X
ISBN 13: 978-0-8439-5745-7

DAWN MACTAVISH

Lark at first hoped it was a simple nightmare: If she closed her eyes, she would be back in the mahogany bed of her spacious boudoir at Eddington Hall, and all would be well. Her father, the earl of Roxburgh, would not be dead by his own hand, and she would not be in Marshalsea Debtor's Prison.

Such was not to be. Ere the Marshalsea could do its worst, the earl of Grayshire intervened. But while his touch was electric and his gaze piercing, for what purpose had he bought her freedom? No, this was not a dream. As Lark would soon learn, her dreams had never ended so well.

The Privateer

AVAILABLE JANUARY 2008!

ISBN 13: 978-0-8439-5981-9

EMILY BRYAN

BARING IT ALL

rom the moment she saw the man on her doorstep, Lady
rtemisia, Duchess of Southwycke, wanted him naked. For
nce, she'd have the perfect model for her latest painting. But
he bared each bit of delicious golden skin from his broad
nest down to his—oh, my!—art became the last thing on
er mind.

revelyn Deveridge was looking for information, not a job.
hough if a brash, beautiful widow demanded he strip, he
asn't one to say no. Especially if it meant he could get closer
 finding the true identity of an enigmatic international op-
ative with ties to her family. But as the intrigue deepened
d the seduction sweetened, Trev found he'd gone well be-
ond his original mission of...

DISTRACTING the DUCHESS

VAILABLE MARCH 2008!   ISBN 13: 978-0-8439-5870-6